I0634547

# TUNNEL
## —•OF•—
# VARANAVAT

**Gautam Chikermane** is a writer, tracking the worlds of money and power, faith and mythology. He is currently the new media director at Reliance Industries Ltd and a director on the board of CARE India. Earlier, he had worked in leadership positions for some of India's top newspapers and magazines like the *Hindustan Times*, *The Indian Express*, *The Financial Express* and the Outlook group. He has served three terms as director on the board of Financial Planning Standards Board India and one as its vice chairman.

His past books include *Five Decades of Decay* (1997) and *The Disrupter: Arvind Kejriwal and the Audacious Rise of the Aam Aadmi* (2014).

His body lives in Mumbai and New Delhi, his soul in Pondicherry.

# TUNNEL

## ·OF·

# VARANAVAT

## GAUTAM CHIKERMANE

RUPA

This is a Print On Demand copy and hence does not have special finishing on the cover.

Published by
Rupa Publications India Pvt. Ltd 2016
7/16, Ansari Road, Daryaganj
New Delhi 110002

*Sales centres:*
Allahabad Bengaluru Chennai
Hyderabad Jaipur Kathmandu
Kolkata Mumbai

Copyright © Gautam Chikermane 2016

This is a work of fiction. Names, characters, places and incidents are either
the product of the author's imagination or are used fictitiously,
and any resemblance to any actual persons, living or dead,
events or locales is entirely coincidental.

All rights reserved.
No part of this publication may be reproduced, transmitted, or stored in
a retrieval system, in any form or by any means, electronic, mechanical,
photocopying, recording or otherwise, without the prior permission of the
publisher.

ISBN: 978-81-291-3727-2

First impression 2016

10 9 8 7 6 5 4 3 2 1

The moral right of the author has been asserted.

Typeset by Saanvi Graphics, Noida

This book is sold subject to the condition that it shall not, by way
of trade or otherwise, be lent, resold, hired out, or otherwise circulated,
without the publisher's prior consent, in any form of binding or cover other
than that in which it is published.

I held her tightly, my head bent against her spine, feeling the smooth texture of her body, one that I had held for as long as I cared to remember. Tomorrow, we draw blood. Again. A surge of energy passed through the iron, filling me up with an intimate strength. *We will protect.* I put her down gently. Then picked up the second spear and repeated the mantra. *We will kill.* The third. *We will hack.* Fourth. *There will be no hesitation.* Fifth. *He, whose time has come, will move on.* Sixth. *He, who still needs to grow, will stay.* One by one, I empowered each of my spears with the death mantra. Then prayed for strength and unshakable resolve. And finally, peace. When I put them down, I sensed them vibrate, ready to slash, aching to kill.

# Contents

# Prologue

A twig cracked and I knew death had found its moment of life. I didn't need to turn, didn't need to see. Or sense. My body knew who it was. From the depths of my being rose the foreboding of battle–possibly my final.

If you haven't felt the blade of a sword slash through your body, you won't relate to this knowledge. If you haven't rejoiced in the flight of an arrow that stops only after it has embedded itself in your thigh, you won't know the joy bloodlust brings. If you haven't killed with your bare hands, you won't understand compassion.

Only a Kshatriya knows the celebration that the dharm of violence places on us.

Vishnu knew. Behind me, I could feel his eyes boring into me.

Soon his spears and knives would follow.

This last battle was going to be my greatest. I would fight it at my weakest. Or maybe at my highest. The Kshatriya in me was dying. I was leaving that deadly force behind, with all memories of slashing, cutting, jabbing, breaking, crushing. I was readying myself for the next battle, this time within myself.

But my body was exhausted. My mind was not ready for yet another bout of killing.

This was no time for that twig to crack.

Wishes seemed to avoid my company. They disliked my constant companion–death. Right now, it took the form of my biggest enemy towering behind me. Powerful, confident, fresh. Armed with not just tools of death but with a burning desire to kill. He was accompanied by trained soldiers, extensions of his weapons, all ready to die for him. I didn't need to turn to see the sneer on his face. Warriors speak a language that only warriors understand. Vishnu spoke to me silently, telling me that my time was up.

Moments ago I had completed what I thought was my last assignment for the kingdom. The Pandavs had escaped and were away from the clutches of conspiracy hatched in Hastinapur.

Exhausted after the killings, I stood alone, the warmth of Janaki's final warrior-kiss still lingering on my lips, passion of her sinewy arms still holding me tightly.

The mountains gave the gentle breeze a touch of cold—winter was on its way. The never-stopping music of the Ganga flowed behind in a melody it had sung for ages. I was in the middle of Varanavat's dark forests, with shades of orange flashing through, as the flames we had ignited rose to touch the skies.

Purochan's palace of lak was now a collapsing ball of fire. Next to the palace lay Kedar's ashram of peace.

And Urvashi...

The cracking of the twig brought me back to the present. I wasn't ready for this battle but it was one I had to fight. It was like a deep, unquenched longing of nature, almost preventing the changes within from taking shape. Like the last note of a long recital. A note that delivers a fitting climax, bringing permanent peace to the heart. A note that completes the raag. Ends it all.

Like death itself.

Through the cracked twig, Yam was playing that note tonight.

After sending the Pandavs to safety, I had returned to the forest carrying an unfamiliar burden of an inner transformation. Something within me was letting the warrior I had been for more than six decades go.

My spears suddenly felt heavy. I didn't need them anymore. The knives around my belt began to hurt. I loosened it, looking for a safe place to hang them until someone from Kedar's ashram could collect it. There was nothing to fear anymore. All enemies were dead.

I was too weak to carry anything but the burden of the dying Urvashi. I knew she was safe; that Kedar would save her. We were entwined by destiny. But still, urgency pushed me. What if...?

The night acquired a darker shade because of the forest, but the small darts of light that the burning palace exuded scraped my eyes. The flames lit up the sky as though the sun god Surya had descended on this wretched earth.

But the light was still tolerable for my weak eyes. Two shades more and I would wince.

I had drifted through the thick forest, found a group of entwined branches and placed my spears between them. Then I had carefully tied my belt of knives around the spears. It was almost like worshipping, bidding a final goodbye to my companions of decades. The weapons felt heavy or perhaps it was just the heaviness in my heart. I was tired. But I felt free, relieved. No more fighting. No more killing. No more hiding. And no more tunnels.

My being was overflowing with a love I had never experienced before. There was nobody—not Urvashi, not my children. There was no idea—not of the kingdom nor of dharm. There was no companion—not the spears, not even death. There was just...love.

A new confidence told me all was where it should be.

The movement had begun. I was leaving Kshatriyahood behind. A new life awaited me. There was sweetness around me. It seemed I was merging into nothingness. Or everything was merging into me. Differences in matter were blurring.

I had begun to walk through the forest. What sort of a Brahmin would I be? A rishi of knowledge? A warrior rishi? A reciter of Veds? Would I follow Kedar? I laughed at my own audacity, stifling further thoughts.

Or was my destiny to serve Ved Vyas as he sprinkled the knowledge of the Ved around the Ganga and set up a stream of institutions around the holy river, making each rishi a repository of knowledge, each pupil a reciter of mantras?

A whole new world was opening out before me...before us. Urvashi was back and her love pulled me deeper. We were celestial travellers and didn't even know it. I needed to hold back time.

I had watched from the river and the twisting forest trail the bright red-yellow glow of the burning palace. Above me were the first signs of Ushas, but the sun was late. Purochan's palace of lak had taken charge and turned the darkness of the night outside the forest into light.

Sounds of the birds were...

There were no sounds. It was quiet. Too quiet. Everything was still. Too still. My instincts got there before my mind could reach them. The threat of danger wrapped itself around me. But there was no reaction within. What was going on? Where were the birds?

The crack of the twig cleared the cobwebs.

That crack revealed a truth I had known all along. I could not die without fighting this preordained battle. For the first time in my life, I was afraid. Not because of death. I had embraced it, courted it so many times that even Yam would have lost count. My body was of no consequence anymore. It had survived many arrows, spears, axes.

My fear rose from a strange, unknown part of me, somewhere near a point that my victories had smothered—survival. For the first time in my life I wanted to live. I needed to live. For Urvashi. For creation. For my self.

How things change.

I had come to Varanavat to die. But fate cheated me of that victory. There was no exit, no light in my tunnels. Just when I thought the flame in my soul, gasping for breath under the layers of guilt would finally be extinguished and bring me the peace I had sought for lifetimes, came this strange longing, fresh whiff of aspiration, a never-before-experienced desire to live.

I had come to protect. But ended up killing. My days of soldiering were long gone, though memories of violence still lived within me, lingered like gangrene, eating my vitals. My task was to take care of a young woman and her five sons, two of them still carrying their last milk teeth, and take them to safety. It was to be a quiet, bloodless exit. It wasn't.

I came to dig. But when I surfaced, it was from complex tunnels that criss-crossed within me, not very different from those I had built. And when the bloodbath came, it was poetic catharsis.

I had come to lose myself. But in a fire that still ignited Varanavat for a krosh or two, maybe more, I discovered my self. As death danced to the slashes and rumbles of weapons, I had sent valiant bodies to the great beyond. In the process of delivering my physical dharm, something shifted deep within me. I finally longed to live for a purpose higher than any other I had pursued.

The sound of that cracked twig changed things. The luxury of exhaustion was gone.

Still weak, I tried to gather my scattered parts. I had to kill Vishnu. It was too much of a risk to leave him and his soldiers alive. But the love in me was flowing too fast, too deep, transforming all my past into a fluid future, where neither weapons nor their wielders existed.

If I didn't kill Vishnu now, I would be wasting another lifetime. Kedar had pushed the realization. The movement of consciousness had begun. I could not betray my destiny any longer.

For the future ahead, my past had to be erased. I may be weak. Possibly on another plane. Perhaps death would finally grant me the release I had been seeking. But I didn't want to die now.

I had to face my fear.

The crack of the twig told me that the time to think was long gone. I had to act. Kill or be killed. There was only one recourse—ride my instincts, honed over lifetimes. I fought the new movement within. I felt my body harden, my back straighten.

Slowly, I turned.

# Rescue

*One hundred and sixty-six days ago*

The sound of hooves below me was muted. Partly by the morning moist soil and partly because of a weak horse, they didn't have the ring I heard when I rode to war.

Besides, war was now decades behind me.

Behind me? No, it lay within. Latent. Like a coiled-up cobra, ready to strike. I shook my head and smothered the snake.

We had an emergency and I was running late. Tunnel 14 had a problem around a bend. The soil above had moistened more than we had expected. Between a lazy water lines designer and an over-zealous young miner, with strong muscles rippling all the way to his brains, a few hits were all it took for the earth to cave in on him. The water hadn't flowed in yet. But how much longer?

I had warned the Tunnel 14 contractor about this. The entire Kuru empire knew my zero-tolerance on safety issues—one error and the contractor's high-flying career would be over. Tunnels were important for the kingdom, creating and maintaining them was my dharm. But safety of the miners was paramount and nobody was going to get in its way. When parents handed their boys to me, they did so knowing that I would educate them, train them, offer them a career and most importantly protect them.

The contractor might as well leave Hastinapur. In any case, his girth, fattened by the high-paying royal work, couldn't fit into the high-risk tunnels of Hastinapur anymore. But then, his sincerity and loyalty were tested. This could be something else.

As far as the miner went, depending on his physical injuries he could crawl back to the elite tunnel squad in a year or two. But it were his psychological injuries, the ones in his control that would finally determine whether he would. Usually, a serious accident meant the end of a miner's career. But I have known many diggers who have conquered and crawled out of the tunnels of their fears, the psychological scars bringing a powerful but humbled wisdom with them.

Not a single chief miner in any country of Aryavart was free of an accident. It was almost a pride, not very different from the scars soldiers carried and boasted about.

I was far away, at the lower Tunnel 53, when the messenger panted in with the news. The incident was three krosh away.

After a long night of intense supervision, Vayu needed rest, so I borrowed the first horse in sight. But Jeevan's ride was not only shorter than Vayu, he was clearly not strong enough.

Not for me, that is. I stood a full dhanush and a dhanurgarh tall with heavy bones and muscles to match. My face was taut, though the lines that would turn into wrinkles in another twenty years had begun to show. Unfortunately, I could not hide my wrinkles behind a beard. To me, being a miner and carrying a beard were not possible. That was because I still dig.

I don't need to. As chief miner of the Kuru empire, I am way past the dirt and grime of physical digging. No chief miner I know in the entire Aryavart, from fertile plains of neighbouring Mastya and Panchal to the far-flung drier lands of Avanti and Vidarbh, digs himself.

With me, the problem was different. I enjoyed my profession and never let an opportunity to dig pass me. And then, of course, there is the light aversion. I can hide from the world I could no longer face. And from the shreds of my being that have been swallowing my sense of peace for decades now.

Maybe what I call 'enjoyment' is really an escape.

All this strenuous and constant work meant that I was as strong as a Kshatriya soldier. And though Hastinapur, or elephant city, a name it got because of the largest elephant army it commanded in Aryavart has thankfully forgotten, I am in fact a Kshatriya.

I was born a Kshatriya, to Rishabh, one of Hastinapur's most respected spies. But I had earned my Kshatriyahood the hard way, fighting bloody battles for the kingdom, under general Bhishm.

As the years of prosperity took their toll on the kingdom's dying memory, long forgotten was the fact that I was a trained soldier, born to protect, to fight, to kill and to die killing if need be. I had lived my life in the hope that I would end it as a martyr, bearing scars to provide evidence. The thought itself was intoxicating. Putting my nation before anything else, the seductive arms of a heroic death over a slow and lingering life.

My years in the tunnels had pushed me beyond the edges of my being. From some of those dark corners, blinding light would taunt me, questioning my death wish.

When I rummaged through ancient memories that scraped through my body, a stranger would hold me in a bright, bluish-white world. Not the physical light that brought the ridges of the tunnels to life. It was a light that came from somewhere else and filled me up. Unknown, yet familiar.

It is hard to explain, but it is akin to what darkness is for those who live on earth, the fear of the unknown. I had given up the glamour of being a Kshatriya and embraced the life of a miner. But for those who don't know, mining is more dangerous than fighting. There is not a moment of peace in the shadowed lives of miners. Instead, there is danger the moment you step into the mouth of a tunnel.

But from that light there was no escape. It was as if something in it was calling me. Not something, it was someone. Maybe both.

And though I tried as I hard as I could to smother it, I knew it lay within.

Waiting.

The sounds of a city waking up filled the silences between the thunder of my steed.

Vedic chants grazed my route as I passed the Brahmins lighting their morning sacrificial fires. The collective resonance of 'Aum' in one street after another, one gurukul at a time, turned the wind rushing through my hair into a light breeze that caressed the being within. The Brahmins chanted their mantras and turned the entire city into a series of magical moments. The mantras seemed to emerge from the depths of every citizen's being.

From fish, birds and cows to elephants, horses and men, this was a period of pause. It felt as if the mantras had bound Kaal, time, within their resonances, asking it to wait until they finished exploring the timeless vast, the unending space and got the gods to sit beside us.

As I looked over the majestic Kuru assembly in the distance, I saw Lord Surya, the sun, threatening to shower his premature blessings anytime now, sweeping our goddesses away with blinding brightness.

From the east came his onslaught, swallowing the purple, starlit sky. Like the arrows of our archers, shafts of gold began slashing at the night. Through gaps between thick mango trees, like an army moving after a siege, unstoppable was Surya's light.

His light moved faster than my horse. Its gleams echoed from pillars and gates, through trees and openings.

The best part of my day was ending.

Don't get me wrong. The mantras brought me deep peace, permeating every pore of my body, filled every cell with a new life. However hard I tried to recite them, I just couldn't get the intonation right. Every home in this capital city of the Kuru empire, indeed in the entire Aryavart, knew the mantras and sang their singular glories stacking! the first prahar of the day, just before dawn.

But nothing could match the sound and the intensity of the mantras that young Brahmins sang after they returned from Ved Vyas's ashrams. He was creating a legion of spiritual warriors. Over the past forty years or more that I personally remember, Ved Vyas's bigger purpose had slowly unfolded before us—he was reworking an entire consciousness, knowledge, and power with a force that was entering and energizing the vitals of our great civilization.

Respected across countries, but living like any ordinary sadhak, Ved Vyas was the most unassuming rishi in Aryavart.

No, it wasn't the mantras.

It was light.

For everybody else, morning was a period of gentle waking. For me, it meant pain. It cut and blinded me. Even the gentle glow of the morning light that I remembered from my youth was hard on my eyes now.

My aversion to light was because of a peculiar problem aggravated by my profession. The chief vaid had said that my pupils had dilated to almost permanently large openings and though I was not even seventy, age was against me.

After spending most of my years in darkness, I had forgotten the splendour of the sun. We miners and diggers worshipped Ratridevi, goddess of the night, and her sister Ushas, goddess of dawn.

As most of humankind slept, our beautiful goddesses worked with us in the tunnels of transport, secret trenches of soldiers, clandestine corridors of lovers, cleansing the evil that chose to reside here. Irrespective of the state of the sun up there, in our tunnels it was the reign of darkness.

Tunnels are a world painted with different colours of shadows—purples, greens and blues. And then, there was black. You'll be surprised at how many kinds of black coexist. No different from men.

Or the innumerable shades of personality parasites that resided in every man, some known. Most unknown.

And so, my tunnels had become my refuge, my protection...my world of darkness, fine-tuned by rough physical edges and unseen imaginary fears.

In my tunnels I was hiding from the devils chasing me from the past, fighting a new war for which I had no weapons, no training, no support. And yet, my body told me I was ready.

When in a particularly happy mood or when my past would sweet-talk me into it, I would join the soldiers in our evening exercises and often beat some of the good wrestlers and spearmen of the king's army. Hearing about my reputation, even Princes Duryodhan and Bhim would invite me for friendly wrestling matches. That's when I took refuge in my age.

There was no point. If I won, it would scar the young princes. If I lost in trying to make it look real, I could break a bone, tear a tendon and some of my pride.

Future kings are best served, not wrestled.

It took a warrior's horse to carry me. Vayu was the best I've ever had—black, tall and strong, one who could read my mind. King Dhritarashtr had gifted him to me. The morning after I had finished the upper tunnels that began from under his palace and stopped half a krosh a short of the Ganga, where the threat of water seeping into the tunnels prevented further digging, I found a foal tied to my stable, neighing to the skies.

We looked at each other and he calmed down instantly, his eyes boring into mine. It was almost as if we had known each other from another time, another world. Dhritarashtr's das didn't need to tell me about this gift. I knew Vayu was mine.

And I his.

This brown mount only seemed tougher than he really was. Maybe he was past his prime. Or maybe I wasn't his usual rider. Every horse follows a pattern with his owner. Over time they get bound to each other, a delicate relationship that goes beyond feeding or caring.

Soldiers know this very well. That's why maharathis and atirathis are so finicky about anyone riding or even touching their horses.

Only some spoilt sons of the king and ministers kept away from stables, a gross error for future warriors, for such behaviour can never help you to lead men in war. These sons will sit on minor thrones without any merit. Such was the degeneration of Arya principles, not just in Hastinapur but across Aryavart.

The other group that steered away from horses was children of some Vaishya merchants on whom Goddess Lakshmi's blessings of excess wealth had turned into an intergenerational curse. Some of them even made their attendants ride for them. These children would pursue trades, become wealthier and seal their irrelevancy to a greater expectation Hastinapur demanded out of every able-bodied man. And woman.

It wasn't the inability to ride that irked, it was the attitude of seeking comfort that was poisoning the value system of Aryavart that I would often brood about when drinking the common som. Expensive wines were not for me.

But right now, my attention was on Tunnel 14.

As the morning wind rustled through my thick black hair in which streaks of white were beginning to mark their presence, the foam around my borrowed horse began to grow.

We were getting closer to the city now and I could see it stretching itself in the morning light—a man pulling water from a well, a young girl running after a dog, a few men walking on the road, their heads bent in deep conversation.

The jamun trees were bearing fruit and a small four-year-old boy stood in the middle of the road, looking up. I took a wider arc to not disturb him in his job of trying to catch that one jamun, which would make his day.

A party of pilgrims, probably on the way to Himavat, and for whom our city was a watering hole, stood on one side. They were cooking a small meal, getting ready to go, their bullock carts waiting by the side. A young man was drawing water from one of hundreds of wells that lined our city.

He looked at me curiously, then turned to a buxom woman next to him, eased a cynical smile and said something. The woman laughed, her teeth shining white against a dark background.

Soon the road would be jammed with vendors carting their wares to the four large markets of the city.

Finally, the parasites would come to do the 'king's work'—soldiers, tax collectors, petty officials, even the nobility. Corrupt, all of them.

I spat the thought out on a lizard looking hard at a group of eagles that had taken early flight.

'Left-right, left-right...' the sounds of marching shook the dawn, cutting the mantras behind like a knife.

Dron's military academy veered close. Some late students were rushing towards the gates. I slowed my horse down to help him catch his breath.

To call Dron an acharya, guru, somehow didn't feel right. Thin of frame, short of height, brimming with temper, Dron was anything but a teacher. He was more deeply entrenched in the petty conspiracies and sordid ambitions of palaces and desires than the lowest bureaucrats.

When you look into the eyes of a guru, you feel peace, strength love.

In Dron's case, you felt his eyes were cutting you, trying to tear the subtle body and see and preen at what lay within. There was a hunger in them. For what, I couldn't fathom. Personally, I didn't like the man. Whenever I was with him, I felt my energy fall, as if he was sucking it all away from me.

While linking the academy and his home with the palace tunnel, after the initial discussion, I supervised it from a safe distance and let my assistant Vajr manage Dron's tantrums.

Nobody, and certainly not I, doubted Dron's competence. There had been many gurus who were brilliant military leaders, two of whom were my teachers—Parashuram and Kedar. Besides, young princes from as far away as Vidarbh in the south and Gandhar in the north trained in his academy. No, I didn't grudge him his warrior craft.

His loyalty too was beyond doubt. Not because he adored the kingdom. But because he had no options and loved himself and his possessions too much to risk them.

No, Dron was no guru. Beneath the armour of 'guru' he was no different from any other high-ranking minister. His sister's husband Kripacharya was equally a military man. But before him you felt the wisdom that holds a Brahmin's consciousness together. In Dron's case, it was pure craving, lust.

'Left-right, left-right,' a loud chorus roared, the warrior sandals of soldiers marching in tune with the beat of war drums.

The horse trough at the entrance was well-endowed, almost

luxuriously so. A dozen or so horses stood by. The attendant folded his hands and bowed his head.

'Pranam, Badri. What brings you here at this unearthly hour? Surely you're not enrolling at the academy this morning.' He laughed aloud at his own joke.

I had no time for frivolities. 'This horse is tired and I am in a hurry. It's an emergency. I need to borrow another,' I said, pointing towards the horses. The request was mere formality.

'Emergency?' his smile vanished. 'At this time? Definitely, Badri. Which one?'

I looked at the horses. The largest, a brown, stood strong but his head hung low. Three horses down I spotted a white, scraping the ground with his forelegs. He was ready.

'That one,' I said, nodding towards him with my chin.

'Good choice, Badri. It belongs to Ratan, a promising young prince who has come from Chedi to the academy. I'll inform him.'

'Take this,' and I handed him the reins. 'It's Jeevan's. Let him catch his breath, feed him well and send him across to Tunnel 53.'

I turned to the white. 'What's his name?'

'Agni.' Fire.

As I patted Agni's neck, the chorus of war cries behind thundered within me as well. An ancient longing ached in my heart. I wanted to be there...I was there.

Not now, not ever, if you can help it, I told myself, shaking away the thought and calming the blood that had suddenly acquired a life of its own, thumping an ancient war-dance in my veins, a memory of slashing and goring.

I violently wrenched myself away from my past, my hand stroking the neck of the white. I gave him some straw to munch on, he turned away. I laughed. 'This one is ready to fly,' I told the attendant.

A cloth saddle lay next to him. As far as technology went, this was as state-of-the-art as any could be—the bridle, the bit and leather straps held the saddle in place. But, I felt a lot more could be done. It was still a crude cloth device that had a short life and constantly needed to be replaced.

Given our mighty academies of science and technology, spread throughout Aryavart and from where any king could draw knowledge, saddle research remained an unexplored field.

I brushed his back clean. Even a single dry leaf under a saddle can irritate the calmest of horses and I had no time. As I placed the saddle on his back, he snorted and looked at me. Sure enough, he had fire in his eyes.

'That's right, Agni, a few moments now,' I told him.

Naming our domesticated animals was getting to be a skill that was now bordering on precision. I double-knotted the cotton strings, and loosened the leather belts to allow the saddle to breathe. Almost reading the urgency in my heart, he grunted and shook his head.

I leaped on to him and steadied myself. Agni barely noticed. This horse had strong muscles that danced to a stronger will.

'Make sure you tell Ratan that it was an emergency,' I shouted, as I walked Agni past the academy. The last thing I needed in my life was another complication. Kshatriya horse-owners are not the easiest of enemies.

'I will,' his voice merged into the marching of a thousand soldiers behind him.

The clang of swords. The whoosh of arrows. The thuds of maces. The grunts of wrestlers. The chorus of formations—heron, needle, crocodile...

I shook the memories away as they began to invade my being.

Nudging Agni, I realized he was indeed fire. He didn't warm up. He just leaped into a surprising run. A few strides later, I let him have his head and he raced into a full-throated thunder, trampling the Hastinapur roads with vengeance, almost as if he was testing their strength.

The sound of his hooves was like the stormy rain. You couldn't hear the individual steps, just a deep rumble, beating to my heartbeats, as he drummed across the horse trail that ran parallel to Himavat Pathh.

The sun was behind us, lighting up the way ahead and I knew in a few nadikas, I would find it difficult to open my eyes without protecting them with my turban, a thin cotton cloth I used to tie around my head, but which was broad enough to cover my eyes like a veil, when needed. It was tied five times around. I pulled one level down over my eyes.

Around us, Hastinapur was waking up. Mantras of the Brahmins were concluding with 'Aum Shanti'. Gurukul bells were calling out to the city to wake up and get going.

The white was crushing the trail as if his life depended on it, ignoring the surprised looks on people's faces on the way. I held him strongly with my legs but kept his reins loose. He had style—a high head that would dash ahead pulling the body and the body pushing hard so that the head would rise. He was born to run, bred to race, trained to fight.

'How long?' I shouted at the guard at entrance of the construction site. Agni was still running through the early pink-going-on-red sky. I gave his neck a few slaps, jumped off his back, and ran a few steps alongside with the momentum, holding the bridle. His energy carried him a few dhanush farther. Then, snorting with disappointment, he stopped to look at me, his left foot scratching the ground. His eyes said it all—he wanted to run.

'Less than two nadika.'

'Give him some water and ask someone to run him down a bit,' I told the guard, who took the Agni's reins from me. 'Then return him to Dron's academy. He belongs to a Chedi prince, Ratan. Take good care of him.'

In the distance ahead, near the fenced area of our construction site, I saw Vajr turn towards me. His constantly grim face was a shade darker. The man exuded authority and had paan in his mouth. He was one of my six deputies, the man I thought would take charge of Kuru kingdom's mining after I retired.

'This is not good, Badri.'

'I know. But we have blessings on our side.'

He raised his head in a question. 'Yes, water would not have seeped through yet.'

'No,' I said, running towards the site. 'That isn't my worry.'

His eyebrows rose in a question.

'If the water is seeping through, it would help him. If not, we have a bigger problem on our hands.'

'Dust.'

I nodded. We had designed various ducts but, however hard I tried, I couldn't reduce the dust beyond a point. I had reached a barrier in my tunnelling laboratory where the circulation of the ventilation duct was able to provide some sort of a survival balance between air and dust, life and death. But I knew my model the miner didn't have much of a chance. The dust could choke him.

'So, his best friend is also his biggest enemy,' Vajr said. I nodded. Talking to each other was like extracting secrets that lay in our combined knowledge of the tunnels we had built together. 'If there is too much water, he drowns. If too little, he chokes.'

Moisture of the breached water line would grab and slow down the moving dust, while allowing air to reach the miner's lungs. Dampening, I had found, is an important mechanism to control the dust created by breaking stones and dry earth.

'It's a tricky point, Vajr,' I said, avoiding the gate and leaping over the fence. 'If the crack is long, the same water could drown him.'

And then, there was the Ganga. From the private citizens' point of view, Ganga was a river in a hurry, narrower than the Yamuna and swifter than the Saraswati. What it lacked in breadth it made up in speed.

'You do know the underground rivers,' Vajr said.

'Yes, but luckily that's not where the breach is.' There were two underground rivers flowing alongside the Ganga, a rift that nature had created when the lands below ours shifted through a series of earthquakes and carried the Ganga waters for krosh together. Apart from the rains, this kept the water table of Hastinapur high and was good for citizens.

But it made life difficult for us miners.

A peculiar challenge was that in the three lower tunnels that began halfway from King Dhritarashtr's fort and went all the way across the river to the other side, we had to dig at least four times deeper than the wells on the way. The smallest of leaks here and the cold waters of the Ganga would not only destroy the tunnels beneath it but could go all the way to the middle and flood some of the upper tunnels.

A single leak here could turn our intricate network of tunnels into a grid of death.

By Ratridevi's grace, the problem was not in this area but towards north, where the terrain was stonier, drier, dustier.

Here, I had discovered a new technology, a complex process of balancing by which we would be able to keep the soil adequately damp and allow air to travel freely. A little excess could cause leakages and slush, a little scarcity could take the miners to a dusty death. It was controlled by tunnel heads, who checked them thrice every day.

The technology itself was more a chance of fate, which had come up by accident, many years ago. So I call it 'discovery' and not 'invention'. My contribution to the technology was in showing how adding water to the soil can reduce the dust quotient in tunnels.

Six years ago, when I tested it and finally with trepidation put it out in public domain for further analysis or criticism, it had proved to be a technological breakthrough. Since then, several mining scholars in Aryavart universities have worked on it, taken it forward. It is still being worked on and a lot of lives have been saved.

But many have not.

I wanted to call the process a simple and utilitarian 'Geela'. But Hastinapur's prime minister, Vidur, had convinced the elders in Dhritarashtr's Sabha that it should be named after me. I had strongly disagreed. For a private person like me, any such public award was uncomfortable.

The conversation was merely a process, Vidur had already decided.

'Geela is so...unimaginative,' Vidur had said over one of our dinners. We'd laughed. To be fair, it was.

'But I am a miner, not a poet, Vidur,' I'd said, handing him a bowl of daal, lentils.

'Says who? You don't know it but there is a rishi inside longing to get out of your Kshatriya body.'

He said it casually, while shaping a ball of rice and daal between his fingers before he flung it into his mouth. But the idea struck. Me, a rishi? I killed the thought. But there was a strange truth it carried, one that lingered on.

'Why not something like "Breath of Life"?'

I tried to get away.

'And you won't get kheer if you refuse.'

I gestured towards my mother.

'*She is my mother as much and a mother has no favourites, Badri,*' he mumbled through his meal, still chewing the morsel, a little slower now, looking into the distance. The silence around him was comforting. '*Yes, we could live with that,*' he smiled.

We settled on '*Kuru Breath of Life*'. The empire got the credit, Vidur his kheer and I my anonymity.

'Have you closed the water line?' I asked Vajr. We were close to the site now.

'Yes,' Vajr paused. 'The new chief engineer was very annoyed.'

'If someone woke you up in the middle of the night, I'm sure you wouldn't offer him sweetmeats.'

'I used your name.'

'Good.'

I was the last word on mining in the kingdom of Hastinapur. They might gripe and groan, call me senile, but after five decades of dedicated service to the nation, four of them in tunnels, nobody ignored my orders. Vidur's commands were clear: 'If Badri asks for anything from anyone at any time, it must be delivered without fail. Discussions later.'

It wasn't just me. This order applied to all the highest-ranked officials in the kingdom. The commander-in-chief, chief justice, chief priest, chief jailor, chief surveyor, chief of police, chief architect...I was one among many. But the many were few.

And the few were dying.

How I missed Diwakar, the chief engineer, before Kailash was thrust on Hastinapur by Shakuni. But how could Diwakar die such a strange death?

He was returning from one of the irrigation canals he had built so the Vaishya agriculturists on the western side of Hastinapur could get water and grow their wheat.

It was said that a wild horse had run him down. But according to spies who reported to Vidur, it had been a planned assassination. We had argued through the night.

'*Why would anyone want to harm someone as inconspicuous as Diwakar?*' I'd asked.

'*Because he controlled the water and the roads of Hastinapur.*'

I had looked at him compassionately. '*Not good enough.*'

*Vidur smiled and began to gaze into the silver vessel he held, as though he was looking at his reflection in the wine.*

*After a while he looked up and said, 'Let's finish this wine.'*

*We drank it in a gulp.*

*When I'd left his house, he walked me to the outer chamber and said, 'Thanks my friend, thanks for not asking. If time and conditions permit, I will tell you everything.' A hint of bitterness hung around the edges of what he left unsaid. I didn't push.*

*Vidur was my friend. He was also the prime minister of Hastinapur. I knew my spaces in both those relationships.*

The waterline was closed but the danger of backflow remained. I turned to Vajr. He had already read my mind.

'The gradient is in our favour. It won't flow back.'

'What is the angle?'

'Badri,' Vajr calmed me down. 'I have checked, relax.'

I was confused. How could the tunnel collapse? The soil had been tested for strength. The ventilation ducts had been reinforced. The scaffoldings were...the scaffoldings!

'Vajra, I can understand a thoughtless hit of a miner. But how did the scaffoldings crash? I thought we had strengthened them only last week.'

'My thoughts exactly. The contractor there,' he pointed out to a sheepish-looking mass of flesh in the distance that once was a handsome man called Vaman, 'followed your instructions to the last nail.'

'Sabotage?' I asked.

Vajr looked at me, his eyes wide.

We turned our heads towards Vaman. He sensed our glance and bowed down low, his hands joined, his face clear and full of remorse.

It didn't make sense.

We reached the site and speared through the crowd of miners, all familiar faces. Like those of soldiers in war.

'Surangraj...' went the whispers.

'Badri...' they hissed as the crowd made way for me to get to the vent.

'Who is trapped?' I asked Vajr.

'Radhe,' a shrill voice answered.

Radhe, I thought with a pang in my heart, as I ran over the rich grassy soil to where the bend was. Why you, of all the people?

'He is holding the scaffoldings,' Vajr said.

My face must have fallen.

'He is a strong boy, Badri, don't be afraid.'

I knew tunnels have a mind of their own. Now, they were telling me that their minds were stronger than their bodies. Tunnels don't care about relationships of their builders. Radhe was the son of Raman, my former assistant, who was now building a career in the neighbouring Matsya kingdom.

It wasn't difficult to find out where Radhe was. A small crowd of night-shift miners had gathered around an air vent funnelling life to him. Luckily, there was still time before the morning shift. The space, just above where Radhe was, had been cleared.

Vajr had quickly built an additional temporary ventilation duct for the trapped boy. As he updated me on the details of the accident, I wondered how long Radhe could hold the weight of the earth, even if the planks stayed.

'How long can you hold on, Radhe?' I had to shout over the din of chaos among other miners, who had nothing to hold on to but their tongues. My voice was gruff, deep, almost gravely, not unlike the medium of mud and stone I lived in. The silence that followed was still.

The precise point, where Radhe was trapped in Tunnel 14 was closer to the middle tunnels. This meant the depth was of about six to eight dhanush. Worse, the duct was a curved structure because of the huge rock between Tunnel 14 and Tunnel 15, so sound would have to bounce through the duct.

'Badri?' the voice was loud but I could sense the symptoms of weakness in it. There was way for air and the dust had been controlled. But his muscles were tiring. The crowd had already got him to speak more than he should have. 'Don't worry,' he grunted. 'I will hold on till you reach.'

I smiled to myself, remembering my younger days. I had seen Radhe grow into a young man. When Raman sent him to me for training, he did so knowing he could trust me. As in all professions, children don't take lessons from parents. Raman wanted me to train his son. I couldn't let him down.

'We are coming for you, Radhe,' I shouted. 'Stay strong.' In the silence that followed, I felt worry cut its way through my nerves.

I turned to Vajr. 'He seems to be around the point where we built the last scaffoldings.'

'...That's right, sir...' a tentative voice slipped in. It was the contractor.

'Vaman,' I said roughly, 'if there has been any compromise in your materials or placing...'

'...I know sir,' his brain behind that pot-belly was functional, his eyes in pain. 'I personally supervised that bend. If you find any compromise, crush me under the first elephant. I can't believe this myself.'

I nodded. Vaman's eyes were speaking the truth. This was no contractor error.

'If the scaffoldings have broken, the palace route would be closed, right?'

'Actually,' Vajr paused to spit, 'the scaffoldings have collapsed from both sides.'

'Both sides!' I swore. 'Vaman, how could that happen?'

'Badri,' Vajr intervened calmly, 'don't you remember? You would tell me anything can happen in a tunnel.'

'Yes, but this is not the moving of earth or the flowing of water. This is our tunnel, Vajr. Ours. Built for the Kurus, by the best in Aryavart. This needs an investigation.'

Vaman was fidgeting on the side. 'By all means, Badri. Please investigate it, get the best men to do it, I assure you...'

'Right now, Vaman, your assurance is the last thing on my mind,' my thoughts returned to the boy. 'We need to save Radhe.'

'Two teams are already working, Badri,' Vajr said. 'From both sides.'

'How far is Radhe from the sides?'

'According to my estimates, he would be six dhanush from the palace side and about four same from the west. I am betting on the western side.'

That was a rocky patch. Those four dhanush could take more than a day. Perhaps two even.

I turned to the forest beyond the site. Beyond the first line of trees, it was dark. I concentrated on Ratridevi. 'Help me, Mother. A life is at stake. Show me your mercy.'

One by one the sounds disappeared then the tension.

In the silence that followed, my mind walked through the intricate network of tunnels I had built over the past few decades.

The answer dropped.

I bowed before Her in gratitude.

'Pull the team off right now, Vajr.'

Vajr paused to spit. 'Pull it off?'

'No point wasting their energies,' I said. 'Besides, digging horizontally has an additional danger of hitting another part of the tunnel that could end up in a backflow which can drown Radhe. And then, there's that untested, unstudied boulder.'

Vajr scratched his head slowly. 'So, what's your plan?'

'To break into Tunnel 14 from one of the parallel tunnels. Get me a new team, fresh. And reach Entrance 2.'

As I ran towards the entrance of tunnels, I heard Vajr give orders behind me. I left my staff at the entrance and grabbed a shovel from one of the junior diggers. 'When did you last test this shovel?'

'This morning, sir,' the man stammered.

'Are you sure? There is a life at stake here.' I tested the shovel for strength and stability.

'Yes sir.' From the look of hurt on his face and the conviction in his voice I knew he spoke the truth.

'Good. Your tools are your gods, always respect them.'

By the time I reached Entrance 2, Vajr was standing with two young diggers in their loin cloths and one senior digger in his dhoti, now tied above his knees. I recognized the senior digger from his stocky frame. Even at a distance, you couldn't miss Sauti.

'Another emergency, Sauti,' I said. He gazed at me intensely.

Sauti had worked with me in a previous disaster, a few years ago. It was the night of Diwali and we had had a small team working overtime to complete a connecting tunnel that had caved in.

As Hastinapur celebrated the festival of lights, we managed to save sixteen lives. That incident wiped the smile off Sauti's face forever. He had suddenly grown older, grimmer. We had lost two diggers. One of them was his son.

Even at the end of the day, or night I should say, the two younger diggers were bursting with energy. One was almost a dhanush tall, the tallest digger I had met in a long time.

How did he make it through the academy? He was lean, all muscle. Rarely do tall people make the miner's grade. This is a profession for dwarfs. Mine was a lateral entry into mining—I had chosen to leave the fighting for a more peaceful but equally vital service of the kingdom, more as an administrator.

All chief miners in any kingdom of Aryavart were shorter than me. The tallest of the rest, Samba of Avanti, stood well below my chest.

This boy was fidgeting, raring to go.

'What's your name?'

'Vyakul, son of the state.'

An orphan.

I looked at him again. He carried a pride that few sons living in families did. Thanks to Bhishm and his each-child-our-child principle, a child without a family was given a larger family of Hastinapur and the accompanying strength that came with it.

Many children were adopted by childless households. From the look of belonging on Vyakul's face, he could well have refused the offer and stayed on with his larger family.

'Thank you for joining us in this mission, Vyakul,' I said. 'You know the dangers, I presume.'

'I wouldn't have given it up for anything, sir,' he said, a burst of sincerity enveloping me.

The other apprentice was shorter, stout. Below the fat, I could sense strength. His arms were well-proportioned.

'And you?'

'My name is Kalu, son of Dwandh.'

'Dwandh...the charioteer?'

'Yes, Surangraj,' Kalu beamed at the recognition.

'You look as though you worked through the night.'

'Yes Surangraj, I did.'

I looked at Vajr, a question hanging between us.

'He insisted, Badri,' Vajr said with a straight face.

'Radhe saved my life, Surangraj. I wouldn't stay back even if you...' he paused out of politeness.

As I heard him, I felt my youth rush in.

'Do all of you know what we plan to do?'

'Yes Surangraj,' they answered in a chorus.

'Do all of you know that we might not return?'

'Yes Surangraj,' the chorus chanted. The voices of the young diggers were a shade louder.

'Is any of you an only son?' The question was redundant as far as Vyakul went but had to be asked according to rules I had framed.

'No Surangraj.' Kalu and Vyakul exchanged a playful glance.

Vajr had chosen well. The two looked like a team.

'A good combination, Vajr.'

Between Sauti's experience and the young diggers' power, we could save a life.

I turned to Vajr. 'Now, you wait here. We'll be back.'

'What?'

'Yes Vajr, we'll be back,' I looked at him. He seemed to be melting away.

'Am I not coming?'

'No you're not. And in case I don't return, you know the drill.'

I turned my back to him to avoid any further argument.

'But sir, I cannot let you go there alone.'

'I'm not alone. You have given me these three brave diggers. That's enough.'

He looked hurt. 'I mean...please let me come, I know what you plan to do.'

'Vajr, we have worked and built tunnels ever since I remember mining. I know exactly what's on your mind. Thank you, my friend. But with the blessings of Ratridevi, I will be back, we all will,' I turned to my team. 'Radhe will be back. Now relax here. Get the vaid, and keep some water and gur ready.'

I didn't want to speak of the eventuality of the danger we were getting into. Or the fact that he would have to take charge if I didn't return alive. He knew the responsibility.

We turned to enter the tunnel. Before I could take a single step, Vajr stood before me. He folded his hands, bent down and touched my feet. I took his shoulders to hug him. He clasped me hard. 'I'll be waiting, Badri.'

'I have to go, Vajr.'

When he moved back, I noticed his eyes were wet. My heart was warmed but I had no time for sentiment. 'Don't weaken me, Vajr.'

'Let's go,' I said to the team.

I led the three diggers to the entrance. The guard at Entrance 2 had been observing us. I looked at him for the security drill.

'One chief miner, one senior miner, two diggers entering lower tunnels,' he shouted to nobody in particular and made four notches on the sal wood plank before him. That was how the tunnel guards remembered.

I looked at the light outside. A white gleam filled the spaces that were dark merely moments ago. Soon the harsh sun would be out. The tunnel was waiting.

I turned to the guard. He was handing a torch to Sauti. It was burning just right, embers rather than fire. The guard knew air was precious, it needed to be saved.

Radhe needed us. My team awaited my command. We looked at each other. I nodded.

Then, in silence that you could call peaceful or fearful, we descended into darkness.

The tunnel welcomed us in its cool confines.

'Sauti,' I began to think aloud, 'Tunnel 14 is a connector. But both ends have caved in. We don't how long the breach is. In any case, I can't take the risk of breaking through them. One wrong hit and whatever space is left with Radhe, will fall,' I paused, letting everyone adjust their eyes to the darkness ahead.

'My plan is to break into it from one of the parallel tunnels. Which one is the nearest?'

'Technically there are two. Tunnel 34 is the nearer one,' his voice fell, thinking. 'But there's the boulder…you remember? You called him "The Scoundrel".' The two boys laughed.

'Yes, I remember and we had to go around it.'

'And instead of going south, I convinced you to veer north.'

I smiled. 'A fact, that you will not let me ever forget. How long is the bend from Tunnel 14?'

'About a dhanush or so.'

'All right, we'll break in through Tunnel 34.'

'Now listen carefully,' I said, turning back to the team behind me. 'This is a military operation. Soldiers fight on land with one another. We fight nature and human excesses beneath the land. We need absolute discipline. One error could mean the loss of five lives.'

Vyakul and Kalu exchanged a glance, then looked at Sauti, who nodded. They turned to me.

'Our goal is to reach Tunnel 34 and dig sideways through the gap,' I said. 'Getting there will not be easy. We will have to pass through the lower tunnels. So though there will be just enough air for all of us, it might get a little suffocating. But like in battle, we have no options. We win or die. Are you ready?'

'Yes Surangraj,' two youthful voices filled the darkness with the conviction of a war cry, again reminding me of my past.

'One last thing.' They looked at me. 'We need to get there fast but also need to conserve our breath and energy for the final battle. Victory is most important. And ours lies in saving Radhe.'

Vyakul nodded, turned to Kalu and exchanged a silent note. Sauti was as still as the tunnel itself.

'Let's go.'

My mind was redrawing the network of tunnels that I had designed, overseen and built over the past three decades.

All palaces had tunnels to help their kings escape, just in case. But Hastinapur's was the only palace I knew of, that had this intricate mesh to help the royal family and the ruling leadership escape in case of the worst, say a siege or even a break-in into the fort.

Not all tunnels were meant for the royalty. Some were used by Vidur to speak to his spies and messengers, for which I had organized pockets. The tunnels were like corridors of secrecy, where you could have a conversation, hide, heal. Nobody could come or leave unannounced.

Or so we thought.

Behind our backs, many of these tunnels were being openly abused by officials and servants who threw names of the royalty at my staff.

Queen Gandhari's perfume attendant Medha, for instance, thought it her right to walk through Tunnel 29 simply because it was a shorter route to the palace and 'you can't keep the queen waiting, can you?' As a result, smells that were sweet on a woman's body turned that tunnel into an abomination. I began to avoid using that passage.

When I spoke to Vidur about it, he laughed it off. 'This is not war, Badri. Learn to live in peace. It's all right. She has been tested for loyalty. She is fine. Loosen up.'

Perhaps it was because Medha was one of the most beautiful women around. Dark, tall, shapely, with eyes that could kill with a glance, she had a voice that was music and a body that pushed you towards the edges of Aryan principles. She carried a grace that came naturally to her. Had she been born a princess, she would have been a great queen, with kings from across Aryavart seeking her hand.

Or perhaps I was just lonely and her perfumes ignited something more than smells.

In any case, there was no way the enemy could reach Hastinapur through these tunnels. I was yet to see any other kingdom venture near ours in tunnelling complextiy.

From the palace, I had built eleven exits and upper tunnels which were two dhanush deep and went on for half a krosh or so. Depending on the soil-water composition, these merged into the middle tunnels at a gentle slope that took them to a depth of six to eight dhanush. Finally, in a series of stairs, rope ladders and slides, these culminated at the lower tunnels, whose depth depended on where they were. If under the river, they could go as deep as twenty dhanush. The way out was simpler, with low-angled slopes opening out into homes, wells, shrubs, forests, rocks.

Though all tunnels were interconnected, these were not linear connections. They were coded. Often, what looked like the wall of a tunnel hid an entrance to a connecting tunnel.

Even as we created paths in the belly of the earth, our eyes remained outside. Being neighbours, the adjoining kingdoms of Virat and Panchal were our immediate concern. They were led by strong and proud kings and backed by a bountiful agrarian and cattle wealth. Our comfort was in the fact that they still lived by the Arya code.

Hastinapur was the most powerful kingdom in Aryavart, though in the distance Magadh was rising fast. But as history had taught us, power is a fleeting moment in the wider span of time.

Some argued that Hastinapur was spending too much of its resources on tunnels. The treasury officials had even calculated that if we stopped all work on the tunnels and their maintenance, we could reduce taxes by a tenth.

They said the high-security preventive network was not needed in Hastinapur along with King Jarasandh's Magadh, ours was the most powerful kingdom in Aryavart. In fact, other kingdoms had greater reasons to build these tunnels, as the Kuru emperors had repeatedly harboured imperial ambitions. From Shantanu to Pandu, it was Hastinapur that had expanded its domains or extracted tribute from neighbouring nations.

Further, the military might and foreign policy of Dhritarashtr's kingdom was unvanquished. Vidur would prevent any alliance against Hastinapur from being sealed through his formidable network of spies and disarmingly charming diplomacy.

But in case that didn't work, Bhishm and Dron were enough, with just a single akshauhini of elephants, chariots, infantry and cavalry to ward off any attack, however large or strong.

The next generation of Kurus also inspired confidence. The repugnant guru-dakshina that Dron got them to extract from Drupad of Panchal aside, we were yet to see their prowess in a full-scale war.

Between Bhim, Duryodhan and Arjun, Hastinapur slept easy. And then, of course, there was Duryodhan's friend Karn.

We had no need of tunnels to save our city from outside attack, they argued.

It was Vidur who patiently explained that the prosperity of Hastinapur was because of the preventive measures taken during peace times. In his world view, tunnels were one arm of an overall policy, whose intricacies lay within his mind.

Our threats were elsewhere. Though the writing on the wall was still being articulated, the fault lines of Hastinapur lay within.

Few spoke of it, but most of us veteran officials could sense that the cracks developing between King Dhritarashtr's hundred sons and his late brother Pandu's five sons went deeper than just sibling rivalry. When Dron's pupils exhibited their skills in a tournament a few years ago, for the first time some of these cracks became public. But most citizens thought they would die away as the boys grew their beards and grappled with responsibilities.

Not me.

I never harboured false hopes. Perhaps that's the way of us miners—there is no space for hope in the small, deadly confines of a tunnel. I could see that the rift would only widen. That's when the powerful Magadh might attempt a siege. It could even be along with Panchal.

I had to prepare for the worst, and when it arrived, this intricate mesh of walkways would come in handy.

Tunnel 14 in itself was a complicated passage. Though it began with the upper tunnels that were two dhanush deep, it also crossed the middle tunnels which could go as low as eight dhanush. That was because of a huge boulder in the middle.

I didn't want to destroy the middle tunnels right now, so I had to enter from the lower tunnels and arrive at the point from where we could get a horizontal clearing.

'We will continue downwards on this Tunnel 2,' I spoke as we walked. 'Then we will make way through 8 and finally to 34. Be careful not to slip because 34 is still under construction and the earth could be wet. We will enter it, walk around the bend that will take us to the height of 14, somewhere close to where Radhe is trapped. There we will dig. We will hit 14 from the south side, probably near the ventilation duct. The last part will be very tricky, so watch every hit. Beyond that we'll just have to take the earth as it comes.'

I looked up and saw three pairs of white eyes, with reddish hues on their face, reflecting Sauti's torch. 'Am I clear?'

'Yes Surangraj,' all three said.

'Let's go.'

I led the descent, with the two young miners behind me. Sauti followed at the end. After the first flight of temporary stairs that still carried the dull light reflecting from outside, darkness embraced us. I waited a few moments, letting the darkness settle down for my team.

Though I could see every ridge clearly, since my pupils were already expanded, I waited for the team to get accustomed to the dark. Sauti's torch, at the end of our rescue party, gave me more than enough light to be able to negotiate the rough edges of our tunnels.

We began our walk.

Ahead, our shadows settled into their eerie but predictable shape-shifting ways. They led us across the twists and turns of the tunnel, now stretching into innumerable shades of black, now gliding over ridges of light, now disappearing altogether, always moving.

Our shadows swept over the rough clay on the sides, the scaffoldings above and the coarse ground below. They flew over the stones and boulders we veered around. They had no pattern except that the previous moment was completely different from the present. And the future would be unrecognizable by any present.

Like dark creatures running away from the light behind, our shadows dug and directed the way ahead for us.

We went deeper. With every step the darkness before us turned a shade blacker, the silence a shade louder. I was home. I touched the walls I had made with my hands. They were smooth, lined with clay we had imported from Mathura through our highly-skilled Vaishya traders. They felt cold. We must be close to where the upper tunnels met the middle tunnels, I sensed.

We continued slowly, deeper into the darkness, measuring each step till we arrived at an opening.

Six entrances invited us into their pitch-dark mouths. This was the end of upper tunnels. The shadows finally settled as all of us caught our breath.

I turned left to enter Tunnel 8. I had hardly taken twelve steps, when without warning, I stumbled over something hard. I didn't fall and regained my balance. It was a carelessly-dug area.

'Watch out, there's a bump here,' I warned the team. 'Sauti, I need to meet the team that did this, tomorrow. This is unacceptable. Also the team that certified it as usable.'

'Yes, sir.' I could sense him thinking.

As we entered the deeper middle tunnels, I left irritation on the surface of my mind and began to concentrate on the emergency at hand. We had to reach Radhe. Fast.

Tunnel 8 was wider than other tunnels. It was meant for soldiers whose thighs could take pressure. The tunnel could also take the breadth of six soldiers at a time.

But since the tunnels were meant for the king and the royal family's safety, they could not be so steep so as to prevent Queen Gandhari from walking. This had been a delicate task and I remembered the intricate planning that had gone into it. For now, I enjoyed the width of the tunnel.

In most other middle tunnels, we would have been panting. But I had adjusted the circulation of the air passage to serve a mini army, so breathing, though a little heavy, was not laboured. The slope was to our advantage.

The air was getting thicker.

'We have reached the lower tunnels,' I announced to a team that had already sensed it. But a drill is a drill. 'Now stay with me,' and I turned right.

Although the stairs were neatly carved out into equal heights, or whatever the earth and stone would allow us, descent was not easy. I could sense the heaviness of breath behind me. 'We need to work on the circulation, Sauti. Remind me tomorrow to speak to Vajr.'

'Yes...' Sauti panted, '...Surangraj.'

As we continued our descent, the air became denser, the panting behind me more audible. The air was not flowing. Something was blocking a passage somewhere. My mind's eye travelled back to the beginning of the tunnel.

'Sauti, the air here is not how it is supposed to be. Check the intersection of 28 and 19 tomorrow. I think we might have a problem there. The water balance was not solved completely. If the earth has collapsed on one of them, we need to rebuild it.'

'Yes,' he paused. 'But the block could be in the circulatory pipes.'

Beyond our heavy breathing that broke the spaces between silences, I sensed the presence of various beings, creatures of darkness.

I had seen many of them. It wasn't worms, insects or bats that bothered me. We had already fixed the rats and the snakes with mini-moats around every entrance, backed by such moats at every junction of upper-to-middle and middle-to-lower tunnels. The strays that still managed to get in were cleared every day.

No, the animal forces were under our control.

Besides, I had realized that animals were more afraid of men. We were the invaders into their homes, armed with modern weapons against which they had no chance. It was only when cornered that they threatened. It was rare for me to hear of any digger being attacked. Just men walking about produced enough vibrations in the ground to keep snakes away. There were random cases of snakebite in winter, if a snake disturbed out of his hibernation fanged his tantrum. But by and large, the animals were fine.

It was the formless ones that posed a bigger challenge. Beings that had no shape, no identity, but who were more dangerous to miners than any other animal or weapon could ever be. They were amorphous shape-shifters, deceptive. They seduced, intimidated, misled. We ruled the terrestrial turf. They were the kings below. Little beings of the nether world, they enjoyed the process of duping us miners.

Rishis told us they were part of the hostile forces nature had created to serve a cosmic equilibrium. They were meant to test our darkest fears, make us face our worst nightmares. And purify us as we passed through them.

Perhaps they resided within us.

I sent a silent prayer of protection to Ratridevi. I also became aware that while Sauti was an experienced miner, the young duo in my team was feeling the first bristling of trepidation. I needed to get their minds off that fear, the worst enemy of a miner. I didn't need that. Certainly not now.

I slowed a step and put my hand on the shoulder of the tall miner behind me.

'Is anything bothering you, Vyakul?'

He hesitated. I turned to look at him, his eyes showed it all.

'I am sorry Surangraj, but yes. I'm feeling afraid.' Straight, honest...I liked this boy. Son of the state, he had said, and like a good son, he put the state above his personal vanity.

'Vyakul, do you remember the miner's prayer?'

'I do.'

'Sing it out for us.'

This was a prayer that all of us were taught by the rishis who had ventured into the earth and stayed buried there for three months. During this time, they did not eat or drink and lived on very little air. So strong was their self-control that they could do all this without any air ducts to help them. One of them told me he didn't even need to breathe.

Their job during this period was to understand the consciousness of the world below, speak to it, tell it about men, their jobs, tunnels and why they needed to break into their silent world. And seek its cooperation.

It was like spiritual diplomacy.

With mantras that spoke directly to the beings there, the rishis had nurtured and refined the art of chanting over centuries. These were handed over to us miners and diggers in the form of mantras. Any apprentice in our profession had to know them. There was no melody here, as in weddings or thread ceremonies. But when recited properly, they carried immense occult force.

As we walked, Vyakul sang.

*Beings of the night*
*Oh, creatures of the dark*
*Allow us to step ahead*
*Pardon this trespass*
*Give us directions*
*So we know you're not in the way*
*Grant us passage, venerable ones*
*So we can travel through your world*
*We bow before you, revered ones*
*We bow before you, oh wise*
*Forgive us, guide us*
*We are all part of the divine dice*

All of us joined him in chorus. 'Aum shanti, shanti, shanti.'

Vyakul sang this prayer from his soul. Very few could do that and certainly not youngsters. They were too self-conscious, too much in a hurry, with too much to prove. But Vyakul's recital touched me.

The silence that followed turned some of the creatures away, not all. As we walked, it felt as if some weight had lifted off our shoulders.

'You sing very well, Vyakul,' I said, trying to spread cheer among the sudden gloom. 'Don't you want to try out a career as the court singer? You'll be much better paid. And it will also be less risky.'

'You might not remember, but you taught us this mantra,' Vyakul said. 'I prefer working with my arms, legs and mind. I love breaking into the earth. Mining is my dharm' and with a hint of contempt, 'not singing!'

'If you come out of this assignment successfully, you can rest assured the road to mining will be smoother,' I said watching the shadows that continued to dance to Sauti's moving torch. One disappeared to my left into a darkness that seemed eternal. I made note of that entrance.

Vyakul's back straightened. 'Thank you, Surangraj.'

'If I might speak...' It was the other young digger, behind Vyakul. 'Of course, Kalu.'

'We just passed an entrance to our left...' he trailed off, hesitantly.

'That's right, Kalu,' I said without slackening the pace. 'Not many diggers can identify tunnels and their entrances so early in their careers.'

Kalu's beam travelled through the darkness and gaps in shadows to me. 'But we need to get to Radhe in Tunnel 14 from below. That entrance is next, not the one we passed.'

I walked for about two dhanush and a huge mouth opened to the right. 'And here it is.'

We entered a narrow tunnel, meant to ward off enemies if they followed. It was also crooked. At points, the rough edges cut our bodies.

'Remember,' I said to nobody in particular, 'this is a safety tunnel. So, it is going to be hard and could scratch you, particularly you Kalu and you Sauti. Be gentle with it. And do not raise your arms too high, you might hurt yourselves against the scaffoldings.'

Each tunnel has its own character. Over a period of planning, digging, finishing, airing, dusting, polishing, they evolve into personalities of their own. Some are gentle, some twisted, some protect, some offer peace.

Not unlike men.

Many change their nature with use. A tunnel used by armies and guards is tense, alert.

One used by citizens for trade catalyses transactions has the pressure of deals in it.

The environment of women and men walking through the tunnels carting their hopes, desires and fears changes the personality of tunnels. Many rugged tunnels have become benign, as lovers turned them into spaces for embrace within the confines of darkness, limitations of air. Love has conquered the hearts of these tunnels.

And then, there are rogue tunnels.

This connector was one such, it had no mercy. I had designed it in a manner that pursuit would be difficult. In an emergency, a few strong pulls on the top of the scaffolding and the tunnel would cave in from behind, leaving the pursuer underground, gasping for air, fighting dust and getting bruised by sharp, uncovered crystals. This would be a short tunnel.

'Just a few more steps,' I said. 'Four...three...two...one...and here we are.'

The opening before us was wider than most. This was the intersection of the middle tunnels with the lower tunnels. As we entered the huge cavity, I heard two gasps behind me. Vyakul and Kalu.

I smiled. Anyone would be wonderstruck at the intricate design of this crossroads. Not everyone had access to this place, only very senior miners or the privileged. Even Sauti, who had been here a few times, was wide-eyed. The only person who had stayed calm on reaching here was Vidur.

But for the height, it had an expanse that would give the Hastinapur Sabha a run for its size. There were eighteen equal, similarly shaped openings around us. Their wide open mouths, shaped craftily to induce fear, hinted at the darkness within. Despite their similar appearances, their individual personalities were intact.

But that could be gauged only after you entered them. When you looked at their entrances, they all merged into a somewhat neutral territory, the rogues and the friends, the compassionate and the vicious.

Like efficient soldiers, they waited. Six of them had further openings about three to five dhanush away. Only four people knew which ones—Bhishm, Vidur, Vajr and I.

With the three of us around Sauti's torch, our shadows pasted themselves on different parts of the round walls, each etching a life, partly on the surface, partly into the open mouth of the tunnels, like a monster eating his prey.

I had named this Crossroads of Confusion. It was meant to leave the best armies bewildered in an emergency, at least for 10 vighati. There would be just about enough time to run ahead and hide or prepare for a fight.

The air was flowing better here and I could sense my team filling their lungs with it.

'Brothers, we will sit for a vighati, catch our breath and concentrate. Ahead lies Tunnel 34. Now listen very carefully,' my tone moved down a few notes. 'We will enter from the third entrance that will take us just half a dhanush from where Radhe is. The earth, as you can smell, is reasonably damp.'

I noticed Vyakul feeling the earth with his hands, testing it here and there. It was largely wet soil with little bits of stone. Despite his height, Vyakul was a natural miner.

'We will have to dig at a slight slant. Kalu and Vyakul, I am banking on your arms to push this through. We should reach the wall in less than 12 vighati. After that, I will dig the horizontal. Clear?'

They nodded slowly.

'Good. Now take a deep breath and concentrate.'

At the centre of the crossroads, four sets of eyes closed in unison to pull all our vital, mental and physical energies together, rid our minds of all distractions. The air caught a charge and I could almost sense a solidity to our concentration. The rishis had taught us well, I thought. Our breath was almost noiseless.

'Aum shanti,' I ended the concentration.

As Sauti, Vyakul and Kalu folded their hands in offering to Ratridevi, I said to nobody in particular, 'Let's go.'

The carvings of mythologies, carefully sculpted across the ceiling by craftsmen brought all the way from beyond the southern Vindhyas, were our clues. We had to enter the one below a crocodile. I led the team.

Vyakul followed, steadier now. We began the climb in silence. Eight dhanush later, we turned right towards our final destination. Our shadows went running across the smooth lines of Tunnel 34. I calculated in my mind the mesh behind. A few steps more. I began to test the walls, hitting them at various places. We were now almost parallel to Tunnel 14.

I hit the wall with my fists.

Dull.

One step...lighter.

Two more steps...sharper.

Five more steps...dull.

Back again three steps...sharp. I slapped again for confirmation... sharp.

I looked at Sauti.

He turned to the boys, pointing to an area about the size of a large dog. 'Here.'

They began well. Every thud pulled mounds of earth. Sauti and I began to clear it behind us with our shovels. The boys were being careful, trying to not throw the earth on our faces.

'Vyakul, Kalu, stop fooling around,' I said sharply. 'You are wasting time.'

They immediately began in greater earnest. Breathing was getting heavy again. Sweats of anticipation and fear began to fill the space. Every hit ended in a grunt. A few mounds of earth hit my bare chest and I knew, they were digging with their very souls.

But I overestimated their prowess or underestimated the earth. Even after 15 long vighatis the hole didn't look any bigger. It took them about 10 fear- and hope-filled vighatis before they reached where I wanted them to.

Radhe's life clung to each vighati.

The mounds turned heavier, damper. I sensed greater amount of water in the soil. Below our feet, the ground had become slippery. I was worried.

'Careful now, don't slip,' I said. The young boys readjusted their stance and continued.

The stench of our collective sweat was overpowering, filling the space. The air felt so thick, we could well be digging through it. This tunnel was not meant for exertion, it was merely a bridge to a larger one. The lack of oxygen got the boys panting.

We had very little time. If the wall didn't give in now, there could be five fatalities, not just one.

The dullness began to fade with their hits, the sound turned a little sharper. Was it my imagination or hope? We were close. No, the sound was real.

'Stop now, get back,' I said.

In the little light that Sauti's torch illumined, I could see their faces drenched in sweat, the whites of their eyes in a slit, standing out in an otherwise completely black area. Vyakul slid across my body, his frame hot with the exertion, his breath coming in spurts. When Kalu went, his thicker gait pushed me to the wall of the tunnel, cutting my back where a rebellious stone stood out.

No time for the luxury of pain. I pulled out my narrow pickaxe and began to push it gently about 2 dhanurgarh from the bottom. Instead of hitting the wall in front of us, I was scraping the soil out from under it. Digging here was tricky work and needed supreme attention.

A shovel was useless here. The more you dig, the more the sand and mud will cave in on you. At this depth, the tunnel faced pressure from both the top and the sides.

All of us experienced miners used hand tools. Our ancestors began with bones, antlers and stones, moved on to wood and then to bronze. Today we use iron. My staff and pickaxe were built from the best iron, the one warriors use to make swords and spears.

The staff was a variant of the spears in my earlier life.

The pickaxe scraped a stone and my heart stood still. The sound brought three sighs behind me and the panting stopped for a few seconds. If we had a boulder before us, Radhe was as good as dead. Starting all over from the other side would mean a risky compromise with time.

I carried on. It was just an errant stone, large, heavy but still movable. With the pickaxe, I carefully removed the soil around it. The devil was smaller than a boulder but larger than a head. I pulled it out and threw it behind me. It rolled off with a thud.

Tentative laughter behind me.

I too found myself smiling with relief. The stone aside, the soil flowed easily and I continued to push.

A few moments later, my pickaxe went in smoothly.

An opening.

I began to move the pickaxe horizontally, using all the strength I had. When I made enough place for my arms to enter, I put the pickaxe behind me and began to use my hands to pull out clods of earth from above the opening. I pulled gently, slowly, testing each clod.

'Radhe?'

No reply.

'Radhe,' I shouted. 'Radhe!'

A groan.

'Hold on Radhe, we are there.' Mother, give me the strength to get him out alive.

Panic doesn't need mind's permission and against my better judgement, it entered my arms and I began to pull at the earth with a madness that grips the frightened. I pulled hard, throwing clods of earth behind me with violence that had been sitting dormant in me.

'It's all right, Badri,' Sauti said behind me. 'We are almost there.'

I could feel Radhe's feet. They were cold. I shook them, as I pulled out the earth. A lump of wet soil fell to the ground. I pushed it behind with my hands. My head entered the hole, I could see him now.

'Sauti, the torch!'

Sauti passed me the torch and I set it next to me to allow me to see what's inside.

Radhe was still holding the planks but was resting his elbows on his chest. Dried blood lay thick on his arms, while thin, fresh streams flowed from his head. His shoulders were stuck to the wall. He had raised his knees to hold the planks across him. He looked weak. His eyes were closed.

'Radhe!' I shouted, my voice quivering in new panic, sharpening the pitch. 'Radhe!'

I dragged myself into the tunnel and stood up. Working around the scaffoldings, I checked their strength. They seemed perfect. Not a bamboo was out of place.

Except one. It was leaning on one side of the tunnel, while Radhe held the other. I looked up and met my worst fears. The break wasn't out of a weak branch or an error of unaccounted-for excess weight that miners often forget.

I raised the torch and lit the truth. The cut was smooth, clean—deliberate. My breath stopped. A breach in tunnel security? Who would do that? Surely it was an insider's job. Why?

I must speak to Vidur.

I looked down at Radhe. His eyes opened weakly.

'Radhe, are you all right?' I asked, my mind still on the cut.

As his gaze met mine, he smiled weakly through caked blood on his lips. 'Badri, you are here? I knew you would come. See, I held on...'

I could see him giving up with relief, transferring the responsibility of his life to me. As his arms gave up the fight, the end of the scaffolding he was holding on to gave away. The wood groaned dully and the earth fell on me with sudden force. I held back the planks and bamboos, but the pressure above was too much. One plank cracked loudly and fell on my back, carrying with it the weight of the earth.

I fell on Radhe, but managed to hold back with my hands and knees. I pushed back to give room to Radhe.

'Sauti!' I shouted.

'Yes Badri.'

'Pull him out,' I said with a grunt. 'Fast. Now.'

The weight kept getting heavier, pushing me down. Radhe was below me now, my feet spread out at the entrance of our breach for Sauti to drag him out, my hands next to his shoulders.

I heard the wood creak. The earth we pulled off had weakened the scaffolding, it was cracking now. A volley of mud and stones hit my back. The wooden planks followed, threatening to break my spine. In the silence of the earth, the noise was loud.

The tunnel was collapsing.

The weight almost crushed me, my arms taking most of the pressure. Another plank groaned. Its pitch rose higher. And with a loud sound it cracked and fell on my back. It took me superhuman effort to push the weight back, even hold it where it was. My arms, strong from the soldier's discipline, held together, my muscles crying out for relief. My thighs protested the pressure.

Pain, acute pain. I invoked Shakti, goddess of strength. 'Just a few moments, Mother.'

I was still on my fours. But the weight had increased. My arms wouldn't hold out.

Sauti was dragging Radhe out carefully. 'Sauti, pull him out now!' it was a shout that ended in an urgency as I felt something in the tunnel give in with a deep and hair-raising rumble.

As more weight fell on my back, I was breathing in gasps. There was dust around my face, I could feel it enter my lungs. I coughed.

'We're pulling, save your breath,' said Vyakul.

I felt a pressure and looked down. Radhe's injured face was limp, his blood-drenched hair following as his body was being pulled out roughly.

The weight above kept increasing. I bent down and saw Radhe's arms follow limply. Someone was shouting, 'Badri, Badri!'

The sounds began to get fainter.

Suddenly, I found a tunnel within and flew away to a battlefield.

I was gone. Into a world I thought I had left behind. Time dragged me back, all the way, to the war I had tried hard to forget. I met my guilt.

The past four decades I spent hiding from that soldier, from my love, from myself, all those years I had spent in the darkness, using tunnels as my shield, my sanctuary, all those hard years vanished. Suddenly, I was facing my inner devils.

There was a flash of light, metal clanged against metal and bore through a body. Blood spilled out.

'*Badri!*' *someone was shouting.* '*No, Badri!*' *It was Urvashi.*

*Too late.*

*I was wounded. A sword had slashed my right thigh. An arrowhead stuck out of my right arm, two others stuck in my back. A spear had gouged somewhere below my chest, resulting in a bloody but harmless gash. I was on my knees.*

*Her back was against an overturned chariot, her sword had fallen. He was walking slowly, knowing her end was near, his sword twisting in* his wrist, swinging with his arm. They were talking, perhaps the final lines before the end.

Urvashi closed her eyes, awaiting the final blow.

He raised his sword. Instinct moved faster than sound, and before I knew it, my spear was gone.

As the thick, heavy metal flew from my left hand, gliding over a sludge of blood, I realized it was too late. The spear stuck home, precisely where it was intended to, through his back where his heart pumped life.

The man's sword dropped.

He turned slowly. I saw death in his eyes, but his were not looking at the spear jutting out of his body.,They were piercing my armour, and through it, shaking my soul.

As the light began to go out of those eyes, they continued to pierce me, turning and twisting my innards.

A shriek...Urvashi.

'What have you done, Badri,' she sobbed. 'What have you done?'

She turned to the soldier before her, the man who would have killed her without remorse and folded her hands. 'Forgive me, Nataraj, this victory was yours.'

Something inside me dried up. I looked at the dying man.

He was standing now, slightly bent in great pain, the tail of my spear behind. The handle of his sword was visible, the shaft buried in streams of black-red puddles below. He looked at it with a poignant longing but was too weak to reach out.

The well-sharpened head of my spear was jutting out of where his heart should have been, now a receding fountain of red beyond his armour. He saw his blood merging with that of others, below him, in marshy mire. He looked up. There was no pain in his eyes, only surprise. Like a volley of arrows, they stung me.

'How could you?'

I was too stunned to speak. My physical strength was draining out. It was my last spear.

The soldier tried to raise his hand to signal but failed. His mouth opened to say something but couldn't. It twisted into a smile of pity, compassion, forgiveness. He was still smiling as he finally fell in a dark red splash around him. He lifted his head. Beyond the soil, now darkened with his own blood, *all I could see were the whites of his eyes. He died looking at me, those eyes bleeding me within.*

I shouted myself back into waking. The relief was a blessing, the darkness comforting. The pain made me feel alive again. I was moving in and out of the conscious and unconscious, present and past, light and darkness.

Alone.

Battling those eyes I had been running from, all my life, all over again.

'Radhe...'

'He's safe, you can come out.'

The mission was over, we had saved Radhe. Almost on cue, the plank above me gave way completely, hitting the right side of my head as I tried to hear what Sauti was saying. My neck twisted and I floated into a darkness of pain as the world around me caved in. Dry dust began to rise and fill my lungs in the small confines of where now I braced for death. My face hit the ground and I swallowed dust that mingled with the blood in my mouth. I choked for a moment. Then I couldn't breathe anymore.

I saved him, Raman, I saved him.

*'You killed him!' a distant voice screamed. 'In cold blood.'*

No, he is safe.

*'You killed him in the most heinous way possible.'*

He was going to kill Urvashi.

*'That's the way of the Kshatriya. To die fighting.'*

But her shield was thrown away, she was unarmed.

*'And that was enough for you to break the soldier's dharm?'*

No, I followed my dharm, I saved her.

*'In a battlefield, there is no personal dharm, there is only the Kshatriya dharm. You breached that. You no longer deserve to be called a Kshatriya.'*

I killed for the kingdom.

*'The kingdom stands on dharm, you destroyed it.'*

I killed for Urvashi.

*'On the battlefield, there are no people, only warriors.'*

I killed but I am ready to die as well.

*'It's not your death that's needed. It's your life. You need to shift.'*

I was numbed into stillness. Shift what?

'Your being.'

My being?

*Urvashi stood up slowly, the sword back in her left hand, her right arm bleeding, her face full of dried tears, her hair scattered.*

*She was panting from the long fight, bracing on the sword to stand steady, taking short, loud breaths as she readied herself for the next charge. Her accusing eyes surged through the battlefield and cut me into a thousand pieces.*

'Urvashi,' I began...

*Her eyes bored into my soul, carrying anger, disappointment and helplessness altogether. And yet, they looked no different from when I first saw her. Through her eyes, her soul spoke to mine directly. We didn't need words.*

I took a step forward to embrace her, calm her down.

*She shook her head at me. Then, with a suicidal scream, she turned and jumped back into the battle behind her, seeking a final dance with death.*

'Stop, Urvashi, stop...'

*'By not moving, you are killing her'...another voice. Kedar...gurudev...*

But I...I saved her...

*'Leave your death wish. Embrace life. Shift...shift...shift...'*

Shift what, gurudev?

That was the question, the last thought in me as I felt rough hands pull my feet and roughly drag me out. The weight of the earth on the broken planks, now covering my back, was crushing me.

Then, with a deafening sound that reverberated through my being, Tunnel 14 swallowed me in its deathly silence.

# Conspiracy

*Thirteen days later*

A survivor, that's who he was. He had a perceptible presence. Silent, yet familiar strength. And it was growing. The first time

I met him, the assassins had almost managed to kill him with swords and maces.

I knew a fighter when I saw one. In moments that could have been final, I've seen many Kshatriyas give up. Not this one. He was fighting back with all the spirit he carried in his young-and-growing but physically-weak, brutally-wounded body.

That was last year.

I was on my way to Tunnel 96, one of the lower tunnels that needed my absolute attention and one that had become a challenging duel. It was a complex tunnel. It suffered from excessive leakage as well as flowing dust.

Tunnel 96 was the main connector to the middle tunnels the royal family would use to escape, if the need arose. Most of all, it had to be built in absolute secrecy. We had to keep it hidden, as far as we could, from the rest of the miners.

I was enjoying the stillness of pre-Vedic morning, the dew-topped grass caressing my bare feet, lending a cold-yet-warm sensation that nobody has been able to understand yet. But for the setting moon, the sky was dark.

Yet it carried the threat of turning dark purple, as the sun would soon play its magic of time and Goddess Ushas took charge of the day from Ratridevi. My eyes were comfortable and I could make out the silhouettes of banyan, neem and pipal trees.

The smell of mangoes filled the air with their characteristic sweetness, teaching Hastinapur more about the changing seasons than any lesson in the gurukuls. There were a few shrubs under them, surrounded by gently-swinging blades of grass, beaten down near the trunk, with impatient children climbing to pluck mangoes still lingering.

The birds had not begun their morning songs yet. Not a twig rustled, but the gentle air cooled the body.

The darkness comforted my eyes and perhaps some others who thrive on it.

Just then, the atmosphere was shattered by a strong, sarcastic command. It was like a violent slap to the silence that descended on Hastinapur between darkness and dawn. I startled out of my reverie.

'Three of you and you can't get him?' It was a familiar tone. The man was a high-ranking soldier, used to giving orders and had sold his skills to the dark side. He may still be loyal to the kingdom but not to the forces within himself.

I've seen power do that to many.

The faint blue light of the setting moon turned the shadowed area they were in almost black. Three soldiers were crouched together, their knees bent, their arms spread out. Their backs to me, they were clearly going for the kill.

The moonlight sent one shaft of reflected light and two dull-blue—one sword and two light maces. Someone was going to get hurt.

'Keecha, get the bastard,' one of them hissed.

'I'm trying, I'm trying...'

'Don't try, just kill him. He's done enough damage.'

'Watch out, you'll get hurt!'

It must be a brave man who stood up to them.

Four men against one was a serious volation of the Aryan code. It disturbed me to no end. But of late, the deterioration in values had begun to accelerate like a horseless chariot running downhill. Across Aryavart, we could see the fall of dharm. Hastinapur was no exception.

This group of ruffians didn't seem to be from the city, though. Their accent placed them outside Hastinapur. Somewhere north, I thought. Part of the Kuru empire, no doubt, and yet not quite.

The north was where rich plains gave way to the lofty Himavat. People from mountains are generally calmer. Mountains, like tunnels or mines, cannot be taken for granted. They offer a measured existence.

There, the natural serenity is amplified by the presence of rishis, the constant hum of Vedic chants, the learnings of the Upanishads, the stories of the Purans and the presence of gods themselves. Or perhaps the absence of men that kept nature's magic still alive.

This was something else, an aberration.

I looked around for the night guard. He was nowhere around. This was the second time I had caught him sleeping. Probably drunk like last time.

I banged my iron staff on a small boulder on the side to alert them of my presence. It had a ring of strength that only Bhola, a weapons blacksmith, specializing in spears, knew how to provide. His subtle tempering of the metal was known to every atirathi in the Kuru empire.

In the past he had made my spears. Now that I needed staffs, he had welded them with a precision that gave them the power to dig. Under my instructions, he ensured they remained weapons, particularly the edges, the holds and one end. So, they were my tools of trade as well as weapons.

'What's going on?' My raspy voice in the silence was loud. It had a peculiar tone, a sharp ring of disgust whenever it spoke to injustice. I leaned casually on the staff, a smaller pickaxe swinging lightly behind my back on a leather string.

The three men bending over stood up with a start, looking at each other, almost as if they were caught. This was clearly trouble.

The leader turned towards me. Slowly. His long sword swung with his body, almost as if it were a part of him, and swayed back, holding in its pendulum the threat of death. A small curve of his shield stood out in a silhouette above his left shoulder, a weapon as well as a status symbol.

His movement was careful and carried in it the predictable intoxication of power that had consumed the man. His body didn't move but an invisible aggressive devil sitting in his being jumped at me. The force was palpable.

As a rule I disliked large men. But this one drove my aversion to the edge. There was something about him I detested immediately.

Rishis say, what you hate resides as a mirror in you—fix that and your hate turns to love. I couldn't fix it within, so I lived with it.

'Who are you?'

His voice was soft, almost like someone not wanting to be discovered, but annoyed at having to be quiet. I looked closely. The man was taller than me, better built, younger, more aggressive. He also carried the arrogance of someone who knew that it mattered little if he was caught.

Someone high up was protecting him—an official, a minister even. No, you can't go so far with officials. It was probably someone from the royal family. Or maybe, I was overreacting.

I took my time in walking up to him. His demeanour annoyed me no end. It could have been the emanation that had jumped out of his body and expanded, making him look larger than he was. In the shadows of moonlight and trees, I made out the well-toned muscles. Somewhere a dart of envy pierced the memory of my youth.

The tunnel needed all my attention and my being was concentrated near my head, trying to figure out the fissures below the rock, the water table and the complexity of either going around and risking the water at a future date or mining through the rock that would be safer but longer.

When you sit in your mind, there is a comfort, as you rise above emotions into the higher realms of thought, ideas, reason. Retreating to the heart is restful. Over the past few years I'd found that despite being a warrior-worker, the heart was calling me and it was slowly becoming my natural abode.

But climbing down from the head is painful. And I was feeling the agony now, as I prepared for a fight that seemed inevitable, and during which my energy balled itself into my solar plexus. Like it would, during wars.

With every step forward, I descended towards the middle of my body and with every fall, my muscles quivered, my body yearned to act, my irritation rose. The domesticated organization man in me be damned, I was back on the battlefield, muscles taut, the familiar bloodlust rising.

I took a deep breath, using the time to allow myself to settle lower as I walked the few steps towards the man. My hold on the staff, steadied with the earth from the walkway to my home in my palms, was reassuring. It was as much a weapon as a tool or symbol of authority.

The pickaxe swinging lightly behind me, invisible to the group in case of sudden fight, gave me additional support. In its natural form it cut through soil and rocks; but if agonized and pushed, a little twist of the wrist could draw death blood. I was ready.

Behind me the purple skies of Ushas were opening up. From the side, the setting moon's rays shone on the leader's face, now visible. It was square and ugly. He had a nose broken by many battles—a close-combat soldier. His forearms were smooth; certainly not an archer's. His upper arms were thick and rounded—a man who once used the mace but had now given it up to the technologically superior and lighter sword. The chin stood forward, head held higher than normal. A senior soldier, an officer.

'I'm a citizen of Hastinapur,' I said calmly, the blood flowing fast in my veins, ready to kill or spill. I closed my eyes and breathed part of my anger out. 'Who are you?' My voice startled one of his men standing behind.

Though I could see him clearly, his eyes were still trying to look beyond my silhouette. A snarl began to form around his mouth. He opened his mouth to speak, when there was a violent movement behind, and a cry that jarred the silence.

One of the men was lying on the ground, his sword on his side. A dark shadow formed on his chest. The man's cry ended in a gurgle, a sound I had heard many times in war. It was the sickening dull murmur of a throat torn off, when an axe withdraws from the neck or a skilled martial arts warrior uses the deadly skill of his fingers to yank it out.

Alert and active, the shadow jumped from the chest of the gurgling man to avoid the swing of a mace that came from behind. It was almost as if the man with the mace was hitting air. But more impressive was that the shadow managed to 'see' the blow come from behind.

Clearly, a warrior, either trained and experienced, or powerfully intuitive. The gurgling man's voice began its predictable sickening coughing, choking.

Through the noise and haze of fleeting movements, I was able to see who I was protecting.

It wasn't a 'who' but a 'what'.

Limping, the black shadow leaped back on his attacker in one roundabout twist, trapping the mace-holding wrist in his mouth.

The mace fell with a thud and rolled away, the moonlit gleam pendulating with anticipation, waiting to be picked up again. This was not a mace of a common man. It was bordered with spikes—not the hundred that only the superheroes of our age managed to carry and control, but still sharp enough to be a weapon of offence.

Why?

The dog didn't let go and the man began to make animal noises. The third man was shaking, unable to decide.

With a measured movement, the big man before me unsheathed his sword, walked up to the screaming man with the dog attached to his right wrist and raised it in a certainty of death. A dull blue-white gleam reflected from it.

Without my knowing, my staff pushed out, catching the rising sword in its upward journey. Using the momentum of his sword, my staff pushed it higher than the solider had planned, perhaps at the point when he would slash it down, twisting it on the way.

It was a technique I had learnt from Parashuram, when he was teaching Bhishm and a handful of us around him. The sword slipped out of his hand, gathered a mind of its own, cleared a graceful double-somersault, before falling behind him. A sharp and sustained clang filled the morning silence.

The sound told me all I needed to know. The weapon was heavy, well-crafted, well-balanced, a weapon only senior soldiers carried. He was definitely a gana-pati—in charge of twenty-seven elephants, eighty-one horses and one hundred and thirty-five footsoldiers, if not higher.

The big man looked up with a sudden start. Maybe he didn't expect it. Maybe it was the darkness that worked in my favour. Maybe the dog had years ahead. Maybe I was just lucky.

Between the dying moonlight and the emerging morning light, I noticed his face closely. It was the face of a warrior with trails of many battles etched on his face. Two scars stood out, one on his left cheek, the other around the centre of his forehead, above the nose, travelling into his black locks, tied back.

But it was the snarl and eyes that revealed that this was a man with no scruples, a Kshatriya gone bad. Probably a spy-assassin. One who killed not for dharm but because he enjoyed killing.

What was he doing in Hastinapur?

The early risers were beginning to throng towards us. The man looked around as a group of rishis tried to figure out what the early morning fuss was about. One of them, chewing on a neem twig, leaned forward, spat out his phlegm to the side and asked, 'Badri, is that you? What's going on?'

The assassin narrowed his eyes into slits. 'You dare challenge me?' he hissed, the sneer making his face uglier than it was. 'Badri,' he said, registering the name somewhere for future abuse.

'Yes, Madhyamaya, it's me,' I replied to the rishi but continued to look at the assassin. 'It's nothing. Just some good folks who seem to have lost their way.'

'You dare challenge me?' he repeated, his hand around his belt. I noticed it carried a dozen or so knives and a larger one, the asidhenu. A dangerous three-edged weapon that close-combatants used, by his side.

When fighting the sword, all he would need to do would be to get into the swing of the opponent's arm. Once there, an expert in asidhenu could kill the best of warriors with ease. A swordsman or even a mace-wielder had no chance.

'Keep your hands where I can see them,' my voice grated out of my throat. The grip on my staff was in the attack position, as a soldier would hold a spear. I saw him note that and store it somewhere. His eyes travelled down my spear-staff to me. A little twist of my arm to the left and his exposed neck was in danger of being spiked from the narrow digging end, carrying my personal signature of a sharpened edge on one side.

'Your hands,' I repeated my words calmly but they carried threat.

His hands moved away from the knives, not in the open palm position of defence but tightly clenched.

'I'm challenging nobody,' I said. 'Who are you? Why are you here?'

'That's none of your business,' the assassin said, looking furtively at the approaching rishis. 'This dog...' he began, realized he looked foolish and stopped.

'But this dog keeps to himself,' Mahamaya, chewing on his twig, said.

The soldier glared at the rishi.

The sky was lightening and I was squinting. A modicum of his brute-self coming together, he stared at me, trying to fix my face in his mind. 'You will die for this,' he hissed. He continued to stare at me but spoke to the two men. 'Pick up that body. We are leaving.'

Even though the anticipation of pain in my eyes was gnawing me from within, I continued to focus on him through narrowed slits, studying him.

'Disappear before I cut you down,' I was surprised by the violence in my voice, my arms steady, my staff ready to kill. All my attention and even my breath was focused completely on the man, his neck and my staff. He was a moment away from next life. I was back in the battleground.

Unflinchingly, he looked at me along the length of the staff. I saw him try to etch my face into his heart. It wasn't bright enough for normal men, only for me. But warriors didn't always need eyes to see, I could feel him grope through the lightening sky, measuring me beyond my body, crafting an image that he stored away for a future kill.

I felt something let go of me and realized he had been squeezing me, smothering me with his vital energy. One of his men picked up his fallen sword and handed it to him. He kept his eyes on mine as he stepped back to take it. His hand was shaking with anger. He turned to go. A final evil glance came my way, as the pointed end of my staff followed him.

The two younger hands picked up the dying man and merged into the adjacent forest. The assassin followed. It was getting brighter, but the night of the forest swallowed them.

It was futile to pursue them at that hour. I must speak to Vidur, though his spies would transmit this information within the next few moments. I continued to look into the forest, as the rishis returned.

The man's face was etched in my mind now And mine in his. Both of us knew our fates were conjoined by the seal of destiny. We would meet again.

Only one of us would walk alive.

A warm, wet feeling on my foot. It was the dog. It raised its eyes towards me, sending a message of gratitude. I bent down to pet it. Instinctively, it stepped back, still limping. It growled a little, still unconvinced about the ways of the men.

I squatted on my heels, put out my hand. The wet warmth returned.

'Who were they, Badri?' Mahamaya's forehead carried a frown that was tighter than what mere curiosity demanded, the neem twig hanging from his mouth.

I looked up at him. 'I don't know. Certainly no friend of this dog,' I said, turning to the black shadow below. 'Nothing to worry about. Just some outsiders.'

No point in alarming citizens. Or interrupting the morning mantras.

The fight over, I could feel my being rise to the comfortable warmth of my heart. How did this transformation happen? I was a warrior, a Kshatriya, one who killed for the king, one who wanted to die for the kingdom. How did this softness, this weakness, enter my being? I should have killed the man or at least attempted to capture him.

I pulled my dhoti till above my knees, sat down next to the dog, cross-legged, my staff lying across my thighs. It was a wild forest dog I had passed by a couple of times on the outskirts of Hastinapur. All of eight months old, with the strength of a bear, the agility of a cat, the spirit of a warrior.

His eyes told me that he had adopted me. We looked at each other. I realized how much time had passed only when the early sunlight began to hurt. I pulled one fold of my pugri, turban, down across my face as a veil, a solution I had devised for times when I would have to face light.

My pugri was longer than usual and tied in a manner that I could pull down upto six folds over my face. They were enough for me to withstand the light, when I ventured out of the tunnels I built. But not the ones I carried within.

'Come,' I told the dog, standing up.

He looked up, now ready to give into his tiredness.

'Come,' I said again, thinking I'll leave him home, get his hind leg treated before returning to Tunnel 96.

He began to follow but after a few limps collapsed. I picked him up. He was heavier than I expected. And wet. In the early opening up of pre-daylight, I moved my hand away from his body. It was smeared in red.

The warrior had bled. But not whined.

'Brave kid,' I said.

He looked up with eyes that carried a past. Then, I felt his body relax.

I brought him home. My granddaughter Sumati gave him his name—Veer, meaning brave. He slept for three full days, healing. Sumati stayed close all the time, feeding him milk. A bond was born—Sumati, Veer and me.

And now, almost a year later, our roles were reversed. As he recovered and grew into one of the largest dogs in Hastinapur, Veer's presence became stronger.

Right now, I could feel his eyes boring through my body, right into my soul, sending waves of invisible strength and uncompromising love. Almost as if he was healing me from within, even as the vaid had applied his skill on my body.

So intense was his devotion and our love that he could speak to me without words.

*Get up, Badri, it is unbecoming of you to be lying wasted.*

*Yes Veer, I know.*

*Get up, there's work ahead. We have to go hunting. Come on.*

*A few more days...*

I smiled. Veer didn't like closed spaces and didn't accompany me to the tunnels, but enjoyed hunting.

And then I sensed there was someone else in the room too. The calm, the peace, the tranquillity...I shook off my haze. What was Hastinapur's prime minister, the brother of King Dhritarashtr, doing here?

'Vidur?' I asked nobody in particular, looking at the dark ceiling above.

'Yes, Surangraj,' he said in his melodious, mantrik voice. Mantrik because whatever he spoke, came from a level of awareness and consciousness that was as close to God's as I had experienced. No less than any mantra that any rishi chants.

Vidur was the conscience of Hastinapur. Had he not been born where he was, Vidur would have been a rishi, like Ved Vyas or Markande. There was something in him that would emanate and touch the deepest in me. The rishis said it was something in us that vibrated to the consciousness of the other. Almost like an invisible exchange of inner energy.

As prime minister, Vidur could translate that idea in the real world, in every act. When he was around us, with his smile that was as generous as it was genuine, we felt close to the peace that resided in us. He opened our souls to the calm within.

For most citizens having Vidur in their homes would have been an honour that would have preceded with ceremonies and announcements. To me, Vidur was a friend and despite being two decades younger, he had sought my company regularly on matters of tunnels and mining.

The nitty-gritty was important to him for the larger role tunnels played in statecraft.

Over time, as we got to know one another and he began to trust me, our discussions got more intense and we looked at related aspects of protection of the kingdom, spies, messengers, other officials and what they were upto. Our friendship grew as he endeared himself to my children and shared his wisdom and laughter with us, often calling us to his large but minimalist home in the palace compound for simple meals that he prepared with his own hands. He did not marry. And as far as I knew, didn't seek out women.

We would discuss the Rig Ved, and how it was shaping our society in Hastinapur and Aryavart. I learnt about how kings lived and thought, what drove them, their passions and motivations, their weaknesses and machinations. I think he learnt about how the commoners lived from people like me.

Well, strictly speaking, I wasn't a 'commoner'. I was well cared for, the Vaishyas would even call me 'wealthy'. I had enough land to house two entire villages, well-managed by my three sons, who oversaw the tilling, milking of six hundred cows and caring for hundred horses. I had gold that would be worth a lifetime's work of a dozen well-to-do merchants. Being a senior official, with six decades of service to Hastinapur, all of this was tax-free. Yes, I was wealthy. But deep within, I was a man of the ground, and didn't think much about my land, cows, horses, gold or houses.

I was the hunted, running from the hunter in me. Burrowing into the tunnels below.

In addition to having wealth that would be multiples of mine, Vidur was an immensely powerful prime minister.

And yet, we were bound together with the knot of dharm. I cared little for my riches. Vidur was as austere as a rishi. We treasured our relationship.

On rare occasions, when he would be distressed with palace intrigue, he vented his frustration here. This dark, windowless room with narrow gaps on top of one side for ventilation was witness to many stories of deception.

Within the paraphernalia of grandeur, power and wealth, Vidur was a lonely man, perhaps the loneliest in Hastinapur.

It was nice of him to come and visit me as I lay, battered by the treachery of Tunnel 14. But today's meeting was not about niceties. It wasn't about the tunnel. It wasn't even about me.

Vidur was here to save the future of the Kuru empire.

As advised by the vaid, my family had ensured I was sleeping straight on my back. When the planks gave way and the earth caved in over me, it left my right shoulder dislocated. I was lucky my neck hadn't cracked. Thank the great lord for Sauti's quick action or else it would have been a journey through a new tunnel for me—to destination death.

Between the waves of strength from Veer and a sea of calm from Vidur, I was healing faster than the vaid's turmeric-based medicinal concentrate that I could smell everywhere—my arms, my head, neck.

I realized I was wearing only my loincloth, tied loose, with a rough cotton sheet covering me. My black angvastr was straddling a stool next to my bed. How did anyone allow Vidur to enter my room? When I tried to turn, a sharp pain hit me on my lower back and I must have groaned. It was embarrassing to do that before Vidur.

He was looking over me, his white angvastr loosely hanging over his left shoulder. As he stood up to caress my head, I heard a soft but firm growl. It was Veer. Vidur laughed and said, 'Come here, you devil, nothing's going to happen to your master.'

As he grew up, I found that Veer was only half-dog. His black-grey body was as large and as graceful as a panther's. His grey wolf-like eyes seized you, sent shivers of fear. His growl was somewhere between.

I know it's not biologically possible, but Veer was probably a crossbreed between a wolf and a panther.

To commoners, Veer was generally quiet and invisible. But his presence was overpowering, his silence a menace. It took him a while before he even allowed my family to fool around with me. Except for my grandchildren, who could get away with anything—pull his ears, count his deadly teeth, hide his food—all were wary of him. My sons didn't like him one bit, their wives couldn't tolerate his presence. Behind my back, I often heard and ignored their comments.

'Veer!' I reprimanded him, but my voice was barely a whisper. The growl subsided.

*It's Vidur.*

I tried to see where he was but could manage to open only my left eye. The right eye felt heavy and pained when I tried to open it. Now fully awake, I could feel the light and almost pleasant burn of the vaid's firm bandages with paste-leaf all over me.

Vidur smiled and walked up to Veer. He raised his ears in alarm but allowed Vidur to pat his head. When he looked at me, his eyes were still cold, sending me a message that he was humouring Vidur only because of me.

*That's right, behave yourself.*

I tried to turn again, but the pain was unbearable.

'Relax, Surangraj.'

Surangraj was the name that Vidur had given me in the Sabha of Hastinapur, when I completed the work in the upper tunnels in record time. The entire junior council had stood up in respect as the senior council watched. Vidur had referred to it only in passing but the name stuck. Surangraj—King of Tunnels.

Vidur was one of the few members of the royalty who called me by that name. And when he used it, he did so with a deep feeling that had the ring of truth. The Truth. The conviction in his speech turned an abstraction into reality. When he said it, Vidur made me feel like a king.

He was fanning me lightly with one of those new contraptions that traders from Mithila had brought for the rich. They needed less effort and delivered more air. Now, these fans were gaining ground in middle-class households, as merchants traded and entrepreneurs across the borders started making them.

With superhuman effort, I gritted my teeth and turned my head to the right to be able to see him. Vidur was sitting on my comfortable chair. In the economy of actions that Vidur stood for, he sat at just the right distance from where we could see each other clearly and speak in low tones.

'How long have you been here? You should have woken me up. Why are you fanning me?'

'Surangraj, please calm down.'

'Som!' I shouted for my son. My voice grazed the mud walls of my room, the largest in our home, and returned with an apology. 'Hira!' My personal attendant was missing too.

'I have asked your family and servants to leave us alone.'

I sensed restrained urgency in his voice that woke me up from within. 'I need to speak to you, in private.'

I was alert again. 'Yes, Vidur, but please stop fanning me.'

He ignored me.

'Surangraj, I have spoken to the vaid and by god's grace, all you have are some minor injuries that will ache for two or three days. That pain you carry is one of healing. Your right shoulder is dislocated, but given your health, it will heal within thirteen days. It will take you about a month to be able to dig again.'

My room glowed in his smile. As always, he had done his background research.

I let out a sigh of relief because the pain told me that I might never pick up the shovel again.

'The pain,' he said, almost reading my thoughts, 'will take some time to leave.'

Vidur's smile began to lose the fight against the familiar furrow on his broad forehead, one that had formed before my eyes. I think it coincided with the Pandavs arriving at Hastinapur. It could even be the times—the Kali Yug was around the corner and all of us could feel its pressure.

'Listen carefully,' he said, his voice going a level lower, a pitch graver, reminding me of us how we miners move into middle tunnels. 'Hastinapur is in danger. I have a plan that only you can execute.' He said it in his straightforward manner. The simplicity carried force. 'We need to save the Pandavs, they are the future of the Kuru empire.'

'Save the Pandavs?' I repeated, possibly sounding foolish. 'What do you mean? Save them from whom? We have Dron, Bhishm. The Pandavs are warriors themselves. Who dares...'

Vidur looked at me vacantly.

As he continued, I felt my pain disappear, replaced by attentiveness, something I thought my body was quite incapable of. My good eye looked at him, carrying a vague question, from my heart.

'Do you remember Duryodhan's Water Sports House, the one he built in Pramanakoti near the river?'

'Who doesn't? In less than three years, it has become one of the most magnificent water sports academies in Aryavart.' I began to get carried away by its splendour. 'Princes and warriors from across the world come to learn there. It is today the pride of Hastinapur, a mark of our soft power.'

'Yes, but do you also remember Duryodhan's first excursion there, when the Pandavs accompanied him?'

'Yes, I also remember that Bhim did not return once the sports got over and you had sent search parties to find him. And a few days later, that naughty giant returned on his own,' I smiled, recalling the baby-faced warrior-in-waiting. 'There were rumours about his returning with far greater strength.'

'Yes, but this is no smiling matter,' he said. I shifted my weight on the jute bed with some difficulty, to face him. 'It is only with god's grace that Bhim returned to Hastinapur. Duryodhan had built the Water Sports House to kill him.'

The silence in the room was cut only by the sweet chatter of my grandchildren playing outside.

'Duryodhan conceived and built an entire infrastructure of this scale, just to kill Bhim?'

'Yes.'

I was shocked. Not because of what Vidur was saying but because it was impossible to imagine that a twelve-year-old boy could be filled with so much hatred. Even if we allowed Duryodhan the concession, that it was Shakuni's brain running his arms, the very idea that he could participate in and execute a crime so complex was difficult to digest. But it also showed his latent organizing skills.

'Why didn't you tell the king?'

'My brother is weak. He is no match for Duryodhan's tantrums or Shakuni's evil mind. A handful of us have put in everything to protect the Pandavs so far—in the Sabha, in the academy, in their very home. Duryodhan has now become incorrigible. And with Karn by his side, he thinks nothing can touch him.'

'With Karn's aid, his military flank is protected and with Dhritarashtr's he has the protection and legitimacy of authority. That's a dangerous combination, Vidur.'

He nodded. Dark silence descended on my windowless room.

About Karn, I had mixed feelings. He had nobility written over his forehead and had clear eyes. His control over archery was as good as Arjun's or even Dron's. The way he carried himself was like a king, not a charioteer's son he as was known.

In an earlier age he could have earned his way to Kshatriyahood. But today, the clasp of the incumbents was too strong for any single individual to breach. My body shuddered at the memory of how Dron had extracted Eklavya's thumb as tribute to ensure that Arjun remained the world's best archer.

Karn was not only a friend and permanent companion of Duryodhan but his physical and moral strength too. He was Duryodhan's armour, archer, ally. He would die for him and also kill. Except for his misplaced loyalty and a rough, uncultured edge to his demeanour, I felt Karn to be more in tune with the Pandavs, sons of Dhritarashtr's brother Pandu.

Karn was a blessing Duryodhan didn't deserve.

I could understand Duryodhan's mind. After the Pandavs came to Hastinapur, the kingdom's attention shifted to them. The five brothers were radiant, unknown, strong. What endeared them to us was the way they carried the innocent simplicity of the forests, where they had spent their childhood, to Hastinapur. They had an inner magnetism compounded with mystery. We wanted to see them, be with them, know them.

Particularly Yudhishthir, the eldest brother, who not only had kingship written on his every action, but also carried an atmosphere of calm compassion wherever he went. You looked at him and you knew a king lay waiting for us, a rishi-king. Will he last the degeneration of Arya values?

Most importantly, their bonds were unseen to us and such love was a delight to watch. It was almost like they were five individual bodies serving one mind. Their moral and emotive guidance came from their mother, Kunti.

That Hastinapur took to the Pandavs and thereby created an able competitor for Duryodhan's assumed throne was bad enough. But when in their games, Bhim turned the Kauravs into pulp, Duryodhan didn't know what to do or where to turn. There was no mercy from Bhim's relentless assaults—playful to the boy-giant, violent to those on the other side.

On his part, Bhim didn't know his own strength. There was not an iota of malice in him. He was merely an overgrown baby gurgling with joy in a giant's body, expressing himself in the only way he knew—physically. He was discovering his own power. Many years later, after their successive ordeals, I thought Bhim had degenerated into a monstrous character. But certainly not now.

Once while returning in the evening, from Tunnel 18 near the forest, I saw Duryodhan and his three brothers writhing in pain on the ground. I looked at the guards. One of them said the Kaurav princes were climbing the tall mango tree and Bhim came and shook it so hard that they fell down. The tree was large and among the fallen branches lay Duryodhan's brothers, sprawled. They were bleeding mildly from their knees and elbows.

The blood didn't worry me. Every prince had to bleed his way to earn his Kshatriyahood. It was the smell of their sweat. Not the sweet tang of exertion that built muscles, strengthened bodies. It carried the bitter stench of fear.

A dhanush away, Duryodhan's face was seething with frustration. Further down, Yudhishthir was admonishing Bhim in his quiet, dignified way. The joy of physical power was still flowing in Bhim's arms, as he waved them about unconsciously, the sunlight glistening from his muscled body. His eyes were looking at his feet.

As if reading my thoughts, Yudhishthir looked at me and smiled his way into my heart. Almost apologetic, he said, 'Surangraj, Bhim doesn't listen to me. You are our elder, please explain to him that what he's done is wrong and he must apologize.'

I folded my hands in a namaskar. As Bhim raised his baby face towards me and smiled wickedly, I felt a dozen Bhims get out of his body and surround me with a playful menace. The emanation of his brute strength was harmonious if you're a friend and fearful if an enemy. Right now, it was happy.

'What can I say, prince?' I frantically tried to revive Vidur's lessons on diplomacy. 'A younger brother must follow what his elder brother says.'

Bhim made a face of mock hurt pride at me and turned to look at Duryodhan. Even though he was beyond leaping distance, Duryodhan took a step back, cringed at that unconscious movement and looked up at Bhim with his head held high, supported by a crutch of history that presumed him to be king. But all of us could see through his attempt to pick up his fallen pride. His eyes were still wary, wondering what new conspiracy Bhim was hatching behind his chubby cheeks.

As humbly as he could, and it wasn't much, Bhim bowed before Duryodhan and said, 'Please forgive me brother, I didn't do it intentionally. I didn't mean to hurt you. I was only playing.'

Duryodhan's teeth were gritted, his fists full, his body taut and his mouth twisted with fury. Trembling, he turned and walked away, shouting at his attendants to help his fallen brothers. His exit was of a king who had lost a battle and badly so.

'Are you also deaf?' Bhim shouted at him. Duryodhan's speed slowed, his chin fell to his chest and his eyes glared through their slant. He didn't turn back, shook his head and walked off.

Are you 'also' deaf? That comment was one of the first tendrils of darkness that poisoned the atmosphere of Hastinapur. It defined the stakes. Bhim had taunted Duryodhan where it hurt him the most—he was a blind man's son, a blind man who had become king only because Hastinapur had no option. This was not acceptable behaviour and my face must have winced at this ugliness.

On its own, being blind didn't matter. The state took care of all disabilities and every person. The problem was despite being younger of the two, it was Pandu who was made the king of the Kuru empire, not Dhritarashtr. It was only after Pandu died that Dhritarashtr sat on the throne he now loved so much. At any time in the Sabha, you could see his fingers caress the elephants on its armrests with love, lost in his light-less world.

Now, with the return of the sons of Pandu, Hastinapur was divided. Should Duryodhan be the next king or Yudhishthir?

Yudhishthir didn't miss my expression. And before I could change it, he had rushed to Duryodhan's side.

'I am sorry, brother,' Yudhishthir was walking to console his cousin. But Duryodhan ran away, his fists brushing tears from his eyes.

I wanted to be no part of this. Even watching the humiliation of a king can be dangerous. I folded my hands and sought Yudhishthir's leave, who by then was lecturing Bhim on courtesies. 'We're not in the forest, Bhim, you need to change the way you behave, you need to respect...'

From the corners of his eyes, Bhim watched me leave, a hint of a smirk on his lips.

'Badri?' Vidur pulled me out of my reverie. 'Where are you?'

'I was just remembering the incident by the mango tree, when Bhim had injured three Kauravs physically and hurt Duryodhan's pride.'

Vidur took a long breath. 'What do I do about Bhim? But then, sibling rivalry is common. Don't your sons fight?'

I remained silent for some time.

'Vidur, please don't misunderstand me, but why have you come here?'

My pain shifted to him. His forehead knotted and he began to stare at the ground. Then he took a deep breath, exhaled and said, 'Here's the truth, Badri. The Pandavs are facing death. There are six people in this conspiracy. And there is nothing anyone can do about it. Not even me.'

The sounds outside were suddenly alive. A distant trumpet of an elephant. Horses in my stable. A flock of birds screeching near the lake behind us. Suddenly, the silence of shock was trying to get out of my room.

'I can count four,' I said slowly. 'Duryodhan, his younger brother Dhushasan, Karn and Shakuni. Who are the other two?'

'The new character is Purochan.'

'That ruffian, who killed some harmless rakshas in cold blood and collected gold from the king last year?' A shameful episode in the history of Hastinapur, everyone knew about the manipulation.

'Yes, I'm afraid. He is now the governor of Varanavat.'

*Varanavat. This was just not my day. The name brought pain.*

*Varanavat. That's where Urvashi lived.*

*Urvashi—my love.*

*Varanavat. Memories of action versus contemplation, passion versus sacrifice, dharm versus love.*

*Dharm. The nuances at Rishi Kedar's ashram on its outskirts.*

*The ashram. She wasn't ready for the ashram life but that's where she was. Life. Miraculously, she had survived the battle. I had won, saved her life.*

*Won? But I lost the war when she moved out. Without a word. Without an embrace. Without looking back. In a fleeting moment, all I was left with were memories.*

*Forgive me, Urvashi...*

I felt a gentle touch on my arm. 'Badri?'

'I'm all right, Vidur. Just some old wounds.'

He understood and allowed me my space for some time. Then, 'How long since you've met Urvashi?'

How long?

For how long have I missed her fiery dark eyes that could warm as well as burn?

*The first time I saw her at the military academy, she was in a squad formation, training to protect the queen. I was waiting by the side for Bhishm to return. As I turned to watch the training, I saw her in the centre of the formation, taking a leap above the heads of other soldiers, landing soundlessly on her toes. She wasn't pretty in the traditional sort of way. But she had the grace of an antelope. A dancer. As I continued to stare, I noticed her body. There was a raw energy of the fighter hiding a sophisticated sensuality. Her arms bustled with muscles. A few scars on her forearms told me she had practised archery, technologically the highest weapon any warrior could aspire for. But her demeanour was one of a swordsperson. Or a wrestler. I would love to get in there. Between the exercises, she felt my predatory eyes, turned to me. Kohl-laced dark eyes, all attentive in the warrior formation. She smiled. And that smile said it all. For me, she was the one. For her, I was he.*

For how long have I missed the embrace that could break the back in a battle hug or fill the emptiness of being desired?

*'She is Urvashi, daughter of the state,' Bhishm said, not looking at me.*

*She had chosen the warrior's path, following the treacherous murder of her parents and siblings. She began with revenge but had now directed that energy towards delivering justice and protection.*

*'I still think revenge lurks somewhere in her thick, dark locks,' he said, jibing me with his elbow and a knowing smile. 'Maybe, you can temper that sentiment. She's the best we have and will join the queen's bodyguards soon. She is much younger than you, not yet eighteen.' I was thirty-five. 'But you will make a fine team.'*

*Team? We were lost souls, meeting after lifetimes of tapasya.*

For how long have I missed the lips that could bring life back into the dead, create a will to live?

*'We are bound in ways that transcend time, Badri,' Urvashi said, her open hair spread out like dark rivers on my chest. 'But both of us have bigger achievements ahead. Fighting is our skill, protection our dharm.'*

*She brought her hand to my face, feeling the rough bristles. 'The love that binds us has a deeper purpose than this,' she moved higher, her lips open.*

*Why is she talking so much?* 'Yes,' I started, 'but...'

*She muffled my protest. Frenzy kissed eternity, echoed on walls of silence, and like a thunderstorm, spread out around me, captured me bathed me in its sweetness.*

*There was nothing but that—I was Purusha, she was Prakriti, we were one.*

'More than three decades now.' I returned to Vidur.

Vidur nodded. 'Maybe it's a good time to cross paths with destiny again.'

I looked at him, the pain in my body giving way to the warmth in my heart.

'But I assure you Purochan will not be easy.'

Duryodhan attracted the worst scum of Aryavart into his dark fold. Evil as he was, Purochan had three things going for him. He was strong in body, skilled with the mace and the sword, and ambitious like Duryodhan himself. Had he been born to a king, the soldier and strategist in Purochan would have made his mark on the political and military folklore of Aryavart.

After the peaceful and voluntary annexation of Varanavat by the Kurus, Purochan realized that his chances of being the king of Varanavat were over. He was now a cog in the wheels of a larger empire and even managing to reach an atirathi status were limited.

Determined, he made his way up the hierarchy, first reaching Hastinapur and from there to Duryodhan. In a series of well-planned moves, he gave the young prince his complete loyalty. His first offering to Duryodhan: the death of former king of Varanavat, who was becoming a nuisance to Shakuni's designs by dealing directly with Vidur and Bhishm rather than with Shakuni or Dhushasan. With the king out of the way, and his children still too young to take over, Purochan was made governor of Varanavat.

Purochan was evil and had found the right atmosphere to develop his character.

But Vidur had only counted five. 'Who's the sixth conspirator?'

Vidur closed his eyes. 'The upholder of Arya values in Aryavart, the last refuge of the weak, the highest aspiration of any political alliance,' he paused, looking vacantly in the air. 'My brother, our king...' he paused to take a deep breath.

'Dhritarashtr?' I said hesitatingly.

'Yes.'

Vidur had dropped the fan and was holding his head in his hands. He was sobbing silently, his shoulders jerking. For infinite moments I didn't know what to do. Here was Hastinapur's best mind, its very conscience. A face that had no expression except compassion and uprightness. A body that demanded nothing but to serve the kingdom. A man who wielded immense power but chose not to carry it on his shoulder. A diplomat par excellence. A strategist beyond compare. A man loved beyond the Kuru empire and throughout Aryavart. A saint whom the rishis respected. This man, this mahatma, was shedding tears in my home. Right in front of me.

Veer walked up to Vidur and put his head on his knee, staring hard. Vidur caressed his head.

I watched helplessly. There was not one word I could speak that would be right. I stayed silent.

Tears over, the conspiracy flowed. On the excuse of spending time with the locals to understand the border districts of the Kuru empire, the Pandavs had been sent to Varanavat. Most of Hastinapur believed this was a plot to get them away from the capital and allow Duryodhan to rebuild his relationships with citizens.

But from what Vidur told me, it was a plot to kill them. 'The plan is to ensure that the Pandavs do not return from Varanavat.'

'What am I to do in all this, what can I do? You need soldiers and strategy to protect the Pandavs, not a wounded miner.'

I heard my father in the next room, dragging himself towards us. Vidur wiped his eyes. Veer looked up, the tip of his tail carrying the beginning of a wag.

As he entered the room, Vidur got up with the agility of a messenger and before I could turn my eye, was at my father's feet.

'Who is it? Oh, Vidur,' he said looking into the distance with his inner eye. 'What brings you here? Why didn't you come and see me?'

'You were sleeping, tauji.'

As a former spy, my father Rishabh had served the kingdom well. Being a spy meant that he worked very closely with Vidur. Now, he was old and ailing.

'Badri, are you up? I kept coming to your room for many days but they told me you were asleep.'

Days? 'How long have I been here?'

'It's been more than sixteen days now, Badri...'

Sixteen days?

'Pitaji, Vidur and I are in the middle of something...'

'Oh good, from the sound of that "something" it looks like I should join you boys.'

Boys?

The old man was silently looking at us but I could sense his vision exploring our minds. He had crossed 110 years and was past middle age. But he looked older because of the toll, including extreme torture, his profession had extracted from his body.

'The kingdom is in grave danger. Is that what you've come to tell him, Vidur?'

Vidur laughed. 'Is there nothing we can hide from you, Rishabh? You remain a guptachar, a spy, long after you've ceased to be one. Don't you remember the cardinal rule of your profession?'

'That I'm to forget my entire life once I retire? Vidur, I told you this when I retired and I tell you now again. This is the stupidest law in Hastinapur. It breeds discontent. I'm lucky to have Badri. But not all spies do.'

'We have a lavish pension scheme...' Vidur began.

'Yes, but at our age, more than money and comfort, we need respect. You see, the information we carry in our hearts that all your techniques of mind control can't bury is invaluable. Use it, Vidur. Don't waste us, don't waste this team. I speak not for myself, I speak for scores of others in Hastinapur. I speak for hundreds across Aryavart. Change this law.'

'I agree with you, tauji,' Vidur was truthful, 'but it's necessary. That's how statecraft has been designed. If you have a better model, I'm always willing to listen. And frankly, we don't expect you to forget, just that you need to lock your memories.'

This was going out of hand. 'Pitaji,' I said in my gentlest tone. 'I urge you. This is important.'

'Yes, yes,' he mumbled, trying hard to sound normal. 'But Vidur, have you had milk and gur?'

'No, Rishabh, but I'm well-fed.' A tiny hint of authority came into his tone. 'We really need to talk, Rishabh. Please forgive me.'

My father's face turned a shade darker, his voice a note deeper. 'I will leave you, Vidur. But my son has already suffered much. Right now, this room smells of conspiracy. And while I'm always ready to sacrifice myself and my family for the kingdom, I cannot let him go unprepared. If I must sacrifice my son, he shouldn't die unknown,' he paused. 'He will not suffer like I did.'

The last sentence hung in the air like an astra, ready to unleash its destruction.

Vidur and I were struck by the force of my father's gently-spoken words. My heart, already under pressure from the beating my tunnels had given me, was melting. I stifled a sob.

'Pitaji,' I held out a hand. He hobbled towards me and squeezed it. His grip was still strong. His lower lip was quivering.

*He will not suffer like I did.*

Like a sharp sword, it seared past our emotions and cut into the dark tunnels residing in our souls. He was referring to his final assignment, when he had to get vital information for Bhishm's attack on the Kasi kingdom, north of Hastinapur to get brides for his incompetent half-brother, Vichitravir. Rishabh had managed to get the swayamwar plan passed on to a messenger, who carried it to Bhishm. But in the process of staying on to support Bhishm from the inside, he was trapped by Kasi's counter spy network.

How he had managed to live through the torture that followed, is a story that few know. He was lucky that during Bhishm's attack, when all the other kings went out to fight, he was able to outdo the cell guards and escape. This, with two broken ribs, a fractured leg, bloody arms and a face smashed to pulp.

It took him more than a month to crawl back to Hastinapur to a hero's welcome. But after that, he couldn't pick himself up. Bhishm offered him a sinecure where he could oversee and supervise the spy network. Rishabh tried that for a few years but realized his skill was in the actual transaction of information, not in organization of an information network. A self-respecting man, he didn't want a dole and left active service.

I felt a warm drop on my shoulder, a tear. Then he left my hand. The warmth went away with it. As he turned to walk away, his stick leading him, I saw the face of my mother at the door. She had been listening all the while. Vidur touched her feet. 'Mother.'

'Bless you, Vidur. I know you will never harm us. But Badri is all we have. Please don't sacrifice him for your diplomatic games.' The last sentence carried a bitterness.

'I won't mother.'

She took my father's arm and led him out. As their shadows tailed behind them into the passage, Vidur called out after them. 'Rishabh, Mother! Here's my promise—Vidur's promise.'

His face, always grave, now had his facial muscles tightly-knit in a warlike stance I had never seen. 'Badri will be back by Diwali. He will light the second diya in this house.' He meant after my father. From the corner of my good eye, I saw my parents' shadows pause and a sense of relief filled the room. 'And I will light the third.'

Veer got up, walked majestically towards me, turned around twice, brushing his body next to my arm, and settled down next to my bed between Vidur and me. He had sensed the tension and the palpable violence underlying it. He turned to me.

*Another journey, Badri.*

*Yes, Veer.*

*I am ready. But you aren't.*

*I will be. Soon.*

*Even if you aren't, I'm there.*

Veer was staring at me, quiet but ready for action. Vidur turned to me, his tone returning to one used to giving orders, as prime minister.

'Badri, here's what I need you to do.'

Veer and I turned to him.

⊱⊰⊱⊰⊱⊰⊱⊰

# Varanavat

*Eight days later*

Freedom can be intoxicating.

My soul was floating with the sudden exhilaration you get when you leave cities. That's when your sense of alertness dulls a little. And without your knowing, you're caught in Yam's loop.

The smoke cover of Hastinapur was now long behind me and the fresher air of the plains filled my lungs and freed my head. The other relief came from the lack of horse-dung smell. The sanitation commissioner still hadn't been able to find a way to control that. Everywhere you went, the smell followed you till a point when your body got so used to it that you realized what you were trapped in only when you travelled.

Right now, I could sense that freedom.

The smell of mustard, wheat and millet filled the air. As did sounds of trade, the dynamism of exchange. This was the hub of Kuru wealth. Bordered by the Ganga in the east and the Yamuna in the West, the plains of Aryavart were an area of rich soil, where the Vaishyas practised their agriculture.

Further north was the Uttar Kuru mountain range, the beginning of the Himavat, the abode of rishis.

Spring was exploding in diverse colours, spreading fragrances. The wind was soft, carrying somewhere the heat that would follow in a month's time, but cool for now. Eight days into the journey and even though I was still in the plains, I could sense the first mountains before they showed up. By my estimate, it would be two more days before we began the climb.

Every breath of air was like drinking the cool water of the Ganga. What am I doing in Hastinapur? The question appeared on every journey. Perhaps this would be my last exit.

Veer had sauntered off, as he usually did when we hit the trails. He too enjoyed the freedom of unfettered expanses that the plains and mountains gave him. The clangs of utensils in homes, the needless voices of people trying to do little more than assert their presence, the march of arrogance under the feet of soldiers, the neighing of horses as chariots steered their way in narrow lanes...freedom from the noise was a restful relief.

*I understand, Veer.*

*I'll be back.*

*Be careful. I heard there are wild dogs around our trail right up to Varanavat.*

*I see them. They bark but from a distance. They won't touch me.*

*I know, but doesn't hurt to be alert.*

Sweetened by the season as earth began its familiar circle of life, the fragrances carried the joy of creation, as one tree after another, one flower at a time, opened up.

Unafraid, as their city cousins were, the chirping of birds was nearer, the squirrels raced closer. A jackal looked at me and wondered what a two-legged animal was doing riding a four-legged one in the middle of her forest. Then she returned to her feast of leftover black buck, probably devoured by a tiger.

Freedom always comes at a price and for the joy of being in the mountains and fresh air, we had to pay with alertness. Tigers were rampant where we were headed.

'Watch out for a man-eater over the shoulder of that hill,' a villager had advised me over a light snack, two days ago.

But the forest was rich with life. We would encounter lions on the way. Maybe, panthers too. The hiss of snakes, particularly kraits and cobras, were as rampant as the screeches of their deadly enemies, the peacocks. In the smaller, calmer rivulets that fed the Yamuna, crocodiles waited as patiently as logs.

The forests had begun and the majestic Himavat Patth, that wide highway that led us all the way to the foothills of the snow-capped Uttar Kuru ranges, veered right. Thick was the jungle, largely padded by shrubs that merged into distant trees. Around this turn, the road builders seemed to have been in a hurry, leaving a large tree cover around the bend.

Silence in forests usually continued for eternities, but right now, it was too silent.

Something within me from a distant past tried to warn me. The chirping of birds had receded to a distance, walled in by the tree cover.

Intoxicated by the freedom, Vayu's steady gait and the air that cleaned the soul from within, I was in a reverie of complete relaxation.

That's when I walked into them.

The man standing before me carried a sword in his left hand and a chakr, the most difficult to wield out of all weapons, in his right. Like any warrior of stature, he had an array of small knives tied around him on a leather belt. He was dark, short and thick. There was no trace of fat. He was all muscles, built in the tough forest of life, where you could be wrestling a python right after escaping from the jaws of a tiger.

Even though it was still day and the setting sun was behind me, there were long shadows on both sides of the trail. On the left the shrubs melted into trees, then the trees conspired to create a canopy of darkness that the evening light found difficult to break through. On the right, the trees, mostly dominated by neems, pipals and mangoes, had almost eaten into the highway.

The sun was milder but still enough to pressure my eyes. I had tied most layers of my pugdi on my head, leaving just one tied loosely over my face.

The bounties of nature had relaxed me and I missed what was an obvious hideout for rebels.

Nature's signals of exceptional quiet were clear, though. In my loosening up, I just chose to ignore them. The forest carries silence, no doubt, but not the kind we fantasise in cities. Under the brush a clucking of birds, behind that rock there a scraping of a monitor, high above the trees the swinging of monkeys…

I ignored them all. You're losing your edge, Badri, I told myself.

Not a trace of doubt marred his stance. Standing slightly sideways to keep the direct light out of his eyes, thick legs slightly apart displaying confidence and stability, mildly bent for sudden and quick action if needed, he looked at me with the strength of a banyan tree and the glance of an eagle. His naked, well-built body sported only a loin cloth to protect his dignity.

A soft smile lit his handsome face.

I knew what that meant. His followers were in the trees, hiding behind the yet-to-ripen fruits. As I glanced slowly around me, I could see some arrows pointed at me that would be as sour as the mangoes in this season.

I cursed under my breath. Vayu, who had understood the situation as soon as we turned around the rock, stopped a few paces before the man. I had directed Vayu on the green at the centre of the highway, where the wheels of chariots had not killed the grass. That kept us quieter. It was an old habit of a warrior which I used to muffle Vayu's heavy strides.

My mule, Kadak, snorted behind us, wondering what the pause was all about. He carried my spears, some tools and food. Unaware of the danger, Kadak wandered to the side of the wide trail, testing a new kind of grass, chomping noisily to let us all know he liked it.

I shifted my weight forward to dismount.

'Keep sitting,' the voice was calm, the pitch almost boyish but so strong was his inner being it could almost give me a bear hug.

I stiffened. The swing of the pickaxe on my back suddenly seemed like a wasted comfort. Two of my staffs that were almost as good as spears hung on the left side of my saddle, pointing to the earth. On the right were two of my best spears, ready to be drawn if needed. My sword was near my right hand, the knives tightly belted around my waist.

All useless right now. One move towards any of these weapons and it would be my last.

'Where are you going?'

'Who are you?' I rasped, trying to capture a shred of courage from my solar plexus.

He laughed. 'You seem to be too filled with the authority to understand simple things of life. You don't ask questions here, you only answer them.'

Almost at the same time that I heard a twang on my right, an arrow whispered in front of my eyes, sending a harsh blow of air at my nose before settling down at the base of the Gulmohar tree on my left with a muffled thud.

'So, Mr Official, where are you headed?'

'Varanavat.'

'Varanavat, he says,' the man raised his right arm, talking to shadows around me. 'What for?' He nodded at a tree to his left. A boy dropped down soundlessly and walked up to Kadak. My eyes followed him.

'What for?' the man repeated.

'I'm going to the ashram of Rishi Kedar,' I said, stressing on the last two words with reverence.

'Rishi Kedar,' he mimicked me. 'What happened, you lost your nerve to fight?' In the few moments, he had measured me well.

'I'm not a fighter, brother. I am a miner.'

'Yes, yes, that's right,' he said nodding at Kadak, whose weight was being relieved as the boy pulled the weapons off and brought them towards this man. Kadak nuzzled the boy's shoulder, happy with the lightened burden on his back.

'A miner, he says,' he looked around, laughing. 'And that's why you carry these spears?' he looked at me, his eyes carrying the sarcasm. 'Who are you? And remove your scarf.'

'I told you, brother...'

'And you are not my brother,' he said, his voice rising, 'so don't call me that. Besides, brothers don't kill brothers here.' His voice grabbed the edge of death: 'Who are you?'

This was getting nowhere and I began to feel the familiar longing to fight flow in my veins again. The knives around my waist yearned to be unleashed but I kept my hands on my thighs. My spear was calling me to act. I shook these dangerous thoughts away. Taking my time to get a sense of the theatre I was trapped in, I turned around.

The hidden rebels were now standing on the trail. Four on the right side, three on the left. I glanced upwards into the mesh of trees. One...two...three arrows were visible without the faces manning them. That meant another two or even three behind the cover.

I was trapped, there was no way out. I invoked the diplomatic knowledge of Vidur and looked straight at the man before me.

'I ask you for the last time,' the man said. 'Show your face and tell me who you are.'

I was afraid but this was no time to show fear. If there was one thing warriors respected, it was courage. Cowards die fast.

'Fourteen men with their arms exposed against one without any. That's not dharm,' I couldn't help the roughness to my voice. 'But I bind you not to the sophistication of the civilized. I speak to you in your language. Is this the courage you are known for?'

In the inner trails of the mind, I was walking a dangerous territory. If my gamble worked, a challenge stood ahead and a combat would follow. If I won, I would walk free. If I didn't, a signal was all it would take for me to walk my final trail.

The man's brow knotted for a moment. Then he smiled. 'Do I sense a challenge, traveller?'

'That's for you to figure out. If it is a challenge you're looking for, it's yours. As for me, like I said earlier, I am a miner recovering from my wounds and on my way to the ashram of Rishi Kedar.'

He began to stride towards me purposefully. I noticed his features. He seemed to belong to the Khasiahni tribe, from the middle ranges of the Uttar Kuru mountains, more from the Panchal side than Kuru. What was he doing here? And if he was indeed a Khasiahni, where were the...

'He speaks the truth, Araak,' a voice behind me said. The soft voice carried a muted but strong authority. This was their true leader. A woman. Araak was probably one of her husbands in this polyandry-dominated tribe.

I dared not look behind. Araak stopped in his tracks.

'Get off the horse,' he said. 'And take off your veil.'

With the cushion of the woman behind me, I pushed my gambler's luck. I got off the horse with a jump and stood before him, towering a full head and a half above. 'The pugdi stays.'

He opened his mouth to speak when he was stopped by the woman's voice behind, now closer. 'Miner, I didn't know men wore veils in Aryavart. Has Manusmriti been expanded by your corrupt and sold-out pseudo-rishis to include veiled men?'

It seemed this tribe couldn't speak without sarcasm.

'No, devi,' I said respectfully and turned around slowly, keeping my arms at a fair distance from my knives. She stood there leaning on a wooden spear, a short and light bow hardly longer than my arm across her body, a small leather quiver showing the feathers of her arrows peering over her smooth naked right shoulder. A coarse brown cloth around her waist accentuated her hips and tapering legs. The angvastr that should have covered her upper body was missing. Instead, it had been folded and tied around her small breasts like a bodice that warrior women took to. Her sinewy forearms were scarred with practice. An archer.

*'I don't understand why you can't shoot an arrow straight, Badri.'*

*'Oh, but I can, Urvashi. It's just that I prefer the spear.'*

*'You're going to get annoyed now but the spear, the gada, the sword...these are outdated weapons. You need to evolve with technology. The future belongs to the man who can pull the bow.'*

*'Or the woman.'*

*'Be serious. This is a session.'*

*'I prefer other sessions.'*

*Her black eyes widened with anger.*

*'But yes, you were saying something, go on...how do you hold the bow?'*

*She burst out laughing. We kissed.*

When she looked at me through her dark, large and luminous eyes, she teased the senses that lay hidden under layers of tunnels within me. She carried in her being a violence that was deadly as it was sensual. It took me all my control not to gasp. In her strength she towered over beauty, in her beauty lay strength.

'Then why hide your face? I'm told Kuru breeds handsome men. Why deprive us of that pleasure?' The three archers around her laughed and soon the entire brigade was laughing.

The joke was on me but I still smiled.

'My eyes are weak, devi,' I said truthfully. 'They can't tolerate the light of day.'

'That's why you dare to choose evenings and nights to travel in our forest.' They must have been tracking me for a few days now.

'It's the only way to travel for me, devi.'

'What's your name?'

'I'm Badri, son of Rishabh.'

She winced, looked hurt, but stayed silent.

'I am a miner at Hastinapur. I dig tunnels. One of the tunnels fell on me and hurt me. I'm going to my guru Rishi Kedar's ashram to recover.'

'Son of Rishabh,' she mimicked. 'But who is your mother? Don't you give her the respect she deserves for having given birth to you?'

'Yes devi,' this debate around dharm and the position of women in society, between a rebel woman and me, in the middle of a trail was strangely surreal. 'I'm Parvati-putra, son of Parvati.'

The woman released a deep breath of satisfaction, measuring me again. Then, her eyes narrowed.

'You taunt my man,' she nodded towards Araak, 'of not being civilized, and yet you treat your women in this despicable manner. But that's your problem. For now, tell me why carry these weapons that you can't even touch, leave alone use?' The scorn was sharp.

'These are for my protection against bandits, devi.'

'Bandits, indeed!' she spat on a lizard to her left, a dhanush away from her bare leg that ended with a bright red cloth anklet. Metals make too much noise for a people that had become rebels. Puzzled, the lizard shook its head and hurried away. Then, she took a few strong steps towards me.

'Like us?'

She was close now. If I put my hand out, I could caress her lips.

'No, devi. Though you try hard to behave like them, you are not a bandit,' I noticed her smooth sunburnt shoulders, her toil-worn eyes and saw the stream of stories she had authored. This woman had led her tribe across many trails, through many forests and many battles and had the scars to support those fights. 'You are the brave Khasiahni tribe, masters...and mistresses,' I fumbled to stay politically correct, 'of the Uttar Kuru mountain forests. Why are you stopping travellers, devi? And why are you so far from your home?'

Her eyes softened at my correct identification. She hadn't hardened yet as many do after spending life under pressure of death. There was still hope.

'Don't patronize. You drive us away from our homes. You deprive us of livelihood. You force us to pick up these weapons,' she twanged the string of her bow. 'And now, you ask why we stop you? The right question is: why should we not kill you?'

'I have nothing to do with the politics of nations or the expansion of Aryavart, devi. I'm just a miner, my dharm is to dig.' I said it with conviction but couldn't convince myself.

'But you enjoy the fruits of that politics, that exploitation, that marginalization. You step on our lands, burn our forests, leave us homeless.'

'Devi,' I repeated with all the sincerity I could muster, 'I'm just a miner, I'm wounded. I'm going to my guru's ashram to recover. And if you think I need to be killed for the ills of my people, do it right now.'

She looked up, surprised. Then I changed my tone. 'It's easy for all of you to hold arms and give me a pravachan, lesson, on crime. But if I must, I will die fighting.'

'Let me make his wish come true Janaki,' Araak said, the gentle confidence missing in his voice, now a bark.

Janaki.

I missed Veer. But there was little he could have done all by himself.

*Where are you, Veer?*

*I'm around. Do you need me now?*

*No, I can handle this group. Besides, there is no point in both of us dying. If I don't return, you can finish my task. But do it carefully, these people are warriors. Go one at a time. You sound happy. Found some friends?*

*Yes. And you have too.*

'No, not this one. He is brave. Though he hides them, I can sense he speaks with his eyes. There's truth here. Can't waste him, even if he's one of them. Let's go.'

'Janaki...'

Her voice caught an edge. 'I said, we leave,' she turned to him and saw him craving for a fight. 'Now!'

In a moment the tension was over. The women and men around lowered their weapons. She turned to me. 'Tell your masters that the Khasiahnis don't kill needlessly, but we won't stop until our lands are returned to us.'

'Devi, I owe you my life. Seek it for a righteous cause, ask for it in battle, demand it for protection, and it's yours.'

'You give me nothing that I don't already own,' she laughed with relief, sending a message that it was she who had allowed me to live for now. They began to retreat into the shadows.

With the shuffling in the forest, an explosion of birds rose to the skies. Monkeys began jumping earnestly and soon, the entire forest was singing and dancing to her laughter. One by one they disappeared into the blackness on both sides of the trail.

The scar on her back was vicious. She felt my stare and just before entering the darkest part of the forest, a little beyond where the wild, flattened shrubs merged into the dense, larger trees, she turned and threw an amulet at me. When I caught it, it still held the warmth of her body.

'Tie it around your neck. Nobody will touch you in this forest, Janaki's forest.'

The copper amulet had a crude reverse etching on it, signifying the sun over mountains. I tied it around my neck and looked up. She was still there, alone, almost vulnerable, holding tightly the burden of her tribe's survival.

'Be safe, Janaki. And remember Badri's promise for life.'

She flashed a poignant smile. 'Another day, it would have been so different. I still haven't seen your face.'

The sun was down. I pulled the veil down. She looked at me for a long moment. Her smile came from her being and touched mine.

'You should shave that beard.' Abruptly, she turned and walked into the dark.

I continued to watch her straight spine, her head held high, her purposeful strides long after she was gone. But what my mind couldn't forget was the gentle sway of her hips.

Alone I stood. Kadak was still grazing, Vayu was still standing, and I was still smiling.

It felt good to be alive.

The stench of the city was now almost erased out of my memory. The smoke, the sweat, the food...nothing came between man and nature.

As in most journeys, I realized, once again, that it is only after you embrace nature that you break the bonds a city gently traps you into, one convenience at a time.

And then there was the delicious uncertainty.

To most, travel represents danger. To me, it's freedom, bringing me as close to nirvana as I can get in this lifetime. There's something special about riding roads to the unknown. From the day I was able to walk and then ride, travelling to mysterious realms had become a part of me.

On the Himavat Patth, I relished every moment of the way.

Something was tugging at my heart, pulling at my soul. A thrill bound my body as I prepared for a long ride ahead, on a terrain that was predictable only within the arms of time. It took less than a month for the semi-forested trail to cover all tracks. Only the trained could remember the shape of trees, the depth of streams, the colours of mountains in different lights.

It helped that I was well-travelled.

I had explored the shrinking green hills of the Aravallis that the desert from the south-west of the Matsya kingdom was gradually feeding into. In the southern city of Ganeshwar, specks of sands entered homes. That was when we realized how close our new neighbour, the desert, was.

I had experienced gods on the higher mountains of the Uttar Kuru ranges.

I had walked trails, swum rivers, ridden the deserts on camels, the plains on horses, the high mountains on mules, even donkeys. The only ride I avoided was on elephants. Even though the huge animal was the mascot of Hastinapur, I was never comfortable on it. It was too pompous for my taste, too slow for war.

The nature of my work demanded me to get intimate with the most inanimate—the underground. Few know how living in the earth below the surface really is. The worms, the snakes, the roots, the bats...all come together and create an invisible but living ecosystem. To the extent that it allows us to see the invisible. Our profession borders on the spiritual.

As a result, I had closely worked with almost every kind of soil. My work underground also served another purpose high above. The Kurus didn't always have harmonious relations with other nations, and professionals like me often served as diplomatic tools.

Because of the cutting-edge technology we had developed in mining and tunnelling in Hastinapur, I was often the glue, binding neighbours, sometimes even the farther nations, as an advisor. Every trip was cleared by Vidur himself, keeping foreign policy and commerce in mind.

To the immediate south, I had overseen two operations in Surasen.

To its east lay the Panchal empire, a kingdom equal to ours in valour under Drupad, and one that had become our biggest headache ever since Dron humiliated him. This was the only place where I had faced direct hostility while directing operations along the Ganga.

Further east, in the kingdom of Kosala, formerly the realm of King Ram, I had lost two of my young miners to the floods-afflicted empire.

To its south-west, I had spent tireless moments negotiating the rocky Aravallis in the Cedi empire.

From soft plains of the north to the stony mountains in the south, I had dug. From agricultural land along valleys to urban conglomerations, and at one critical point even under river Narmada of the Avanti kingdom, I had seen the underbelly of Aryavart.

As a younger man, I had travelled the rich plains between our three great rivers, Ganga, Yamuna and Saraswati. I had waded through them and merged into their souls.

Ganga, the violent, action-oriented, like Kali—cold. Yamuna, the calm, deep and quiet, like Maheshwari—warm. And Saraswati, whose waters cleansed my body and soul alike, gave me a rebirth—moody.

You could say I was a global citizen in the truest sense of the word.

My work had brought me closer to humans across the civilized world. Though a Kuru by birth, I had no nationality as far as my work went. Or, you could say, I was a citizen of countries you needed two hands to count. With some pride I could lay stake to the claim that there were at least a dozen or so very senior officials, even kings, in each of these nations, who knew me by name, and where my goodwill still counts. My professional seal resides in their tunnels, reminding them of the passages I built for them.

Even in places I hadn't been invited, I was respected. The proud Magadh empire for instance, now ruled by the terrible Jarasandh. He routinely sent his miners to Hastinapur for apprenticing with me. I kept them away from the palace but, under the eye of Vidur, gave them the theoretical grounding in tunnelling technology that was one or two generations behind ours.

But howsoever deep our diplomatic bond, no king allowed me to build tunnels for his palace. That was like handing over your defence sovereignty to outsiders, who could turn into enemies tomorrow. I understood and was happier for it. I just left them with the knowledge of their soils, the tools in their hands, and strategies around their geographies.

Along with friends in high places the one unique advantage I had gathered with my experience was that I knew the greater Aryavart like very few non-Brahmins did.

People sought me out for information, the nobility and kings for strategic inputs, the citizens for stories. My travels to these places, also led me to my deep friendship with Vidur, a friendship that rode the banalities of protection and information but over time went way beyond it.

Apart from kings, their empires, citizens and cultures, I had had first-hand and experiential knowledge of villagers, tribals and rebels, who lived along the main roads that connected kingdoms as well as the trails that cut forests, ridges and deserts.

Dark was the night and I was prey.

This was not the time when the sane or the civilized ventured through forests. A half-moon behind me, my eyes were comfortable and gave me a distinct advantage over any other. Time changes land and the same geography on which men traded, walked and fought now belonged to cannibals.

Vayu, Kadak and I rode on, steadily.

The first part of the night takes time to settle, and so did we. I had found a wide open plain next to the Yamuna with a few trees. The day was in transition, a point where things almost come to a standstill. Predators of the night were not quite awake and those of the day not quite asleep.

I offloaded my weapons, released the saddles of Vayu and Kadak and rubbed them down before allowing them the luxury of enjoying the lush grass and water.

Then, I opened my food-bundle and began to eat the packed roti, onion and mango pickle. I had enough for one more day. And that was all I needed before I reached the ashram.

Vidur's plan was simple. He wanted me to build a tunnel under the small palace that the Pandavs would be living in and through which they could escape. They were to be directed into the thick forests on the foothills of the lower mountain ranges. They were to cross the forest until they reached Ekachakr, a village deep in the forest, where they were to wait for further instructions.

The murky details bridging the two were my responsibility.

The plan was destined to fail and I had told Vidur that. One miner, or even a squad of miners, could not accomplish this in such a short time.

'Don't worry, Badri,' he had said with a confident smile. 'The Pandavs will help you.' At some point I wondered whether I was to help them or they me.

'There is one more thing, Vidur. The breach in Tunnel 14 was not natural. The scaffoldings were broken by man, not weight.'

'You mean, someone sabotaged the tunnel?'

'Yes.'

We were both silent, asking the same question: 'Who?'

'I'll have it investigated. But now you should plan your journey.'

'Who knows about this plan, Vidur?'

'Just you, me and Yudhishthir.'

'Did you discuss this with anyone else?'

'Why do you ask? Where are you leading?'

'Just speculating if someone knew what you were planning.'

'Well, when the Pandavs were leaving and the people of Hastinapur were following them, I too joined the crowds. A little way off, when people were few, I spoke to Yudhishthir in the language of the Mlechchh. I used this language because no prince, neither Pandav nor Kaurav took those lessons. Only Yudhishthir did. For everyone else, knowing this language of the "low" was not something kings wasted time on. This was an optional subject and many avoided it,' he paused. 'I think I should make this course a basic requirement.'

'But there could be spies in the crowd.'

'Yes, there could be.'

'What exactly did you say?'

Vidur related the conversation.

*He who knows the schemes his foes contrive, in accordance with the dictates of political science should, knowing them, act in such a way as to avoid all danger.* Meaning, your journey is filled with danger, there are enemies around. Watch out, stay alert.

*He who knows that there are sharp weapons capable of cutting the body though not made of steel, and understandeth also the means of warding them off, can never be injured by foes.* Meaning, it's not only steel that cuts or kills, there are other weapons too. Get to know them.

*Be on your guard. The man who taketh a weapon not made of steel given to him by his foes, can escape from fire by making his abode like unto that of a jackal.* Meaning, stay alert, alert, always alert. Have many routes to escape from, the way a jackal does. Use tools to make escape routes.

*He liveth who protecteth himself by the knowledge that neither the consumer of straw and wood nor the drier of the dew burneth the inmates of a hole in the deep woods.* Meaning, fire (the consumer of straw) would not burn in a tunnel. Make it.

There was more, but that was beyond the scope of my work.

I enjoyed Vidur's escape recital. 'Surely, if I can understand it, someone who knows the Mlechchh language could have understood what you meant by building a tunnel.'

'Probability is low, but possibility exists.'

'And who would you trust to build that tunnel?'

Vidur was silent. 'You.'

'Isn't it possible that Shakuni would have figured this out?'

'Yes...' he said slowly, 'that is possible.'

'Is it possible that the breach in Tunnel 14 could have been a trap to get me out of the way?'

'But you were at 53 when the breach happened.'

'Yes, but I was supposed to be in 14 that night. It was a last-minute change in plans that I decided to go to 53.'

Vidur was silent.

'Now, you are announcing my departure to Varanavat,' I continued. 'Wouldn't that be playing into their hands?'

'Not really. They may have wanted you out of the way but instead have only injured you. The extent of your injuries is unknown but for outsiders it is serious. Your guru lives in Varanavat, Urvashi lives there. It's only natural for you to go there to recuperate. When you do, you leave Vajr, who is really Shakuni's man and not ours, in command of the tunnels.'

I winced. 'You're wrong there, Vidur,' I said. 'Vajr is as loyal as Veer, he can't be Shakuni's man.'

'I know you don't like hearing this, Badri, but get used to it. It is the truth.'

'So, I'm supposed to go to Varanavat pretending I'm more injured than I really am. Fine. Once there, I'm supposed to give Yudhishthir a message. And then, begin the tunnelling.'

Vidur nodded.

'Even if all of this works out to edge-of-the-knife accuracy, there are two problems.'

'Go on.'

'One, I don't know the local terrain, I only have a broad idea. So, a lot could go wrong in building the tunnel.'

'Yes, that's why you're going and not one of your deputies or one of my spies. What's the other problem?'

'It's related to the first. I don't know how long it will take.'

'That's true. But I think we have some time. If I have read the man right, Purochan will not burn the Pandavs immediately. It would be too obvious and Shakuni won't agree either. My study of evil says that a few days before the Pashupati festival would be the time. That's when the run-up to the celebrations begin.'

I looked on grimly.

'There's another piece of information I received last night. Shakuni's plan is to first build a house of lak and then, at an appropriate time, burn it down, with the Pandavs in it. This has been planned for a while now. Purochan would build the house, Duryodhan would push King Dhritarashtr into sending the Pandavs there and when all eyes are away from them, Shakuni would give the signal.'

The wine suddenly tasted bitter but I swallowed it in a single swig. 'So, I have about five months.'

'That's right,' Vidur smiled, taking the last sip. 'More than enough time, don't you think?'

Distant drums from villages within the forest. Hooting of owls.

Slithering of snakes.

Shades of bats.

Predators of the dark were on the prowl. The night had woken up.

I cared little for them. The rare man-eater aside, most predators left men alone. It was the two-legged predators I had to be careful about.

Particularly, the Aghoris.

Usually, they didn't bother us. But anyone travelling in the dark was easy prey. A few sects of Aghoris had turned spiritualism into barbarism. Eating human corpses and excrement was one thing. You keep them out of the cities, call them un-Aryan, try and 'reform' them. But cannibalism went beyond all notions of civilization. They had taken the worst of the Kapaliku sect and transposed it to Aghorism. So, cannibalism was not merely a form of nutrition or a protest of the marginalized.

It had been raised to the pedestal of religion, as a sacrifice to Chamunda devi. No Aghori of this sect was worth being called so until he had killed and offered to the tribe a feast of a man. They believed it greatly empowered their sadhana and their ego-transcending spiritual practice.

And if that man was a Kuru official, so much the better for its politics.

They hunted with dogs. It was comforting not to hear their barks and the yelps. But I needed to hurry.

A woman's cry filled the spaces in the night's silence.

Instinctively, I nudged Vayu forward. The moon was rising and the shadows of the trees to our right had painted the Himavat Patth black.

In the light of stars I saw a broken chariot.

It had been dragged to the left side, towards the bushes and pushed just enough to keep it hidden. I looked carefully. The dragging hadn't left any tracks. There was grass growing comfortably.

Watching us slow down, Kadak gave me a careless look and headed there as if it were the most natural thing for him to do.

Kidnapping strangers on the way was the most common tactic of Aghoris. That's why, unless it was an emergency, few travellers dared venture out after sundown. What was this woman doing there?

The cry came again, a little stifled.

I got off Vayu with a jump, pulling out spear as I landed firmly on my feet. I looked around and sensed danger in shadows. Slowly, I pulled out two more spears, went to the side and dug them in the ground, one at a time, a distance of two dhanush separating them.

'Who is there? Come out, I mean no harm,' my voice sliced the silence like the spear I held, my left hand caressing the knives in my belt across my waist.

'Help!' it was almost as if the woman's cry had got a fresh lease of life.

'Whoever you are, let the woman go,' I said to the shadows in the forest, knowing fully well I must be alert to my back. Since it was night, they wouldn't risk an arrow. If it missed, it could hit one of their own.

'Don't meddle in our matters, stranger. Carry on and nobody will be hurt.' The voice carried little conviction, almost testing.

'A woman has asked for help, I have no options but to give it,' I said slowly. 'Let her go and I will leave.'

A long pause filled the darkness. Then something slithered.

'Run,' a weak voice lined by desperation said. A man's voice abruptly ended in a gurgle-grunt. 'Run!'

I began to walk toward the voice, my spear raised my knives ready. Some movement in the distance. This was possibly a small party, probably three or at most four people. Most likely, they were not soldiers or fighters, just bandits.

A shapely form in white angvastr came out. Possibly it was the woman who had cried for help, her left hand wiping tears. She walked slowly and stood next to me. I didn't move my gaze from the darkness.

'Are you all right?'

'Yes,' she whimpered. For a woman in distress, that didn't sound convincing. The eyes of my body were awake. Besides, vision was clearer to me at night than under the sun.

'Who is the man?'

'My husband,' she said a little louder. 'We were on our way when they chased us and our chariot broke down.'

'Let the man come out,' I spoke to the shadows. The woman moved behind me.

Around the same time, two men, their hair and beards matted, came out. Both carried weapons. The shorter one wore a garland of human skulls. The other held a short axe in his right hand.

I smiled at this drama.

Why would they open themselves so easily. Unless...

I sensed the woman behind me move. Keeping my eyes on the two men, I quickly shifted three steps to the left, near my other spear. From the corner of my eye, I could see a shaft of dull moonlight. I continued to look at the men.

A soft moan behind the men.

The hairs on the back of my neck stood on end.

Just when I felt the blade slash the rising mist, I jumped around the spear I was holding and turned around in a circular swoop, my left leg in position.

In the tiny moments before impact, I saw the woman's face. It carried hunger.

But I wasn't dinner tonight.

I straightened my leg and hit her on her ribs. The force was enough to make her fall but not hurt or break her bones.

As she fell with a cry, I completed my circle, landing on my feet, facing the two men. They spread out. The man with the garlanded skulls nodded to the one with the axe. He began to slash it openly now, trying to frighten me. The man behind me started muttering some chants.

The trick was old, too old for someone who had travelled as much as me. The chant was supposed to invoke fear into men, while the taller man would plunge the axe at the right time.

I stood still.

The eyes on my back told me the woman was taking a long nap and wasn't going to disturb anyone tonight.

The man before me edged forward slowly. Two more men emerged, one behind the chanter, the other from the side. I pulled out my spear.

'Look, my friends, it will take me less time to kill and offer all of you to Chamunda devi than it would to blink. Take my advice. Stop this right now.'

The man with the knife was young, probably in search of stature in the tribe. He had to draw blood. He moved forward.

With a mind of its own, my spear rose. It hit out like a cobra. The blade passed through his heart all the way to his back. I turned it slightly and pulled it back. In less than a moment, the silhouette of a black blood-fountain filled the Himavat Patth.

It was still coming out in spurts when he fell.

It was there in his silent scream, as he tried to hold on to his life.

It was still there, when I walked over to him, stepped on his face with a force, crushing his skull and spilling his thick, warm brain on my sandals, ending his misery.

It was there when I turned my gaze on the other man.

His chanting had stopped. The man was now quaking. The one on my side had disappeared. I felt the blood-fountain continue to surge for a few more moments before turning still, a warm puddle of fluids around my feet.

I walked up to the man with the skull-garlands. His eyes were wide, trying to create a trance-like atmosphere but I suspected it was more out of fear.

I slapped him violently. The ash from his face broke out like a shower of silver dust, each speck reflecting the constellations above. He fell next to Kadak.

Kadak looked at him, then at me, then moved aside to a greener patch and continued to enjoy his meal.

'Go away before I kill all of you.'

The man wiped the blood now streaming from his mouth.

'Take this miserable body,' I nodded at the dead man near Kadak, 'and the woman with you.' It was futile to kill those who didn't know how to fight.

A jackal howled in the distance.

As the cannibal party slithered away, I entered the woods. In a few steps I found a man. Or what was once a man.

An open abdomen, ripped apart just below the sternum; his entrails lying on the ground, some of them pulled as far as a dhanush. The white of the bones of his right thigh was mixed with the flesh and blood there. He was being eaten alive. I looked at him. There was no hope.

'Let me get you some water.'

'No,' he whispered weakly. 'Just stay with me.'

I looked closer at his face. The jugular had been slashed and an earthen pot was placed next to a reed that was directing the blood there. In frustration, I kicked the pot into darkness. Some warm fluid licked my foot.

'Thanks for the warning, my friend,' I bent over him. He looked like a worker.

'No...' he gurgled. 'Too...late...' He was calm.

'What is your name? Who are you?'

'Vi...Vihi...' he gathered his strength. 'Vihikal,' he gasped.

'Is there anyone I need to inform about this?'

'Lak...lakh...'

He held my arm tightly. I cradled his head with my other arm. We looked at each other. Something in his eyes continued to construct words that his lips couldn't speak.

As the glint of the stars above vanished from his eyes, I recited a silent prayer.

Yam was on his rounds and had found one soul to carry to the next body.

A village was approaching. It's funny how humankind's biggest rebellion against nature lies in the way it attempts to create a day out of night. Light in the skies beyond the dark indicated a settlement was coming up in a krosh or so. As I walked closer, little lamps in tiny huts told me we were almost there. The smoke capturing the smell of meat and daal hung over the area. It triggered a memory. I hadn't eaten a freshly-cooked meal for days now.

I had two options. Take a diversion, move away from the river and return to it a few krosh later. That would keep me on my path. The quicker I reached Varanavat, the better.

The other option was to ride straight, find a shop that served food and drink and catch up on the local gossip. This was the final outskirts of Varanavat.

As I considered both options, the growling in my stomach provided the answer. I signalled Vayu forward. A warm and happy meal in the company of information would be better than cold and lonely nutrition in the arms of danger.

Wrong decision.

I was two refills down, when the woman brought the leather pouch to my corner.

A jute cot was under me, my back against the wall, so I could see the goings-on. For a small town, this wine was conspicuously large. Next to me on my right was a fat man, whose stomach jiggled when he laughed. Diagonally opposite was a quiet tribal, nursing his vessel.

To my left was someone clearly wealthy. Looking at his ornaments, he looked like a Vaishya trying to buy his way into respectability. A trader, possibly. He would look at my way, ask an innocuous question to someone across the table, and retreat, as though storing the information, all the while measuring me. He would periodically, over three cots, glance at the man across the room, on the other corner.

The man was clearly a soldier and made no attempt to hide it. He was staring at me, something nobody did unless it was a direct challenge. There was danger written all over him, the kind of danger that is backed by strong arms from wide shoulders, wearing an armour of authority. He was the only man armed in this den. Probably, a mid-ranking official.

Next to him was a cot of foreigners. Short of height, dark of skin, they seemed a delicate bunch, probably from the south of Vindhyas. Their long, thin fingers with reddish tips, told me they were artisans. They spoke in low tones, in a language nobody understood. They held leaf plates filled with meat and rice. The oldest of them was a dignified man with a white beard. His brow was knotted with worries. Possibly their leader.

'One more?' The woman with the leather pouch asked. She was stocky and made sure I got a glimpse of her endowments when she bent down, her dark eyes openly inviting.

'Go on,' came a thin voice belonging to the fat man. 'Surely you're not going to refuse this pretty woman.' Laughter filled my corner. Others turned to look and smiled in sympathy.

'Yes, why not,' I said.

This was good wine. Not as good as those imported from the eastern state of Magadh. But good enough and definitely better than the local poison they served in Hastinapur. It was a mix of the texture and colour of milk that had run through a vat of acid. Some family of the milkweed som mixed with local herbs I couldn't identify.

'This is good stuff. What is it?'

I hit a happy nerve and her smile filled the room, as she recited the process. 'Oh, this is som juice, plucked up by roots. We collected it from the mountain last week when the moon was high. On the way we collected the herbs. They're secret, I can't tell you,' she giggled. 'Then we handed it to Nasiv, who did his business and gave us this nectar yesterday.'

That was good information. Nasiv would know more. I stored it somewhere.

'Tell Nasiv that this is good wine but the milk was little more sour than it should be. He mildly over-fermented it.' Being close to the mountains, som was easily available and was cheaper too. Else, for most common people, the affordable high was Sura.

Her smile began to disappear. 'Everyone says the beverage is divine...'

'Yes, it is, but if you serve this,' I raised my copper vessel, 'to the gods, you might call their wrath.' I smiled and she joined.

The fat man began to test the wine again, a thick knot on his forehead.

'But what are you waiting for? A thirsty traveller couldn't ask for anything better from anyone prettier. What's your name?' The man across the room shuffled.

The woman smiled and bent to pour the wine, grazing her naked thigh against mine, unconcerned about the hungry eyes ravishing her. 'Rasilee,' she said coyly. I raised my eyebrows in approval and looked at her. My thigh suddenly felt cool. She had finished pouring and had stepped back. Rasilee gave me a meaningful glance and deliciously swung off to the next corner.

The fat man put his vessel down. He was probably down five or more. 'It's getting impossible to trade here,' he said to nobody in particular, a resigned sense of loss tightening his tone.

'Why?' I asked.

'Why? Have you noticed any lak ornaments around here in markets?' The question was redundant, but told me he traded in lak. 'Soldiers are drinking it all up.'

'Drinking?'

'Yes,' he looked at me, his eyes reddish and carrying a frustration that went beyond his happy frame. 'See that man there?' he nodded to the man staring at me. 'He is Durjan, a soldier from Purochan's army.' So, my speculation was confirmed and I was suddenly alert. 'Do you know his job?'

I remained silent, noticing a needless hostility in Durjan's stare. It bothered me that he was the only armed man in the room. All the rest of us had deposited our arms in the open space outside. His sword stood next to the cot, his knives tied around him. The knives were new, the kind that seemed to have been imported from Hastinapur blacksmiths.

'He has single-handedly destroyed the lak trade in the region,' the fat trader continued. 'Varanavat has imported so much lak that it would take the kingdom more than six months to consume it,' he paused to gulp a sip down. 'But where does all the lak go?'

'Where?'

'To Purochan's vaults.'

'I'm not a trader, but if there is one person buying the entire market, prices should kiss the skies.'

'Yes,' he gulped the liquid loudly and burped. 'Except that he has cut off all traders and deals directly with the Lakheras, there is no space for us.' He looked up, his eyes drifting in a haze, then found what he was looking for. 'Rasilee, one more.'

'Why does Purochan need lak? Is he marrying off all the girls in Varanavat?'

'Girls? No way. In the past six months not a single girl has been able to procure lak bangles and jewellery. Leave the people aside,' he paused to allow Rasilee pour his drink, 'even I, one of the largest suppliers of lak to Varanavat, haven't been able to get more than a fistful.'

'So, what's he doing with it?'

The fat man looked across the room at Durjan. His eyes were wide with fright. The armed man's eyes were now focused on the trader. He turned away and looked at me.

'He's building a house of lak for the Pandavs.' His face turned ashen. He seemed to have said more than he should have. He threw a furtive glance at the armed man. 'I must leave.' He rose, stumbled and fell back with a noise.

A shadow covered his face, then its owner.

'You've had enough, Hridai,' said Rasilee, with strange firmness, a new command in her voice. There was something more to this woman.

The fat man smiled at her, his focus about a hand-length below her eyes.

'Time for you to leave.' Her voice had an edge.

She looked at me.

'What about you?' The smile returned to her round face.

'No, I'm fine.'

'Just call, if you need anything,' she waddled back, throwing a glance of invitation over her shoulder. From the corner of my eye I saw the armed man stand up. I could sense his gaze on me. I picked up my vessel.

'You!'

I sat back, my legs sprawled over the cot, my eyes closed. A tumbler crashed on the ground, spilling the drink. It was the fat man, trembling.

'Not you, Hridai. You.' Everyone under the thatched roof knew whom he was referring to. This was not something I wanted right now.

Strong strides moved closer. Hridai gave me a nudge with his elbow. 'He's calling you.'

I opened my eyes and looked at the man. He was now towering over me, a dhanush from my cot, his hands by his side, ready to fight. A series of light shafts reflected the lanterns around from his polished knives.

I looked up at him slowly. He was handsome and powerful. Probably a senior official. No, he looked more urban, possibly from outside. Either way, serious trouble. The fat man was sweating.

My eyes focused on him as I continued to nurse my drink.

'I'm talking to you, stranger.' That newly-acquired authority in the voice told me he was a recent convert to the dark side. There could be hope here.

My body was quivering for a fight. The cannibals didn't offer much resistance. It barely quenched my thirst. My arms were aching with anticipation. That's the trouble with Kshatriyas. Once the bloodlust has been ignited, it has to be seen to the end.

In less than a moment I sensed this man had more than a designation to carry. He had to prove himself, he wanted blood.

'Look warrior, you don't want to do this,' I took a long sip and looked away carelessly. 'Leave me alone. I have enough troubles of my own.'

Someone laughed in the background.

'Stand up when you speak to me,' the man was close to shouting. His hand was on his sword.

My weapons, like those of everyone here, were outside. So it would have to be a hand combat. My annoyance was becoming real now. But this was not the time. I couldn't risk my assignment. Vayu was in the fenced area further down. I had to get there without a fight and without loss of dignity.

'I am unarmed,' I said a little louder for all to hear. 'And you're close to drawing your sword. Be careful. This is Aryavart.'

The man stepped back in shock. Shaking with anger, he unbelted his sword and knives and threw them to the side. The sword fell with a heavy ring, a well-made specimen. Two men jumped aside as it landed near their feet.

'You be careful, stranger.' It was Rasilee. 'This soldier here is Purochan's man. You don't want to fight him.'

I looked up at her. She seemed tense. Not a trace of playfulness. She bent down, but there was nothing coquettish about her swaying cleavage anymore.

'Leave,' she hissed.

'What are you whispering to him?' the soldier snapped. He grabbed Rasilee's shoulder and pulled her back with a force. She fell reeling to the floor and cried in pain.

By the time he turned to me, my right forearm found itself on his neck and the left one pounding his side. He crashed against the wall and bounced violently back into me. I had to take a step back but caught his throat and stared into his eyes, now wide with surprise.

'Ideally you shouldn't hit a woman. If you must, don't do it in front of me.'

He recovered from the first shock and I felt a strong blow in my solar plexus. I fell over a cot. Revellers were now on their feet, their crashing vessels and plates creating an orchestra of sounds and beats that made no musical sense.

Durjan recovered from the blow to his neck and walked towards me with a menace. I was still getting up when I felt a kick on my ribs. I fell again but rolled up standing.

He kicked again. I took it on my thigh, bent and raised it, putting him off balance. He fell with me. I was up first and waited for him to stand. He roared in anger, his fisted arms spread wide for long punches.

I slipped into his arms and let him have two quick blows in the stomach and retreated. He was bent. I moved to his left, hit his kidney. He fell on to his knees.

I stepped back to breathe.

A big jump and he was on me, his shoulder throwing me over a wooden bench. I felt the hard edge and then the floor. He kicked the bench aside, then kicked me again. My ribs caught the blow.

He bent down to pick me up. But I beat him to it, pushing him with two heavy blows on his face, standing up in the same movement. He covered his face. I saw blood beginning to flow from his mouth.

Moving aside, I grabbed his neck from behind, stood him up violently, locked my right forearm around his throat to my left upper arm. He began to flail and kick.

His foot caught a pillar and I felt myself being pushed towards the wall. I pulled him back with me, leaving nothing in the way of his legs, looking for a hard support.

I began to tighten my grip, choking the flow of blood to his head.

He weakened slowly and fell to the ground, just shaken and not yet unconscious. I lay him on his stomach, put my knee on his back and pulled his head up with his hair.

'I'm leaving now. I want no trouble,' my breath came in spurts. 'If you cross my path again, I will kill you.' I said the words, but regretted them immediately. I was here on a secret mission and had allowed my bloodlust to announce my arrival.

I turned him roughly on his back, looked around and found his sword. I picked it up, unsheathed it and stood over him. Loud gasps filled the room. 'Don't kill him, stranger,' a voice said.

A bleeding mass of the soldier's face looked up at me with strange nobility. I stared back, held the sharp end of the sword in my left fist, the hilt in my right and slowly bent it until the end met the hilt. I threw it on the floor next to him and as it bounced harmlessly next to his face.

'Next time, that will be your back.' A shadow ran out of the shop. It was probably a spy, running to call for help.

Panting, I took three steps back to lean on a wooden pillar, still looking at him, feeling deep satisfaction that filled the vacant spaces of my killing urges.

A soft hand touched my elbow. I looked up sharply. Rasilee was looking at me with concern. 'Be careful, stranger. Purochan won't like this.'

I looked into her wide eyes and smiled. 'I don't like this either.'

The height of the village was new and I was panting more than I would have on the plains and took a few moments to catch my breath. 'But now I'm hungry. Can I get a plate of rice and meat?'

'Yes, certainly. What is your name?'

'Badri.'

'I'll get you a plate,' she said, turning her head.

'A little spicy please.'

She smiled. 'Hari,' she screamed, some of her vitality returning, 'a large thali for the stranger. Spicy!'

My breath was returning. I turned around and spoke loudly. 'Everyone here saw what happened. I wanted no part of this. He,' I pointed at the fallen soldier, 'called it upon himself.'

I walked up to the earthenware pot, lifted it bodily and walked out of the den, into the open, noticing Vayu and Kadak grazing freely on the way.

The air was cooler suddenly and I kneeled on the side, lifted the pot and poured it over my head. Cold water of the Ganga pulled my being from the violent recesses of my solar plexus to the rational realms of my head. My anger was gone. A trick my guru Kedar taught me very early.

I looked inside and saw the group of foreigners on the soldier's table, now sitting by him, trying to help him up.

Their leader, a man with a stony face, clear eyes and long white beard walked behind me. 'What you did was right, but it won't help you.' He took the pot from me and placed it gently on the ground.

'Why? I only protected myself and followed the laws of Aryavart as well as Kuru. Since when did defending oneself become a crime?'

'There is nothing Arya-worthy about Varanavat or Purochan. Your laws belong to the city, not here in forests or villages.'

'Laws are the same for all. And anyone who doesn't follow them or thinks otherwise will face the wrath of the king,' I said, the receding sting of the fight still flailing about in my body. 'It may seem that law-breakers escape the king's danda for a while. But finally, they fall. All of them. And when they do, the sound of justice is loud.'

The soothing air was beginning to cool me from within. 'You don't look like a mountain man, where are you from?'

The man smiled. 'You seem well-travelled, stranger.'

'I am. And if I can guess correctly, you seem to have crossed the Vindhyas to get here.'

The man laughed in good humour. 'We are Lakheras. I'm Varad, leader of the party inside as well as those not here.'

Lakheras. Workers of lak, this tribe from the south made colourful bangles and jewellery for the lower and some poor middle castes with lak. Because the colour of lak is blood red, the upper castes have a superstitious repugnance to these products. Up the income ladder, lak was replaced with copper, silver and gold. With prosperity growing in Kuru, the trade in lak was on its last leg. But they said that every other year and as fashions changed, entrepreneurs adapted.

'How many of you are here?'

'All told, forty seven.'

'That's a large number. What brings you so far?'

I suddenly sensed a wall between us. 'You speak like an official interrogating me,' he said gently.

'I'm sorry, Varad. It is a force of habit. I too lead large groups.'

'We were here for trade,' he glanced at his co-workers inside, helping the soldier get up and limp back to a cot. Then he nudged me to a corner, out of range. 'But,' his voice dropped, 'what we're doing has nothing to do with trade.'

I looked at him silently.

'Varanavat is buying all the lak in the area. He has also pulled us all here.'

'Who is this Durjan inside?'

'He is Purochan's man, who has brought us here,' he said. 'We are constantly under his watch.'

'Why? Is Purochan planning to set up a lak industry in Varanavat?'

The sarcasm was lost on the old man. He smiled politely but his eyes were unconvinced.

Then I threw the bait. 'Or does it have something to do with the palace?'

The small flicker in his eyes gave me the answer. In the relative darkness he wouldn't have known I knew. 'Palace?'

'Yes, it seems you're giving the finishing touches to the palace?'

'Your speech carries danger, stranger,' he said, a little graver. 'You don't refer to the palace here. You're not supposed to know. And if you do, you're not supposed to speak. And if you speak, you're not supposed to do it in public. Careful.'

The water had trickled off my head and beard. I stood up, splashing silver droplets into the lamp-lit blackness.

'Look, Varad. I'm not one who cares very much beyond what I'm supposed to do. I follow my dharm and know little beyond that.'

He looked inside, I followed his gaze. Durjan was reviving.

'I know who you are, Badri,' he said simply. I was surprised he knew. 'What I don't know is why you are here,' he chewed on my surprised expression.

'How do you know my name?'

He laughed gently. 'You think only Kuru has a spy network?'

I smiled.

'So, what are you doing here?'

'I'm recovering from my injuries, Varad. On my way to my guru, Rishi Kedar's ashram to rest.'

'How do you know about the palace?'

'I keep my ears open. And like you said, everyone knows but doesn't speak. What are you doing here?'

'We've been trapped into building the palace. On the surface, we're simply decorating the palace, but what I didn't understand is, where the huge amount of lak that was transferred here, disappeared.' He paused.

'Any speculations?'

'Not speculation, but certainty. The pillars, the beams, the walls... all of them hold lak inside.'

'What?'

'Yes, that's why traders like Hridai,' he pointed with his chin, 'who have grown fat by buying cheap from us and selling dear in the northern areas, are confused. It almost seems that Purochan is now in the lak business.'

'And that Durjan inside is one of his arms?'

'Yes.'

This was more information than I could digest. 'Do you know for whom the palace is being built?'

'Yes.'

'And right now, you and your tribe are being held here...not really wilfully. Is that correct?'

'Yes and no. Yes, because we can't leave without taking our payment, which we will get only after the completion of the palace. And no, because if we want we can leave but we have been assured that if we did that, we won't be able cross two villages without being killed.'

'Killed?'

'Yes,' he paused. 'The forests around the Himavat Patth have become homes of the cannibals.'

I turned to him, suddenly seeing the man who died in my arms. 'Cannibals? In the area? What do you mean?'

'I mean that if any of my tribe tries to return, they are food for cannibals. We are trapped here, Badri.'

'Varad,' I looked at him. 'Did any Lakhera leave in the past few nadikas?'

His eyes were grim. 'Yes, Vihikal.'

'He is dead.'

'How...' he walked up to a rock nearby and steadied himself. 'How do you know?'

'I'm not sure. But just before I reached this place I found a cannibal party feeding on a man. His last words were "lakh". I couldn't figure out what he meant. But he was probably a Lakhera.'

Varad put his head in his arms, looking down. He wept silently. I brought him a vessel of water. He drank slowly, then looked up.

'So, now we share a common prison.'

'Me, I am free.'

'That's what you think. But really, are you?'

'What do you mean?'

'Badri, did you really need to come so far to get rest?'

I looked up at him.

'And do you think that if I know this, Purochan won't? You are very much in a prison. Probably of you own making. Perhaps it is part of your job or of dharm, as you say. Both you and us, we are in this prison.'

This man was no ordinary leader. He was trained. The gentle manner in which he got information out of me was startling. Suddenly I realized I was dealing with a high-ranking spy. I smiled and remembered my father, Rishabh.

'Do you know Rishabh?' I asked suddenly.

His face didn't flinch. 'Rishabh was one of my teachers. I also know you're his son.'

'And you know that I serve the kingdom.'

'Yes.'

'And you probably know that I can fight.'

'Yes.'

'Stranger,' a voice floated out. 'Your food is ready.'

'So, here's the deal Varad,' I turned to him in a gamble. 'You look like someone who can be trusted. I'm here to protect the Pandavs. Come what may, I will save them. Or die in the process. We can work together. But if you cross me...'

'...there is no reason to get there. We need our freedom as much as the Pandavs need theirs.'

'But nobody should know this.'

'Nobody will.'

'We'll meet soon. I will be at Rishi Kedar's ashram.'

'I know the place. It is within a spear throw from the palace,' he said. 'In fact, the ashram is under siege too.'

An ashram under siege? This was unheard of. 'Why?'

'Because it's too close to the palace.'

'But the palace could have been built anywhere.'

'No, only there. You remember the decrepit ancient building that was falling apart?'

'Of course, I played there as a child.'

'That's the basic structure of the palace. We're building over that. Purochan has been asking Kedar to move his ashram out of there. Kedar has been standing firm so far. But it has become difficult for the ashram inmates to go about their business freely. His guards surround the ashram and the road to the palace has been closed.'

*Urvashi.*

*She is fine, Badri. Leave her alone. She can fend for herself and for us at the ashram.*

*But gurudev, she is not ready for ashram life.*

*Who are you to decide that? Let her come. Let her try. I am hopeful. She is different and has always followed her instincts. Neither you nor I can stop her.*

*She is here because she feels I have wronged her.*

*There are at least 108 villages she could go to if she wanted to do that. She has chosen this ashram in Varanavat. Respect her wishes.*

*Can I see her one last time?*

*No. She has told me specifically she doesn't want to see you.*

*I understand, gurudev. Tell her I'm going but will be waiting for her.*

This was worse than I had imagined. Surely, the ashram would not be attacked. But who knows, with the sort of mercenaries Purochan had unleashed here and the general sense of fear around, an ashram would be insignificant collateral damage. Particularly if Duryodhan was backing him.

'Food is ready, stranger,' Rasilee came up next to us. 'What are you two upto?'

I smiled at her. 'I'm coming, Rasilee. Just enjoying the cool breeze here.'

'It's more than a breeze here,' she said, her voice changing. 'Do you really think that pathetic Durjan could throw me off balance, that I needed your help?'

I looked at her. She opened her palm and showed me an amulet, no different from the one hanging from my neck. It carried the same code—Janaki's. My eyes widened and I looked at her again. She stood taller, looked stronger. The coyness was an act.

'Rasilee, I think it would be better if I left now. No need for more provocation,' I saw Varad nod. 'There are bigger fights ahead. How far to Varanavat?'

Varad looked at Vayu. 'On that glorious machine, you should reach by the next prahar, it's just a few krosh away. But better to eat while you can.'

Quickly, I devoured the food, not quite enjoying it but not missing the taste either. 'Spicy!' I looked at Rasilee with a smile.

She raised an eyebrow, mischief back in her eyes. She handed me a vessel of water.

'Be careful, stranger,' she said as I drank. 'We may not be able to protect you.' She handed me a small bundle. 'For the way.'

I looked ahead.

Beyond the trees, a jackal howled. Another joined him. Yam was still hunting.

⊰⊱⊰⊱⊰⊱

# Purochan

*Two days later*

'Surely you don't think that rishis have a divine right to life, Badri?' Kedar's eyes twinkled with their traditional mischief, half mocking, half serious. He was sitting in the lotus position, stroking his thick white beard that merged into his hair. In the reflected light of the sky, he looked like a white lion, crouching.

I kept silent.

'Purochan won't think twice before burning us up.' Through the thick mane, his piercing eyes looked right into me.

'Burn this ashram?' An ashram...my ashram?

I looked around. It was still dark, but the ashram was lit up by diyas in various corners, bathed in the sky's blue. The moon was setting. Soon, the cycle would turn. In the distance, the gates of Kedar's ashram were, as always, wide open. Two young men sat in the darkness, between the steady but humble pillars and a tree-lined trail that led to the guru's home in the centre of this huge tract of land.

'Nothing special about this ashram either,' he looked beyond the window behind me. 'Yes, things had begun to change even when you were here...how many years ago is that?'

'More than sixty I think.'

'Yes, you had barely begun to lift the mace...' he smiled, then laughed aloud.

I knew why. Less than ten years old, I was trying to be a man, as smart, as tall, and commanding as much respect as Sanjay, the brightest and the strongest boy in the ashram then.

*I stole into the weapons room and searched. There it was. That magnificent piece of art, beautiful as it was deadly. Keeping as quiet as I could, I reached out.*

*When I touched it, I felt an unnatural force, as if it was talking to me... warning me. With great difficulty I picked up the handle and pulled it, leaving* a dull, dragging sound on the clay floor that filled the room. Carefully, I rolled it down the four steps, out into the practice area.

I was panting.

You should not be doing this, Badri. I smothered the irritating voice within me with my pride.

My eyes searched the area. Nobody there. Now's the time. Enough of gurudev not allowing me to even touch, leave alone lift, the mace.

I gathered all the strength I had in me in a stance I had seen Sanjay and the senior inmates do. I took a deep breath, bent and picked up the handle. Putting all the energy I had, I lifted the iron mace in one swipe. I held it above my head, my arms shaking with the force and fear.

One voice continued to warn me. The other gloated over the impossible.

Like the first waters of a melting glacier, the warmth of celebration began to flow in my body. I closed my eyes and relished the feeling.

My mind diverted, I felt myself weaken. The mace suddenly felt heavier. I tried to retrieve my concentration. Too late. My quivering arms and wavering mind couldn't hold it any longer.

The weight of the mace shifted behind me, almost dislodging my arms. With my deepest fear embracing me, I fell with a quiet thud and a humiliating cry.

For long moments I lay there helpless, flailing with pain. Then I heard steps, followed by laughter, as other disciples crowded around me. My arms had stretched beyond their capacity. I was crying, now more out of shame of being caught than by the pain.

'What's going on there?' A sharp voice cracked the silence like a whip. It was Kedar.

The boys dispersed towards him, explaining my misfortune.

Gurudev took one look at me. Peaceful strength filled me. The pain began to recede. 'Get up, Badri.'

Sheepishly, I stood up, dusting the mud and my mortification away.

'Look at me.'

I looked into his eyes, the twinkle now reflecting the first distant light. I don't remember how long I stood there, almost an eternity, during which I travelled to realms of strength that probably lay latent within me.

'You broke the rule of this ashram by bringing the mace out without permission. Now, return it.'

'Gurudev...'

'Go on,' the eyes narrowed into a command that seemed to be an instrument of something beyond, something higher than him.

I looked down at the piece of metal, almost my height. The blood in my veins was surging now. I bent down, picked it up and lifted it high above, then rested its head across my right shoulder, my arms steady with a new strength.

I turned around to look at the weapons store. I took a tentative step forward. The skies didn't fall. I took another. Nothing happened. And another. I was walking back.

Behind me I could sense the other disciples and some senior inmates looking on in silence as I climbed the three steps, entered the room and gently placed the mace back in its place.

This was a miracle.

I returned to Kedar, the fear of a whipping lurking. He smiled. 'Your gada vidya begins today. Get ready.'

Gad-vaidya—mace studies.

A murmur of admiration ran through the bystanders.

I remembered and re-lived my first major achievement of sixty years ago. How do I explain it? It was like first love.

'That one moment could have been my tryst with failure, gurudev,' I folded my hands before him and bent my head. 'That one moment was the turning point for me.'

'And now, we stand at another turning point,' he said. 'Only this time the stakes are much higher.'

'What is the problem? Why is our ashram being targeted?'

'This is no longer just an ashram, Badri,' the shine in Kedar's eyes was back. 'Over the last fifty years, this has become a strategic piece of geography that has kindled the eternal darkness of lust that all men have been carrying for millenniums together.' His all-knowing smile had a hint of bitterness.

There was a knock on the door. 'Gurudev, we are ready.'

'Come,' he looked at me, 'we can return to matters of men shortly. But first, let's finish our morning prayers.'

I had reached Varanavat from the south side, behind the village. Boats of various sizes bobbed on the Ganga, waiting for the morning, so that trade between southern village tribes and the northern town could begin.

Vayu's gait didn't change as we entered the river and his silent steps turned into noisy splashes. I jumped off his back, enjoying the cool water around my knees. We walked on until the water reached my chest. Then I began to swim.

Behind us, Kadak stood for a while drinking fresh water to wash down the new variety of grass he had just eaten. I looked back and saw his silhouette, still like a rock, gazing at us. Almost in panic that we might be leaving him behind, he jumped into the waters and not used to them, stumbled for a step or two, gathered his wits and began to follow us.

A few strokes down and I felt a nudge. The lightening of fear passed through my back. A crocodile? No, the skin was smooth. But the push was hard. My strokes began to get longer and faster.

Another nudge, this time from below. Someone, or something, was playing with me. Then, I recognized the smooth skin. I slowed down, turned over and floated on the water quietly, staring at the sky.

It brushed past again. I put my hand down, feeling its smooth scales. It was susu, the river dolphin. Sediments at the bottom of the Ganga made the ground thicker as you went deeper. So, these lovely creatures tended to stay closer to the surface.

I had entered through the shoulder of a wide meander of an otherwise narrow river, enjoying the swim. Halfway, I saw a small port. A ghat, the hub of worship and washing at every riverfront in Aryavart, lay further down. The Ganga was flowing from northwest and we were crossing from south to north.

The water had washed my tiredness away and I was awake and suddenly fifty years younger. I sensed the dolphin come before it did and turned around. Its snout passed by my chest and I grabbed it. Alarmed, it began to swim faster against the river. I rode for a while and let it go. This one was longer than a dhanush, certainly not one of the larger ones I had seen.

As I swam to the shore, I felt its final glide around my ankles. I was careful not to move my feet too violently. Dolphins are delicate creatures, full of love. I felt the ground get closer and stood in the water, my head barely above it, facing the other side, where the heads of Vayu and Kadak were bobbing closer. The dolphin faced me and I patted its permanently-smiling snout goodbye.

We walked on till we reached a large tree cover at the foot of the mountains and rested. We had time, so I stripped and put my clothes to dry, unsaddled Vayu and Kadak, and brushed the water off their backs. Both wandered off leisurely, Kadak testing the change in grass. We were now at the foothills of a mountain, where the land-water mix changed the flavours of food.

The Varanavat I remembered was to my west. That was now Old Varanavat, still underdeveloped, still a village.

To the East was New Varanavat, which over the past decades had become a mid-sized town. I needed to know the topography of where I was going and what the town looked like.

I whistled and Vayu cantered in, Kadak following behind. I led them to the forest towards Old Varanavat and left them in a clearing with the edge of the mountain on one side and thick shrubs on the other. It was unlikely that they would be found at this dark hour.

Then I began the climb.

I saw a few trails that shepherds must be using, but for now I declined to be discovered. I knew this mountain almost as well as my spears. Given that the movement of mountains can blind the best of men, the broad structure was in my head. I knew all the trees and most shrubs. This was the place where I had spent long hours in solitude, whenever I could steal away for a break from the intense schedule at Kedar's gurukul.

The trail was now far enough for me to not be discovered. Keeping it in sight, I began climbing parallely. The smell of air here was sweet and intoxicating. Not quite as thin as near the lower Himavats but not easy on the lungs either. My breath became shorter.

An owl hooted. It was long moaning hoot, travelling through the darkness. He was probably declaring his territory. I looked around. There, through the silhouettes of the holy rudraksh trees, between two branches he sat. Almost as tall as a sword, this was a powerful owl. His eyes were wide and alert, talons ready to prey on peafowls or even a small jackal. Its horns, close together, stood out, its legs fully feathered. He was staring at me, unmoving. I smiled at him. He turned his head, indicating that I wasn't prey.

For both of us, night was clear as day.

As I climbed, I could hear the scurrying of rats, the sliding of snakes, the hum of crickets, all bound together in an interdependent ecosystem. It was a food chain that moved from plants to animals, each of its components living in god's delight.

On the top was a flattened open peak. I looked up; the saptarishi constellation stood above in the skies, confident in its strength. It was a physical as well as a spiritual compass, always ready to guide travellers on earth as well as in their inner journeys.

Over there, close to the hedge, jugnus or fireflies, created their own mobile constellations, now a random motion, now a pattern, only to break into another one. Change is the currency of nature and the jugnus lived it moment to moment.

The air was moist, breathing it was almost like drinking cool water. The ground below me was thick with the soil the trees held, even as rebel rocks made their presence felt. I climbed slowly, savouring every step on the mountain of my memories.

Further north, the mountain ended at the edge of a precipice. Through a secret path, one that only I knew, I climbed down. The fall was short, just two dhanush or so, but invisible to all behind a foliage of thorny creepers that had grown as thick as trees since I had last been here. It was almost an armour of thorns. I worked around the thorns and squeezed past, a few pulling at my dhoti and welcoming me with familiar scratches. The trees had grown taller, the shrubbery thicker.

And there it stood—my cave.

It had a small entrance, hidden by shadows even during the day. I tested it for animals. A whoosh from the wings of a hundred bats brushed past my head. Then silence. I entered, tapping my staff to warn and ward-off a stray tiger or wild dog. No movement. No sound.

Here I had spent moulds of time, watching the mountains, living them, being them. Here I had practised my concentration. Here I would come to cry when I failed Kedar or lost a fight. Here I had built a parallel universe of fantasies for myself. Here was home.

And here was work. Time to put the landscape in perspective for the war ahead.

From my perch behind the bougainvillea branches, as I moved my head and captured the horizon, I saw the old and the new towns clearly.

You could say, Varanavat was a mountain that stood on the edge of the earth. Off the Himavat Patth, if you took the Varanavat trail, it was a one-way ride that ended at this tiny territory. You could not pass through it; there were no roads, not even trails to go anywhere.

You took the road to Varanavat only to get to Varanavat, period.

To that extent, it was the end of the Kuru world, safely ensconced among, and protected by, the harsher mountains to the north and north-west, where it bordered the kingdom of Yaudhey. At some future point trade routes would open between the two nations. But for now, it suited Hastinapur to keep Varanavat as its last strategic vantage point.

Apart from the annexation to Hastinapur, this tribal town had for centuries seen nothing but peace and tranquillity. Annexing territories was not the Aryavart way. But in this case, I clearly remember from my studies, a tribal territory wanted to be part of the Kuru kingdom. The progressive king wanted access to military power, wealth and comforts as well as knowledge, technology and industry, to raise the standard of living for his people.

Looking east, I found the entire row of market and officialdom appear as a straight, long stretch moving from the ghat to the mountains in the north, about half a krosh long. That was New Varanavat.

A wide road in the middle segregated the military and administration on the far east from the markets to its west. Beyond it stood impressive houses of the officials, which ended at the king's palace, now occupied by Purochan, the governor.

To call it a palace would do the word injustice. It was smaller than Dushasan's outhouse in Hastinapur. Torches circled around the palace and the road, almost like jewels of moving fire. Armed sentries stood impressively, taking their purposeful walks, stamping hard on the ground.

Compared to the main palace, the stable along with makeshift housing next to it, was considerably larger than needed for this town. Meaning, Purochan had invested in military matters. Or to control the citizens. Most likely, both.

Further down, in the open, I noticed four elephants wandering around the area. There would be more in that enclosure, now hidden behind the palace. At this height, Varanavat didn't need them. So why did Purochan have them? Probably to impress Duryodhan and place the stamp of Hastinapur on Varanavat. Or to indulge in his illusions of grandeur.

Towards the mountain, on the western side of the road was the market, behind which were homes of the townsfolk. To the north, near the foothills of a range that joined the mountain where I stood, were the smallest houses, probably of the Shudras and tribals. A little south were the larger, and given the simplicity of mountain life, ostentatious houses of the Vaishyas. Eight of them were three storeys tall, destroying the beauty of the place. The first two rows near the ghat, just behind a large temple, seemed to belong to the Brahmins.

Turning to the western side, in Old Varanavat all was dark...except for the old palace, now a little taller. Large torches illuminated the dark there. A few guards stood loosely. We used to play in the ruins of that palace years ago. It didn't seem like that anymore. The light of the moon sent a dull-red reflection from its terrace, probably the lak. It seemed as if the architects had kept the original structure intact and were merely building on the foundations there.

This meant I wouldn't have to dig new tunnels. The old ones were intact and it was only a matter of finding the exits and clearing them.

Further down towards the western foothills was Kedar's ashram. It was a forest really that had adapted nature's ecosystem. No trees had been cut. Little thatched huts stood out in the clearings the forest had provided. A stream ran through it, cutting the ashram into half, beyond which were the plains, where the inmates grew wheat, millet, pulses, vegetables.

Kedar's ashram wasn't a spiritual retreat. He believed in karm, work. As a result, the yog in his ashram of 150 inmates was organized around work. Inmates could choose one of the departments and offer to work there as their sadhana.

Children in the gurukul, of course, had to do everything—milk the cows, till the land, understand trees and their medicinal properties, study statecraft. They had to build the physical muscles to wield weapons, muscles of the mind to use the weapons and learn warfare, all the while toning the psychic muscles of their inner lives. Some would join the military, some would become advisors to kings. A rare few would continue to stay on and conquer spiritual realms.

I was returning after a long time. The town was much larger today. All told, about 6,000 people, give or take a couple of hundred.

More of a give than take.

There must be more than a thousand soldiers there. Not all of them could be from Varanavat. The peaceful town needed no more than 400 soldiers. Where did the rest come from? And why?

Mountains carry strong silence within them. And in that silence you can hear the sounds of life—crickets, owls, snakes, the hiss of trees being washed with a light wind, the flow of river Ganga, even some distant sounds of last revellers in New Varanavat.

Every mountain, even a small hill carries it. In the solitude of stones, grass and trails, under the expansive universe of the moon, planets and stars, surrounded by an atmosphere of darkness, threat and danger, this silence echoed in my heart. I felt one with it.

*The universe lies within us, Badri.*

*But I can't even feel my own body, or my emotions. How can I see the universe, gurudev?*

*In silence, Badri, in silence.*

*I don't understand.*

*You don't need to 'understand'. Be silent, the knowledge will flow in.*

The growl of my stomach pulled me out of the past. Rasilee's food packet was handy. I tore a chappati, captured a piece of deer meat, smelt the preparation and put it into my mouth. Instantly, the spices brought tears to my eyes. These mountain folk loved their chillies.

I wasn't complaining. After days of living on litti, Ganga waters and fruits of trees on the way, any change was welcome. The breeze cleared my head.

I had a few ghatikas with me before the moon would begin to set and the ashramites started their routine. In the darkness, I began to open the last doors to my plan.

The palace where Purochan planned to burn the Pandavs was small. I could see three storeys, but still small. Not surprising, given that it was built four centuries ago. But even in those times, tunnels were in place.

Tunnels had been present during Ram's time in Ayodhya. The experts of the time were the miners from Ravan's golden city, Lanka. I hadn't crossed the seas but from what I heard, Lanka's extensive tunnel system surpassed the best in the world. I was told there were hundreds of tunnels that connected a parallel city underground. At some points, they told me, they were more than a krosh deep. I knew the power of exaggeration in such matters, but still longed to see them for myself.

But even if Varanavat's tunnels were not as elaborate, I was yet to come across a single palace anywhere in Aryavart that had less than six tunnels. They must be there. They had to.

'Relax, Badri, you're getting wishful,' I told myself. 'Work with facts, stay grounded.'

Finding the tunnels was only the first part of the problem, the easy part. The bigger challenge was to find out whether Purochan knew about them. He couldn't have. Soldiers cared little for such things. Even in Hastinapur, apart from Yudhishthir of the Pandavs, and Vikarn and Yuyutsu among Kauravs, no other prince was willing to attend my lectures on tunnelling, organized by Vidur and Dron.

It was an optional subject, not mainstream enough. I neither pushed nor cared. The few students I had were good enough for me.

At the time, I was a little irritated to see Bhim, Duryodhan and Arjun wander off. I had given them the freedom to not attend my classes if they didn't want to. I only wanted to teach the interested. But I didn't expect that out of the hundred sons of Dhritarashtr only two would attend and of five Pandavs, only one.

*Why are you so disturbed? If they don't want to come it's fine.*

*It's not fine, Urvashi. Future rulers must know the technology of tunnels. We may be powerful today, but that doesn't mean we keep our defences down. We must prepare for the future.*

*Don't bother the poor kids. Let them have a good time with their maces, swords, bows and arrows. Over time they will understand and learn.*

*Yes, they will. I just hope it's not too late.*

*Badri, you're too attached to your tunnels. There is a brighter side to life. Enjoy that.*

*You mean tunnels are not bright?*

*There you go again. Relax, they're only tunnels of the king, not your children, for god's sake!*

Today, I was glad Duryodhan had not attended my classes. Chances of his alerting Purochan about tunnels were thin unless Shakuni had infected him with ideas. That was a risk I had to take.

Finally, assuming the tunnels were there and Purochan was unaware of them, they had to be revisited and opened up.

The palace I played around during my childhood at the ashram had two that I had explored then. Relocating them now wouldn't be difficult. The king's chamber was the first point. The armoury was the second. And then, there was that insignificant outhouse. I looked closely. Yes, the outhouse blended well into the forest...too well.

Could it be the third tunnel?

If I guessed my ancient colleague's mind correctly, he would have opened the tunnels up in four directions. To the southwest, a short tunnel that should open up near the Ganga. To the north, a longer one that should reach the foothills of the range. The northwest would certainly open into the ashram, which then was part of the king's estate. But to the forest on the broad eastern side, it could open anywhere from the turn in the Ganga towards the south, the mountains in the north or the shorter range in between.

I had to get into the mind of my ancient colleague. For that I had to see the palace. But it was still under construction, teeming with artisans.

Varad?

The sky was changing colours. Time to meet Kedar.

And Urvashi. I closed my eyes. Sweetness rained upon my soul. And drained my exhaustion.

Then I felt the whip of acute pain, like being hit by a crocodile's tail.

The penance of Kedar lay stretched all across the ashram, from the gates close to the Ganga all the way to the foothills in the distance. As I chewed on the comfort of familiarity, the situation at Varanavat began to get clearer.

'This not a free town at all, Badri,' Kedar said, stroking his white beard that had grown longer since I last met him. His room was as I last saw it—large, sparse, airy, clean, and teeming with an indescribable presence.

'But isn't Purochan from Varanavat?' Despite its annexation, the Hastinapur policy of leaving territories structurally unchanged meant that there was a certain administrative independence Varanavat exercised in managing its own affairs. So, while Dhritarashtr was the king of the Kuru kingdom, territories like Varanavat were given a special status. A local would govern the area, with least interference from Hastinapur as long as taxes were paid on time. So, administratively Varanavat was more or less free to do as it liked.

'Yes, but over the past decade, the political conditions have deteriorated. Purochan wants to transform Varanavat into a trading hub in the region...'

'The only way to do that is to open a pass through the mountains to Yaudhey kingdom and then further to Madra,' I said. 'But that's merely geography. Surely, you can't be a hub if your citizens are not free.'

'...and for trade to flourish you need freedom,' Kedar completed my thought with a smile. 'I didn't say Varanavat has become a hub. I said Purochan wants to turn it into a hub. Till that happens, he can do anything he pleases. More so,' his tone changed, 'since he has the support of Hastinapur. Duryodhan has turned blind to all atrocities Purochan is inflicting on his people under the garb of loyalty.'

'Such people are loyal to none,' I spoke to myself.

'Within the confines of its domain, the emerging Varanavat along with its adjoining villages is riding the ambitions of Purochan,' he said picking up the herbal mix one of the inmates had prepared, and taking a sip. 'This is good, Badri, drink it before it gets cold.'

I brought it closer to my nose. The smell was sweet. I took a large sip and drank it noisily. A light drink, mellowed by honey.

'While reporting to the commanders at Hastinapur, Purochan as Varanavat's governor and military head, has opened direct lines with Duryodhan, Shakuni and Dushasan,' Kedar said.

'These three are predictable,' I said. 'What about Karn?'

'I haven't heard Karn's name here. I'm told he is a great warrior, as good or even better than Arjun,' he said, his eyes peering below his knotted head. 'Is that true, Badri? Is he better than Arjun, Dron's favourite pupil?'

'I can't say. At Dron's tournament, Karn wasn't allowed to challenge Arjun,' I paused. 'It is very difficult to say, gurudev.'

We sat in silence, as our minds began to grind the future.

'And then there is Kanik,' he said. Dhritarashtr's advisor. 'Evil to the core!'

Kanik was Hastinapur's shadowy strategist, who poured his poison into Dhritarashtr's ears, a fair king, except when it came to handing over the throne and pandering to his son Duryodhan's lust for power. Vidur told me that the night before the idea of the Pandavs spending time in Varanavat was announced in the Sabha, Kanik had spent a long night at Dhritarashtr's palace.

'Yes, gurudev, if Shakuni is the chariot on which Duryodhan is riding towards kingship, Kanik is the road. But he can make all the dark trails he wants, finally, it is the execution that matters.'

'Right, Badri, execution. It's always in the execution.'

'And in that theatre, the main character for my assignment,' I felt his smile coming before it reached his lips, 'is Purochan.'

'And his band,' Kedar laughed.

'Rumours at home say that he is one of Duryodhan's six followers, closest to him outside Hastinapur. A rich career awaits this man.' I paused. 'Is he really as great a soldier as he's being made out to be? Often, legends are built around one battle or two achievements. Mostly they don't sustain.'

'Purochan is a great warrior. He was my student for a while, one of the best in armed combat. After you, he is the one student I remember,' his eyes drifted into the past as he continued talking.

'Unlike you, he was ambitious, brutal. Maybe that lust gives him the edge...and the fact that you've been underground most of the past decade, while he has been flourishing with the force of his sword.'

'He is also younger,' I reminded him.

Kedar looked at me compassionately. 'You will need a lot to fight him, Badri.'

'So, Purochan is my guru-bhai,' I smiled ironically, trying to place the man. Guru-bhai or brother, because we had the same guru. The mud wall cooled my back. The rough floor was comforting in its familiarity.

Where is Urvashi?

'But it is not merely Varanavat that Purochan is seeking. No, Varanavat is but one small, probably the first and the most important one for now, but still a small arrow in his quiver of desires,' Kedar continued. 'From what I can guess, he wants greater control over all adjoining former-tribal territories.'

'Ambitions of a king,' I said softly. 'Hastinapur may not appreciate that. Bhishm, Dron, Vidur...no, he won't be allowed.'

'As far as I know Shakuni, he will give Purochan a loose rope for as long as it suits him, then yank it. I think Purochan knows that too.'

After the reorganization and prosperity of Varanavat, the neighbouring tribes had followed in a series of annexations. Vidur's diplomacy helped, of course. As did fears of the Panchal expansion, subtly fed by Hastinapur spies into the ears of the people, so the information rose in an inverse manner right up to the king. Now, Purochan wanted power over those tribes. Not a happy proposal.

Ambitions can be blind.

'So,' I thought out aloud, 'the cannibals coming so close to the Himavat Patth could be part of Purochan's plan?'

'Yes. The cannibals create the right amount of pressure on citizens to prevent them from getting out.'

'The Lakheras...'

'Them too. Varanavat has become a one-way street to death. If you're on the wrong side, you get killed. If with Purochan, you do the killing. And the governance infrastructure ensures both. It is as simple as that.'

'But why has nobody brought this to our notice in Hastinapur?'

'Who will dare cross the cannibals, Badri? Besides, who will they complain to? That too, against their own governor? Complain of what? It is just too much of a risk. These are simple folks, with families. They're happy with their food, their dances and their som.'

'I feel, once the Pandavs are out of the way, Purochan will push the cannibals back inside. And the cannibals must be knowing it.'

'You are right. And those who get too used to eating easy human meat, would be killed,' he paused. 'Badri, you look distracted. What is it?'

I shook Urvashi away from my thoughts.

'The soldiers,' I said after some time. 'That Durjan I met...he didn't look like a solider.'

'Look like? What do you mean?'

'I mean, he wasn't from Varanavat. And he didn't seem to carry the Kshatriya discipline.'

'He must be a mercenary. Purochan has broken the rebels surrounding the Himavat Patth and pulled some of them into service. They're here to do his bidding. Clearly, there's a reward ahead. But I'm not sure.'

They were participants in the glorious offering of the Pandavs that would consolidate Purochan's position at Varanavat and hand him a position from Hastinapur. Already close to Duryodhan's head, the charred bodies of the Pandavs would help Purochan climb into his heart and seal his place as one of the strong generals of the Kuru kingdom. Like Karn. After that there was no looking back for Purochan.

'He can't risk this project, gurudev.'

Kedar nodded but I could sense him trying to break through the layers of my mind, find out what I sought.

'How is Purochan financing all this? A small town of this size and just six thousand families can't sustain a thousand soldiers. Where is the money coming from?'

'Where did you get that figure from?'

'Oh, before coming here I had gone up to my cave and calculated.' Kedar smiled.

'The money can't come from Varanavat taxes,' he looked into my eyes. 'But he has lavished enough power down the line. So, mercenaries like Durjan have taken to manipulating trade on the side. Overnight, lak has become a strategic commodity, under his control.'

'...leaving real traders like Hridai helpless.'

'Yes. But Durjan only controls the lak trade. Then there is food, cotton, handicraft, saddles, swords, leather, oil, incenses. Each has been handed over to leaders of groups. The same conditions apply. Mercenaries control prices, pocket the profit and allow Varanavat traders to keep what's left,' Kedar paused. 'They call it the Purochan tax.'

Trapped in the middle were the Lakheras, who not only supplied the lak but were the only tribe in entire Aryavart with the knowledge of how to use the substance, dye it, harden it, mould it. For Lakheras, who came to build the palace all the way from south of the Vindhyas on the promise of high wages and huge profits, Varanavat had become a living crematorium.

Led by the promise of a better life, they embraced Purochan's extended ambitions, only to realize that once in, the exit walls had risen to cover the skies and all memories of their homeland. Within Varanavat, they were kept on a tiger-leash, never getting a moment when a mercenary-soldier's eyes were not on their doings. Money would follow only after the palace was ready. And if some, like Vihikal, decided to leave half-way, cannibals would ensure they didn't cross the border.

A cosy relationship of Purochan, his soldiers and criminals bound together with a common ambition kept the citizens of Varanavat and the Lakheras under control.

'And then,' Kedar continued, 'we hear about direct grants headed this way from Hastinapur.'

'Direct grants? That must be Shakuni on the sly; no official transactions can happen without Vidur's knowledge. He could be using Gandhar wealth.'

'The coins are in gold and silver, all freshly minted. With the Kuru seal on them.'

'There must be a leak somewhere. I must alert Vidur. Do you have a specimen?'

'No, we have no need for symbols of the money force here. Perhaps, when you go to New Varanavat and meet the moneylenders, you'll get the evidence you need.'

*Where are you, Urvashi? I've been waiting for such a long time...*

*I'm here. There was some last-minute change in the queen's bodyguards.*

*Should you be working so hard in your state?*

*My state? Oh, you mean this? Don't worry, she will be a rishi.*

*This is no laughing matter, Urvashi. And how do you know it's a daughter?*

*I know.*

*And how can the daughter of two warriors be a rishi?*

*She looked at me with eyes that stood beyond time.*

*I know.*

'You want another cup?'

I shook Urvashi off. 'No gurudev, I'm fine.'

The Pandavs were more vulnerable than I had imagined. Despite all their strength, their skills and their unity, they were alone. They were just five young men, barely out of their childhood, with a mother to care for. And the might of Hastinapur's military infrastructure ready to burn them down.

And with it, annihilate the future of not only the Kuru kingdom but a potential hub of dharm in Aryavart.

'And our ashram? Why was I stopped at the entrance? By armed guards? Ashram guards!'

'So far, Purochan has not touched us. But the threat looms,' he looked outside through the door. Kedar's tone suddenly carried a worn-out bitterness.

Suddenly, there were sounds of running feet. They came closer. 'Gurudev,' a loud, distressed voice broke the silence through the door. A shadow followed.

'Gurudev...' A young boy stood, panting. Behind him, a group of six to eight inmates were rushing to keep pace. 'They're here again. This time with weapons,' he paused. 'They say Urvashi is a terrorist and has injured the soldiers.' The boy collapsed at the door.

Urvashi?

When Kedar looked at me, there was no trace of a Brahmin left in him. He had become the feared warrior he once was...as part of Parashuram's army. Before I knew it, he was up on his feet. Out of nowhere, a quiver of arrows hung on his right shoulder, a large bow on his left arm. Two horses from behind his house stood ready to take us to the ashram gate.

In the early morning light I saw Vayu eating from a sack around his neck. Kadak was taking a drink and looked up, contented.

'Loma take care of him, give him some amla drink,' Kedar nodded towards the fallen boy. Then he looked at me with the hint of a smile, 'Time to meet Urvashi.'

His eyes narrowed. 'Don't leave your weapons behind.'

'Take one more step and it will be your last.' The voice was soft, calm, almost sweet. But it carried a deadly finality. Age had brought it a little heaviness since I had last heard it. But that inner strength was still there.

Urvashi.

The solider didn't know what to do. He was few steps from the ashram gate and looked up as Kedar and I jumped down, our horses still running. Two inmates led them aside. I looked around. On every tree, I saw someone sitting, each with a bow drawn, ready to deliver death.

'Kedar, what is this?' the soldier's tone carried a false grouse. 'Has your ashram turned into a terrorist haven?' Behind him stood a squad of twenty men on horses, all armed with spears and swords. They wore armours and helmets.

A planned operation.

'Depends upon how your master behind chooses to define an ashram, my child,' Kedar said. 'Is it a temple of learning, ceremonies and the Veds, where children and adults come to discover themselves before they set out in the outer world?'

Kedar paused to let his psychic strength sink in. 'Is this a sacrifice, where each act is an offering, an attempt to reach out to the divine?'

He looked beyond the solider into the eyes of the squad behind him. 'Is this a boundary, which has a history of more than a thousand years, a thousand years of purification of lands, waters, trees and humans? Is this a sacred idea that the greatest warrior-guru Parashuram blessed? Is this an extension of Ved Vyas's organization, as he travels around the holy rivers, putting the Veds together?'

The soldier was losing his bearings. He looked around, almost helpless before the might of the mind.

'Or,' Kedar's voice caught a cold edge, 'is this a piece of land to be grabbed by cronies of the kingdom—the fallen Vaishyas, the cowardly mercenaries, the ambitious land-grabbers?'

'Kedar,' the solider glanced at the leader of the squad behind him, 'this is no way to speak to...'

'This is no way to come to an ashram, soldier. Get out before you cross the line,' Kedar's voice rose. 'Get out before you force me to cross the line.'

'There is no need for that, Kedar.' The voice was stronger now, surer. The man behind the voice dismounted. A soldier rushed to catch the bridle. He walked slow, taking sure steps. This was a real solider, someone used to giving orders, taking them and killing. And...and I knew this voice.

'Looks like you've sent a contingent of fighters here, Vishnu. What's going on?'

I looked around but couldn't see Urvashi. Where is she?

'What's going on? What's going on, he asks,' the man said, a vulgar mocking in his voice, as he looked around. 'What's going on Guru Kedar,' you couldn't miss the sarcasm in the false respect, 'is that your ashram has turned into a terrorist den. You are harbouring and protecting terrorists.'

The sword still clung to his body even today, the shield too. The menace jumped out of his body and created a ring-fence of evil around him. Since I last saw him, he had matured shoulders a little higher, chest a little fuller, arms a little thicker. In his home turf, his voice carried many shades of arrogance, more confident strength.

The two scars I saw that night stood out proudly. The one on his cheek was partially covered by his helmet. But the one on his forehead was clear.

'The only person I'm seeing doing the terrorizing here is standing before me,' Kedar said.

The soldier's anger was physical. His hand reached for his sword.

'Put that hand right back where it was, otherwise you will return without it,' Urvashi's gentle voice floated through the mango tree. I looked carefully through the branches. There, behind those green mangoes, I saw her.

Vishnu froze right there, his anger uncontrollable, his permanent snarl becoming uglier. I suppose service to evil does that to people. They tend to get physically uglier. I heard his fists clench.

'That's what I mean, Guru Kedar,' he barked. 'That's the terrorist I'm talking about.'

'A woman? An ashram woman? You call her a terrorist? What has she done?'

'She has injured my soldiers.'

'How many?'

'Vatan,' he spoke to someone behind but continued to look at Kedar, 'how many, he asks. Tell him.'

'Three are serious,' a voice behind said. 'Five have light wounds and another eight are terrified of coming to this area.'

'Your terrorists are preventing the kingdom from functioning, Kedar,' a sneer began to form on his face.

'Speaks a lot about your soldiers, Vishnu,' Kedar smiled. 'Just one woman has done that? They don't deserve to be soldiers, send them to my ashram, they need lessons.'

Vishnu's fists tightened.

'Who is this man?' he pointed towards me with his chin, trying to take the discussion away from his growing humiliation.

'Not that it matters, but he is an ex-student of this ashram and has come to recover from his injuries. As far as you or your false state is concerned, he is a guest of this ashram. So, technically, he is an ashramite.'

'What's your name?' he shouted at me.

A soft growl from the trees behind.

Veer?

Vishnu's brow knotted. 'Find out which dog dares to growl at me,' he shouted at one of his soldiers, his eyes moving from me to Kedar. 'And kill him.'

'I would think twice about that, soldier,' I said, making sure my voice reached the mango tree. I thought I heard a gasp from that side. 'Last time, he almost killed three of your compatriots.'

Vishnu moved his neck in my direction, trying to place me. As recognition hit him, his eyes widened. He took a step forward, his hand moving towards his sword. This time the growl was louder. An arrow whizzed past and buried itself noisily, half a step in front of his foot. He almost tripped.

'Next time it will hurt,' Urvashi said.

Confounded, Vishnu didn't know what to do. His men shifted from one foot to the other, awaiting his command. Those behind tried to keep the horses, which had sensed the primordial danger behind them, still.

I stood calmly in front of him, leaning on my spear. Among the trees was a deadly woman who could kill him. Protecting them was an ageing but one of the most feared Brahmin warriors after Parashuram and Dron. And before him stood a man who had thrown his sword off once.

He opened his mouth, 'Kedar...'

'Not that it matters to you or your masters,' Urvashi interrupted him loudly, 'but the men you speak of were attacking a group of ashram women at the banks of the Ganga. They need to know that simply because they are ashramites or women doesn't mean they are easy game. If you attack, you will suffer.'

She raised her voice. 'And all of you here, know this,' she paused to let the violence in her voice sink in. 'I could have killed all of them. I can kill all of you right now, before you dismount.'

A lightning of discomfort passed through them. Two horses moved a few steps back. Others started turning back but were kept under control by the soldiers, now uncertain.

'I didn't then. And I won't now. Because I'm not a killer. But cross the line into our ashram and I will forget...'

Kedar raised his hand, signalling her to keep quiet.

The only sounds we could hear for a long time were the harsh, screaming shrieks of peacocks in the distance and the fluttering of wings, as an explosion of birds rose above the thick, tall tree cover behind Vishnu. It came from the direction of Veer's growl. The horses were edgy. I hoped they wouldn't jump. The tension would turn into a battle right here.

'Control your horses, Vishnu,' I said. 'Otherwise, we might think you are attacking us.'

His facial muscles clenched tighter.

'Go Vishnu,' Kedar said gently. 'You know the truth. So, stop fooling around. This ashram will stay, as will its inmates.'

Vishnu's eyes shifted their meanness from Kedar towards me. 'So, you are here,' the smile did not reach the eyes and didn't carry any conviction. He was wary of me. 'We will meet.'

I scratched my ear, pushing the humiliation further. 'If you want, we can...'

'Quiet!' I was shocked by the force in Kedar's voice.

I kept silent, but completed the message with my eyes. My emanation travelled beyond my body, met his halfway, pushed him.

*Last time you were lucky. This time I will kill you.*

He didn't expect it. As a bully, you get used to pushing. Finding little resistance from simple, unarmed tribals or Brahmins, you tend to think you are invincible. He recovered soon.

*You have come to your death, stranger. And it will be in these hands.*

He raised his clenched fist to his chest and turned to go.

'Wait, Vishnu,' Kedar's voice was on the edge. Vishnu half-turned. 'If Purochan wants to take over this ashram,' Kedar said, 'he will have to kill me.'

'And me,' I said.

'And me,' Urvashi spoke from the trees.

'And me,' the group of inmates around us said in a chorus.

'And me,' came the voices from everywhere in the ashram and echoed in unison before burying themselves in the forest. A flock of green pigeons flew past from one tree to another, their mellow whistles filling the heaviness of the situation with a delightful and untimely humour.

'Nobody wants to kill you, Kedar,' Vishnu's voice was a little sedated. 'But what are we to do if you harbour our enemies?'

'Who is your enemy? That woman who protected ashramites from your mercenaries? Or this man who has come to rest? Or these people,' Kedar pointed towards the ashram huts, 'who have nothing but their tapasya, their sadhana, who seek nothing but the blessings of gods?'

'Since when did ashrams raise armies?'

'Ever since armies meant to protect ashrams turned rogue,' Kedar was smiling now. He had moved the war to his turf, not physical weapons but the power of arguments.

'Are you saying that soldiers will sit back after terrorists attack them?'

'Looks like your soldier's terrorist is my ashramite's protector,' Kedar paused. 'Reality is multi-layered, not as straight as you believe or like it to be.'

'I came to warn you, Kedar. Control that woman, or else we will have to do something.'

'Like I said, Vishnu,' his tone was final, 'if you want to attack any ashramite or take over this ashram, you will have to kill me.'

Vishnu laughed. 'You speak of an ashram and talk about killing in the same breath,' his sneer was back. 'But in the name of the state, if we need to kill you, we will. Have no doubts about that.' Vishnu turned to go.

'A final message for Purochan,' Kedar's voice dropped a shade as the morning sun peered over the trees. Vishnu paused.

'Ask him if he would be able to live freely anywhere in Aryavart with the tag of guru-hatya on his head.'

Guru-hatya, killing one's guru, was one of the most severe crimes in Aryavart. If the word got around, there would be no kingdom that would spare Purochan. He would be a fugitive for life.

Over the trees, the sun was painting its glory on Kedar's face, now intense, as in war as much as in poignancy. I pulled down one layer of my pugdi over my face.

In the distance, I could see the reflection of the morning sun in penetrating eyes. Not one, not two, but dozens of dogs and wolves stood beyond the clearing. Their cold, expressionless eyes were looking through the soldiers and their horses, and at Vishnu through reddish embers.

*Veer, what have you been up to?*

*Your fight is my fight.*

*Yes, this is the same man. But this is between him and me.*

*Really?*

*And who are these wolves around you?*

*My brothers.*

*Brothers?*

*Urvashi is waiting, go.* I thought I heard him chuckle.

Vishnu and his men dispersed into the distance. The wolves continued to watch them as their shortening shadows under the rising sun rode past, neatly in rows of two. The light began to hurt and I pulled the second layer of the black veil on my face, easing the intensity.

'All right,' as Kedar turned around to speak to the ashramites, I saw his taut forehead ease, his muscles relax. He was back to being the guru, the spiritual guide. 'Come to the meditation ground. We need to realign the vibrations.'

Young men and women were jumping down from the scattered trees around, their arrows back in the quivers, their bowstrings loosened. My eyes were fixed on the mango tree. Nobody came down.

'Urvashi,' Kedar said gently. 'Come to my room after the meditation.'

'Yes, gurudev,' the voice came from behind me. I turned around, startled. She was standing there, looking at me. She had more scars. One travelled all the way from her left shoulder, through her tightly knit bodice, right down to her navel. Her arms and thighs had become more sinewy. Her hair was tightly wound behind her head.

She put one end of the bow on the ground and leaned on it as she always did. Her face carried the new radiance of tapasya that erupts from deep within by the power of asceticism that worldly men call 'hardship'. The unfathomable depth in her eyes had gone even deeper to spaces that are visible only in a different dimension, an alternate reality. They were now more almond-like than ever before; steady, unwavering, full of love that goes beyond the body.

It took all my willpower not to step up to her, embrace her. She nursed a small limp when she moved towards Kedar, the injury on her left leg, probably from the last battle we fought together years ago. Her black eyes, now a little softer, continued to look at me through the veil, reading my thoughts from another plane.

'And show him,' he pointed at me with his bearded chin, 'to his room.'

A long pause. 'I will.'

'Gurudev's room is at the centre of the ashram,' Urvashi said. Kedar had told her to show me the reworked ashram premises, particularly its defences. She simply nodded.

We were riding back to the entrance in silence that was broken every few moments by 'Pranam, Urvashi-di'. She would nod or smile. 'You taught that Vishnu a good lesson, Urvashi-di,' a child said laughing. 'He almost tripped!'

Her back, with two new scars on it near the shoulders, was straight as my spear. It moved with the horse as though the two were one, each an extension of the other.

'Gurudev has organized the ashram like a lotus. The central area is where we get together for group prayers, concentration or festivals when people from other academies come here. Behind that is his room.'

I knew all that. The questions in my heart were different...

'Broadly, the ashram is a straight line, from the entrance at the east to the military areas bordering the foothills in the northwest. That's where we grow wheat, millet, barley and vegetables. Fruits come from the mountains and the forests there. Then, there are the homes of the inmates, divided among permanent ashramites, students of the gurukul,' she paused. 'And guests.' She meant me.

'Gurudev said you were the military mind here,' I cleared my throat that suddenly found itself constricting. 'How are our defences planned?'

She nodded at me to follow her.

I noticed small huts built in circles with attached patches of flower or vegetable gardens moving in circles. Three large concentric circles of such huts around the prayer room, opened up, like lotus flowers.

We crossed the first line. 'The first two huts, in this line from the entrance to the combat areas at the back, are where armed inmates live. Also the four huts bordering the forests and two towards the stream.'

Too much focus on militarization of the ashram, I thought. What a waste.

In my time the ashram was a place of learning. Lessons on warfare, weapons, strategy and foreign affairs were little incursions into the realm of knowledge. Its practical ramifications, as Urvashi was explaining today, had been irrelevant. Today, the plan of the ashram looked no different from a fort under siege. But my mind was elsewhere.

'Urvashi,' I hesitated a moment to get the tone right.

She pretended not to hear me. 'And the trail from the entrance goes all the way there through the huts around it. Those two right in the front that you see,' she nodded at the huts along the road, 'are meeting rooms. Next to them are living space for guests,' her tone hardened. 'This is your room.'

'How many are part of your armed command?'

'I have twenty-two archers, fourteen swordsmen and thirty students.'

'How many can fight?'

'Leave the students, all others are trained warriors, who can kill, but haven't so far.'

'Which means that, including Kedar, you and me, we are about forty fighters here. If all are as effective as what I saw earlier in the day, we would be enough to ward off the thousand or so mercenaries, whose motives are little beyond the chink of coins.'

'Yes, I would agree. But blood would flow at our end too. When you have never killed or maimed anyone, it is not easy to draw weapons to deliver pain.'

'So, just the three of us, really…' I tried to fill the hardened silence.

We were quiet for a long time. But this time, the silence was screaming for cover, hanging on a cliff of tension.

Her eyes were looking around furtively.

'What happened, Urvashi?'

'Nothing. You have any more questions?'

I paused, cleared my throat, took a deep breath. 'Yes, Urvashi. I do.'

'Are they,' her voice became cold, 'about the ashram?'

'No. And you know that.'

'In that case, my task is over,' she unfolded her trembling arms and patted the neck of her horse. 'Take rest. Gurudev will see you in the evening.'

Urvashi turned her horse away, ran with it as it reached a gentle pace and a few strides later jumped on it with a grace that defied her limp. I continued to watch her go. I saw her hand reach out to her eyes, clearing a hair or wiping a tear. I felt her eyes boring into my soul.

Ash filled my mouth and liquid salt my eyes.

'And that, over there, is the palace,' Kedar pointed towards a three-storeyed structure, standing like a monster in the middle of a forest. From the ashram side, behind the natural boundary now lined by Ashok trees, we could see the top two floors. The rest of it was hidden behind an overgrowth that had not been cleared. Perhaps, even nurtured to hide the goings on. But it couldn't contain the voices near the ashram border.

'Place it here.'

'It's too heavy.'

'I know, but do it.'

'It's the home of our future kings.'

'You think they will sleep on straw?'

'I understand, just let me take a breath.'

'Hurry!'

The new structure was crude, very different from the palace I had known. However old in its technology, there was a certain dignity the palace lent the place. It was built, keeping the environment in mind, large enough to command authority yet not breaching the trees, the grass, the terrain.

Voices on the walls.

'I need a new bucket of paint.'

'Getting it...'

'Hurry up, I'm already behind schedule.'

'Why didn't you ask for it yesterday?'

'Stop asking questions, just get it.'

The two structures on top of the original palace stood out as loud symbols of ostentatiousness in an area that neither cared for nor looked up to it. There were large swathes of colourful strokes on walls. A painting depicting the king with a hunting party. A large canopy covered the top, made partly of logs and earth and partly as flexible canopies of vines that provided cover and still allowed light and air to flow through.

'Notice the reddish tinge to the earth and logs?' Kedar asked.

'Yes, it's lak. I met Varad and he updated me. Do you know him?'

'I couldn't figure him out, Badri. On one side he seems very sincere and worried about the future of Lakheras. But there is something shifty about him. Difficult to trust the man.'

'That could be because of his profession. He is a spy. His loyalty lies with the state, not with people,' I laughed, 'or gurus.'

Kedar laughed back heartily, 'So, let's keep him out for the moment.'

We walked, hugging the boundary and keeping a respectful distance between the armed sentries that stood every 10 dhanush or so. As we passed, a couple of them joined their hands and bent their heads towards Kedar, looking furtively over their shoulders. Kedar was back to being his jovial self, indulging in some small talk here, asking about a child there.

Contractors were overseeing the work.

'You said you had dusted it...look it's still there.'

'Clean it up.'

'There is no time...'

'Who was the fool who wanted them to come tomorrow?'

'Hey...don't shout.'

'Do you want to be killed?'

Three layers of veil on my eyes, I kept them on the palace. We reached a point from where we could see the entrance. Two large pillars stood there that merged into the shrubbery, creating an artificial space that gave the impression of a wall without being so...surely a part of the original fort. The road to the palace had been widened recently.

A child was crying.

'Why have you brought children here?'

'My son is not well, soldier. I will quieten him.'

'We are not paying you so much to do this.'

'The palace must be finished by this evening.'

'It will, my lord, it will.'

'Stop crying, my child...'

All through, there were the sounds of nails being hammered, furniture being shifted, grunts of men lifting, dragging, pushing.

Soldiers were doing what they do best: controlling.

'Where are you going?'

'Just to ease myself, soldier.'

'The toilets are at the back.'

'They're too far.'

'Go, or else I'll send you further than you can imagine.'

Sound of a slap.

'Fine, fine...why so angry?'

I kept my eyes on the palace. I needed to know three rooms—the first points of most tunnels. The king's chamber and the bath. The queen's chamber and the bath. And the armoury and the inner chamber that housed firearms. Besides these, tunnels could sometimes begin from the kitchen. This was too small a palace for most other sophisticated options.

'I need to see the palace from inside, gurudev. Is that possible?'

'I'm not sure, Badri. For the past two months, ever since the reconstruction began, we have been told to keep away from the palace. And you've seen the excellent relations we have with Purochan,' he smiled. 'I think you'll just have to live with what you have.'

'Gurudev,' a voice sailed through the trees over a cantering horse. 'Gurudev...soldiers...'

We looked up.

'They're here.'

Kedar looked at me, his forehead knotted.

'Again?'

The contingent this time was larger and fittingly so.

First came nine elephants, covered with armours, trumpeting their glory to the forest. Each had four armed men riding it, with a mahout sitting on the head, leading the large animals.

I could see collections of spears on both sides, about eight to twelve each. All were handy to the soldiers above. There was one bowman on each elephant, with a quiver peering over his shoulders. But still they were just bowmen, not archers to be feared, yet.

An equal number of chariots, drawn by two horses each, followed. Two flags fluttered on each chariot. The larger one, on top, carried the Hastinapur symbol of elephant. The smaller one below was the tribal flag of Varanavat, expounding its relative autonomy, three mountain peaks with a sun above. The rathis, charioteers, wore armour, carried a sword and a shield. In the first two chariots stood two men, strong, tall and vicious looking.

One of them was Durjan.

Surrounding the chariots and behind them, followed a battalion of twenty-seven soldiers on horses. Scattered around the horsemen, the chariots and the elephants must be forty-five armoured foot-soldiers carrying spears and swords on them. The horses were armoured too. The riders stood tall, rode straight.

We had before us an army gulma.

Antelopes in the ashram were confused by the heaviness of the atmosphere, running towards the stream. Moving shadows dotted the evening sky above the party, awaiting a feast. It was as if it was a wedding and vultures from villages beyond Varanavat had been invited.

Urvashi stood at the gate, her bow held loosely. Behind her, on every tree were two archers. Near the gate stood nine men and six women with swords and shields. This was Urvashi's rag-tag army. Before the huge contingent of Varanavat, they were dwarfed.

We had requested Kedar to stay back. Our most powerful weapon would not be exposed until absolutely necessary.

Almost magically and together, the contingent stopped. Not a movement. Even the elephants were quiet.

I now had a sense of what these mercenaries were all about and knew that even if they thought they could crush the ashram, they would hesitate. Sacrifice was not the currency of mercenaries.

*This is a show of strength, not attack, gurudev.*

*You're right, Badri. If they wanted to attack, they wouldn't have alerted us. There is something else going on here.*

*Have they come to take Urvashi with them?*

*I doubt it.*

*Then?*

*Let's wait and watch.*

*Urvashi, unless they attack, no movement from your team. Got that?*

*Yes, gurudev.*

*And keep your tongue in check.*

*I will, gurudev.*

*Badri, you know the armoury. If things turn violent, get the weapons, we'll manage the first onslaught. I'll plan the second line after that.*

*Yes, gurudev.*

*All right. Now, not a sound from you.*

'Pranam,' Urvashi said to the gathering before us. 'I welcome you to Guru Kedar's ashram. Now, if you could tell us why you are here maybe we could go about our business.'

'Silent, woman,' it was the man on the first elephant. 'The king's representative, the governor, is on his way.'

So, finally, I get to see the tool that was going to attempt the most audacious assassination in Aryavart. This was the man, who would be one of Kuru kingdom's strongest generals. The man, who had waited patiently to get here, and for whom this assassination would seal the deal. Trained by Kedar, he was now directing the training against his guru.

This man, Purochan.

'Speak I will,' Urvashi said, her stance and her tone unchanged. 'If you have it in you, try and stop me. Or take one step inside the ashram and I will show you what pain is.'

A war cry rose from the trees, as dozens of arrows from the ashram trees hit the ground before the elephants. They stepped back. She glanced at me. *Ready?*

I nodded.

Through the lines of silence, beyond the clearing, I saw the eyes again. Dozens of them. A long, blood-curdling howl filled the air, another joined in. Veer's brigade was here too.

The horses shuffled, the elephants shifted and moved their heads violently.

Only the vultures above continued to float patiently.

'There is no need for weapons, Urvashi.' It was Durjan. 'We are not here to fight.'

'Is that why I see hundreds of your mercenaries, all armed for battle, standing at the door of an ashram?'

Durjan swallowed loudly, the hold on his sword, a new one, I noticed, got stronger. 'As always, you misunderstand. We are here only as the advance party. Purochan is on his way—Purochan,' he stressed.

'As long as you stay where you are, nobody will get hurt,' Urvashi pushed. 'Else, I hope you're prepared to shed blood and men.'

Durjan was furious. 'My hands are tied, Urvashi. Otherwise I would have given a fitting answer.'

'Like the one you gave me at Rasilee's inn?' I joined the conversation.

He suddenly noticed me. 'You...? What are you doing here? I will have to take you in my custody.'

'You can surely try. Last time I was unarmed. You tried and lost. This time I am armed. Come on, give it a shot.' The challenge was like a slap and he began to look around, helpless.

'Durjan!' a voice behind boomed. Vishnu rode up. 'Not today.'

The powerful man swept the ashram with his eyes and stopped at Urvashi. 'The rest of you,' he suddenly raised his voice and shouted to the battalion behind him, 'prepare the patth!'

With surprising efficiency, the mini army before us parted, opening up a gash in the middle, wide enough to carry two chariots.

A deep rumbling followed.

From the distance, a flock of mynahs flew into the air, screeching their irritation. On trees towards the palace a streak of black rose into the skies, breaking up like a mushroom—the jungle crows, cawing their deep and hoarse cries. A howl came from the trees ahead. Far behind the huts of ashramites, cows in the cattle-shed mooed their confusion.

The army was at attention. Vishnu stared at Urvashi with his sneer, knowing and evil. Urvashi stared back, her intense force of tapasya forcing Vishnu to avert his glance. I smiled at the inner play of forces.

The vital power of the Kshatriya Vishnu was now bending low before the psychic-powered force of Urvashi.

The rumbling turned into the familiar sounds of charging horses, pulling chariots. Even on the relatively moist earth of Varanavat, a mix of dust and chunks of earth rising high into the air, over the horsemen, signalled a grand entry. It marked the presence of a king, no less. I looked at Urvashi, smiling contemptuously at this outlandish behaviour.

'What a lout,' I said, spitting to the side.

And finally got a smile out of her, a smile after which I was ready for anything.

My spear felt good as I balanced it in my hand. One accurate throw was all I needed. With their leader gone, others would disperse. I wouldn't even need the escape tunnels.

Vishnu's eyes measured my actions. He moved his horse away from the neat line and stood blocking the way into the ashram gate, his right hand close to his sword and the left running over the knives around his waist.

The chariot came closer, its sound now sharper, as the cloddy earth gave way to a road, partly hardened by crushed stones, covered with thick clay.

The vultures above continued their lazy hovering. The wolf eyes behind them were still, all focusing on one or the other soldier, silently marking their kill. The crows had finished their cawing. In the distance a peacock screech, followed by a jackal's howl. The sun was setting, making the light comfortable, I removed one layer of my veil.

I heard running steps behind me. A young girl, maybe eight or nine, with a worry sketched her forehead, appeared. She pulled my spear arm, unafraid. I got to my knees and bent my head.

'Gurudev,' she panted between breaths, 'wants no fights today. If things get worse, you are to call for him.' I smiled gently, caressed her head.

Before I could say anything, she was on the other side, giving the message to Urvashi, who simply picked her up and laughed when she whispered something in her ear. With a hug, she put the girl down. 'Off you go now.'

When she looked up, her eyes were wide with the joy of anticipation, the smile was back. No, it was not for me. It was the smile that warriors give one another just before the final attack.

The chariot rumbled behind Vishnu's horse and came to a standstill, six dhanush or so from the ashram gate.

Still grinning into Urvashi's eyes, I nodded at the chariot. This is it.

Battles have a way of washing the past—loves, sins, anger, errors, anguish...everything. Perhaps this last battle would do that for us. We turned to face our enemy.

Purochan jumped down, and I felt the earth vibrate all the way under my feet.

I had seen large men. I had heard about gandharvs. I had even met some giants.

But this creature before me was a breed apart, a species that had not quite evolved into man but still not an animal.

On the inner side, there was a force, almost physical energy, which reached out like venomous snakes, poisoning and paralysing parts of you even six to eight dhanush away. Maybe, even farther.

I felt the force and it was strange. Urvashi smiled at me, noticing my discomfort. When I looked at her, she slowly turned her hand into a fist and placed it above her navel.

*What's that?*

*Before any fight, there is a ritual warriors need to do, Badri.*

*What ritual?*

*It's a technique that pulls all parts of your being into a centre. When it's a battle, move it to your solar plexus.*

*How does it work?*

*I'm not sure. All I know is that it works. The theory, which I must admit I didn't quite understand, is that the solar plexus is where the fire chakr sits. It is the seat of power, of warrior energy, of strength.*

Most of the love we celebrated was around fights, weapons, strategy. This technology of empowering ourselves from within that the rishis had passed on, was meant essentially to grow our souls and equally our strength.

Two layers of the veil were still around me. Leaving the talking to Urvashi, I closed my eyes and ignited the fire ball in the seat of my power chakr. I felt it rise slowly, then expand, until I felt I had bathed in the fire of the sun. I was ready.

'Purochan, is here, Urvashi,' Vishnu said, watching a pack of well-trained six hunting dogs get off the chariot and head towards the gate.

'I only see a few forest dogs,' Urvashi replied, unmoving. 'Most of them on two legs.'

Vishnu glared at her.

'And keep your glares for the cowards or the weak. This is Rishi Kedar's ashram. Your position, your power, and any other crutch you may have brought...they mean nothing here. Now, what do you want?'

The dogs felt the force and began to growl. One of them barked.

From behind them, in the direction of the wolf eyes, came replies. Deeper, louder, grated. The domesticated dogs shut down. Two of them whined. Another put his tail between his legs and slowly tried to return.

'Watch them, Vishnu,' Urvashi was unrelenting. 'And learn from them.'

'You...' Vishnu began a shout.

'Silence!' The voice was strong, carrying the authority of a king, the power of an unvanquished warrior. A shaft of gold hit my eye from behind Vishnu's horse. It was a helmet reflecting the setting sun. It came from above the head of the horse. The man must be one-and-a-half dhanush tall.

When he finally arrived, there was no missing his commanding presence. The soldiers and mercenaries suddenly got a bolt of new energy. I could sense new revival within them, as it expanded to cover the confidence they got from Purochan's being. Whatever else this creature was, there was the leadership running through him.

Put your wildest imagination to work and create a symbol of evil. Then find the sweetest honey in Aryavart. Now, dip the symbol in that honey.

What you get is Purochan.

The scars of battle stood all over his shoulders, chest, face. But his eyes, untouched by the blade, were harder than a blacksmith's hammer. When they looked at you, you felt the physical force of that hammer on your chest. I had to look up to get to his eyes.

'It's not polite to speak to a woman in this manner, Vishnu,' his voice filled the ashram with its poison. The words were right, but the tone was noxious. It was almost like, 'You don't speak to a subject, you crush her.'

He looked at Urvashi, who to her credit was unmoved, though I could sense the struggle within her. 'I apologize on his behalf, Urvashi.' Each word was like a blow of a mace.

'Your apology is accepted, Purochan,' she said dismissively, to the chagrin of the mercenaries, their hands ready to draw swords, spears, arrows. 'Now, what do you and your mercenaries want from our ashram?'

Purochan smiled lightly. Brute force of his warrior energy, could not only attack, it could defend as strongly. On the physical side, when you're sitting in your navel, it becomes very difficult for anyone to push you. And in the inner battle, no words, sarcasm or threats move you. Purochan, it seemed, had perfected both. He was as steady as the mountains in the distance. Living in them and being trained by Kedar, he had internalized both nature and technology.

'Mercenaries? You humiliate us, Urvashi,' his eyes narrowed even as his smile widened. 'I'm here to talk to gurudev. May I?'

You needed a blade to cut the silence.

'About what?'

'If you don't mind, that is a discussion between elders,' he said. He took a step towards the ashram.

'Stop right there, Purochan,' Urvashi said, without moving a muscle. 'Stop before you get hurt. Do not enter these premises without permission. This is not your den of debauchery.'

Behind him, I saw the soldiers half pull out their swords and spears, their eyes wide with anger, the muscles of their jaws tight. A sharp voice broke the quiet. 'How dare you speak to our lord like that?'

'Who was that?' Purochan shouted, his head turned slightly back.

'I, my lord,' a young soldier, fresh from the academy, not a scar on his body came running to stand before Purochan, his anger at the way his leader was treated visible in his eyes.

'I had asked for silence, do you not understand?'

The soldier was deflated. He began to say something, instead blood spurted out of his mouth. He looked down and found a long knife, almost a sword, had passed through him, twisting as it crossed his innards. As the soldier fell, choking in his own blood, Purochan said, 'Will someone get rid of this,' and kicked the man. He flew three dhanush in the air, falling at the feet of an elephant, where two soldiers picked him up.

He turned to Urvashi slowly. 'Will you please inform our gurudev,' the word came with a little pause, 'that Purochan is here and seeks his presence?'

'Yes, Purochan,' I felt my intervention was necessary. Urvashi was pushing the limits of decorum too far. One life was already wasted, I wanted no more bloodshed. I turned to a young sadhak. 'Ask gurudev, should we bring Purochan in?'

I sensed the lash of Urvashi's irritation.

'Please have a seat, Purochan,' I said, directing him to a small wooden bench within the premises. 'Your message has been sent.'

Purochan walked up to the bench, six of his soldiers following.

'You,' I pointed with my spear at the soldiers. 'Stay out.'

They looked at Purochan. He nodded calmly.

'And who are you,' he asked, sitting, 'why do you hide your face?'

'That's not the point today, Purochan,' I said. 'Wait for gurudev.'

Within moments, a rider came up to Urvashi. 'Gurudev says he will meet Purochan.'

Urvashi turned to Purochan. 'Come.'

As Purochan began to walk, Vishnu and Durjan marched behind him. She looked at me. I nodded gently.

'You may leave your weapons with Kartik,' Urvashi told the three of them. Purochan paused. 'But you'll have to hurry. It's time for our evening prayers and dinner and the ashramites have had a long day.'

Kartik, a young sinewy senior student took the weapons from the three of them. As the others began to follow, I said, 'The rest of you can wait outside.' I turned to Shiv. 'See if they need anything.' He nodded.

'But make sure,' I spoke to the trees, 'nobody enters without Urvashi's permission.'

Towering over Urvashi, almost double her height, Purochan followed, with Vishnu and Durjan shadowing behind. I was at the end of the party. Over his shoulder, Vishnu kept throwing darts of anger at me.

All three observed closely the ashram activities. Cows and horses being tended to. Mace training was going on, by the side. Sounds of mantras in the distance.

And then, something strange happened.

As soon as we passed by the children's enclosure, they rushed towards Purochan with glee.

'Stop!' Urvashi shouted. 'Go back.'

'But...but it's Purochan chacha...' a young boy said.

'Go back!'

A flush of disappointment on their faces, the children returned. One of them was crying.

'Not today, my child,' Purochan's voice was gentle like a mother's, 'I'll come back later. Then I'll see you. Now get along.'

The children smiled at him and nodded. One of them glared at Urvashi.

This was unreal.

Children are the compass of human psychology. If they like someone, most of the time he deserves to be liked. How did a wretch like Purochan enter their hearts?

When we reached the visitors room, Kedar was waiting outside.

'Come, come, Purochan,' Kedar smiled from within. 'Good to see my former student after so many years. What do you want?'

To everyone's surprise, Purochan bent down. Urvashi and I tensed. With the agility I didn't think he had, Purochan touched Kedar's feet and sought his blessings. Kedar patted his shoulders, testing the muscles. 'I'm happy to see you have kept the training going, Purochan.'

'It's your training, gurudev,' Purochan said, a smile on his face that however hard I tried to call false, didn't seem so.

'True, but what have you been eating? These stony shoulders can't be created out of fruits, vegetables or meat,' Kedar laughed. Purochan joined in. Vishnu and Durjan kept quiet. Urvashi and I glanced at each other.

'Get some warm milk for our guests, Daya,' Kedar said to an ashramite as we sat in the meeting room. 'Urvashi, you wait outside.' He looked at me and signalled me to get in.

The room was large, but there was a corner where small groups could sit and debate. Kedar took us there. I noticed, it was in the line of Urvashi's sight. The evening light was dimming and my eyes needed no more protection. I removed the veil.

First Durjan, then Vishnu, stared at me, fixing my face in their beings.

Purochan waited till Kedar was seated, then placed himself before him across the circular room, airy with long and wide windows. I sat on Kedar's right. Vishnu and Durjan sat on either sides of Purochan.

'Are you comfortable, my son?' Kedar's voice was filled with love that belonged to the past and to another man—surely, the creature before us couldn't have lasted in this ashram for more than a day.

'Yes, gurudev,' Purochan said, as the milk was placed before them in earthenware vessels. Purochan picked up his cup, gazed at it with a strange longing, put his thoughts together to say something. Then resisted, smiled to himself and took a long sip.

'So, what brings you here?'

'Gurudev, you know the Pandavs are living in the governor's palace.'

'Yes, your palace,' gurudev stressed.

'They're moving into their own palace there,' he pointed at the direction of the newly-constructed death trap. 'Tomorrow.'

'That's nice. After years, we finally have royal neighbours,' Kedar looked at me, smiling with enthusiasm. He turned to Purochan. 'We welcome them.'

'They could get no better neighbours,' Purochan paused to put himself together. 'Especially, Prince Yudhishthir. He enjoys the company of sages, rishis and Veds.'

Kedar looked at him quizzically, his brow knotted in a question. 'And...?'

'Prince Yudhishthir wants to seek your blessings before he enters his new home.'

'My blessings are but a medium of cosmic energy. They belong to everyone, for everyone, and I don't need to tell you, they reside in everyone's hearts,' he paused, looking at me. 'Yudhishthir will receive them too. When does he want to come?'

'Tonight, if possible.'

'Tonight? That's a strange time for a king to meet a guru,' I remarked casually. Three meetings in one day was too much for one ashram.

Kedar looked at me silently.

'Usually, the first prahar is reserved for such meetings,' I continued. 'Unless there is an emergency.'

For the first time, Purochan put his gaze squarely on me and I felt the direct onslaught of his force. Even in his relaxed moment, the animal within couldn't be controlled. Since I was prepared, the invisible force bounced back to him. He noticed it and smiled.

'Who is this man, gurudev?' he asked Kedar looking at me.

'Oh, he is your guru-bhai. A former student. He was here...how many...fifty years ago...' Kedar refrained from giving my name. Vishnu leaned over, craned his neck high and gently spoke to Purochan, who looked at me and nodded.

'But matters of kings must be resolved first,' Kedar continued. 'What's the hurry? We could meet Yudhishthir tomorrow morning. In fact, he could join us for the morning prayers.'

'Yes, he could. But you understand the needs of the royalty, gurudev,' I felt a burden move away from me as Purochan shifted his attention to Kedar. 'Yudhishthir is a very different prince. Given a choice he would rather join your ashram here. But right now, he wants to seek your blessings before,' he stressed on the word, 'he enters the palace.'

'In that case, he is welcome. He and I could have a late dinner.'

'Please forgive me, gurudev,' Purochan pushed further. 'But it's not him alone. All five Pandavs and their mother, queen Kunti, will be here. Since I am their host here, I would burden you with their attendants and the three of us. Would that be fine?'

Kedar was quiet.

'The Pandavs and Kunti are welcome. So are you. But leave their attendants outside,' he paused to glance at Vishnu and Durjan. Then, with a smile, 'And yours.' Vishnu's jaws clenched. 'In this ashram, we do all our work ourselves.'

The signal was clear. The Pandavs were welcome, Purochan could accompany them, but nobody else.

'That's perfectly fine, gurudev,' Purochan smiled. 'They can wait at the ashram gates. I wouldn't want to burden the ashram.'

'If they need to.'

He turned to Daya. 'Their vessels are empty, Daya, fill them up.' Daya filled Purochan's vessel, then Durjan's. He turned to Vishnu, who refused.

'I believe they need to, gurudev,' Purochan said, the vessel untouched before him. 'Haven't you heard of the rebels and the cannibals in the area?'

Kedar was quiet for a long moment. 'You are right. Keep your soldiers at the gates.'

Purochan exhaled visibly.

'That was not difficult,' Kedar beamed at me. 'Daya, prepare the seating. Tell everyone I will not be having dinner with them this evening and ask Govind to make his special kheer, befitting our future king.'

At the mention of 'future king,' Purochan threw a knowing look at Vishnu. A light smile played on both their lips.

Kedar saw it all but pretended not to notice. 'All right then.' He looked at Purochan. 'Let's meet the Pandavs.'

# Pandavs

*The same evening*

'A few ghatikas with Yudhishthir, gurudev,' I said. 'That's all I need.'

'Can be done but may not be easy, Badri.'

'I know, gurudev. But my message is for his ears only. I cannot give it to anyone else.'

'I understand that,' Kedar said, throwing a grape into his mouth. 'Here,' he tossed a bunch at me. I caught it. He smiled. 'Try them, they are the sweetest grapes I've had this season.'

I put one into my mouth. The first bite removed all the bitterness pervading there.

'But Purochan is unpredictable. If he chooses not to leave Yudhishthir's side, and that would be the right thing to do as far as protocol goes, you may have to wait for the Pandavs to move into their palace before you get your chance.'

I continued to relish the grapes.

'Unless,' Kedar paused, as Urvashi and I looked at him, 'we can organize a special session of night raags by the children.'

He noticed my surprise.

'Why are your eyes so wide, Badri?'

'Exposing children to a monster like Purochan...'

'So, you've forgotten the important things. Don't let the outer world mislead you.'

I kept quiet, enjoying the comfort of the grapes. Another riddle was on its way. We expected rishis to speak in riddles and Kedar was no different. But this went beyond my comprehension. Purochan was nothing but the collection of asuric forces.

On the physical front, he existed to destroy all good, the Pandavs for now. On a personal level, he was my adversary. On the inner scale, he symbolized the power of individual ego, a representation of a blind and complete identity with the body and mind.

For simplicity, he was the face of what we called evil.

Perhaps Kedar had something. 'Don't you remember the last few classes, on how to live in the outer world and still continue to grow within?'

'Yes, gurudev...' I tried to mumble my way out of this direct question.

'What did Rishi Markande teach you in the two months he was here?'

He waited for my response, then decided to be kind. 'Every good man has a dark side...'

'...yes,' I remembered, 'and every dark being has a bright side to him, a tiny hole in his hardened body from where light can get in and touch him, purify him.'

'The psychic,' Kedar said.

'The psychic,' I repeated, not quite understanding the direction of where this was headed. 'Yes, but what does the night raag have to do with Purochan or the psychic?'

'Not the night raag. But the children singing it.'

I thought I didn't hear him clearly, for this was an absolutely unbelievable turn. Expose our ashram children to this evil? I looked away.

'Did you notice how good Purochan was with children; how much they loved him, danced around him, celebrated his arrival?' Kedar was getting carried away with this compassion, love.

'Yes, quite perplexing. Maybe it's the symbol of authority he carries. Or his magnetism, honed by an overwhelmingly strong force within him?'

'You give our children too much credit,' Kedar smiled. 'Children will always be innocent, equally open to forces of darkness and light. But this has nothing to do with children. It's to do with Purochan.'

There was a chorus of celebration. Outside, we could sense the excitement of children. The information that Purochan would be headed to the ashram tonight was out.

'Gurudev, I enjoy your riddles, but time is short...the Pandavs would be here any moment.'

'Then handle Purochan yourself,' Urvashi glared at me, her eyes fiery, 'why come to gurudev?'

'Urvashi, I understand tension. But Badri is our own,' Kedar said. 'In more ways than one.'

'No, she is right, gurudev. I'm too much on the edge; the safety of the five brothers and Kunti is a burden weighing on me.'

Kedar looked around the windows dotting his hut, then turned to me. 'Come here.'

As we moved closer to him, he closed his eyes. There was a hint of pain in his brow laced with compassion. The kind you feel while hunting a deer for food. Kill him you must for you own survival. But just before you cut his life out, you seek his forgiveness.

'I am the only person alive who knows this,' his voice dropped an octave. 'And now you will.'

Had it been anyone else but Kedar, I wouldn't have believed this story. It just couldn't be true.

'After the annexation to Hastinapur, King Goran hand-picked Purochan, Vishnu and six other children of the state to study military tactics and weapons at this ashram,' Kedar's eyes wore that distant look. 'I told him, they were too old to join the ashram. But Goran persisted.'

Kedar adjusted his saffron angvastr, freeing his right hand.

'One look at him was enough to tell me that this child Purochan was living in pain. He looked at me with a resigned trepidation and confusion. Those eyes I still can't forget. He couldn't trust anyone, and I was no exception. Gradually, as he began to live the ashram life, he left his past behind. Or so I thought.'

There was the sound of crickets outside, almost singing a welcome song for Ratridevi. In the quiet of the mountains, every hum was many shades louder.

'He was always calm, helpful, quiet. The only complaint I got during his entire stay here was from a guest teacher, a Kshatriya who was spending a season here to learn defence strategy and to teach hand-to-hand combat. It seems he had pushed a child too far, hurting his back in the process. Purochan almost smothered him in the wrestling pit.'

We looked up without speaking.

'He was obedient, punctual, hard-working, skilled, a natural warrior. But there was something going on in his mind all the time. He pushed himself further than all other children in military training. Hand combat, knives, spears, gada...' Kedar trailed off into silence. 'Purochan was my best student. His rigorous tapasya bore fruit. In less than three years here, he grew the body that you now see honed, almost to perfection.'

Kedar paused.

'A few days after he graduated as the undeclared best student of this ashram, the keeper of the boys' dormitory, where sons of the state lived, disappeared. We couldn't find him for four days. When we did, and I was there with the search party that discovered him; he was hanging upside down from one leg, on a branch of a mango tree, on the outskirts of Varanavat. His eyes were open wide. They carried a terror I've never seen. His legs, arms, ribs, back had been broken. Slowly. One bone at a time. His groin was battered beyond recognition. He was tortured to a ghastly death.'

Our silent questions laid siege around Kedar. He looked up.

'Years ago, when Purochan was at the state dormitories, Varanavat wasn't as well-developed. There were no checks and balances then. Impressed by the idea that it was the job of the state to take care of orphans, King Goran had borrowed it from Hastinapur in good faith.

But, as you know, a lot lies between an idea and its execution.' Kedar looked out of the window, welcoming the darkness of Ratridevi.

'There, as a child, he was abused by the keeper of dormitories,' he sighed. 'Repeatedly. Over years. And do you know what was the worst part?'

Urvashi and I were all attention.

'These children didn't know that it was not acceptable. It took Purochan a long time to realize that he, and some other children in the care of officials, were being abused. That it was wrong. That it was criminal. That it carried the death penalty. For many years, even after the first flush of facial hair, he didn't know. To him, this was part of growing up. Like eating, playing, breathing,' Kedar exhaled, his eyes pained. 'It was life.'

A cool breeze passed through the room. But Urvashi's face was beginning to melt. I was perspiring with a mixed feeling, angry at the treachery, sad for child Purochan.

'Gurudev...' Daya's voice floated into the hushed atmosphere. 'Pandavs are almost here. What would you like me to do?'

'Tell Kamalendr to receive them. Urvashi and Badri,' he looked at us, 'will join him. Get some lime water and tell the cooks to keep the food ready. And most importantly,' Kedar's tone changed, 'no celebration, they're just another group of citizens here, not kings. No special treatment. Keep your enthusiasm under control.' Daya's chuckle was audible in the silence as he ran back.

'Is that what happened to King Goran too?' I asked.

'Not exactly, you can't go around killing kings. But Purochan didn't forgive Goran. He worked his way to Shakuni and Duryodhan, got their blessings, and then on a hunting expedition, the king reportedly fell over a rock, landed on his head, cracked his neck and died. Purochan was on that expedition.'

Urvashi's was looking down at the floor, her hair, now open, making invisible forms on the hard clay. I found it difficult to breathe...a child abused.

I suddenly figured out what had transpired. The dark force of cruelty had entered Purochan's very being. It was not a reaction, not surface anger, not even rage. It was now part of who he was.

'What about the children?' Urvashi's voice was soft.

'Ah yes, the children.' Compassion swept over his face. 'Today, the only citizens safe in Varanavat are the children. They love Purochan. And he loves them. Each and every child is precious. Today, Purochan oversees the dormitories himself—the food, the care, the education, the games, the learning. And god save the man or woman who hurts a child in Varanavat. Even parents are scared of him.'

'A devil incarnate for all,' I said, 'but a godfather for children.'

'And by default, he is raising a new generation who will become women and men, and carry a loyalty to Purochan that kings would envy. Vishnu, Prakash, Maithili...they are only three out of hundreds out there. They will happily embrace a dozen deaths before allowing a scratch on Purochan.'

'What about Durjan?'

'Oh, he's just a mercenary. But dangerous nonetheless. He is one of the finest warriors with the sword and knives. I investigated him after you told me about the incident at Rasilee's.'

In the distance, ashramites were lighting the night diyas for the performance. We could hear the excitement of expectation in the children's squeals as they passed the meeting room.

'He'll get my sweetmeats this time, watch,' a boy was telling a group. I looked at Urvashi about the same time as she did. It sounded like our sons.

'I'm going to play with his sword,' a girl, her voice trembling with anticipation. We smiled.

'Not tonight, children, tonight is a little formal. The Pandavs are coming,' an inmate's voice. 'Tonight, you have to control and sing the night raag.'

'But why not...' the children's voices trailed off as the group walked on, taking the squeals of delight with it.

In the silence that followed, we found ourselves fighting the human side of this evil giant called Purochan.

'He still has to die,' Kedar shook the past from his eyes. 'Now, go and receive the Pandavs. I'll prepare the children.'

At the door, Kedar put his hand on my shoulder. 'And you will get your few moments with Yudhishthir.'

*Night*

The notes of Kedar's composition, employing all seven notes, merged into the sounds of the tributary behind. Eight children sang the pure notes of the post-sunset to early-night raag, moving their way up to the next scale in a rising circular motion and returning on a different structure. This was sam gana, a mix of the local mountains music riding a complex structure built by the rishis.

It was almost like crossing a mountain, ascending from one side, descending from another. The tune was familiar to anyone used to folk music. It carried the peace of simplicity, often missing in complex raags. Yet it had the depth of maturity in the notes and their relationships that had been honed and perfected over millenniums by rishis.

At the background, a mix of voices, young and old, women, men and children together, filled the silences with a never-ending chant of Aum, taking the composition, a devotion to Varanavat's residing deity Pashupati, to a higher plane, transforming it into something sublime, creating an atmosphere of sounds that carried the sounds of eternity.

They told creation to lie still until the notes ended.

Behind the simplicity of the notes, the innocence of children's delight and divinity of the background Aum, we hid.

The children were seated on a raised platform next to an ancient banyan tree, with long beards hanging in the air, some of which had become supporting trunks that spread wide, going as far as the edges of the forest in the distance. As I tracked the sounds into the forests, I saw a few eyes looking back.

*I didn't know you enjoyed music so much, Veer.*

*This is not music.*

*I know, this is something beyond...*

*No, this is war. We are ready.*

*War! Not yet. Wait for my signal. No bloodshed now.*

All of us, Purochan and Pandavs included, were seated on the ground. The ashram offered no special privileges to anyone.

Kedar sat in the centre of the audience, his eyes simultaneously blissful and alert. Whatever the Brahmin-Kshatriya relationship might be, a future king needed care and even though Kedar's word was law in this ashram, he ensured the Pandavs were given the respect they deserved.

Yudhishthir sat to Kedar's right, a well-built young man, bunched up by the responsibility of taking care of his mother and four brothers that had thrust itself upon him. He sat with quiet dignity, wore a faint smile that widened as children raised the pitch of the raag. He looked more like a seeker of knowledge than a pursuer of territories, more an explorer of inner countries than a soldier expanding the imperial might, more Janak in his demeanour than Ram. Irrespective, Yudhishthir looked every bit the king Hastinapur deserved.

But for that stray thread of self-doubt every now and then that got him to scratch the back of his neck with his left hand, there was not a flicker of expression on his stoic face.

A girl launched into a solo pitch, holding the high note with the skill of a veteran. I had goosebumps, afraid that she might lose the note, resting only when the group, smiling with delight, joined in the chorus and released the tension.

Kunti sat on the other side of Kedar, Urvashi next to her. Intrinsically, a strong woman, Kunti had been beaten down by fate, bringing up five children in a hostile environment. Her eyes carried fear and apprehension as they furtively glanced beyond her eldest son and rested on Purochan beyond him. As Urvashi would whisper a few words into her ear every now and then, the knot on her brow would smoothen. I'm not quite sure whether she heard the raag.

Next to her sat Arjun. Although he had the grace of a dancer or an artist, his eyes, I noted were not on the children. While taking minute care of Kunti, they kept shifting towards Urvashi's arms. At some point he was talking to her silently, showing her the scars on his forearms. They smiled at one another, bonded with that unique intimacy between professionals. Both were archers. I regretted not learning archery from her. A dart of jealousy tore into my heart.

A head higher than the tallest person around barring Purochan, Bhim sat next, a symbol of extreme strength and out-of-place irritation. Restless, he was constantly fidgeting, the sound of his gnashing teeth, reaching us between the breaths the children took. Despite the calm atmosphere that was nursing all around into a sweet surrender before a higher consciousness that seemed to have descended in the ashram, Bhim was seething with rage—uncontrollable, on-the-edge, dangerous. The muscles of his arms rippled like Saraswati's waves over a rocky terrain, as he clenched and unclenched his fists. His eyes were red. I shuddered to think that this was the man who would work on the tunnels with me.

The twins, Nakul and Sahadev, calm as a still lake, sat next to Bhim, looking at him with eyes that held love, devotion and respect, altogether. Quiet, almost irrelevant to the rest of us, they brought a sense of calm foresight and inner healing to the family.

To the right of Yudhishthir sat Purochan, surrounded by children, two of them sitting on his shoulders, another three on his lap. Even as he sat, he was almost as tall as most women in the ashram and some men. Another child, stood in front of this mountain of a man with anticipation. He smiled, bent down, picked him up and nestled him in his left arm, offering a sweetmeat with his right. As the child gurgled with pleasure, Purochan looked at Kedar, and shushed the child with a face so filled with love that you would think he was their doting father.

I almost began to like this demon.

The sam gana had reached the climax, the children were singing to the higher pitches, still in tune, the constant Aum behind reaching beyond beats and melodies, words and meanings, time and space, to create an alternate reality, a universe where nothing but That existed.

Ashramites, some scattered around the platform, others leaning on various trees, were engrossed. It was almost like a group meditation. From the forest, a family of deer walked into the area, unharmed by and unafraid of Veer and his band in the distance. A female inmate offered some leaves to a baby deer, which ignored her, his entire being focused on the platform from where divinity itself was emanating and filling the forest beyond. A male deer walked proudly upto the platform, shook his antlers, turned to look at Kedar for a few moments, then trailed off majestically.

Sitting far to the side of the Pandavs, beyond Bhim and the twins among other inmates, I shook myself from getting carried away. Still looking at the children, Urvashi sent me a message with a glance, telling me the sam gana was on its last notes.

When it ended, there was a deep silence that resonated for many incalculable moments, almost as if eternity had come visiting.

There was no sense of time. Or space. Or life. Or being.

Eyes closed in unique stages of bliss, all sat quietly. Just six of us were alive to the dangers of physical life.

Kedar, the seer.

Kunti, the mother.

Yudhishthir, the light.

Purochan, the darkness.

Urvashi, the protector.

And me.

'Aum shanti,' the deep, resonating voice of Kedar filled the silence without breaching it. In unison, the rest of us joined him. 'Shanti, shanti, shanti.' From the corner of his eye, he looked at me.

It was time.

'How are you, Surangraj?' Yudhishthir never forgot courtesies.

It wasn't easy getting him alone. Urvashi was in charge of Kunti and Arjun. Kamalendr was to host Nakul and Sahadev. Gurudev would handle Purochan and Bhim. Even though Purochan was busy with the children I could sense his eyes tracking us. I was responsible for accompanying Yudhishthir around the ashram before dinner, to work up an appetite.

'I'm well, prince. But pardon me, we don't have the time for niceties.'

Yudhishthir remained expressionless. 'Then, let's get to work.'

A squeal of laughter rose from where Purochan was fooling around with children.

A dangerous pause was on its way and I smoothened that. 'Vidur has sent me,' I said in the Mlechchh language.

'Vidur?' his eyes lit up, with enthusiasm and relief. 'He is the only one in Hastinapur who is concerned about us. But for him, we would be long dead.' He paused, his mind adjusting to a new freedom that allowed him to speak to anyone without holding back. 'Speak freely, Surangraj.'

'The palace you will shift into tomorrow has been laced with lak, prince,' I tried to make it sound as truthful as possible. 'The idea is to burn all of you to death.'

'I know that,' he said calmly; a faint smile of the condemned began around his lips but didn't complete. 'That's why Bhim is so agitated. But we don't know what to do. If we show that we know, we will be killed on the spot. So, we're waiting to enter what Purochan calls "The Blessed Home".'

'Blessed, indeed,' I repeated with a hiss of disdain.

'Have you been there?'

'No prince.'

'The Blessed Home is built of inflammable materials. It's more than lak. You can smell the hemp ready to burn. You can sense the resin ready to explode. You can see the ends of straw, the bamboos sticking out,' his hand reached behind his neck again. 'That overpowering stench of ghee...Everywhere you look, a shade of red stares back...' he stopped mid-sentence and struggled to put himself together.

The two months in Varanavat had taken their toll on Yudhishthir. Even though he carried himself like a prince in public, his venting before me was a sad reflection of the tensions he had harboured at this young age. It also showed his faith in me, placing a new weight to my burden of responsibility. I felt a cry emerge from within. Our future king, perhaps even an emperor, to be reduced to this.

'Prince, I am here to ensure that you live through The Blessed Home.'

Yudhishthir looked up, his dignity back.

The gentle hissing of trees swaying to a gentle wind filled the silences. 'Purochan wants to burn you down. My task is to ensure he fails.'

'Protect us, Surangraj,' he said with a quiet simplicity. 'I don't know when Purochan will light up the palace, but of one thing I'm sure. It won't take more than a few ghatikas to burn us down.'

The delightful laughter of children broke through the night around the dark hut.

'If we die here, it would be Duryodhan's victory,' he said, adjusting his yellow angvastr.

'And the end of dharm, prince,' I said. 'You have a great mission ahead. We look up to you for providing the leadership Aryavart needs.'

'You are very kind, Surangraj,' his eyes became hard. 'What is your plan?'

'Vidur has asked me to build a tunnel for your escape.'

Three shadows grazed the earth near us and both of us fell silent. 'This is where we live,' Urvashi's voice floated into the gaps, as she showed Kunti and Arjun the ashram. 'That's the room for group concentration...' She glanced in our direction and turned away, her voice trailing.

We walked away, near the trees. In the distance, I sensed Purochan's eyes tailing us, even as he fooled around with the children.

'The twins are still young. But is there anything you want from Bhim, Arjun or me?'

'Yes, you will need to create an atmosphere, where a few ashramites can come and go at will,' I said. 'Not too many. It will be just gurudev, Urvashi and me...maybe a few others.'

'Of course, Surangraj,' Yudhishthir said. 'You can come to the palace anytime.'

'I need that to be made official,' I said. 'Nobody should stop us. I need to see the palace with you. When you move in tomorrow, there will be a puja. Urvashi will accompany gurudev. Get her to see all the rooms carefully.'

'And you?'

'I'd rather not be seen around so early.'

'Thank you for thinking so much for us,' I couldn't help notice that this young man before me belonged not to palaces but to ashrams.

'It's my duty, prince,' I paused. 'One more thing...'

Yudhishthir looked at me, his hand reaching out for his neck.

'At any cost, this plan must remain only between you, your brothers and your mother. It should not get out. Don't trust anyone.'

'I understand, Surangraj. In fact, we need to show that we trust Purochan, even as we survive,' he smiled, looking in the distance at Bhim, glaring at the earth before him, his fists clenched. 'But it is very difficult to control him,' he nodded towards the giant, sitting alone, trapped in his thoughts, aching to protect his family but frozen before the word of Yudhishthir.

'Where is the weaponry?' Arjun's voice floated, as they walked past us again.

'There,' it was Urvashi, 'but it's too dark. I'll show you tomorrow.'

'I can shoot in the dark,' Arjun said quietly. He was young, handsome, skilled. Was he trying to impress Urvashi? No, the thought was silly. But still...

'Yes, I've heard. But we still can't open the weapons chamber now,' Urvashi said, adding a hint of finality to her voice. 'And certainly not without gurudev's permission.'

They walked off, Arjun still trying to convince her. He was too much of a warrior to give up so easily.

'Prince, I know the palace fairly well,' I said to Yudhishthir. 'I used to play there as a child. But of the two storeys above I know nothing. They are new. I'll need to understand them. So, if you can, call the contractor. Say some finishing here, a bed there, or something is needed. His name is Varad.'

'You seem to have planned everything, Surangraj,' he smiled. 'Yes, I know Varad. He came to me to plan the area for public meetings; a decent man.'

'Yes, but also a spy,' I whispered. 'Do not fall for his innocent questioning.'

He looked at me blankly, as a king should. But I knew he was disturbed—the itch behind his neck had returned.

'Where is Yudhishthir?' it was Kunti's voice, edged with worry.

He looked at me. 'Mother is calling, we should go.'

I nodded.

'I'm here, mother,' he said, taking long strides towards Kunti's voice. 'What happened?'

'Ah, there he is,' said Kedar, standing next to Kunti. 'Come, come... food is waiting.' He turned to me, 'Badri, get Urvashi. Our guests must be hungry.'

We guided the royal family towards the dining hall on the other side of the tributary. Halfway, I realized Purochan was missing. Turning back, I noticed he was talking to a girl who pulled at his red angvastr. 'Weapons are not allowed in the ashram, child,' he said, bent on his knees and still looking down at her, 'but I promise to show you the sword tomorrow.'

My heart melted again. I didn't have so much patience even with my sons.

As he stood up to join us, Purochan turned his gaze towards Kunti fussing over the twins. They were walking together. Kunti had a hand on Sahadev's shoulder, caressing Nakul's hair with the other hand. Both were revelling in the love that still lingers when boys stand on the threshold of being men, laughing like children, unconcerned about the death hovering over their heads. The three walked in a world of their own, a world where love provided the nourishment, not food. Completely immersed in one another, a single unit.

I turned to see Purochan following behind, looking at them with deep attention, his eyes carrying the look of a man searching for a memory, long abandoned in the intricate maze called life, in a complex phenomenon called fate.

What can a mantra do? However strong, whatever its power, it is merely a collection of words if not recited properly. In the hands of a weakling, no weapon can fly. It is the same for mantras, the signature of evolved Brahmins, the medium of rishis. But tonight I was going to see how the path of knowledge can strengthen the arms of a warrior.

A chariot-wide bridge swayed over the tributary that cut the main ashram from its agricultural land. Small diyas lit the path with their flickering light from the banyan tree to the wooden bridge and then carried on all the way towards the dining hall. As we walked over it, the music of the tributary had a new ring, of water hitting stone. The constant sound was almost like a metallic flow.

Once on the other side, small diyas carefully protected from wind, very different from the large lamps of Hastinapur, guided us towards the circular structure that merged into the agrarian fields. The sound of cows mooing filled the air, as did the snorting horses next door.

'I've kept the dining hall as close to the farms as possible,' Kedar was explaining to Kunti and Yudhishthir.

'But there is enough space near the living areas,' said Yudhishthir. 'Why make the ashramites take this walk?'

'The idea is to speak to the wheat, the barley, the pulses, the cows, the goats...to see, to live the food chain. It is different in the outer world. But here, we try and be as close to nature as possible. We speak to our farm, our vegetables, our animals. We thank them for giving us nutrition. It is not enough to simply tend to them for consumption.

There has to be a stronger relationship of man with the ecosystem of food.'

All of us had paused around them, listening to gurudev. 'But don't let me stop you from your dinner,' he said jovially. 'Come, come.'

A series of ten flat metal drums awaited us at the entrance of the ashram's dining hall. It was large, almost like a Sabha of a small kingdom. Except that the grandeur of colours, seats, pillars and the paraphernalia of officialdom were missing. In their place was a mud boundary, about half a dhanush high, circumscribing the area. A mud and limestone roof protected it from sun and rain.

'Let me help you, queen,' Urvashi said. As Kunti bent and adjusted her hair, Urvashi filled a copper vessel with water from one of the drums and gently poured it into Kunti's hands. Kunti collected the water in her hands and splashed it on her face before rubbing her palms. The water flowed down through an open drain towards the tributary.

It was so easy for women to get along on such matters. Left to me, I would never have done this. As I waited for Yudhishthir to clean his hands, he turned to me and offered the water. 'Come Badri, you go first.' I paused for the briefest of moments, then cleaned my hands. I took the vessel from Yudhishthir and poured water for him, as he gracefully accepted it.

Purochan was standing next, pouring the water for Kedar. I looked back and saw Kunti help Urvashi, as the twins waited for their turn.

I had become too urbanized, corrupted by the worst elements of cities. Even though I prided myself on leading the simple life, there was within me this gigantic ego that needed to be fed every now and then.

The Pandavs still carried the ways of the wild. It was less than five years since they had come from the forests and the innocence of equality still ruled in them. I was once a part of this ashram but they seemed to belong here more. And now I was rejecting the basic courtesies, simply because I didn't want to bow before a prince in this ashram?

Time to embrace humility, I told my ego. When I looked up towards the forest, I saw the eyes hanging in the darkness.

*Bless you, Veer. But this is Kedar's ashram. Don't worry.*

*Doesn't hurt to be ready.*

*For what? What are you doing?*

*Familiarizing my army with friends and enemies.*

*What army?*

*You'll see.*

We entered the hall. Six separate open spaces lined the circumference. A stack of twelve wooden stools, each about three fingers-width high, stood at the entrance of each compartment. Ashramites could pick up one, take it to the chamber, sit on it cross-legged, keeping their food on the leaf-plates before them.

The six compartments circled a larger area at the centre that could seat about forty.

One of the smaller spaces was attached to the kitchen behind, where the rattle of large vessels and smaller utensils filled the air. From here, a few ashramites would carry the food in copper vessels and distribute it to the rest. We were to sit in one of the smaller chambers, the one opposite the kitchen.

This was no ordinary meal and we needed all the silence we could get.

The Pandavs sat on one side, Yudhishthir and Kunti at the centre, the twins Sahadev and Nakul next to her. Bhim filled the space between Yudhishthir and Arjun.

On the other side, Kedar sat opposite Yudhishthir. Purochan, sitting next to gurudev, left little space beyond. Urvashi and I took the spaces next to Kedar.

'Welcome to my ashram, Prince Yudhishthir,' Kedar said. 'And on behalf of Varanavat, I welcome all of you to this beautiful town. May the next few months,' he leaned towards Purochan meaningfully with a graceful smile, 'give you the rest you deserve, rejuvenate you and help you understand the hill people.'

Purochan nodded, the smile on his face partly in tune with Kedar's welcome and partly looking into a future where Pandavs existed only in history.

Purochan's silence was perplexing. I had expected him to be overbearing. Maybe it was gurudev. maybe it was the children. Or maybe I was wrong about him.

'Thank you, gurudev,' Yudhishthir replied. 'The gods are kind to us that we have you as our neighbour. I have heard great things about you from Bhishm. It is a privilege to be with you in your peaceful ashram. It is soothing to the soul.'

'I hope my best student,' Kedar jabbed at Purochan, the only man who could do so and get away with it alive, 'has shown you our growing town.' I sensed a strong force of disgust from Yudhishthir's side as his hand returned to scratch that periodic itch behind his neck.

But the source of that disgust was Bhim, sitting beyond him.

'Do meet the citizens here, they are different from the people in the plains of Hastinapur,' Kedar continued. 'Simpler, but warmer.'

'Yes, gurudev,' Yudhishthir said slowly, 'Purochan has been an excellent host.'

I was watching Bhim and admiring the superhuman control he was exercising in these small confines. Left to himself, Bhim would have died fighting Purochan. Perhaps the children's sam gana had calmed him down.

Three ashramites stood at the entrance of the chamber, with vessels, ready to serve food. Kedar looked up. 'You must be famished. Let me not keep you away from food,' he paused, 'One last crossing,' and he closed his eyes, changing the mood of the area.

'If I might interrupt, gurudev,' it was Yudhishthir.

Kedar looked up, a gentle smile on his face. 'Yes, prince?'

'May I join you?'

'Do you know the verses?'

'I know some,' Yudhishthir paused. 'Which one are you planning to recite?'

'Praise of Food.'

Yudhishthir smiled with enthusiasm. 'Yes, I know these verses. If you permit, may I join you?'

'It's hard to get future kings to even hear them,' he turned to all of us, his eyes twinkling with enthusiasm. 'And here we have a prince ready to recite. If there is anyone else who knows the verses, join us.'

A few moments later, when he began the recital of this hymn from the Rig Ved, I heard Yudhishthir join him in correct pronunciation, right intonation, in perfect unison.

*Now will I glorify Food that upholds great strength,*
*By whose invigorating power Trita rent Vrtra limb from limb.*
*O pleasant Food, thee have we chosen for our own,*
*So be our kind protector thou.*

Yudhishthir's voice matched Kedar's, syllable for sacred syllable. The Pandavs seemed unconcerned. Perhaps they were used to this sort of thing. But when I glanced to my right, Urvashi and Purochan were wide-eyed. These were two voices from two worlds. One was a future king, the other a rishi of the future. The were chanting one mantra that carried the unity of life, non-life and everything beyond.

*Come hitherward to us, O Food, auspicious with auspicious help,*
*Health-bringing, not unkind, a dear and guileless friend.*
*These juices which, O Food, are thine throughout the regions are diffused.*
*Like winds they have their place in heaven.*
*These gifts of thine, O Food, O Food most sweet to taste,*
*These savours of thy juices work like creatures that have mighty necks.*

The symbolic significance of this ancient chant was known to less than a thousand people in Aryavart. But the realization of what could be construed as illogical pining of a tribal society obsessed with the material was lived by perhaps less than a dozen rishis. The chanting showed me that Yudhishthir was one such. He was a Brahmin in Kshatriya's skin.

*In thee, O Food, is set the spirit of great gods.*
*Under thy flag brave deeds were done he slew the Asur with thy help.*
*If thou be gone unto the splendour of the clouds,*
*Even from thence, O Food, prepared for our enjoyment, come.*

The smell of the food suddenly was more alluring. The hunger turned more intense. The mantra had done its magic. A few more verses and the cosmic vacuum created within us would be filled with matter.

*Whatever morsel we consume from waters or from plants of earth, O Som, wax thou fat thereby.*
*What som, we enjoy from thee in milky food or barley-brew, Vatapi, grow thou fat thereby.*
*O Vegetable, cake of meal, be wholesome, firm, and strengthening: Vatapi, grow thou fat thereby.*
*O Food, from thee as such have we drawn forth with lauds, like cows, our sacrificial gifts,*
*From thee who banquetest with Gods, from thee who banquetest with us.*

By the time the hymn ended, it changed our attitudes to nourishment: food for the body was divinized into food for the soul. Now, our bodies would do the eating but it would be the hunger of the gods that this purified food would fill.

*Aum shanti, shanti, shanti.*

In the absolute silence that followed, Yudhishthir was glowing. The mantra had transformed him. A strong radiance, physically visible, surrounded him like a thick sheath of an outer skin. His eyes were bright, looking straight into Kedar's with the confidence of knowledge, a soul equality. A new force flowed through his arms. An element of destiny stood above his head.

Even Purochan, who so far had given him a reluctant false respect as he was expected to, couldn't keep his eyes off Yudhishthir's changed aura. He craned his neck to get a better look. Shadows of the diyas created dark patterns on his face, morphing it into structures of curiosity. There was confusion in his eyes.

And a strange whiff of regret.

In the near future, Yudhishthir would be able to not merely create but keep this energy flowing constantly within him. With Bhim and Arjun beside him, in Yudhishthir, I finally saw the king Hastinapur had been waiting for. He was the king, who had been missing for three generations, from Shantanu to Vichitravir to Pandu and Dhritarashtr.

A conviction forced itself into my heart. Yudhishthir was a king, who must be protected. My task had suddenly expanded, the realization of the stakes had hit home.

No sacrifice would be too big for Yudhishthir, for Hastinapur, for Aryavart.

So far, Yudhishthir had been a king I would die for. Now, I was ready to kill for him.

'But what brings you all the way to Varanavat?' gurudev asked, putting a morsel of chapatti dipped in pulses into his mouth. 'There are,' he munched the food to the side of his mouth, 'better places for princes to spend a vacation,' he paused, suddenly serious. 'Not that you are not welcome here.' Everybody laughed.

'As you know, gurudev,' Yudhishthir said with a smile which did not reach his eyes, 'as yuvraj, my life is decided by everyone else but me; even my holidays.' The joke was forced, but we smiled politely. 'I serve Hastinapur and whatever my elders say, I do. But having been here for a few months now, I can't thank the king enough for sending us here.'

'Yes,' a loud, guttural voice painted with frustration said, 'the king takes very good care of us. Some day, we might die of so much love.' You couldn't accuse Bhim of being diplomatic and the irony was not lost. Arjun glared at him.

'May that day never come, Bhim,' it was Purochan. 'Don't speak of death, when we are celebrating life,' he held up a small bowl filled with pulses and drank it in one go. 'At Varanavat, life is a constant celebration,' he looked meaningfully at Kedar, as Bhim's face darkened.

'Yes, that's true. Our festivities are never-ending, our people are always happy, and our governor,' he looked up at Purochan, 'takes care of every need.' He turned to Yudhishthir and then to all the Pandavs, 'You must explore this place. There is a lot to see beyond palaces and ashrams.'

'We have been to the ghats and the foothills,' Kunti said. Then, she leaned over and looked at Bhim with love, 'If Bhim allows, I would like to climb the hill beyond the Ganga, the one with the large trishul on top.'

'Why Bhim,' gurudev joined the moment, 'do I hear a complaint? If so, I appoint Urvashi right now to ensure Kunti's wishes are fulfilled,' he laughed. 'Urvashi, would you?'

Bhim's ears turned red. With embarrassment or anger I couldn't figure out. I could see the effort he was putting in not to speak. He took a full chapati, collected potatoes into it and stuffed it whole into his mouth, gnashing it to pulp.

'Yes, gurudev,' Urvashi said turning to Kunti, 'let me know when you'd like to go. I'll take you.'

'We are grateful to you, gurudev and to you, Urvashiji,' Sahadev said with a calmness that exceeded his years, 'but that's not what mother meant.' He smiled, 'What she meant was that Bhim needs to enjoy this place too. He's too busy missing our loving cousins, particularly Duryodhan and Dushasan.' A private joke between them, the Pandavs laughed.

Bhim eased up as well, and the first hint of a child-like smile on his chubby face in the evening lit up the area.

Purochan's eyes shifted from Sahadev and Kunti to Bhim. He looked without blinking them. 'It's nice to see such love between cousins.'

Bhim looked up. I felt a menace climb his back and move into his mouth. The tension was sharp and I wondered what he would say. But before he could say anything, Arjun joined in. 'Yes, Purochan. Do you know Duryodhan fed Bhim ladoos with his own hands at the Water Sports House?'

'That's so touching,' Purochan said. 'You are blessed, Bhim,' he said, the words warm, the tone cold.

Bhim was caught between the urge to laugh at Arjun's sarcasm and the welling of a shout at Purochan's celebration of it. He looked at Purochan, felt an invisible tug from Sahadev, gave way to it and silenced himself by stuffing another chappati into his mouth.

The twins had that magical quality to calm, to heal. It was an action beyond arms, a vision beyond now.

'So, what are your plans for the Pashupati festival, Purochan?' gurudev asked.

'Now that the Pandavs are here,' he paused and looked at Yudhishthir, 'and with their permission, I plan to use the occasion to invite every citizen in and around Varanavat to participate.'

'Of course, Purochan,' Yudhishthir replied spontaneously. 'No better time to meet the people.'

'We want to build a statue of Pashupati, the tallest our people have ever seen,' he suddenly turned to Yudhishthir, as if remembering something. 'Prince, I was wondering if we could build it in front of the The Blessed Home.'

Bhim's brow knotted again and I saw his jaw muscles ripple. Arjun stopped midway while drinking water. Kunti's face fell.

But Yudhishthir stood steady, like a rock.

'I have no objection at all,' Yudhishthir paused to look at Kedar. 'But isn't it close to the ashram? I don't want celebration to be a cause for any trouble for you, gurudev.'

'Trouble? That's the problem with kings. They think ashrams are meant for the depressed,' Kedar laughed. 'We will join the celebrations. But just one thing, Purochan...'

Purochan looked at him, a little tense.

'Where will the outsiders stay? They will need camps.'

'I'll put them up at the foothills of the mountains that divide old and new Varanavat.'

'Yes, perfect.'

I glanced at Urvashi. She felt the look but didn't turn her head.

'But wouldn't placing the statue near the palace be risky?' I let loose the animal nobody was willing to go near.

'There would be enough space between The Blessed Home and the effigy.' I noticed how Purochan was using a subtle change in vocabulary from 'palace' to 'The Blessed Home', reducing the sharpness of the threat. 'It will lean outward, away from the palace.'

'Still, I'm not too sure whether this is a good idea. Where have you been placing the statue so far?'

'In New Varanavat,' he paused. 'But the prince wanted to meet the people in a non-formal setting,' he looked at Yudhishthir. 'So, our council felt we might take the festival to the Pandavs rather than having them come to the festival.'

The lie wasn't lost on us. But this was not the time to call a bluff.

I looked at Urvashi and we spoke through the silence.

*This doesn't look good to me, Urvashi.*

*Don't worry, we'll be able to get our people in the crowd.*

*But the Pashupati statue near the palace is risky. I'm sure he will fill it up with lak. It will burn and fall on the palace.*

*True, Badri. But that risk gives us cover as well.*

*How? There will be Purochan's men everywhere, monitoring everything.*

*As a result there will be a lot of noise outside the palace. It will help you dig better.*

*There is the danger that we could be discovered. I think this whole scheme is to ensure that the Pandavs stay within a specified perimeter, under close watch. Maybe, to ensure nobody else gets hurt.*

*Yes, that's possible.*

*They will also know each and every person who comes in and out of the palace. I'm not getting a good feeling about this.*

*Look, if there is trouble, you could get the Pandavs to go to the camps. It could provide cover for future escape, in case the tunnels don't work out.*

*Beautiful.*

*What?*

*You look very beautiful when you plan for war.*

Urvashi threw an angry glance towards me.

'So, tomorrow we have the grih pravesh for The Blessed Home,' Kedar said. 'We could begin in the second prahar. Would that be fine with you, Kunti?'

'Yes, gurudev. In this domain, we leave everything to you.'

'Yudhishthir?'

'If you must have an answer, the only semi-qualified person among us is Sahadev.' He turned to his youngest brother. 'Is this fine?'

Suddenly, Sahadev was alert, his back straight, his eyes looking up, somewhere distant. All were silent. For the first time in this evening, I saw Bhim carry a light smile that came straight from his heart. Kunti looked on proudly. Arjun's face was intense but his eyes were smiling at Purochan's surprise—a young lad, barely out of his teens, had been given this task by Yudhishthir and Kedar. A few moments later, Sahadev returned to the terrestrial plane.

'We can do the main yagn in the second prahar,' he said, his eyes a little dreamy, 'but the initiation should be done in the first prahar, gurudev.'

'And why do you say that Sahadev?' Kedar was curious.

'The southward movement of the sun has begun.'

Kedar smiled like a teacher proud of his student's first learning. 'Your knowledge of the stars is worthy of emulation, Sahadev. While you are here, why don't you take some classes in astrology for our students?'

'It would be a privilege, gurudev,' Sahadev's innocence was back. 'But my assessments are based on intuition; I'm not sure whether I have the rigour to strengthen an argument or logic to teach.'

'You can. I will help you crystalize your intuition and convert it into theory.'

Nakul nudged his twin with his shoulder, smiling. Sahadev looked at Kunti's eyes, filled with tears of pride. Bhim reached out and patted his shoulder, almost throwing the poor boy on the food before him.

'Gently, Bhim, gently,' Yudhishthir smiled.

Laughter filled the hall.

'All right then,' Kedar concluded the dinner. 'If all is decided, we must rest. Tomorrow is going to be an early day.' He turned to Urvashi and me. 'Would the two of you see the Pandavs to the ashram gate?'

We arose and started walking towards the drums to wash our hands. Halfway there, Yudhishthir turned towards the kitchen. 'Badri, a moment?'

Ashramites in the kitchen were surprised. 'Please accept our thanks for a wonderful meal,' he said, his hands folded. 'Tomorrow, as we move in as your neighbours, do come and bless our home.'

A surprised group accepted his gratitude but stayed silent, not sure how to deal with a future king. As we walked out, Yudhishthir whispered to me, 'Your work begins now. The danger has multiplied. I'm worried about mother and the twins. Would it be fine if Urvashi stayed with us?'

'Yes, prince,' I said gently, walking slowly towards the drums, where Kedar was pouring water for Purochan. 'But I'm not the right person. You need to seek gurudev's permission.'

'I know, but before I did that I wanted to ensure you are comfortable with it.'

'I am, prince.'

'Tomorrow then.'

'Yes, prince.'

The diyas were living the last few drops, the flames were dying. But for Urvashi's army, the ashram was asleep. We stopped at Kedar's chamber. Yudhishthir, still resplendent with the mantra, bent down and touched his feet. Kunti and the four brothers followed. Gurudev blessed each of them.

Urvashi walked with Kunti, the five brothers next to her. A few steps ahead, Purochan alerted the chariots. I followed at the end. In the distance, near the ashram gate, we saw torches lighting up the area.

Voices muffled into silence as we reached the ashram gate. Their chariots and horses ready, Vishnu and Durjan were waiting outside. They seemed as alert as the owls hooting from the distance, there was no sleep in their eyes.

In silence we moved, each of us carrying our demons within us.

Yudhishthir and Kunti fought the uncertainty of survival.

Bhim and Arjun engaged with destruction.

The twins wrestled to keep the balance.

Purochan raced towards his kill.

Urvashi prepared to get her small army for defence.

Yudhishthir folded his hands and thanked us again. Then, he climbed the large chariot with Kunti and the twins. Bhim and Arjun mounted the other chariot.

Behind them, Purochan climbed into the third. 'Shall we go, prince?' his voice boomed in the silence. In the distance, a jackal howled.

Yudhishthir nodded.

Led by horse guards, the cavalcade moved towards New Varanavat. In the fading light, I saw Yudhishthir turn his head towards the ashram, as if he were leaving his home. He continued to look for as long as I could see.

Behind me, Urvashi called her army down from the trees and merged with them, planning for tomorrow. One day at a time.

In the stealth-like darkness, full of expectation and danger, I pulled myself together for the battle ahead.

# Palace

*Three days later*

'The pack came again last night,' a thin voice cut through the din of Rasilee's shack.

The words jolted me out of my reverie. It took me considerable power to not turn around. Varad, sitting in front of me, noticed. We exchanged a glance. He was nursing his drink.

I continued to look at the som in my vessel, it was better this time. Rasilee must have spoken to Nasiv. The flavour was just right. But right now, it was the flavour of the conversation that interested me.

'I heard it too,' a more mature voice said. 'The palace dogs were whining.'

'Much as I dislike being disturbed in my sleep,' the first voice paused to burp, 'I wasn't unhappy to hear them.'

'Good thing no citizen was hurt.'

'But have you noticed something? The street dogs have disappeared. Instead, we now have those forest dogs strutting around, as if they own the place.'

'They haven't disappeared,' the thin voice said. 'But towards sundown, they slink away near the palace drains.'

A pause of individual confabulations filled the room.

'Have you,' the voice was hesitant, 'seen the dog that leads them?'

'Dog?' a voice shot from across the room. 'You call that a dog? It's a crossbreed between a wolf and panther, with danger lurking around him that he's inherited from both sides!'

'He was walking in the middle of the main crossing, when a mother began to shout and scream. Her child was playing there.'

'I didn't hear about that one.'

'Yes, but you know something strange happened.'

'What?'

'The dog walked up to the child, gazed at it, wagged his tail, turned to the mother and walked on.'

'He didn't harm the child?'

'No. Not a growl.'

'But the soldiers weren't so lucky...'

'Yes,' the voice dropped, 'you're talking about those three soldiers, right?'

I continued to look into my vessel. Information in any form was always welcome. But there was no need to show excessive interest. I realized sooner or later, it had a way of coming to me. The trick was to not seek it actively. Mostly men find the burden of silence too heavy to cart and are usually aching to end it.

Like now.

'Yes,' a whisper. 'Very gruesome deaths.'

'Unbelievable. I've never heard of such things.'

'Tau, weren't you around when the bodies were being taken away?' a third voice joined them.

A long pause.

'What happened? Tell us.'

'Rather not,' a cracked voice, an old man.

'Oh come on, don't be afraid,' the voice turned a shade jovial. 'Rasilee, get him a refil.'

Tentative laughter followed. Then it subsided.

'Vishnu was shouting,' the cracked voice said.

'Why?'

'You remember Danu?'

'That guy who follows Vishnu like a shadow?'

'Followed,' he corrected. 'He's dead,' the older man paused to gulp down a sip. 'Half his neck had been bitten off.'

Silence hung in the air. The din ended. Everyone in the room was listening to this conversation.

'What about the other two?'

'A trail of blood led the soldiers to the second body. He had been dragged halfway to the foothills. Mutilated beyond recognition.'

'Mutilated?'

'Yes, almost as if it was a personal fight. His sword arm lay near the first attack, the sword still in it. A large chunk of his thigh had been bitten off and lay half a dhanush away. He had ugly bite marks on his shoulder, his back, his chest. It seems as if the jugular was cut only towards the end.'

'Didn't they...eat him?'

For long moments, the only sound we heard was the mooing of cows in the distance.

'No,' the cracked voice continued. 'And that's the mystery. If these dogs are not attacking humans for food, then...what for?'

'Also,' a younger voice chirped in, 'why only target the soldiers?'

'Could be,' another voice, 'a war...'

'What nonsense is this?' a high-pitched voice rolled over, but sounded unconvinced. 'How can dogs fight a...' the voice lost its energy, '...a war?'

For some moments the only sound was of men swallowing the som.

'What happened to the third?'

'I think he died of shock,' haiving drunk the som, the cracked voice was more confident now. 'There was no mark on his body. But his eyes were wide open. Terror-struck.'

'Maybe he saw what happened to the other two.'

'Maybe. One of the guards watching from the tower said he didn't even try to run or protect himself. He just stood there frozen and then fell dead. In all his years as a guard, he said, he had never seen or heard of such fear.'

'Didn't any of the other guards try and save them?'

'I asked him that. He said, the dogs kept the men before them. It was almost as if they were trained.'

'Trained?'

'That's what the guard said.'

'I'm sure they must have tried,' the older man continued. 'The shrieks of the dying men were frightening. But it was the growls and howls of the dogs…or were they wolves…that froze everyone. The whole thing seemed to be organized by that black leader. Others just stood around and prevented them from running away. They also growled the other guards into numbness.'

Branches rustled in the wind outside.

'I don't like what Purochan and his soldiers are doing in Varanavat, but such a death is ghastly even for the worst criminals.'

'It's divine justice, brother. Looks like Pashupati is finally smiling at us again.'

'I'm not so sure about the gods. The question is: who are these dogs?'

'That's something Vishnu has been looking for. It seems they're planning to hunt them down.'

'Brave.' The sarcasm was loud, the laughter following it hesitant.

'Or just foolish.'

'Careful brother,' a soft voice said, 'someone might hear you.'

'I think they're too busy saving their hides right now.'

Laughter.

The tide in Varanavat was changing. The first signs of fear receding were before me. More should follow.

Varad's face was a shadow, his gaze trapped in the distance. He seemed to have been affected by the conversation.

'Relax,' I whispered. 'You are a friend, they won't attack you.'

Varad gathered himself, smiled weakly, finished the drink in one long swig. 'Rasilee,' he said, 'one more.'

I sent a signal of delight to Veer.

## Two days later

'The question is: how would architects and miners think 400 years ago? How would they build?'

'We'll have to get there, Surangraj,' Sahadev said. 'Otherwise, it will be just guesswork.'

We were standing on a flat clearing on the mountain on the other side of my cave. One of Sahadev's attendants accompanied us, but kept his distance.

As did four of Purochan's guards.

'Or a mental construct. I know.'

I had identified Sahadev as one who had the gift of being able to see the future. That meant the past too. It was more to do with a wider sense of wisdom, sensitivity and perception, the currency of inner worlds than any tangible acts of building, fighting, ruling in the outer world. For the latter, I needed Bhim. For this, it was Sahadev.

'What you want to do is to go back in time, right?'

'Yes, prince.'

'And you think I can.'

'Yes,' I said, my eyes covered by three layers of the veil, on the soldiers moving. Nothing to worry but I needed to see them all the time. 'But I'm a miner, not a seer.'

'I can try, but I'm not sure if I'll be able to,' his voice was soft like the grass under our feet, in the shadow of a rudraksh tree. 'You see, these other worldly things happen to me, I don't pursue them.'

'Whatever works is good for me, prince,' I said, watching an eagle soar into the clear sky, close to the next mountain. 'Once I know what to do, the task is half done. Building a tunnel is not very different from going to war. Both need preparation. The physical act of digging or cleaning or discovering can happen only if we can figure out what my ancient colleague did with the palace.'

'Let's try logic,' Sahadev came straight to the point. 'For starters, I suppose mining technologies were not as advanced as they are today. Does that mean anything?'

'Yes, even a hundred years ago, there were no ventilators.'

'And what would that mean?'

I was enjoying Sahadev's questions. Usually, I analysed my job alone. But this time, I was racing against time. 'No ventilators meant, that the escape routes would be short, like in the palaces of some smaller tribal kings.'

'How short is short?' Sahadev's eyes began to look upwards. I wasn't sure if he was trailing the eagle or shifting into another realm.

'I'm not sure. But depending upon the need for fires to light up and how many torches you need, I would say if the tunnel is not naturally ventilated, it should be between twenty to fifty strides of a charging horse.' I paused to think. 'A good horse', I clarified.

Sahadev was silent. A handsome boy. Even though he resembled Arjun in looks, Sahadev leaned more towards Yudhishthir in his character. He was great at cattle management—the animals loved him and he took good care of them. From the west, we were hearing tales of Krishn, a cowherd-turned-strategist, now driving the destiny of Mathura. Sahadev seemed something like that but without the body of a Kshatriya.

He turned to me and opened his eyes. 'But exits are limited by geography. The advantage we can get if we escape to a distance is not the same as fifty strides of a charging horse.'

'I agree, prince, but this is what we have. Geography as well as time, both are not in our favour at Varanavat. And yet, escape we must.'

'Do you have any options?'

I nodded. From my cave further up, I had seen four possibilities. The moment I thought about it, I wanted to be there. My cave of tapasya, a place where I could think and often reach the deeper parts of myself, gave me a sense of spiritual safety.

'The shortest route would be the one that goes southwards towards the Ganga, in less than fifteen strides of a charging horse. This is sort of a private ghat for the king's family around where the river turns and is wide enough for five large boats to provide cover.'

'Yes, we swim there regularly. I've also seen the boats. The danger is that Purochan's men could be sitting in them.

'Right. And that's why the shortest tunnel is not necessarily the safest. Apart from Purochan, we have another enemy. This palace is 400 years old. There is the issue of seepage. We don't know if the tunnels were reinforced or how. Four hundred years is enough for rivers to change their minds. And if it has come closer underground, it could do what Purochan's soldiers can't—drown us. Risky.'

'Very risky,' he said thoughtfully. 'So, that's out.'

'The next two exits would probably be across. To the west is Kedar's ashram.'

He looked at me blankly. 'That should be safe but how long can we stay there?'

'Right, at some point you will have to leave and you never know how information travels and to whom.'

'And in the process, we could even put the ashram in danger. Not right. As Kshatriyas, it is our job to protect, not seek protection, even if we are outnumbered. We can stay there at best for a night or two, no more. We will have to leave. And once we do that, we could be caught.'

The attendant brought us drinks. We took the silver vessels. Sahadev nodded him away.

I took a sip, long enough for the attendant to be out of hearing. The lime water was sweet, cool, refreshing.

'The third exit could possibly be to the east, where these mountains,' I ran my hand in the air to show the range before us to him, 'divide the old Varanavat from the new. These would be about three or four times the distance but would be relatively safer as far as the water-dust balance goes. The problem here is this,' I pointed down towards the empty settlements.

'That's a trap.'

I nodded.

'Finally, we could go northwards, towards the lower Himavat, there,' I pointed to the snow-capped range in the distance. 'This would be a very long tunnel, about double the length of the ashram route.'

'Ventilation would be the problem here, right?'

'Yes, ventilation and the long walk,' I paused. 'But once out, you could disappear into the forests there, catch the tributary behind the mountain and go further north.'

Sahadev turned to look at the range. 'Arjun and I went hunting there. The game is good, the forest is rich. I wonder why it is so empty.'

I signalled to an attendant. He came and picked up the vessels. 'Do you want some more?'

Behind me, I noticed the guards take two gentle steps towards us. They continued to look the other way and talk among themselves.

'No,' I said. 'Get me a large water pouch.' He ran back and handed me the pouch.

I walked into the thick tree cover and in the relative darkness, poured the water on my head. It was colder than I had imagined, colder and strangely comforting. I wet my veil and put it on again. This darkness is where I belonged, the light outside was no longer for me. I lingered on, watching Sahadev through the veil, my body ready to rush in case the guards decided to get closer.

I enjoyed the smell. It was earthly yet filled with the misty air of the mountains. Barely the beginning of the lofty Himavat, these mountains held a promise, almost calling to the higher peaks.

It was time to return. You can't disappear with a prince, however close you are or however important the work, for too long. Purochan's army would be desperate by now. Kunti would be worried. I shook my head, sprinkling water drops around, they shone like jewels...little specks of jade, reflecting the green in the sharp light outside the forest cover.

Suddenly, I sensed a presence, strong, intense and warm. I sensed him before I saw him. Looking up, in the darkness of the thick trees, four sets of eyes reflected the light outside. I smiled at Veer and felt safe.

*You've been busy.*

*So have you.*

*Except that I haven't done any killing. So far.*

*The two I killed were those who wanted me dead when I was young.*

*I thought so. How did you know who they were after so many years?*

*They still carried their peculiar smell.*

*You still remember?*

*Smells are a tool that humankind has given up in favour of eyes.*

*Why did you kill the third one?*

*He died of his own fears. We didn't touch him.*

*We? You mean these eyes next to you?*

*Yes, you'll meet them at the right time.*

*I'm missing you, Veer.*

The presence faded away. I suddenly felt lighter. Not giving into needless sentimentality, as abruptly as he came, Veer was gone.

## Four days later

'Who goes?' the growl was louder. 'Take that veil off.'

The evening was still young and I was approaching it from the south. The orange glow of the sun to my west was still hard on my eyes and the veil was tied twice around my face.

The distance between the palace and the ashram was small, within spearing distance. But you can't jump over fences into palaces of princes.

I had come from the ashram along the curved Ganga Patth. It was about a yojana before I reached the turn towards the palace gates, now made majestic for the Pandavs. I slowed Vayu and nudged him towards the gate, Kadak followed.

Ahead in the distance, the palace stood proudly, its decrepit history buried under Purochan's walls of death. One look told me that in its prime it must have merged with the forest, an architectural pride in the neighbourhood.

But pride has different meanings for different cultures. The newly-constructed two storeys above the ground floor showed how the needs of civilization had grown, as man sought more space for himself.

Or to ensure escape was impossible once it burned.

I had avoided the palace altogether. Kedar had taken care of the rituals and Urvashi had stayed on for security. No need to be everywhere. Besides, the further I stayed away from Vishnu and Purochan the better it was for Pandavs. In any case I was supposed to be recovering from my injuries.

Today was different. There are only a few things you can do alone.

'Who goes?' the booming voice belonged to a thickset man on the left gate, a chief sentry. I looked down. The face was familiar. The beard was thick and grey, the indigo dhoti tied like a soldier's, a sword dangling around his thigh, still in its sheath. But it were the eyes, always the eyes, black and piercing.

I halted Vayu, Kadak shook the flies off his head and snorted. 'A friend,' I said softly.

'I'm nobody's friend,' his eyes wore a puzzled look, trying to pull out a memory from the deep forest of discipline and habit. 'State your name and your work.'

'Do you still take yourself so seriously...' I paused to let a memory travel. '...Chiroo?'

In less than a moment, the eyes melted, their ferocity gone. 'Badri!'

I jumped off Vayu, stumbled on a loose stone and dove straight onto the floor. Before I could hit the earth Chiranjeev's strong arms caught me. 'Watch out, old man,' he said, picking me up bodily and holding me in his signature bearhug.

'Who,' I grunted as he squeezed hard, 'are you calling an old man?' And then, using a trick Kedar had taught us, I slipped out, tying another knot of the past between us. 'You have a reputation here, Chiranjeev,' I panted, 'so I won't embarrass you with a fall. But the next time you call me an old man, I'll forget it.'

We laughed loudly, embracing again. 'Such a long time, Badri,' his eyes were moist. 'How have you been?'

'I'm well, what have you been upto?' I looked at his sword. 'A weapon of aggression,' I said, nodding at it, 'hanging on Chiranjeev's body. Nobody will believe that.'

His eyes lost their humour. There was something there. He signalled his deputies away.

'Let's not go there, Badri,' he smiled feebly. 'What brings you here? And what's this veil? Don't behave like a newly-wed bride. Off with it.'

'The veil is because of my eyes...a rare disease. I'm a miner now and being underground has cost me my sight.'

'Never heard of such a disease,' Chiranjeev looked at me closely.

'Neither had I. Rare it is. But it's mine. And with this veil we live together.'

'So, you can't take it off?'

'Let the sun set, I will.'

He stared at me, curiosity bordering his restraint.

'So, what brings you to Varanavat?'

'My horse.'

He laughed. 'You will never change! I mean, why are you here?'

'To recover.'

'What happened?'

'One of my rogue tunnels fell on me. I almost died. I'm here to heal at gurudev's ashram.'

'Why,' he cleared his throat, 'are you going to the palace?'

'To meet Prince Yudhishthir and take this sack of apples for him. Gurudev has sent them. Do you need to check it?'

'It's my duty,' he said, a regret in his voice. He was gurudev's student too.

'All right,' I exhaled and smiled. 'Don't let me come in the way.' I turned around and shouted, 'Kadak!' The mule looked up from the new grass he was munching, hobbled over and offered his head. 'All yours, Chiroo,' I said, stroking Kadak's head.

Chiranjeev nodded to his deputy, who began rummaging through the sack of mangoes. Kadak lost no time in trying out the new grass.

I looked around. A large contingent guarded the palace. Soldiers on horses walked about. The young ones oiled the chariots and fed the horses. Swords gleamed in the sun, some reflecting its rays directly. Elephants were missing but that could be the nature of the place rather than a conscious decision. Under normal circumstances, this would befit a senior official. But in Old Varanavat, with the sole neighbour being Kedar's ashram, the number was overwhelming and jarring.

'These sacks are fine, Chiranjeev.' The young soldier, more a Vaishya than a Kshatriya, stood aside.

I looked at Chiranjeev. 'Can I go?' He had been observing me closely; too closely. Another good man, who had been dragged to the dark side? Or just another soul degenerating into the cycle of an aimless life, a life defined by processes, orders, fears.

'Yes,' the smile was back on his lips. It didn't reach his eyes this time. They were suddenly furtive.

From the foothills that divided the old Varanavat from the new on my right and all the way ahead in the north, where the forest merged into the higher mountains, the palace grounds seemed larger than what I had estimated from my cave high above. Then there were the disorganized settlements, now vacant. Which meant danger—under the protection of soldiers, hostiles could hide here.

They were not as well-manicured as the Hastinapur gardens but not wild either. Lined by mango and neem trees, a temporary two-chariot road, large by Varanavat proportions, meandered to the palace. From my cave, it looked like a snake. Now, as I rode Vayu towards the palace, it didn't seem as sinister. I noticed the trees as I passed them by. Lots of open spaces. So, there was little chance of hiding. A disadvantage for us if my tunnels failed and Pandavs had to use the land.

Halfway to the palace, the road bent around a thicket. Even on horseback, it came in the line of sight. The bend itself was sharp. I wasn't comfortable. I slowed Vayu down and examined it closely. The thorny shrubs had been carefully removed. There were only softer, leafy plants here. This was clearly, a place to hide. And sure enough, out of the thicket emerged two soldiers with spears.

'What do you want?'

'Nothing,' I looked at them, mean creatures both. 'I am just looking for a tree to go around.'

'Here?' the man raised his spear. 'Go away, before I dig this into you.'

I moved on, their laughter behind mingling with Vayu's and Kadak's strides.

The smell of horse dung hit me around the time I saw the palace, tapering above a raised mound. It was a quadrangular piece of man-made structure vying with the natural geography for attention. A reddish hue covered it from all sides, remnants of lak that hadn't been painted over properly. The oily walls gleamed in the sun's rays in a surreal mixture of gold and red.

The broad directions of the tunnel were ready. Sahadev and I had finalized them. Now, I needed to see where they opened in the palace. If my guess was right, it would be the armoury or the sleeping chambers of the king...five princes and their mother in this case.

Two spear-holding soldiers stood guarding the entrance to the palace walls.

'Who goes?'

'Badri,' I slowed Vayu. 'From Kedar's ashram.'

'Never seen you before.'

'Is seeing me important?' I was getting tired of this bureaucracy.

The stocky guard looked up, his spear casting a shadow on his face as it moved from right to left.

'Check the sack,' he said to his aide, still looking at me.

'Let him go,' a commanding voice said. It was familiar. I turned.

Vishnu.

The guard was all attention. He stepped back.

'Grateful,' I nodded at Vishnu.

'I'm in charge of The Blessed Home,' he said, that ugly sneer returning. 'If there is anything you need, speak to me.'

'Appreciate your offer, Vishnu. But right now all I want is to obey the royal summons. Yudhishthir, our prince, has called me.'

His glare dug into my heart. He was a very strong warrior. Our fight would not be easy.

'A friend of the royalty, huh?' he said, a taunt underlying his tone.

'No friend,' my voice recovered its rude rasping. 'Just a servitor. Like you.'

He gave me a knowing look. I had seen it before. And the words in that look had said pretty much the same thing in Hastinapur—I will kill you.

The slightly twisted smile on his face added an extra word—soon.

The strong stench of death overpowered my senses as I entered the palace. I isolated the different substances—hemp, resin, ghee, fat—all mixed together to hide the sharper smell of lak. The gleam of the sun shone on every wall. This was worse than I had imagined.

In the comforting shadows of the palace walls, I removed one layer of my veil and waited for my eyes to adjust. There was excessive use of wood. With a large number of trees around, it was the favoured material for homes, of course. Still, the area seemed as if it were a warehouse of wood...carefully collected dry wood.

'Badri!' the voice was unmistakable. Bhim sounded cheerful. Like he used to be in Hastinapur. I remembered the evening at the ashram, when he was gnashing his teeth, almost insane. This was a completely different young man. Maybe he didn't like giants.

'Yes, prince,' I jumped off the horse. Bhim signalled an attendant to take Vayu and Kadak to the stables. As they were being led, Kadak turned towards me, restraining the attendant.

'Wait,' I told the attendant, 'the sack has fruits from the ashram.'

'Only one?' Bhim mocked. As we laughed, he nodded at a man, who picked up the sack and carried it into the palace. 'Come,' he said, lowering his voice, 'and observe carefully this mansion that our dear cousin Duryodhan has got made for us. This, what does that hyena Purochan call it?' he scratched his head, 'yes... The Blessed Home,' he spat. 'Blessed indeed.'

Bhim led me through a dark passage that opened out to the right wall of the palace. Innocuous eyes looked at us from everywhere.

There, right before us, at the back of the palace, with the forest and the scattered, illegal and empty settlements as the backdrop, stood the scaffolding of a statue under construction. Tall, majestic and almost godly.

'Whose statue is this?' I asked.

'Pashupati,' Bhim replied.

Pashupati or Rudr or Shiv. Three of the hundred names for the versatile god—an ascetic, an archer, a consumer of poison, terrible, yet benevolent. All contradictions resided together in one deity.

Pashupati.

We walked up to his feet. 'Where is the head?' I asked a worker tying ropes.

'Still being built,' he grunted as two men at the top pulled the rope tight from above and he held them down, his muscled arms taut. He stood up, wiping his sweat with a gamcha around his shoulders, his body gleaming in sweat. The ropes I noticed held the statue straight from behind, three strands pulled tight—one at the centre, two on the sides, held by thick maces dug deep into the ground. 'They should be here in a few days, prince,' he said, addressing Bhim, his eyes wary.

'I guess you'll have to hurry then,' I said.

'Yes, almost forty Lakheras are working full time on the head.'

'And you? Are you not a Lakhera?'

'No sir. I'm from Varanavat,' he said, raising his head a little. Clearly, there was local pride here.

'So, what do you do?'

'I make sure the Lakheras do their job,' he said with hesitation. 'I'm the local contractor.'

'What is your name?'

His face wilted. A hint of hesitation, 'I'm Charak.'

'Charak, you are serving the future kings of Kuru,' my voice now had an edge. 'Be careful, very careful, in how you build this. There should be no error,' I paused before I unleashed the bigger weapon. 'I will remember you by name.'

'I...I will,' he stammered. It was important for him and all others in this conspiracy, however small their part, whatever else their proclivity, to know that their heinous work would not go unnoticed.

'Where are the other Lakheras?' I asked roughly.

'They are still in the palace...helping the Pandavs settle down.'

Bhim glanced at me, then smiled at the worker, as we walked on. 'Go on then, get on with your work,' he told the shuddering worker, 'you don't want us to miss the festival, do you?'

As Charak walked away, he took out a gamcha and wiped his forehead.

I turned back to see the workers. They were looking at us, their eyes carrying a strange expression of apprehension.

As we walked back towards the palace, I could see three tracks from the three effigies leading there. The tracks had been brushed well, but to a trained eye, they were clear.

'Charak,' I called him again. He turned with a start, dragging himself to us. 'What's this?' I pointed to the tracks.

'The Ganga.'

'Ganga?'

'Yes,' he paused to put himself together, 'as you know, from Pashupati's head falls the Ganga. We are building a fountain from this statue. The water will follow this track and then,' he walked hurriedly towards the palace and pointed to the edges, 'flow down here.'

'Good,' I said. 'Why towards the palace?'

'I...I don't know sir...I'm only executing the design given to me.'

'All right,' I said roughly. 'Get lost.'

We walked on towards the palace walls. 'You pushed him too hard, Badri,' Bhim gloated, happy that someone else was matching his roughness.

'Yes, I want him to know that he's being watched. He is a very small cog in the bigger wheel of this conspiracy. But each cog has a role. Each cog has to be responsible for the role he plays. And each cog has a family, children, property he doesn't want to lose.'

A tool box lay on the ground between two tracks that would carry the Ganga. I walked towards it, and deliberately tripped myself, falling hard on the ground, my fingers digging into the soil. I felt the solid texture of lak. When I got up, my fingers had a thin layer of oil.

Bhim tried to pick me up but I raised my other arm. 'I'm fine, prince,' I said as I watched two workers and six soldiers run up to us. 'Just getting old, let me catch my breath.'

Turning to the soldiers, I sent a harsh force that told them to stay where they were. They stopped in their tracks. No words were exchanged.

I continued to sit for a while, catching my breath, while my hand put the soil back as it was.

'Prince, where are your sleeping chambers?' I asked Bhim as I dusted the dirt off my dhoti.

'Right here, Badri,' he pointed to the back of the palace. In the distance, two soldiers looked at us.

'There are three tracks from the statue, leading to the palace, towards the sleeping chambers. The one I fell on is lined with lak underground. At some point, the Ganga water will turn into oil, someone will open the ground between the effigies and the track, and a fire will be lit. The fire will then rush to the palace.'

I saw Bhim's fists clench, his eyes getting that mad look. 'Control yourself, prince,' I said, 'we don't want them to know that we know.'

As we continued to walk to the palace, we passed a group of Lakheras giving finishing touches to the swinging beds hanging from neem trees.

'The heights are uneven on those two,' a familiar voice sounded. 'Fix it properly.' As I looked, Varad shot me a glance.

'I've changed it twice,' a worker protested.

'It's not enough. Change it again.'

'Varad, when are the swings going to be ready?' Bhim asked.

'Give us one more day, prince.'

'You're late,' I said. 'We need more speed.'

'We are going as fast as we can,' Varad said. 'But we are new to this area, the trees here are wetter than the one we are used to. By tomorrow they should be ready.'

'Let them be,' Bhim said, nudging me towards the wall. The soldiers at the corner were suddenly all attention. 'Overall they've done a good job. But there are more important matters here. Come.'

We walked towards the wall. 'I'm getting used to it,' Bhim said, 'but did you smell anything strange when you came?'

'Yes. A heady smell of oils.'

Bhim smiled, happy to be proved right. 'Since morning Arjun and I have been investigating this palace,' he paused to create a sense of drama, looked at me expectantly, a bubble of delight just waiting to come out.

'And?'

'It is built with inflammable materials like hemp and resin. Worse, it is laced with oils. Between the stones and the wood is lak,' he sounded relieved. Here was a completely different character from last night's. I must advise him to steer clear of Purochan. 'It's particularly obvious in the top two storeys.'

'That's because the base structure was already standing. They would have had to pull down the existing structure if they wanted to lace it from within. That would take time. That's why the smell is stronger up there, on new construction, where they are free to use whatever they want.'

Bhim scratched his head.

'And that's why,' I looked around for soldiers, lowering my voice, 'we need to build the tunnel.'

But Bhim wasn't finished yet. 'I told Yudhishthir to avoid staying here. Give any excuse. As a prince he has the right to not like it. Delay it. Whatever.'

'What did he say?'

'That in fact we should live here so that nobody knows that we know what's going on,' Bhim paused, now mimicking Yudhishthir playfully, his tone graver. 'Stay alert and seek out opportunities to escape. If Purochan finds out that we know what he is planning, he might act now. We need to delay his action. We need to lull him into believing that we know nothing.'

He laughed heartily. I didn't know what to do. You can't laugh at a future prince. So, I just turned to a corner. A soldier was staring at us from there. Bhim saw me look at him. He turned to glare at the soldier, who walked away. Strangely, without any hurry. Such confidence in soldiers didn't feel right.

'Careful, Bhim. There could be lip readers here. We need to prepare for the worst.'

Bhim nodded. 'You're right, let's go inside. Yudhishthir is waiting.'

'Yes, prince,' I said, though my attention was focused on finding the mouth of the tunnels, if any, in the palace.

'Surangraj, the question is, who will cry for us if we are killed?' Yudhishthir turned to see Arjun walking around the central room checking if anyone was overhearing the conversation. 'Our great-father Bhishm? Our teachers Dron and Kripacharya?'

It was a large room that had four large doors, opening into a rectangular corridor around it. Around the corridor were six rooms—individual bedrooms of the Pandavs, two along the lengths and one on the sides, with corridors in between, leading towards the gates of the palace.

The chamber we sat in was the family room. A carpet, imported from Gandhar, swept the central floor, leaving the white floor around exposed.

This was where the Pandavs lived, a fair distance from the modest Sabha, the kitchens, the dining rooms. Two other rooms adjoined the living quarters, the armoury and an extra room.

'I feel we should just crush them before they do,' Bhim said, stamping his foot on the hard floor. It was white marble, almost as good as those in Hastinapur, with black streaks running through it. The imperfection made the marble stand out for its simplicity. I never liked the pure white marble slabs. They seemed somewhat artificial. But for now, I wasn't interested in architecture or floor design. I was looking for gaps, cuts, edges.

'Bhim,' Yudhishthir was indulgent towards his giant brother, 'do not underestimate your enemy. See where we stand.' He got up from the easy chair, his arm behind his head, as he began to walk around the room. 'We have no rank, no power, no positions, no soldiers to command. We have no friends, no allies. We have no wealth to fight Duryodhan's full treasury.' He paused to smile, 'Your strong arms, my dear brother, are not enough to fight a battle leave alone wage a war.'

'So, what do we do? Wait for Purochan to burn us?' Bhim looked into the distance with anger. 'Die without a fight?'

'No brother,' he went up to Bhim and placed his arms on his shoulders. 'Let us pretend we know nothing. Let us lead normal lives. Go hunt a deer or two. Meet the people of Varanavat, get into their hearts, win them over.'

He turned to me with a smile but continued to speak to Bhim. 'And while we do that, Surangraj will do his magic underground. In the meantime, nobody should even suspect that we know what's going on.'

I continued to shuffle through the room. Occasional streaks of the orange evening sun from the windows in the adjoining rooms flooded the central chamber with light but there were no direct rays. The armoury was clean, I had scraped every corner. The outer rooms were too open.

It had to be this central chamber.

'What are you doing, Surangraj?'

'I am looking for the escape hatch, prince. But don't let me bother you. Please carry on.'

Yudhishthir's brow knotted but he turned to the door of the chamber. Arjun stood there, quiet.

'I don't know about you,' Arjun came in silently into the room and said in his quiet, dignified way, 'but I'm not going to wait for Purochan to burn us. Bhim and I can face the Varanavat army. I have enough arrows to fight the vahini of Varanavat.'

A dramatic silence filled the room. Then Bhim turned to him and asked, 'How do you know it's only a vahini?' The mere thought of action brought a smile back on the giant's baby face.

'I'm not absolutely sure, but from what I see and what we saw at Purochan's palace, even a vahini would be a higher estimate.

'What have you found?' Yudhishthir asked.

'That the gan employed at this palace is a third of the entire Varanavat defence system. War elephants are of no use here, so they are only ceremonial props. This means, the total army comprises a vahini, that is, eighty-one war chariots, two hundred and forty-three horsemen and four hundred and five foot soldiers,' he walked up to the fruit basket near the window, picked up an apple, took a bite, looked out and smiled at its sweetness.

Then he turned around and continued. 'I can see familiar soldiers that comprised the gan in Purochan's palace here. I don't think

Purochan would have involved the entire vahini. So, it is this gan we need to take care of. Which means, twenty-seven chariots, eighty-one horsemen and one hundred and thirty-five foot soldiers. Add the mercenaries and we are roughly dealing with about two hundred and fifty soldiers, of which we need to worry about thirty or fifty; others are irrelevant.'

I was struck by the insights in Arjun's calculations. Of course, there could be no other way. It was risky enough for the gan to be here. Calling the entire vahini would shame Purochan and Duryodhan across Aryavart. But I continued to focus on the floor, running my fingers across the room. The marble was smooth. Even the edges of the stone were tightly wound together by lime. I scrapped some lime off between the stones at the corner of the room. No, this was not it.

I turned to the next one.

'That's a good starting point, Arjun,' Yudhishthir said. 'But will you be able to fight them all alone?'

'Alone?' Bhim's brow was knotted. 'Who said Arjun will fight alone? I'll be there next to him.' He turned to Arjun, 'Leave all the chariots and half the horses to me. You handle the rest.'

'Bhim, this is not the time to joke,' Yudhishthir said.

'What joke? Didn't we vanquish Drupad's army a few months ago?' he paused to think, walking around like an elephant in the room. 'We will need more information about the soldiers, their prowess and all of that. Give me a fortnight and I'll have those details. I feel, it would be easier than we suspect, but we should not lower our guard,' he rubbed his hand with glee. 'I would go with Arjun's assessment.'

'I only wanted to let you know that while our lives are at risk, the risk itself not so great,' Arjun said, running his right hand on the scars of his left arm.

The fourth line of marbles checked, I rose slowly to move towards the bed. Yudhishthir turned to me. 'How long will it take you to make the tunnel?'

'I don't know. There should be a tunnel already. The palace is old but not really ancient. Tunnelling as a form of defence system should have been in place when this palace was built...'

A shuffling outside. Cloth against the floor. Movement. We looked at each other, our hands instinctively on our weapons.

Someone was listening to us.

By the time I turned my head, Arjun was at the door. He signalled me to carry on talking. Itching to squeeze a neck or two, Bhim walked out of the other door, surprisingly quiet, nodding to Arjun on the other door. The idea was to trap whoever was there.

'So, it's a question of finding it,' I said continued tentatively. 'Once I find it, all I would need to do would be to join the links inside the tunnel and ensure that the point where it opens is safe. I'm sure it is in this room...I can sense it.'

'You can...' Yudhishthir paused, 'sense it?'

All through my eyes were towards the door. Who was it outside?

'And look who we have here,' Bhim's voice boomed into the room before he entered.

We looked up. Urvashi.

'You scared us,' Yudhishthir said.

She was silent.

'What brings you here, Urvashi?'

'I don't think you're prepared,' she said calmly, standing steady at the door. 'How did I get in without being noticed by any of you?'

Bhim looked at Yudhishthir, Arjun at me.

'You are underestimating your enemy,' she went on, talking to Yudhishthir. 'That could mean death for you, your brothers and Kunti. All your planning,' she turned to Arjun, 'your information,' then to Bhim, 'your strategy of attack and how many you can kill will come to nothing if at any point Purochan decides to attack you in this room. All of us know the theory of war, but this is real danger. And you are behaving as though you are still in Dron's academy!'

Her words were like darts, cutting through ego and pride of men not familiar with such open criticism. There was not a shade of pleasure in her words, just disinterested, deep concern. The future kings of Hastinapur stood stupefied. Nobody, not even their worst enemies, had spoken to them in this manner. I controlled my laughter.

I was leaning on a wall, my fingers feeling the smooth surface with the oil plastered on it, a light shade of pink under it...lak. But I knew enough about the walls. It was the floor I was studying. If there was a tunnel, there had to be an exit. If there was an exit, it had to be on the ground floor, in the sleeping chambers.

The sudden silence in the room was deafening. I looked up.

'Tell me, prince, are you ready?' Urvashi limped two steps towards Yudhishthir and looked straight into his eyes.

As Bhim began to open his mouth to speak, Arjun silenced him with a glance.

'Urvashi is right,' Yudhishthir turned to all of us. 'We are presuming as though we are completely safe.'

'You need constant vigilance at critical points.'

'Like?' Arjun asked gently.

'Like,' she turned to him, 'this room should be covered by two trusted people all the time. Whenever Yudhishthir goes out, Arjun or Bhim must be with him. I'll stay with Kunti and the twins. Your attendants have to become warning signals for anyone moving towards this chamber.'

She looked around. 'And where is the escape door?'

'Escape door?' Bhim repeated slowly, sounding foolish.

'Yes,' she walked towards the left circular pillar in the room. 'If suddenly you are attacked, which door are you going to run from?'

'I didn't think about that,' Arjun said, 'but there are four doors to the adjoining rooms...'

'...three of which,' she interrupted, 'look into open spaces. Only that one,' she pointed at the south door, 'has some sort of defence potential.'

'That's the armoury,' Bhim said. 'But it has no exit door.'

'There is a small window that opens out to the south side. It's a short run to the Ganga from there. That's what you need. Your attendants must stay in that area. Have them build tents in that direction. Say they need a clear passage so Kunti can bathe in the river in privacy.'

Bhim began to open his mouth but thought better of it.

Urvashi noticed it. 'What is it, Bhim?'

'Nothing, Urvashi...you are right. We are far too confident about our prowess in war. This is not war,' he was talking to himself, softly. 'This is a battlefield of treachery. Neither Arjun's arrows nor my mace can fight this.'

'Good,' Yudhishthir said, 'now, let's not berate ourselves. Urvashi has alerted us. We need to take extra care.'

Yudhishthir looked at me, 'What is your opinion, Surangraj?'

'We have to be careful but not so much about a frontal attack. I've been studying the soldiers. They are all like me—swordsmen and spear-wielders, apart from some mace-wielders. These are all weapons of the past. They don't have a single bowman, unless he's hiding somewhere.'

'Chances of them having archers are low,' Bhim nodded. 'If there was an archer, he would have shown up by now.'

'And so,' I turned to him, 'they can't fight us and win if we have Arjun and Urvashi with their bows and arrows.' As Arjun looked at Urvashi, she looked at me with warmth.

*It was your eyes, Urvashi.*

*I thought it was my body.*

*Yes, that too. But your eyes captured me from within.*

*I don't know what you're talking about. Most men I knew only wanted my body. When I looked at you, I felt something open through a wall of lust, something deeper, something of the beyond.*

*Most men? You mean...*

*Yes. But now he's gone. I could have gone with him but I loved Hastinapur more than him. Why are you disturbed?*

*No, nothing. I'm surprised that I can be jealous of a man who no longer exists in your head or even in our country.*

*Jealous? That's good.*

*Good?*

'Yes,' Bhim said, looking indulgently at Arjun, admiring the scars on his forearms.

'Bhim can support Arjun and Urvashi, but thats all,' Yudhishthir said. 'Only if they break through and reach us close enough for body combat, should Bhim lead. Then, Arjun should be the backup. Our biggest challenge would be to stay alert to them congregating and coming close to this chamber. Close combat is our tactical weakness, we need to keep it as far away as possible.'

The situation was grim and I allowed it to seep in.

I looked down. What's that? A curious gap in the tiles below. It seemed a slab had a strange pattern. Small, almost minute, but a pattern it was. There, just near the bed, going under it. I ran my foot over it.

The smooth marble floor had a rough but invisible line running across. I squatted and followed the crack with my fingers. It looked no different from others, except that it was a little narrower.

I pulled out my pickaxe and cut into the crack, shredding it. The lime peeled off with difficulty, revealing a gash. My heart began to beat faster. Around me, I felt the pressure of attention.

'Surangraj?' Arjun's question hung in the tension.

'Give me a few moments, prince,' I shaved more of the lime. 'Bhim,' I turned to the giant, 'can you pull this bed away?'

As Bhim dragged the large wooden bed effortlessly, an innocent, standalone marble slab, no different from any other in the room or outside, looked up at me. The architect had tried his best to merge it with the mother slab. The grey lines were running clean. But that was colour, not the stone's natural lines. The gashes in between the stone had been painted to follow the lines, to give an illusion of a full slab where there was none.

'What is it, Surangraj?' Yudhishthir asked, coming closer.

Looking up, I saw the eyes of the three brothers looking with hope and expectation. Outside, the chirping of the evening birds suddenly sounded louder.

Arjun put his hand on my shoulder. I looked at him. His eyes carried Yudhishthir's question.

'Give him a moment, Arjun,' Urvashi said, standing calm as ever, the beginning of a smile on her lips. She knew. My breath had shortened.

I saluted my ancient colleague who must have thought of this technique 400 years ago. What amazing foresight! All I now needed to do was to get under the palace, find the escape tunnel and see where it led. A prayer of gratitude left my heart and went up to Ratridevi.

My hand went towards the wall for support, where Bhim grabbed it urgently and pulled me up, his cheeks red with holding back, his black eyes, turning even more intense as his eyebrows joined together.

'This, dear prince,' I turned to Yudhishthir, trying to prevent my voice from shaking, 'is the door to your lives.'

It took me four days to clear the tunnel from the ashram to the palace. From the foundations I understood the approximate placement of the room above. My guess was right. The place where the bed stood was the point of the tunnel's opening.

'This is where we'll clear the tunnel from,' I told Yudhishthir, pointing at the slab. 'This bed must be on top of the slab at all times. Nobody should enter this chamber, whatever the reason.'

'And that would apply to you too,' he said. 'How will you come?'

'The farce of helping you settle down is over. The grih pravesh is now a month behind us. Today is the last time you see me here. From tomorrow, I'll be gone. Nobody will see me here anymore. Maybe, once or twice I'll come to keep up the appearances. It will also be our update meetings. Otherwise, we will communicate through Urvashi or Bhim if he can reach the foundations. We have skeletons of three tunnels. We only need to clear them up, join them at strategic places.'

Yudhishthir nodded.

'But if that's the case, wouldn't Purochan know about them as well?'

'I hope not,' I said slowly. 'It would be naïve on our part to presume he wouldn't. But however intricate the planning, there are some things that only experts know. My feeling is that the architect would have been called in a hurry and told to finish the two storeys above fast. That's where most of the new construction of inflammable materials is. That's where most of the energy and attention would have gone. In any case, it's a risk we will have to take. We have no options. By choosing to stay on the ground floor rather than on the top, you have already made your first move.'

I paused to let the thought sink in. 'What we do know is that Purochan will light the fire. What we also know is that when he does, all exits around the palace will be blocked, and you will be prevented from escaping. We also know that he will light up on Pashupati festival...'

There were heavy steps outside. Was it Purochan? My hand instinctively wound itself around my knifes.

'No need, Surangraj,' Yudhishthir smiled. 'Those steps can belong to only one man.'

His raw strength and great vitality entered the room a few moments before his body did. It was so difficult to distinguish Bhim from Duryodhan, both of them from Purochan. All three carried a force, bordered by a menace that reached out and gripped people, froze them before they even showed up.

'You're late, Bhim,' Yudhishthir said. 'Go on, Surangraj.'

'...and we know how it will be lit.'

'Are you talking about the fire?' Bhim interrupted.

'Yes.'

'In that case we also know how it will be lit, how the ropes holding the Pashupati statue will be cut from behind and how the lak-laced path to the palace, here, will burn,' Bhim stressed with a thump of his foot.

'But what we know,' I said, 'and what Purochan may not, is that when he lights up the palace, we will have this tunnel. In fact, apart from the tunnel per se, it is the information about it that must be guarded at all times.'

'We don't have much time,' Yudhishthir said.

A shadow in the passage quietened us. In three quick strides I was at the door. Nobody there. No rustle. No sound. Arjun smiled at me from the corner, sharpening one of his arrows. I turned to Yudhishthir. We smiled.

Our panic bonded us like soldiers on a battlefield.

'We'll need to guard every step of the way,' I said. 'If all goes well, you will escape from one of the tunnels.'

'And if not?'

I didn't answer. The thought didn't occur to me. Was I losing reality in this high-stakes assignment?

'How will mother endure all this?'

'The queen is a tough woman, prince. And with Urvashi by her side, I assure you, nothing will touch her.'

Yudhishthir's arm returned to the back of his neck, his poise thoughtful. After a few moments, 'How many tunnels are there?'

'Over the past month I have cleared three. They all lead to the foundations of the palace. During those early times there were no dungeons in palaces. Varanavat didn't need them.'

'If I had my way, I would wring the neck of that Purochan and the rabble he calls soldiers,' Bhim rubbed his hands with glee as his eyes wandered off into a fight.

'Bhim, ' Yudhishthir said. 'This is not a wrestling pit...'

'I know, I know,' Bhim said, his nostrils still flaring. As he turned to me, I felt the direct onslaught of his force on my chest. He walked to the corner, filled a large clay vessel with water from an earthenware pot, and in one large gulp, drank it all. Bhim wiped his thick moustache with the back of his hand. Looking pleased with himself, he walked to a corner and placed the vessel down carefully.

Yudhishthir turned to me. 'Where do the tunnels lead to?'

'There are three exits,' Sahadev said, his voice calm. 'One opens out to the east, between the empty settlements and thick forest, close to the lower ranges. The danger here is of wild animals and soldiers hiding,' I noticed Bhim getting ready to speak and Yudhishthir stopping him with a raised hand. 'But these can be easily managed.'

'The second opens out in the west towards the ashram, under Kedar's room.'

Bhim's eyes widened with surprise, throwing a bolt of questions at me.

I smiled at him. 'The ashram is a gift from an ancient king of Varanavat,' I explained. 'At that time, it was part of the palace and hence the tunnel. Following the annexation to Hastinapur, the landholding changed, but the poor tunnels don't know that.'

Bhim guffawed like a general, Yudhishthir's lips stretched. Their future roles were cast in their smiles, I thought.

'That,' Yudhishthir said, scratching his head, 'should be the safest way out of the palace.'

'Yes,' said Sahadev, pulling out our older conversation, 'but you can't stay there for long without being discovered. Besides, we'll end up putting the ashram in danger.'

'Then?'

'The third tunnel goes all the way under the forest to the lower Himavat there,' I pointed north. If you go to the terrace of the second floor, you'll be able to see the area. That's the tunnel I would prefer. It's long, twisted, complex; but the safest.'

'Why not the one that leads to the Ganga directly?' Bhim asked. 'It's the shortest.'

'Because there are far too many people there, prince. The danger of being caught there is high. It opens out to ships and boats. Our problem is not the tunnels or the exits...'

'I don't like this running away,' Bhim said, interrupting me. Turning to Yudhishthir he said, 'Give me just three days, brother, I'll bring you Purochan's head.' He looked in the distance, his fists clenched, an evil smile lighting his lips.

'Let Surangraj finish,' Yudhishthir's arm returned to the back of his neck.

Bhim turned to me, and raised his thick, bushy right eyebrow. 'You can leave the fighting to me, Surangraj,' Bhim said, clenching his large fists. The waiting game was taking its toll on Bhim. He was aching to crush a few skulls, break a few ribs, club a few men.

He needed death to live.

'Killing or fighting won't help us, prince,' I said as patiently as I could. 'Our problem is to escape without being noticed. That's what Vidur has asked me to ensure. You are to escape from Varanavat without anyone knowing. You are supposed to die in the fire. That's the message that needs to reach Hastinapur.'

'I'll wring the neck of that Duryodhan,' Bhim said, his voice rising, 'and send a message to the other realm.' A mean smile stretched his lips as he fantasized killing his cousin.

I must tell Yudhishthir to control this giant. He could be the biggest weakness in our escape plan.

'Purochan and his men will be keeping a watch on me. Now that I won't be coming here anymore, they may rest easy. But I'll need help from here,' I looked at Yudhishthir and pointed towards the large bed. 'And this is the place that needs to be dug.'

'That's no problem, I'll do that in two days,' Bhim said.

'I know, but it needs to be done silently. You can't dig. You can only scratch out chunks. Below the slab is refurbished clay, hardened by time. I'll be digging upwards. The advantage we have is that the floor is not very thick. But you'll have to be careful not to break it entirely.'

'Leave it to me, Surangraj,' Bhim said, flexing his arms, gleeful at the prospect of action. Both Yudhishthir and I were silent and sceptical. Our exasperation must have been visible.

'I said, leave it to me,' he turned to Yudhishthir, 'I care about mother as much as you do, brother. Don't let this outward action,' he flexed his biceps, 'mislead you. They carry my brains too.'

'Come, mother,' we heard Arjun's voice outside, as Urvashi limped into the room, with Kunti behind her.

'Welcome Urvashi,' Yudhishthir said. 'Come, mother, sit here.'

He turned to Urvashi. 'Any update?'

'Purochan's men have seen the friendship develop between Kunti and me. Kunti is now going to ask me to move in. Once here, I will be her personal assistant as well as bodyguard. That means being with her, wherever she goes, whatever she does, every moment of the day,' she paused. 'And night.'

Sahadev went and sat at Kunti's feet.

'Mother, is that fine?' Yudhishthir asked Kunti. 'Where will Urvashi sleep?'

What a wonderful relationship. Nakul and Sahadev were not Kunti's biological sons, they were her husband Pandu's younger wife Madri's children. And yet, after Pandu and Madri had died, Kunti lavished all her extra attention on them. Maybe it was out of a sense of duty. Maybe it was because the twins were the youngest. And to see Yudhishthir and Bhim so indulgent towards them gave a new meaning to sibling love.

'I can move into this chamber. It is larger. Your throne moves out and we get her a bed here,' Kunti said. 'Is that fine, Urvashi?'

'Kunti,' Urvashi smiled, 'I am an ashramite, I don't need as much space or privacy as you might. If you are fine, I am fine. Besides, this is not a holiday. This is for your protection. I'm here to guard you.'

She turned to Yudhishthir. 'But before I move in, you will need to send a formal invitation to gurudev. I've briefed him and he's fine.'

'What this means,' I thought aloud, 'is that this room will be the safest place in the palace. From Purochan's point of view it would help to have all of you in a cluster. He will think it's easier to kill.'

'We must make it a habit to congregate here every evening,' Yudhishthir said, control returning back to him. 'Maybe we can pray together in this room in the morning and have post-dinner drinks too.'

'Things are moving too fast, Yudhishthir,' Kunti said. 'The only signal I'm getting is that we need to trust Surangraj, Urvashi and gurudev. But I sense this is the right choice,' she turned to me. 'We'll follow you, Surangraj.'

They all looked at me and I realized that I had to decide. 'Yes, that works.'

The Pandavs were safe for the moment, I felt. As for escape, the tunnels will open into the inner chamber, under the bed. The six adjoining rooms will guard that escape chamber. Nobody would enter here, unless accompanied by the Pandavs. Standing guard would be Urvashi. Another group of her archers would be waiting near the ashram boundary, barely a shout away.

The plan was almost in place. Escape tunnels had been thought through. The information inflows were limited to Pandavs, Urvashi, Kedar and me. The only work ahead was to open the tunnels out, clean them and make temporary ventilators. I would work outside-in to the palace and Bhim would meet me at the foundations.

Everything was working to the movement of the sun. But like the sun itself, the entire glare of attention was on me.

I needed a pair of hands in the tunnels. Already too many people knew about what I was planning—the Pandavs, Kedar, Urvashi. Information has a way of spilling out. It seeks its own redemption. And time was against us.

There was only one man.

## The next day

It wasn't difficult to convince Varad. Chances of the Lakheras being allowed out of Varanavat after the burning of Pandavs were almost nil. And even if they escaped from Varanavat, it would be impossible for them to cross the cannibals in the forests. The Lakheras would be the last gift Purochan would hand the cannibals, before pushing them back into the deep jungles.

Varad knew that.

'Frankly, it is only if Purochan dies that you can return to your lands, Varad,' I told him as we drank som, outside Rasilee's shack. 'Otherwise, you are trapped.'

'I know, Badri,' he said, looking into the distance. 'But how do you propose to fight his army? Wouldn't it be better if we waited for things to stabilize here and leave once trade brings peace?'

'You know it as well as I do that none of that is going to happen. It's just wishful thinking. The fact staring at you in the face is that once Purochan thinks your task here is over, you'll be asked to leave Varanavat,' I paused, looking at Vayu and Kadak enjoying the breeze, now cooler, eating grass. 'And beyond the urban boundaries of this town, the cannibals are awaiting their feast.'

In the long silence that followed, the sounds of the forest intensified.

'What makes you think that once Purochan is dead, we'll be allowed out?'

'Because, Hastinapur will need to put in an immediate replacement. That should take about three months, during which there will be real soldiers, Brahmins, merchants coming in and out of Varanavat. My guess is that Vidur will be here. There is no way the cannibals will be able to run the riot as they are now. They will be forced away.'

We were walking and were now at a comfortable distance from Rasilee's shack, closer to the forest. Behind us, the first birds were returning to individual chatter that would soon mushroom into a cacophony of homecoming. Only if you listened carefully, from your heart and not just the ear, could you sense their complex harmony of conversations and reliefs. 'We are home and happy to be back.' Not very different from humans.

Varad broke nature's silence by throwing his clay vessel into the forest, swearing with a violence that didn't belong to him, but reflected the pent up frustration of his entire trapped tribe. It cracked against a tree, disturbing the tranquillity of the forest. A scurrying of feet, a flapping of wings, a shaking of branches. Then things settled down.

So did Varad. He nodded slowly, his eyes intense. 'What do you want us to do?'

'There is no "us" here. Only you. No other person, Lakhera or local, must know this.'

'You put too much faith in me, Badri,' he took a long sip, swallowed it slowly. 'Or yourself. Just two of us against Purochan's army?'

'And you carry too little faith,' I smiled. 'Besides, even in the stray chance that you are right, it's better to go down fighting for your freedom than to sit like an innocent deer waiting for an arrow.'

We were silent. In the distance, through two layers of my veil, I could see vultures soaring, possibly where the Himavat Patth cut the forest. Was there another victim?

'Varad,' I asked gently. 'Tell me, has any Lakhera tried to leave Varanavat in the last few nadikas?'

His eyes were furtive. 'Why?'

'Because I don't think he's going to make it.'

Varad turned to where my eyes were still stuck. Apart from the signals they sent, the gliding of vultures was always majestic. They waited for the animals below to finish. Usually, the whole prey could not be eaten; there was always some extra. They had the patience of rocks.

'Naman, his brother Ankash and wife Revati,' for a few moments, his eyes held the pain in his heart, then the tears fell like a stream only to disappear in his beard. 'I told them not to leave.'

He wasn't the type who needed a hand on the back or a shoulder to cry on. He was too proud for that. I knew the type. I was one. Not the time to console him. I handed him another vessel and once again we began to stare into our drinks.

Something was not right here. Varad had told them not to and still they left. Why?

'How many Lakheras have you lost?'

'Counting these three, fourteen.'

'That's a lot of death for one tribe.'

'They don't listen to me,' he said, almost speaking to himself.

Something was going on here and I couldn't place my finger on it.

'When is she coming?' I tried to change the topic.

'Anytime now. Rasilee has sent the signal,' Varad's eyes, now red with pain, looked up. 'If Janaki is late there must be a reason.'

### Twelve days later

'This is the fiftieth time I've hurt my head. That's why you need dwarfs to dig, not warriors! Why in god's name did I listen to you?'

Varad was annoyed. But he was smiling. One of the first things you need to learn about mining is to keep your head cool and away from the edges.

'Look, if you tie that cloth around your head, it will protect you,' I told him, digging further. Behind me I heard a rustling of cloth. It was best to not pay too much attention to whiners in the tunnel. The best of men find it difficult to work underground.

The tunnels were almost ready. Like in Hastinapur, I had given them codes. The one to the ashram was Tunnel 1. That to the Ganga was Tunnel 2. The third one, the longest and the one I had planned to use, was Tunnel 3. There should be another tunnel but so far it had evaded me. We were now working on Tunnel 3.

Unlike Tunnels 1 and 2, this one was wide and high. By high I don't mean that you could walk straight in it. I mean, you could ride in it. Actually, three horsemen with their arms on each other's shoulders could ride in it and still not touch the walls. It was a fascinating piece of tunnelling that I couldn't imagine an ancient miner, with little access to knowledge or technology, building.

On their part, the walls had been smoothened with clay, giving an impression that you were in a small Varanavat home.

I was wonderstruck by the planning and the meticulous cuts my colleague of three or four generations ago had made.

Why? Why would any miner seeking the safe custody of his king make such a luxurious tunnel? Was it an attack tunnel? But attack what? There was nothing around as far as the eye could see and the eye could see all the way beyond the first slopes of the distant lower mountains.

It was in the turns that the width narrowed. It was at one such turn that Varad had hurt himself. I sighed.

'Now what are you sighing at?'

'Nothing, I'm wondering who this miner was. This is such primitive work on such an important tunnel.'

'What do you mean?'

'Let me begin with what's good. For starters, this is one of the three escape tunnels out of the palace. So, it has been thought through. The slopes, the soil study, the direction,' I ran my hand on the smooth walls, 'all are in the right place. This knowledge was available a hundred years ago. And I give him full credit for it. You will have no leaks here.'

'Then?'

'Then,' I said, talking as much to myself as to Varad, 'the descents into and out of the tunnel are gradual, keeping the elderly in mind, perhaps the gradient of the place.'

'I still don't see the problem...'

'Finally, it is completely frictionless, with enough room for three horses. This means, the royal family can escape along with its bodyguards, comfortably.'

Varad raised his shoulders and thrust his neck out. A question hung in his eyes.

'Look, I...I can't point it out...I don't know...but something's not right.'

'You're going to make this a commentary on a miner of three or four generations ago? Relax.'

I looked at him blankly.

'Maybe you're thinking too much. Maybe you need rest.'

'Yes, maybe, let's dig.' But the feeling, that invisible feeling lingered.

A little way towards the palace I saw my opening. 'All right,' I said, testing the roof for the roots of a dying rudraksh tree I had identified in the morning, 'this is where we make our fourth ventilator.' The trunk was hollow all the way down. All it needed was the clearing at the bottom.

'You mean the part where the roof caves in on me as you watch from a distance?'

He laughed heartily. I joined him. But the discomfort didn't let go of my throat.

*Seventeen days later*

'Where is he?' a shout, faintly familiar.

A woman's voice followed. She was trying to explain something to him. 'I don't care, get him now.' The two walked out of the shack and saw us in the distance. It was Rasilee. The shout had come from Durjan. He was holding his sword.

'You,' Durjan pointed at Varad with his sword.

Varad turned to him, his fists clenched. There was suicide in his eyes. Maybe, it was the burden of deaths on his shoulders. Maybe, it was the hard work in the tunnels. Maybe, it was just a hot day.

'Keep sitting, Varad,' I spoke softly, just so my voice could reach him. 'Let me handle this.'

Varad turned to me to object, but I was already up on my feet.

'What is it you want, Durjan?' I paused to shake his mind off Varad completely. 'Another beating?' That slowed him down with the right amount of distraction. Behind him Rasilee stifled a giggle.

I took the gamble of challenging him, knowing fully well that he wouldn't dare attack me. Irrespective of his hatred, he couldn't hurt me. In that single evening, when Purochan and Pandavs had come to the ashram, the stakes had changed. For the moment, they were to my advantage. And I pressed.

'Wh...what are you doing here?'

'Enjoying a drink with my friend,' I said, raising my vessel. 'You can join us, but you'll have to leave your sword behind,' I paused as he looked at his weapon. 'And your anger too.'

'I'm not angry,' he said quickly.

'Ah, my mistake. Just that soldiers don't bare their swords unless they want to draw blood. Maybe, in Varanavat, it's different,' I smiled.

He looked foolishly at his sword. There was a snort behind him. It was Kadak, enjoying the grass.

'At Hastinapur,' I repeated, firmly this time, 'we don't show our swords to friends, unless we are at the akhada. Or to our enemies unless we are in a battlefield or want a fight. This is neither an akhada nor a battlefield. And I am neither your friend nor your enemy. I suggest you keep that sword back, or return to where you were.'

Durjan was caught between his pride and anger. If he chose either, he knew he would be dead. Purochan must have warned him. He chose life. Putting his sword back in its sheath, he walked up to us.

I picked up a new vessel, poured som into it and gave it to him. He looked around and held it gingerly. I saw him exercise supreme self-control. Suddenly, his face was blank, expressionless.

Slowly, we walked away from Rasilee and Varad.

'So,' he took a long sip, 'who are you, Badri?'

'Like I told you the last time, I am a citizen of Kuru. I live in Hastinapur and I am here to recoup from my injuries at Rishi Kedar's ashram.'

'No, really,' he looked straight at me, trying to use his mind instead of his hands, 'there is something more to you than just being a citizen. You stand like a soldier.'

'I was a soldier once,' I said, continuing to walk away from Varad, who was looking perplexed at this rather surreal conversation. 'But not anymore. Maybe, the bad habits of soldiers have stayed.'

Durjan laughed with relief and I granted him a smile of approval. We continued walking, now more than four dhanush away from Varad.

'I know what you are doing here, Badri,' he said.

'Glad to hear that,' I answered. 'But I didn't know I was so important that you or those whom you serve would be interested.'

'Not me, it's...' he stopped. Clearly, he was too much of a soldier to understand verbal wrestling. I let it pass.

'Look Durjan,' I said, my legs slightly parted as I stood facing the forest. 'I don't know what you are doing here. From the first look it seems you have trapped yourself into something you don't want to be a part of anymore. I understand loyalty, but there are limits to it,' I paused to see my words sink into his head. 'I fear you maybe crossing those limits. A bigger dharm awaits all of us. Just be careful so that you don't end up crossing dharm while embracing loyalty.'

'Is that a threat?'

'A threat? No, not at all,' I said, taking a sip. 'It's the way of the world. It's destiny. It's life itself.'

'I don't understand all this, Badri,' he said, putting himself together. 'All I know is that when I serve someone, that service becomes my dharm. Everything else is a matter of opinion.'

'That's a fair assessment, I agree. But have you cared to see where your service is finally leading you to?'

'Have you?'

I sensed movement in the forest. Perhaps it was Janaki. For me, this conversation was over. Something in me pushed towards this bandit-warrior leader. Dangerously close to a raw, physical attraction. And yet, it was far enough for restraint. It wasn't just the Pandavs I needed Janaki for, there was something more. My mind tried to hide it, but my body and the pounding heartbeats sang another song.

'Maybe you're right. Both of us are puppets in larger games,' I said looking into his eyes. 'Just so you know, I respect your loyalty. I may not get the chance to say this again.'

He seemed moved. 'And I yours.'

'Also,' I said, smiling, 'that in our last fight, I didn't beat you fairly.'

His eyes showed movement but not a muscle moved. 'And how's that?'

'I don't think you were prepared to deal with a skilled fighter. You probably thought I was a passing traveller.'

He smiled. 'Yes, actually I did. You were good, very good. You could have killed me that night.'

'Yes, but my dharm wouldn't allow that, would yours?'

He was silent.

'You seem like a good man, I wish there was some way to help you cross over,' I said with a tinge of regret. 'I wouldn't like to fight you again. Either way, the loss of a good warrior would hurt Aryavart.'

'You are still a soldier, Badri,' he said, a tone of regret rising in his voice. 'But for me, soldiering has become a matter of a few coins. I fight here today, tomorrow elsewhere. My sword is for hire,' he caressed the leather sheath, hardened on the outside by weather but softened inside by repeated use, and I read a brief history of this warrior before me. He had been betrayed and was now finding his feet with Purochan. 'But when I give it, I complete the task. I slash to cut. I cut to kill.'

'Would things change if I told you that what you propose to do this time would go beyond individuals, that it would affect all the kingdoms of Aryavart?'

'Nobody asked me when my family was butchered in the...' he stopped midway in a memory that he had buried under his new reason for existence.

'Durjan,' my tone changed, 'when you and I will die, our families will weep, maybe our community or even our village may shed some tears. Then, life will take over.'

His forehead knotted.

'But if what Purochan proposes to do works out, the entire Aryavart would be engulfed in a never-seen-before darkness.'

Durjan looked at the floor, then at the distant foothills. 'My world has already been painted in the darkest shades of black. I'm standing at the edge of what you can imagine to be the furthest shadows. Aryavart,' he spat, 'means nothing to me anymore.'

'If you have suffered injustice, I promise you that I will stand by you, fight next to you and help you fix it, Durjan.' I meant what I said and when he looked at me he knew I wasn't lying. 'But what you have embarked on will only haunt you for the rest of your life. Return to light, while you still can. Nothing's lost.'

'It's too late, Badri.' He paused to look at the foothills again, reliving another memory, 'you are a few months late.'

We finished the som together and looked at each other—a smile of destiny in our eyes, a smile only Kshatriyas know, a smile that seals the future more eloquently than any number of words: we'll meet in the afterlife.

## Nine days later

'Now step back,' I said. As Varad, drenched in sweat, turned to me, I tested the wall before us. 'Yes, this is it. Get some rest.'

I knocked gently. No response.

Then a few hands to the right. Another knock. No response.

How could that be? My calculations couldn't be so wrong. I was sure I was knocking on the backside of the palace, right under the wall that joined the armoury. Nobody could be there. So, where was Bhim? Could some of Purochan's men have been around? It must be the seventh prahar now. The meals must be long over. So, why the delay? I was beginning to get worried. Banging harder would put the project in danger.

In the faint light of smouldering coals, the whites of Varad's eyes were staring at me.

'We wait,' I said putting my staff gently on the ground.

Varad put down his tools with relief. We had been digging almost continuously for the past two prahars. He pulled out his leather pouch and nodded to me. I bent down, put my palms under it and as he raised it, I drank like I always do after a long session. Then he drank straight from the pouch and poured a little water over his head.

'What makes us so ready to die?' Varad's question was directed at the darkness.

'I don't know, I think that's the way we are.'

'The way we are,' he paused, 'or the way we've been trained?'

'That's a dangerous trail you're walking on, Varad.'

'With a friend beside me, I can negotiate any trail, friendly or dangerous. So tell me.'

'I'm not sure. I think we are all born with a dharm within us. As we grow, we get trained. Not all who are trained become soldiers, only a few. So, I suppose, you and I are a mix of dharm and training.'

'I often feel that the way we can be left to die, at the slightest whim, shows that we are nothing more than instruments for those who wield power,' he paused. 'No different from the pickaxe on your back or the sword hanging on Purochan. You, me, Vishnu, Durjan, Purochan...all of us are instruments of power.'

'Then we need fulfill the dharm of the instrument. A sword has to cut. A pickaxe has to dig. A soldier has to fight. Neither your sword, nor my pickaxe, nor our soldiering asked to be made. As instruments, we simply allowed life to carve out our personalities, determine our dharm. The sword doesn't weep when it cracks, a soldier celebrates death. So, why bother?'

'Your simplicity is endearing, Badri. But if you look at it from the perspective of kings, you may see the futility of it all.'

'And yet, I assure you, I will do what has to be done. I don't know about others, but I can't escape my dharm. It is the only thing I have. There is no other time I feel so alive as I do when I'm in harmony with my dharm. That's meas in, the real me, the man inside this body.'

We were silent. The air was heavy but not yet strained. 'How is your breathing?'

'Now that you ask,' he inhaled deeply, 'it is a bit difficult. Do we need another ventilator?'

'Yes, I think so. Maybe the ventilators we've made are fine for the smaller tunnels: Tunnels 1 and 2. But this beast needs more.'

'Oh god,' his whites looked at me with despair, 'not again.'

'I'm afraid, but yes. All our efforts in opening up the tunnel from the forest and reaching all the way here would go to waste if they can't help the Pandavs escape.'

'How many more?'

'I would say two more—one between Ventilators 1 and 2 and one between 3 and 4. Beyond them, the openings will take care.'

Varad paused to visualize the ventilators. 'That's where the bends were.'

'Yes, I didn't pay attention then, but now we must.'

'Fine, but just to point out, how do you think that the ancient king and his family would have escaped? And if they could, why can't our Pandavs?'

At that moment, something fell into place.

'Varad,' I said excitedly, 'this was not an escape tunnel at all. This was to distract pursuit. The real tunnel lies elsewhere.'

Varad groaned. 'Frankly, after all the work we've done, I don't quite share your excitement.'

The weight of the unknown lifted from my chest.

## Eighteen days later

My knuckles were raw from hitting all the points on the wall which I possibly could. But the sound didn't change. The hollow I was looking for remained evasive. This wasn't working. Perhaps I was wrong. Perhaps hope had drowned reality. Perhaps I was losing it.

Varad saw my frustration. 'Badri, I'm not a miner, but this much I can definitely conclude: your banging is leading us nowhere.'

'Your comments, my friend,' my irritation yanked those words out involuntarily, 'are leading us nowhere.'

'That's not what I meant, Badri,' he said gently. 'The point I'm making is this banging could take you forever, more time than the Pandavs have.'

From the depths of my frustration, I began to relax. 'The answer is not in this banging,' he continued. 'I think you'll have to get into the mind of your ancient colleague—his mind, Badri, not his hands.'

*Our hands are mere instruments. The real fighter is our mind. Give that up and your instrument is useless.*

*But gurudev, you said the instrument, after a while, gets a life of its own.*

*Yes, it gets that life. Intelligence seeps through the cells, the tissues, the arms. But the mind is necessary for their final expression. Focus.*

*On what?*

*Right now, on your adversary. Start.*

'Badri, are you All right?'

'Yes...yes, Varad. I need to be alone. There's rubble in Tunnel 1... can you...?'

Varad left without a word.

This was a different battle. Winning it was crucial. It could mean the difference between life and death of the Pandavs.

It could mean the victory of dharm or adharm.

But I wasn't thinking right. The tension of time was in the way. The tools in my hands were of no use in the tunnel I now had to enter. I gently dropped them to the side.

Before they hit the ground, I was burrowed into the realms of the subtle. I was trapped in the creation of my own making and nobody could help me here. One by one all thoughts ceased.

*Get into the mind of your adversary, Badri, his mind.*

What would he do? The tunnel technology wasn't as developed as it is today. The tools were different.

Would he have had iron staffs? Unlikely.

Would the tunnels have been planned while building the palace? No idea.

Would he have planned a single tunnel or more? Don't know.

Was it the work of one miner or many? Nobody knew.

This needed an altogether different sort of mining. I needed to dig into the past. I needed more time.

*Six days later*

'Not for me, Janaki,' I said as clearly as I could. 'It's for Aryavart.'

'What has Aryavart given us?' she spat out. 'Just marginalization! Words like justice or dharm have no meaning beyond the cities or riverside ashrams. To us, they are meaningless.'

'I will get that fixed, Janaki. You will meet Vidur. I will ensure you get justice—your lands, your honour, your rightful place in Aryavart. I will fight for you...with you. But don't abandon dharm.'

'We were driven out in the name of dharm.' Her eyes lit up with violence. 'Our lands were taken away from us in the name of Aryavart, of establishing what you call dharm,' she stressed the word. 'And sitting in your palaces, you allowed that to happen.'

'Janaki...'

'And now you want us to save these,' a lash of contempt filled her voice, 'princes.' Her eyes brimmed over with tears of anger. 'So, they can finish whatever is left of us?'

'They know nothing about this, Janaki, nor does Vidur. The injustice done to you and your tribes is not acceptable to Hastinapur.'

She turned her face away, wiping a tear, the knuckles of her right hand white as she clasped her bow tightly.

'Look at Varanavat. Despite the annexation, it is a local who rules the territory. It is unfortunate that right now it's someone like Purochan. But as far as independence goes, the Kuru kingdom values it.'

Janaki was silent. 'More than eighty of our people have been butchered. And not just men and women, but the old and ailing,' she suppressed a sob. 'Children. My child...'

'Janaki.' It was Araak. 'May I speak?'

'No!' She wiped her tear with her angvastr, once white, now brownish with dust, frayed by use. Even now, the rippling muscles of her archer's arm sent waves of youthful aspirations through my being.

Slighted, her young husband began to measure the grass around his foot. This was an embarrassing moment for Varad and me. Varad was staring into the distant forest. I was fidgeting with the som vessel.

Then Janaki's features softened. 'Speak,' she said to Araak with rough intimacy, hinting at love that transcended words or tones.

'Not here, Janaki,' he moved a few dhanush towards the forest, 'come here.'

Janaki looked perplexed. As she walked to him, I couldn't miss the grace of her hips. Or that scar.

They spoke for a while in their language. It was more like a younger brother and an elder sister speaking than a husband and wife. This bond was too precious. I almost felt guilty about my longing. They argued softly.

Like a good husband, he was persistent.

Like a good wife, she was impatient.

Like a good leader, she listened, argued.

Like a good queen, she took a decision.

We looked up expectantly.

'No, I am not going to sacrifice more of my people for your petty palace intrigues.' The finality in her voice ended all further discussion. 'But if you are comfortable, I will fight alongside you.'

'And me,' Araak said quickly and with a decisive look at Janaki, 'you are not going there alone.'

'Who will lead the Khasianis after me?' she asked, irritation building in her tone. 'Right now, there is only one person. That's you, Araak. After a few years, maybe, if she shows leadership, Bindu could take charge. But until then, you will have to keep our tribe safe.'

'I am not going to allow this, Janaki. The tribe can't lose you. I...I can't...'

Janaki's eyes softened. 'We'll talk in the evening.'

Araak hesitated.

'Go!'

Reluctantly, he dragged himself away.

Janaki's eyes were shut in pain when they turned to me. 'Like I said, I'm not doing this for Aryavart or for Hastinapur.'

'Then?'

'I'm doing this for you,' she said, her eyes expressing the truth of her words.

'Me?'

'Yes,' she turned to the forest and her tone changed. 'I need one thing from you.'

'What?'

'You have to get our rights back. Else, our tribe will keep diminishing. In every battle we lose five or six people. We are constantly moving. There are children. Elders.'

'How do you expect me to do that?'

'By being our ambassador.'

'But I'm a Kuru citizen.'

'That you are,' she turned to me and smiled, 'and will remain. But until our lands are returned, until we are given the dignity we lost, you will be our ambassador.'

'Me?'

'Yes. Araak can't lead, nor can Bindu. If I die fighting, I must be assured that you will take care of my people, lead them to safety, give them dignity,' she was speaking faster, the pitch of her voice rising. 'Do you agree?'

This was going to be difficult. How could I, a senior official of Hastinapur, speak on behalf of the Khasianis as an ambassador and lead them? It was as close to treason as I could imagine. And yet, the Khasianis now belonged to the Kuru kingdom. They were 'our' people, our family. Marginalized but still part of our political boundary. Every family has an angry corner, where the victimized or those left behind nurture their angst. The proud Khasianis had to be integrated into Hastinapur.

'I can't be your ambassador, Janaki. I can speak for you, argue for you, push the Kuru officialdom for you. But I can't be your representative.'

She looked downcast.

'But Janaki,' I said, 'here is my promise. I will take the Khasianis to Hastinapur, I will get you the full attention and the reason of Vidur. It will be my next task. And I'm confident that we will be heard. But whether justice will be delivered or not, I can't say. Hastinapur is in disarray, we are fighting from within and are not on the best of terms with our neighbours. But I give you my word...'

She interrupted, 'You don't need to. I believe you.' Her eyes were closed, partly in pain, partly in relief. 'Now,' she opened them slowly, a new sense of alertness, an intense force visible in them, 'what was your plan?'

The warrior in her was back.

*Seven days later*

From the haze of a bluish, cloudy screen, a clearer picture emerged. Slowly, the haze lifted. The terrain was the same but everything was different. I was walking but not on the ground. Each scratch on the tunnel told me a story. Each jutting stone showed me the mind of its architect. Each segment of its snake-like twists opened out into a saga. Now, suddenly, I felt transported into another era. The walls, the floor, the size, even the darkness of the tunnel...everything was the same. But still, it felt different. My steps felt lighter; I was almost floating. I could not feel the comfort of the physical being, or even gravity.

I was tracing the footprints of time. I was tracking my ancient colleague of hundreds of years ago. I was with him.

I was him.

'Run, Jambu, run.' Jambu paused. Asmi?

*A sword slashed through his right arm. As his spear fell, Jambu clenched his teeth and looked into the cruel eyes of Vrindhak. Then, instead of withdrawing, he pushed into the sword, his left hand holding a knife.*

*Vrindhak's expression changed to one of surprise. Jambu twisted the knife, now firmly lodged from the side, above Vrindhak's kidney. Vrindhak's arm, suddenly flaccid, fell from the sword, his eyes wide. Jambu pushed the knife.*

*The huge warrior, two heads taller, thicker and more battle-scarred, couldn't move. Jambu raised the knife higher, and twisted again.*

*'This...' Vrindhak's whisper was barely audible, 'can't...be.' When he fell, he was bleeding.*

*Jambu turned to go.*

*'Kill me, Jambu,' Vrindhak gasped softly, gathering all his energy. 'Don't leave me to die in defeat.'*

*'Killing may be your profession, Vrindhak,' Jambu paused to pull the sword out of his arm, taking time to withdraw the entire blade without cutting any more flesh. He grunted loudly as the blade left his arm, now a stream of blood flowing from the metal. 'Protection is mine.'*

*'Jambu...' it was Asmi in the distance, at the second twist. 'Jambu, save the prince, go! I'll hold the army here.'*

*'How many of you are there?' In the darkness of the tunnel, it was difficult to make out.*

*'Enough,' she said over a spark that lit her face briefly. There was blood dripping from her head, leaving trails of red, almost like rose petals on a bride's crown.*

*She pushed the sword, finished her kill, then turned to look at Jambu with a love that transcended time, and stood beyond the edge of space. For a fleeting moment nothing existed but Asmi and Jambu. That moment carried life, dharm, love. It was a moment of unity. A moment where creation seemed to bow before its creator.*

*A moment of death.*

*'I'll see you in the cave,' she broke the spell, 'now go. Save the prince!' She was smiling. 'And watch out for that archer.'*

Jambu pulled the prince's foot, 'Get down, prince, run with me!'

The prince jumped off the mule and ran, his breath heavy. Arrows whizzed past above their heads one after the other. That must be the archer, Yavan, from Gandhar.

Yavan was leading the army behind Asmi, shooting. Arrows were hitting the sides of the tunnel and littering the ground. One grazed Jambu's thigh. The mule began to follow the prince.

That was too close. He shoved the prince ahead of him shielding him from the arrows.

They ran till the third twist. Around it, Jambu pulled the prince's arm and jerked him back all the way. 'Wait here, prince.' He took three steps backwards and with his left shoulder broke into the wall. The thin clay gave away and Jambu fell, the rubble falling all around him. He got up, coughing from the dust, holding his right arm.

Pain.

'Come, prince.'

'Jambu, you are hurt,' the prince panted.

'Yes, prince. I may not be able to last for too long. There,' he pointed in the direction of the dark forest, 'lies freedom. Go, you will find a horse. Get on it and ride towards the river. Loma has a boat waiting. Ride across and stay in the forest with Loma until I come for you.'

'Where are you going?'

'My work is not over, prince,' Jambu said controlling a spasm. 'I have to go back. My friends,' he paused. 'Asmi...'

'Go, Jambu,' the prince said, the light torch reflecting his watering eyes. 'I'll be waiting for you. Return with Asmi, with valour, with victory.'

The prince walked into the shadows.

Jambu turned, his eyes bloodshot. He walked two steps into the tunnel, reached out to the top and pulled out the scaffolding. The bypass tunnel collapsed before him as if it never existed.

'Jambu, no...' the prince's voice muffled in the rubble. A wall of stone and soil, raising dust now blocked the prince from the rest of the tunnel. The prince was safe.

Jambu coughed.

It was time to die, as a patriot, for the kingdom. This was all Jambu had ever wanted, this was his reckoning with truth. Death was his moment of life.

He pulled out his hunting knife, tore off a strip from the mule's saddle and tied it around his right arm with his teeth and the other hand. Satisfied, he pulled out four spears, three in his bandaged arm and one ready for assault.

Jambu hugged the mule's head, then slapped him hard. 'Go!' The mule ran to the other side of the tunnel to safety.

In the distance he could see Asmi receding slowly. She was injured. Badly.

The last fight had taken hope away from her. All her soldiers were dead or injured. She was alone.

An injury in her abdomen was now beginning to trickle down, draining her strength with it. Her left foot had been crushed by that ugly mace wielder, now lying in the distance, his neck three steps away from the body. She dragged her foot, still fighting with only a sword. She ducked as an arrow flew past her head, landing a dhanush away from Jambu.

With all his energy, Jambu threw his spear towards Yavan. The next moment, the archer lay on the floor of the tunnel, a long spear leaving behind a fountain of blood, as it passed through him. The scream of another man behind told Jambu the spear had sought and found another victim to quench its bloodlust.

Asmi looked back. Jambu didn't stop. The soldiers paused for a brief moment. Then, with a battle cry that infused new energy into them, they rushed towards Asmi.

Jambu reached her from the back. They looked at each other, smiled, and stood as one, holding each other's injured arms, their fingers slipping through the blood and sweat, finding a grip that would hold the soldiers as long as there was life.

Yavan was gone, so it would only be swords and spears. Like the fusion of dancers they backed off, one careful step at a time, fighting two or three soldiers together, avoiding swords and knives until they reached an area where the tunnel narrowed.

Two more steps and they could hold the army.

'You lied to me,' Jambu said, warding off a knife coming in her direction with his spear, 'you were alone.'

'You lied to me,' Asmi answered, 'you planned to die here. Did you think I would allow you to?'

The soldiers stood still as they heard two of Varanavat's deadliest warriors laugh.

Then they attacked.

*The sound of laughter, coated with an unearthly delight, interspersed with grunts, clangs and cries, echoed through the tunnel, all the way to the mule, who had reached its end.*

*When the laughter abruptly stopped, there was a pause, like a moment between inhaling and exhaling.*

*Then an angry thunder filled the universe and the skies poured out their grief. A longing for the completion of an unfinished song filled the emptiness. And a well-rehearsed raag, violently torn off halfway through its final performance, yearned to relive the missing notes.*

From the rough and airless confines of Tunnel 3, I stood with new vigour flowing through me, vitality empowered with the mind, power of knowledge that came from the past. Was I Jambu? And Asmi, who was she? Was this the endless cycle of karm? Was there an unfinished agenda that needed to be completed in this lifetime? The past had revealed the present. But would I be able to change the future with that knowledge? Would I be able to break out of this destiny-chakr? Or would I, as commanded by kaal, time, keep digging tunnel after endless tunnel? And unleash yet another birth-and-death process of nature that would repeat again, and again, and again? No, I had to end this. All this while, I was ready to die for Vidur, for Yudhishthir, for the Pandavs, for the Kuru kingdom, for Aryavart. But now, I had emerged from that tunnel. I had to live.

For a purpose beyond my life.

# Dharm

*Twenty-one days later*

What I heard in the inner chamber that afternoon haunts me till today. I had had to exercise supreme self-control not to run out and vomit. The idea of murder was taken out and raised to the level of statecraft!

And I agreed to it.

In the horrors of war, I had seen enough darkness to fill many lifetimes. I had seen prosperous towns being plundered, trails of gold coins crisscrossing blotches of blood. Proud and unarmed soldiers, who should have been captured and convinced to join us, had been speared in frenzy, their heads crushed under elephants in an organized massacre. In the blindness of bloodlust, weapons flew in any direction, killing men.

Mostly, it is the bloodlust that doesn't go even after battle. Kshatriyas work themselves up to this lust and only the sounds of swords slicing flesh, spears tearing organs, maces cracking skulls can quench this thirst. That's why before any battle, there is a long lull where kings and their advisors try to move towards peace.

But what Kunti proposed that hot afternoon was cold-blooded murder. The slaughter of innocent people. No different from what they were escaping from. Quite like what Duryodhan and Purochan had planned.

Perhaps worse.

I was in the tunnel, discussing exit strategies with Bhim in very low light—the ventilators were feeble and the air had to be preserved. We were testing the tunnels for ease of escape, airflow and looking out for manoeuvres around narrow ridges, clearing the path for stones and rubble, smoothening out the uneven floor. I had asked for the trapdoor in the palace to be left open as far as possible so that fresh air could flow through the crude gradient I had prepared in the tunnel. We were thirsty.

'Come to the palace, Surangraj,' Bhim said, the whites of his big, bright eyes shining over a chubby face, perspiring with strain. 'My throat feels like sand, let's have some lime water.'

'All right,' this giant was completely focused on eating and fighting, with no other sentiment in him.

No greed for power like Duryodhan. No seductive skills that women swooned over like Arjun. No deeper pockets to his personality like Sahadev. No time to waste on dignity like Yudhishthir. No love or empathy for horses like Nakul.

He was an innocent giant, with just the protection of the family on his mind and longing for his brother to sit on the Kuru throne. Nothing else. Not a speck of ill-will, except that which was reserved for

Duryodhan and Shakuni. And now, for Purochan. In his later years, this would grow to include Dushasan and Karn.

'Come, brother,' Arjun offered his arm to Bhim and pulled him out. In turn, Bhim lifted me, almost wrenching my shoulder. Such amazing power.

The light from outside hit me. It was still the fourth prahar of the day and the doors of this inner chamber opened into the four walls outside, three of which had wide windows. I closed my eyes, pulled out my veil and wound it around, twice.

A sense of grim brooding greeted us. Suddenly, the air in the tunnel below seemed lighter than this room's. Nakul tried to lighten it. 'You're just on time, Bhim. We were preparing our exit.'

Bhim's eyes opened wider. 'You were preparing an exit without me?' he asked with a mock hurt in his voice. 'But first we need two pots of lime water,' he turned to Nakul. 'Can you ask someone to get them?'

I sat in a corner and looked at the room. Everything was the same as I had left. But in the inner recesses of our beings, we could feel the discomfort, the disharmony.

Sitting next to Kunti, even Urvashi's otherwise clear and smooth brow was furrowed. An expression of helplessness underlined her now perpetually calm face. Sahadev sat at Kunti's feet, looking away. Arjun was running his fingers on the scars of his arms, trying to hide his face. Yudhishthir, his hand behind his neck, stared into the distance.

Nobody was looking at anyone.

Except Kunti. Completely poised, steady as a warrior, her presence had an iron-edge.

You needed a mace to break the thick tension in the room.

Bhim provided that.

'Give him a vessel,' Bhim told Nakul, pointing at me, raising the earthenware pot in the air, tilting it and drinking the lime water in loud gulps.

By the time Nakul had finished filling the silver vessel, I was by his side, 'Thanks, prince.' He smiled gently and walked back to sit by his twin's side.

'What is the problem?' Bhim asked over a burp, half a pot down.

When nobody answered, Yudhishthir raised his chin towards Arjun, asking him to speak.

'I'm not in favour of running away. We should fight for our lives. That's the way of the Kshatriya,' Arjun paused. 'I agreed to escaping, because of you,' he looked at Yudhishthir and then turned his gaze on Kunti. 'But this is murder. Every cell of my body says "no".'

'What murder?' Bhim said. 'Will someone tell me clearly what's happening?' He gulped down the first pot loudly, wiped his face with the back of his powerful hand, waited for a burp that refused to come and left his brow knotted with irritation.

'Mother says we need to leave bodies behind, when we escape,' said Nakul.

'Bodies?' Bhim put the pot aside, eyeing the second one. 'Where are we going to get bodies from?'

Four terrible words filled the silence.

'Damyanti and her sons.'

We turned towards the voice. Kunti.

The terror of her words hit only later from the implied meaning. That she could say it so simply was stunning. Her eyes were expressionless. Not unlike the command of death-lord Yam. So matter-of-fact that for a moment I thought I hadn't heard the words right. A wave of cold passed through the room and everyone stayed frozen.

'What?' It seemed even Bhim couldn't believe the words. He held the second pot in his hands, now unmoving.

'That's right, Bhim,' she said, her expression unchanged. She took a moment to gather herself. 'If we are to live, we need to show that one woman and five men have died. Otherwise, nobody will believe it. Duryodhan wants a body count, not just a fire or words. By giving him this Nishad family, we will ensure our freedom.'

This was the first time I gave my complete attention to Kunti. Still a handsome woman, you could call her attractive in her own way, though the toll of life had extracted much out of her. First, as the wife of Pandu, a king who was extending the domain of Kuru kingdom, she had travelled and seen more battlefields than rooms in the luxury of palaces. Then, she had to fight for Pandu's attention alongside the younger and exceedingly beautiful Madri. The harsh life in the forest followed. And then, after Pandu's untimely death, she was back in the palace, negotiating intrigue lurking in every moment, around every corner. There had been also these five young children to look after. It was admirable that she was still sane. A weaker woman, or man, would have fallen by now.

Bhim looked at Yudhishthir, almost pleading for sanity.

'But that's murder,' Yudhishthir said, quietly. 'It makes us no different from Duryodhan.'

'What do all of you feel?' she lashed her eyes on her children, one by one. 'Does any one of you have a better way? Anyone has a safer option?'

Bhim and Arjun looked at her, then lowered their gaze.

'And you, Badri,' she turned to me. 'Is there another route to our safety?'

'To be honest, I haven't thought about it, queen,' I mumbled softly, looking into my silver vessel of lime water, my throat suddenly dry. I felt my hand shake. In all my minute planning, how did I oversee this? I didn't know what to say, how to react. Her eyes pressed against my chest, pushing me over the moral edge.

'Then think,' she hissed, turning around the room. 'All of you. If you can find a better way, I'll be happy to walk on it. But remember,' her tone sharpened, her breath shorter, 'after we escape from Varanavat, neither Duryodhan nor his spies must follow us. Hastinapur should do the customary pretence of grieving for us. We should be believed,' she stressed on the word, 'to be dead.'

The neighing of a horse floated in through the south window, voices of boys followed. In the stable beyond the kitchen, it seemed they were trying to tame a young horse.

'Badri,' Yudhishthir turned to me, 'you've been trained in statecraft, you've served the realm with Bhishm, worked with Vidur, you should know. Tell us.'

I picked up the vessel, finished the lime water and walked to the second pot. Bhim lifted it easily and gave me a refill, his shaking hands spilling some. I walked back in silence, sensing all eyes on me. I had to get out of this tunnel...it was too dark. Even for me.

'Prince,' I looked at Yudhishthir, 'these are decisions best taken by you. I can lay the board for you.'

'Do that,' Yudhishthir said, a compassionate smile on his face. He knew what I was doing...escaping from this battle. Arjun looked away. Sahadev's face was expressionless, his eyes vacantly looking into another space. All were waiting. There was no hiding.

'There is no doubt that we need to send the message to Hastinapur that the Pandavs and Kunti burnt to death in the fire at The Blessed Home,' I began, trying to assemble the rushes of reason, even as my being revolted against the idea.

Kunti's face softened.

'But do we need to leave bodies to do that?'

'How else?' Nakul asked, holding his mother's hand.

'Let me frame it in a different way. Will the Pandavs allow themselves to die in a fire? Without trying to run? Without protecting themselves? Do you think that would be acceptable?'

'No, that would seem too far-fetched,' Kunti said. 'The Pandavs won't die without fighting or at least trying to escape.'

'So, leaving five bodies may not do the job. The Pandavs could have run out and burnt among the many other bodies that the fire will consume.'

'The bodies can be strewn around, in groups of three, two and one,' Kunti said after a moment. 'That would show that we tried to escape and help each other but failed.'

This woman was pure evil!

Her senses had been hijacked by the need to save her children, perhaps rightly so. Examples of martyrs having given their lives for kings and queens flashed before me and I realized how over generations we citizens had been systematically brainwashed into believing that we need to protect the king at any cost, even with our own lives.

Worse, the way we treated the marginalized people of our kingdom never ceased to shock me. But killing an innocent, vulnerable Nishad family in cold blood? I wanted to shout at her, but kept quiet. I walked towards Bhim for a refill. Water flowing gently into my vessel was the only sound in the room. I returned to my corner.

'Badri,' Kunti continued her relentless assault, 'your body seems to disagree. Speak your truth freely. What does strategy teach you about the protection of a future king, the lesson on the interdependence of king and kingdom?' she looked at Yudhishthir, pausing before unleashing her final weapon of words. 'Do you remember the Eternal Duty?'

I felt my being stretch as it bounced between my head and my heart. Blood was pumping angrily within my veins. It took me superhuman effort to not lose my cool.

*Gurudev, give me strength.*

*The strength lies within you, pull it out.*

*Not this, gurudev. I have never fought such a battle.*

*Now is your time. Just remember to do your dharm. Focus on dharm. Everything else will fall in line.*

I thanked the gods for the veil around my face.

'Do you remember?' Kunti's tone was so sharp that Sahadev was pulled out of his meditative reverie. I saw Nakul squeeze her hand. She visibly calmed down. The twins had that healing touch in them.

I nodded.

'Would you care to recite it for the benefit of the princes here?' She was calm but continued to push me to the edge of my tolerance. A wave of nausea rushed to my throat, I smothered it with a sip, my veil pulled up till my nose. I looked at Yudhishthir.

'A Kshatriya should not live relying upon destiny, especially he who is desirous of ruling,' Yudhishthir said, saving me the embarrassment. 'The king and the kingdom should always mutually protect each other. This is an eternal duty. As the king protects, by spending all his possessions, the kingdom when it sinks into distress, even so should the kingdom protect the king when he sinks into distress.'

Her argument across, Kunti sat back. Bhim was staring at his feet.

'What would Bhishm do?' Arjun asked. 'What would Vidur do?'

'Vidur,' I said, recovering my strength but trying my best to keep the acid away from my tone, 'would not agree to this.'

'And Bhishm?' Yudhishthir asked.

'Nor he,' I said.

'Then tell us,' Kunti was breathing fire again, 'how do we convince Duryodhan that we are dead? How do we ensure he doesn't follow us? How do I protect my children, the future kings of Kuru kingdom?' Urvashi placed a hand on Kunti's shoulder.

'Prince,' I said in defeat to Yudhishthir, 'you expect too much from me. I leave it to you to decide what is to be done and how. My job is to take you to safety.'

'We will not be safe unless Duryodhan believes we are dead,' Kunti continued. 'It is not enough to escape the fire, the palace, or even Varanavat. Our safety lies in Duryodhan's head—he needs to believe we are dead.'

A long pause filled the air, now seething with sparks. 'She is right, Surangraj,' Yudhishthir said.

'I know, prince,' I turned to Kunti. 'Queen, I completely understand what you are saying, believe me. It's just that killing innocent people to save ourselves is not something I would do. It is against dharm.'

She had won the fight. It was there in the slight smile when she spoke.

'Surangraj,' she said, her tone softer, now that victory was hers, 'we are not talking about your dharm. Or mine,' she looked at each of her sons, pausing for effect. 'We are talking about the future king. Let me recite another line from statecraft,' she said, closing her eyes and pausing to take a breath.

'If by slaying a single individual a family may be saved, or, if by slaying a single family the whole kingdom may be saved, such an act of slaughter will not be a transgression.'

Kunti opened her eyes to look at me, but I had lost the battle. So had the strongest warriors around me, Bhim and Arjun. As had the epitome of justice, Yudhishthir. A mother's love had vanquished us all.

Dharm had won.

Dharm had lost.

And we were left holding its carcass.

## Eight days later

The symbol of Pashupati stands for the heights His idea stretches to. And here, at the foothills of the Himavat range, the god of destruction merged into the mountains. He stood as though he belonged here, this was his home.

A large statue of his stood in front of the palace, about thirty strides of a charging horse away. It faced east, welcoming the dawn in the morning with the Ganga, that symbolically flowed from his hair in a fountain with a crescent moon on the right, gurgling behind. The Ganga fell behind him in an artistically-built wooden support and meandered to the ground before ending just before the palace entrance. A simple lever mechanism carried water from the ground, all the way up to the head of Pashupati before falling around him like a twisted curtain and flowing into the drains of the palace.

Thick, black, matted hair merged into the snakes running all over him. The snakes shone in the light, as real as their skin. A benign face looked into the skies above in a trance. His third eye, terrifying to the weak and the evil, was open, emanating an invisible force. One large snake wound itself around Pashupati's bluish neck, while more than a dozen smaller ones spread out over the body. Eight came all the way down to his feet. The points of the trishul stood taller than the palace, thick, strong, firm.

Yudhishthir and Purochan stood together, the prince looking like dwarf in front of the giant, both insignificant before Pashupati's majesty. Vishnu shadowed Purochan. Arjun and I tailed Yudhishthir. Varad followed a dhanush behind. All of us slowly walked around the statue, admiring the work. We had asked Bhim to stay away.

'What a magnificent piece of art, Varad,' Yudhishthir said, a genuine admiration filling the words. He took off his pearl necklace and handed it to Varad.

'Your words are enough for me, prince,' Varad said, bowing his head, accepting the pearls. 'But this is an honour.'

'Purochan,' Yudhishthir looked at the giant, 'you have done well to employ the Lakheras. When I return to Hastinapur, I will invite you to organize this for King Dhritarashtr too. It is delightful to see such attention to detail. Arjun, look at the way the Ganga flows down all the way to the palace.'

Nodding mechanically, we followed the waterway that would in three days be filled with oil to burn the palace.

Purochan bowed gently, glancing at Vishnu next to him. I tried hard not to look at Arjun, but sensed his concern through the air.

'Every kingdom celebrates its festivals in its own ways, Purochan,' Yudhishthir continued. 'How is it done here?'

'The Brahmins know it better, prince,' Purochan began, 'but I'll try and sum it up to the best of my abilities. You should forgive me because this is not my area of expertise.'

'Come on, Purochan,' Yudhishthir laughed. 'You can do better than that. Go on.'

'As part of the Brahma-Vishnu-Shiv trilogy signifying the Creator-Preserver-Destroyer, Pashupati (or Shiv) matches the very lives of us who live in the foothills and even more so for kingdoms in the mountains,' Purochan said, the air around him changing to one I remembered at Kedar's ashram. 'Worshipping Pashupati, another name for Rudr, is an extension of our being, prince, with the added aspirations of tapasya, strength, compassion. We offer prayers so all evil is destroyed.'

How could this man, who was plotting the deaths of the Pandavs, speak with such authority on Pashupati? The clarity of his speech, the depth in his words, were curiously irritating me. I had to get it off my chest.

'Pashupati remains a contradiction I have never even attempted to decode,' I said, creating tension.

'A contradiction?' Purochan was visibly perplexed. Behind him, Vishnu's brow knotted. 'You mean because there are such few references about him in the Veds?'

Oh, this was getting worse. Purochan was a scholar. And we were about to fight in a territory that didn't belong to us Kshatriyas. The gods were the domain of Brahmins. But I had to go on.

'What do you mean by contradiction, Badri?' Yudhishthir said, switching to my formal name.

'Certainly not the Vedic references that Purochan suspects. As far as I remember from my ashram days, even though the hymns are few, the intensity is overpowering.'

'Then, what contradiction were you referring to?' Purochan asked.

I paused and looked up at the grand statue. 'See that bow, that trident, that third eye? These are symbols of a fierce warrior. The Veds illuminate him as a force, The Mighty One of Heaven.'

'And in the subtle realms of yog,' Purochan interrupted, his eyes clear 'this force is what leads the upward evolution in the ascent of consciousness.'

I was annoyed now. 'And sinners fall before him, evil flees when it sees him approach. Even the fearless, evolved Brahmins, for whom nothing is any trouble, approach Pashupati with trepidation. He could well be another name for destruction.'

'So, where's the contradiction?' Purochan asked, his entire being curious. Not a shred of aggression, just pure devotion, an intellectual curiosity. This was unnerving me.

'There is also a completely different view of Pashupati—compassionate, to the weak, generous to the point of being naïve.'

'Naïve?' Purochan asked, his tone slightly changed.

'Yes, naïve.' my arrow had found its mark. 'That's why he is known as Bholenath or innocent. Call him with devotion and your wounds will be healed, pray to him in surrender and you can walk away with any wish. Mythologies are being created now about how he grants wishes to even the Asurs, those who identify their being with the body,' I paused to turn the knife. 'And to those who have even crossed to the dark side.'

Yudhishthir began to scratch the back of his head. Purochan remained unperturbed.

'That's a very simplistic view of things, Badri' he said gently. 'You need to look at Pasuptai as the spirit of what lies within you. Once you touch this spirit, you can get what you desire. Whether it's a Dev or an Asur is irrelevant. Pashupati grants you access to your desires through surrender.'

'You speak like our guru, Purochan,' I said, somewhat disturbed by the depth and conviction of his knowledge. This giant, this evil soldier lived his dharm. And there was something disconcerting about that. Like Pashupati, he too was a paradox. 'But you leave me unconvinced. And more than me, it is our people, the large numbers, who take this contradiction as given.'

We reached the feet of the statue and looked up. A crescent moon stood on the other side of his head, from where the Ganga was flowing. The body, each rippling muscle well-defined, was perfect, designed keeping in mind the best warriors. Varad's craftsmen had built an outstanding piece of beauty. At any other time, in any other place, this statue would have got awards and the team that built it would have been invited to the king's Sabha.

'The entire Aryavart is in awe of Pashupati, either in fear or in greed—the two emotions that have driven the evolution of man eternally,' Yudhishthir said.

'That is true, prince. But you do see how people in Aryavart are veering away from him,' Purochan said. 'Our prosperity is weakening us. There is a definite shift in the religious preferences in Aryavart. A large part of the world now seeks the blessings of the wealth gods, the lavish Vishnu and his money-bestowing wife Lakshmi.'

'Yes, Purochan.' Yudhishthir said, his eyes holding back a smile. 'We are giving up the ferociousness of our Kshatriyahood and rigorous tapasya of Brahminhood in favour of comforthood.' We laughed loudly. I was glad that Yudhishthir had ended the tension. Religion has always been a difficult subject for me to speak freely on.

'What do you believe in, Badri?' Purochan asked. The question was lined with curiosity which was deeper than the words.

I looked at the imposing statue, then towards Kedar's ashram. 'I live among the rituals of my family.' I said 'Particularly the families where my two daughters are married into.'

Everyone laughed. 'You do very well, Badri,' Purochan said.

'But as far as my beliefs are concerned, Pashupati, or for that matter Brahma, Saraswati or Kali, are mere symbols. All of them reside within us. We just have to reach out into the recesses of our consciousness to find them, express them.'

I must have hit a nerve, as everyone went silent. But I failed to dislodge Purochan. He was strong from within. He was a complete man, if I ever saw one. He continued to look at me with steady eyes. And did I sense a hint of respect?

We were behind Pashupati now. The tall structure was well oiled. You could see a strong gleam in the air. The statue was leaning towards the palace, its centre of gravity a few feet ahead of where it should be. Ropes held it back. They would be cut at the right time, I knew. Once down, the stream meant to be Ganga, would fill with oil and lak and flow into the palace. The fire behind would do the rest. Arjun's eyes were concentrated on Pashupati's bow—an impressive piece of equipment, well-designed, exploding with power.

'What do you see, Prince Arjun?' Purochan asked.

'His bow,' Arjun said slowly. 'Pashupati's bow. That's what I want.' Arjun's single focus was something like a legend. And today, Aryavart's best archer proved the legend was not wrong.

A thick smell of wax, oil and lak filled the place. Purochan's people had tried hard to dilute the smell with leaves, incenses and sacrificial fires. But there comes a point when you get so drunk with confidence that you miss it all. Worse, you believe, everyone else misses it.

We didn't.

Despite being a small and fringe tribe, Varanavat had invested a huge amount in the adjoining ecosystem they believed was protected by Pasupaati. That's how ashrams like Kedar's filled the former kingdom. And that's how the status of Pashupati, a simple, tantric ascetic, rose to heights unseen anywhere south of the Himavat.

'People from the adjoining villages have begun to come in, prince,' Purochan said, his voice positively jovial. 'In two days, they will congregate here and stay on for a month. We will leave the gates open and allow them to come in. They are looking forward to get a glimpse of you and your brothers and the queen. I hope that is fine?'

I had seen people from beyond gather around the palace to celebrate one of the most looked-forward to festivals in this area. Despite its numbers, Varanavat was gaining prosperity. As it got wealthier, its faith in Pashupati increased.

'Yes, Purochan. In fact, some of them have already begun to come. A small group from the north was here yesterday. Very warm people.'

Purochan turned to Vishnu, a question in the air. 'The Nandi tribe...' Vishnu clarified.

'Oh, the Nandis,' Purochan smiled, his eyes distant. 'Did you meet Suksham, prince?'

'Yes, Purochan. He is a happy leader, full of life. It was a joy to meet him. But what is the plan for the festival?'

'The main puja will happen here,' Purochan pointed at the large expanse in front of the statue. 'You will lead the puja with the priests. Kedar will be the officiating priest.'

'Perfect.'

'Then, food will be served.'

'Where will the Brahmins sit?'

'Right in the front.'

'I would like to serve food to them myself. My brothers will join me. I hope we will not get in the way of your customs.'

Purochan paused, his eyes reflecting new respect and strange irony, compassion as well as regret. 'No, prince,' his voice quivered. 'The Brahmins will bless you.'

'Not me, Purochan, I want them to bless our great nation. I want them to bless Varanavat, Hastinapur, Kuru,' Yudhishthir's eyes looked into the great beyond, 'I want them to bless the entire Aryavart.' He turned to Purochan, 'We have reached this prosperity and peace with great bloodshed. We now need to bring back the Brahmins. They will help us settle Aryavart to a newer, higher state of being.'

Purochan silently bowed his head beneath the weight of genuine respect, his lips slightly open in awe of this man destined to rule.

Regret lingered in his eyes.

## Thirty-four days later

The cool breeze refreshed my climb to the cave. A strange smell greeted me. I threw two stones. They bounced on the walls and settled down quietly. No animal.

I looked down at Varanavat. Prosperity was hurtling towards this town, transforming the place and allowing its citizens to breathe, live a life of greater comfort than they ever had. My meetings with Pandavs, particularly the last one with Kunti, were tiring me out.

I allowed the silence and the simplicity of the mountain to cradle me.

From my perch high above, I could see the lavish homes of Vaishya merchants. Most had two chariots standing within their walls, some even three. A few were decked ostentatiously, as a rebellion against the simplicity of the area, probably belonging to a handful of merchants who traded with Hastinapur or Magadh and needed to show that they did. Most chariots were two-horsed.

But even beyond the tony areas, towards the outskirts, away from the Ganga, where the Shudras lived, I could see a few small, modest, single-horse chariots. Some were structurally two-horsed that seemed like hand-me-downs. Almost all homes had horses tied.

That tells a lot, for unlike cattle or goats, horses are expensive, mostly used by Kshatriyas for war, Vaishyas for trade. For Shudras to own them meant there had been a trickle-down of wealth.

That's why the first sense of wealth in a kingdom or area comes from the smell of horse dung. That smell was dominant in Varanavat.

Which in turn meant that whoever was in charge here, was doing his job well—Purochan. Perhaps Varanavat was doing better than Hastinapur or some of the larger town conglomerations.

Despite the immense wealth seeping throughout Aryavart, there was a social wall that had not been broken. The segregation of higher castes from lower ones, for instance, annoyed me to no end. The commendable culture ended up being an abstraction, now visibly restrictive. As populations grew, perhaps the entrenched castes wanted higher barriers to retain their positions.

Corrupt and small-minded Brahmins gave religious seals to what was essentially self-preservation. This, in the land where rishis like Kedar, Markandey and Dhaumya walked, preached and bridged the material with the spiritual.

They forgot that the most knowledgeable among them, Ved Vyas today, and Valmiki before him, were born in lower castes. Valmiki was a Shudra. Ved Vyas's mother was a fisherwoman, also a Shudra. The flexibility and mobility of castes had gradually been restricted. How a large number of the lower castes allowed this to happen, I couldn't figure out. The process had been slow but firm.

But that is how it is. Ever since civilizations began to mushroom, inequality had been a handmaiden of money and power the mistress of control. Over time, perhaps, Aryavart will overcome these divisions.

A golden glow fell on Varanavat as the sun began to set. Shadows of uncertainty were being cleared in this town, still coming to grips with the reality of its strategic position and aspiring leadership. So quiet was the place that I could hear Kadak snorting down below.

And when I looked beyond the prosperity at Varanavat, there was one man standing behind it all—Purochan.

For all his plotting, all his evils, the well-being of Varanavat showed Purochan was an able and efficient administrator. Perhaps his people even loved him. Had the kingdom been independent, he would have been a good king.

He was probably acting in what he saw was the best interests of Varanavat. If in the short-term he was able to get direct access to the existing as well as the potential kings, Dhritarashtr and Duryodhan and their advisors Shakuni and Karn, it seemed a more secure relationship than backing the isolated Pandavs.

Legally, the claims of the Pandavs to the throne were at best dubious. Practically, they were powerless. And physically, they were alone. The best of generals need an army and the Pandavs had none.

There remained the question of dharm, that abstract and invisible notion that guided Aryavart. But dharm is easily twisted. Just as Kunti found dharmic justification in killing Damyanti and her sons, Purochan could have built his logic with equally-strong arguments of statecraft, but in an inverse manner. If by killing six Pandavs, six thousand citizens of Varanavat could be happier, safer and more prosperous, the sacrifice was well worth the trouble.

It was time to go.

The final confabulations of escape needed to be run through. Tonight was all we had. I began to get up. Varad and Urvashi would be waiting.

A twig cracked nearby. Then, another. A shuffling. Then all was quiet.

Someone had followed me. Maybe not one, but more. The hair behind my neck stood up. They were waiting. I didn't want a fight now. Tomorrow was crucial.

I had one spear and my knives. They should be enough.

I walked backward into the shadows, allowing the cave to engulf me. There was a strange smell in the air.

'You can come out, Badri,' a harsh voice whipped the air, disturbing the birds into violent screeching. 'We know you are there. Escape is not possible.'

I slinked further inside, the smell intensified.

'Come on,' the voice carried an edge of impatience of someone used to killing. 'Let's get over with it, I'm hungry.'

A few laughs. But nobody came near the mouth of the cave.

'Go slow, Keval, he's dangerous,' another voice floated in, a confident man, but practical, not given to undue danger.

'He was a soldier, remember?' the third voice was shaky, afraid.

*This is no time to go, Badri. You need to conserve every bit of your energy for the escape.*

*I know, Urvashi. But I have checked the tunnels dozens of times. Even Tunnel 3, the longest and the most winding, is ready; you've seen it yourself. I can walk through it blindfolded. There is nothing for me to do. I can't sit, I can't sleep.*

*Let him go. It was Kedar.*

*But it's just a question of two days, gurudev. Surely, he can sit for two days.*

*You can capture a lifetime in a moment. Kedar spoke slowly. Two days can change the world. Then he smiled. No, two days can change creation itself. Let him go.*

*I have to go. My energy lies in the cave.*

*What if something happens to you? Too much is resting on your shoulders.*

*Rest Urvashi, nothing will happen to me.*

And now, here I was.

'Badri!' the leader of the group said, loudly. 'Come out and get it over with.'

I went further into the darkness. Soon, I would reach the end of the cave. It was a tunnel-like structure, tall in height but short in length. My foot slipped on something wet, but I didn't fall. I squatted on my haunches and felt around. There was something soft. I froze. But it wasn't moving. There was a piece of cloth, then a body.

Cold.

Dead.

The smell was of blood.

In the darkness of the cave, I looked at the body, clear to my dilated eyes. A soldier. His eyes were open in fear. His neck yanked off, the head barely hanging to the body with neck tendons. There was blood all over. Most of it had caked on his body, some on the stony ground. It was a little damp. The man must have died a few ghatikas ago.

But who had killed him, and where was the murderer now?

This man had been waiting in my cave—my cave. I almost felt violated. His sword was gleaming from the fading light outside. How did I allow this to happen to me, how did I risk everything? Urvashi was right, I shouldn't have come here. There was too much at stake.

The voices outside continued to taunt me.

'Enough,' the leader shouted. 'Keval, it's time, get ready.'

They didn't know Keval was dead. They would come in anytime now. But someone had killed this soldier.

Who?

'If you don't come out at the count of three, we'll come in, Badri. Keval, we're coming in.'

'One...'

It was a do-or-die for me. I had to think up something fast. A thick rock of mountain blocked me from behind. There were enemies in front. Nowhere to go. I had to fight. I had to win, because I, couldn't not die. Not yet.

'Two...'

I checked my knives, pulled out one in my right hand, my spear held low in my right. I thought I heard a sound. A growl. Veer?

The man began to say 'Three,' but couldn't complete it. I heard his throat being torn off, as he gurgled on the number.

'What's that?' one of his supporters shouted.

'It's the wolf!' another cried, his voice high-pitched.

I threw myself outside, my spear exiting the cave before I did. To my right, the leader was in spasms. One of them tried to run away. He slipped and I heard his scream as he fell over the cliff. As I looked up at the third soldier, I heard a dull thud. The first soldier had died before he reached the ground far below.

The other two soldiers were frozen. Veer was standing still, blood dripping from his mouth. They looked up at me. 'Save us, Badri.'

'Too late, my friends,' I turned to Veer. 'Get them.'

As Veer jumped on one of them, the other tried to slash him with his sword. Before he could drive it in, my spear went all the way through his armour, into his chest. He took three steps back as the spear got caught in the armour behind. He looked at Veer stuck to the other screaming soldier's hand. Then, with fear in his eyes, he fell, almost grateful for the spear rather than the jaws of death.

The third soldier's hand was now lying on the side, still holding the sword. He was screaming in pain and fear.

'What's happening?' a voice came from below. There were more soldiers there.

'How many soldiers are there below?' I asked.

He continued to scream incoherently. 'S...Six...'

'Who sent you?'

'Vish...Vishnu...Vishnu.'

'Why?'

'T...t...to...to kill you, please forgive me.'

I nodded at Veer. His voice ended in a muffled grunt. By the time

Veer looked up, his mouth dripping blood, I had picked up the leader's sword. 'Let's go.'

I went towards the shrubbery, Veer climbed higher. He must have found another way.

Four soldiers were climbing up. I steadied myself behind the bushes, sword in my right hand, spear in my left. The knife was back in my belt. I waited.

The first soldier grunted, looked around and saw the dead. He turned to pull the others. 'All dead, come fast!'

He pulled the first one, then the second. The fourth soldier climbed up himself. It was futile to return to the cave. I stood there, waiting. Veer was up there, I knew.

'There he is,' one of them saw me. I walked back slowly. As they moved towards me, I carefully stepped around a body. They were bent, spreading out, ready to attack.

Out of the bushes behind me, I heard a rustle. I turned. Janaki was smiling, an arrow carelessly hanging on her bow. She looked so attractive.

'Who are you?' one of the soldiers asked her.

'The right question is: why am I here?'

'Yes,' the soldier looked puzzled, irritated, 'why are you here?'

'To kill you,' Janaki said casually.

'To kill you,' the soldier mimicked her, drawing laughter from behind. His sword now gleaming menacingly, he began to walk towards me.

'I warned you,' Janaki let the arrow go. It whizzed past me, sending a breath of air that stirred my angvastr. It hit the soldier in the heart. He continued to look at me, with surprised eyes as he fell to his knees and rolled over.

Behind the other three soldiers, one more had climbed up. That made five. Where's the sixth, I wondered.

'What about the four of you?' Janaki said. 'How would you like to die?'

They looked at each other and nodded purposefully. Three of them charged at Janaki, one towards me. I braced myself, the sword ready, the spear low, my knees bent. But as he reached a dhanush or so near me, a dark shadow intercepted his charge. Veer.

The momentum of the man kept him running, but the gash on his jugular was sending fountains of red in the golden light of the sun. The man shook violently at my feet for a few moments, then slowly the light faded from his eyes.

By the time I looked up, Veer was gone, as if he was never here.

Behind me, two soldiers were down. One had an arrow in his heart and was dead.

The second had an arrow sticking out from his neck. He was holding it with both his hands, a muted silent pain sending the last sounds he would hear in this life.

My mind stayed on the sixth soldier. Where was he?

Janaki was nowhere to be seen. Her bow was lying a dhanush away where she had stood, arrows from the quiver strewn around. The third soldier had raised his sword high above his head in a lethal striking stance. He towered over Janaki, now lying on the ground. The arm would fall and Janaki would be gone.

'No,' I shouted, pulling out my knife, knowing fully well that there was no way it could reach the man before his sword slashed Janaki. But before the soldier could bring the sword down, a flash of light and the soldier's hand fell away.

The soldier screamed in pain as the sword fell with a clang on a rock. He looked to his right. 'You?' a look of surprise and pain. 'But...' But before he could say anything more, there was a swipe and his head was rolling down the mountain.

I looked at our saviour, my knife suddenly useless in my hand.

Durjan—the sixth soldier.

Durjan?

'What are you doing here, Durjan?'

He suppressed a cynical smile. 'Cutting heads.'

'Janaki,' I rushed to her, her body glistening with the fight, a few drops of blood on her cheek, probably a spray from the man who would have killed her. I held her close to my chest. She was still recovering her breath. 'Are you fine?'

'Yes,' she said, pausing to breathe. Still holding me, she turned to Durjan, her brow knotted in annoyance. 'You needn't have interfered. I had him.'

'Interfered?' Durjan took a breath, his chest still heaving from the climb and the fight. 'Had him?' His sharp look was back. 'You were dead, woman.'

'Dead?' and Janaki raised her hands. Both carried knives. 'That man was moments away from a double death. But thanks, I will remember this.'

Nine bodies, in various states of death, lay strewn around us. I felt cool air on my body as Janaki eased away and began to look at the bodies.

'You said your dharm was the coin,' I smiled at Durjan, walking up to him. 'You're not getting any here.'

'I have a good collection. Now, I need...' he paused, cleared his throat and put himself together. 'Badri, I've been thinking. I was deluding myself. It's not coins I need. I need justice.'

We were silent for long moments.

Justice. At the end of the day, finally, it all comes down to this word. The word that had created most rebels, powered the most anguish, led the most upheavals. And yet, it was a word that we took so lightly. Justice.

I looked straight into his eyes, now brimming with pain he had not allowed to erupt. 'Whatever the atrocities, whoever the person, you will get justice. I assure you. If it was in the Kuru empire, I will lead you to Vidur. If outside, I will fight next to you.'

He nodded.

'But right now we have an immediate question. How will you return to Purochan?'

'I won't. This is it. I'm here now.'

I held Durjan by his shoulders and brought him close to my chest. He hugged me hard, almost clinging on to me. I felt warm tears roll down my back, a silent sobbing on my shoulder.

Durjan. The dreaded Durjan. He had single-handedly managed the Lakheras. Single-handedly, he had manipulated the lak trade in the region.

Durjan, whose loyalty was to coins.

Durjan, a mercenary to be feared.

Durjan, a warrior.

Durjan, who had a trail of deaths leading to him but searching for the one that would grant him peace.

Durjan, now weeping his past away.

In the silence during which the sun set and turned the skies red, I looked over Durjan's shaking shoulder. Veer was staring at me from a distance. Then, like the long shadows now creeping up at a speed that you see only on mountains, he merged into one and disappeared.

## The night before the fire

Tomorrow we light the fire. Tonight was our last meeting.

'Let's go over it once more,' Yudhishthir said. 'Surangraj, speak.'

Ushas was still to awaken and Varanavat was silent. The birds were just about stirring. And the rays of the sun—still many yojanas away to the east.

In the dim and flickering light of the night torch, I saw six pairs of eyes, all attentive, focused on me. Seven shadows flitted about on the walls of the inner chamber of the Pandavs. I wore no veil. We sat in a circle, next to the bed.

Outside the room, the four doors and passages were guarded by Urvashi, Janaki, Varad and Durjan. It was completely dark in the passages there. But for the occasional sound of the night guards, nothing broke the silence.

As far as Purochan went, for all practical purposes, Durjan had disappeared after the incident on the mountain. As night descended, I told him to move into the ashram. In the dead of the night, the four of us had been working on the tunnels, checking the ventilation, the ducts, the floor, the twists. I had given control of each tunnel to one person.

This was almost beginning to feel like an army operation.

'There are four tunnels, prince,' I said slowly. 'Tunnel 1 opens out to the Ganga. This is the shortest tunnel, about fifty strides of a charging horse. Because of the danger involved, Durjan and Varad will be in charge of this tunnel.'

Arjun nodded.

'Tunnel 2 leads to the ashram. This would be around 150 strides long and opens in the centre of the ashram. Urvashi will be in charge of this one.'

I paused to let the information sink in.

'Tunnel 3 is the longest we have and goes all the way to the foothills. This is about five times longer than Tunnel 2, or about 700 strides. This is the one we will use first. Janaki is in charge here. It opens into the forest. Once there, Janaki will take you to a safe spot in the interiors, where I will meet you. This tunnel is high and I will have six horses waiting for you.'

'Won't the horses make noise?' Nakul asked.

'They will, prince. But I assure you the sound of horses will be muted in front of the large fire that we will light. The fire will also pull most soldiers towards it.'

'And then there's Tunnel 4 that leads to the settlements, but one that I'm not going to use. It is a tunnel for quick escape if we are pursued. Maybe, I will pull it down.'

I looked at the giant next to me, 'Bhim will guide you all the way. He knows the tunnels backwards.' Bhim was the only Pandav to have walked the tunnels with me. Arjun had come and gone. The others had stayed on ground.

'Varad, Bhim and Arjun will light the fire at critical points.'

'That's as far as the escape goes,' Yudhishthir said. 'What about the soldiers? Are you sure the tunnels haven't been discovered?'

'There is nothing to suggest that we've been discovered,' I said slowly. 'But never underestimate the enemy. They could meet us anywhere. The advantage we have is of attacking first. Purochan would like to light the fire on Pashupati puja night. That is two days from now. Instead, we will light it a day earlier.'

'What about the bodies?' Kunti's voice was soft, gentle but firm. A chill hit me from behind.

'Has Damyanti moved in?'

'Yes, Damyanti has been helping mother with odds and ends for three days now,' Nakul said.

'And the sons?'

'They mostly hang around her. Or get water and other things.'

I was beginning to get irritated again. But I had agreed to this. And now, it was too late.

'Make sure they stay for longer tomorrow.'

'Leave that to me,' Kunti said.

'Are your clothes ready? You will need to leave your expensive dhotis, jewellery and crowns here.'

'Yes,' Yudhishthir said. 'Urvashi has got us simpler clothes. And to be truthful, we like them. They give me the feeling of being one with the people. They,' he looked away, 'remind me of our simple forest life.'

'And,' Arjun said, 'they make less sound than our silks.'

'They also burn less easily,' said Sahadev.

A dog wailed into the disappearing night. Another answered.

'Sandals,' I continued. 'Make sure you wear the warrior sandals. They should be flat, strong, light. Check them properly, test them well. You too, queen.'

'Don't worry, Badri,' she pulled out an artificial smile. 'I'm the mother of warriors, I know what you are talking about.'

Then Yudhishthir turned to Arjun, 'What's troubling you?'

'Our weapons,' Arjun said, looking at me, 'What about our weapons?'

'The bare minimum. Bhim should carry his sword,' I turned to him, 'a light one if possible. Your quiver should be light and tight, like you would in a battle. Nakul and Sahadev should carry four quivers each. And all of you must have knives. Nothing else.'

'My mace...' Bhim began.

'...will stay here and burn,' I ended. Bhim nodded reluctantly. We smiled.

'Durjan, Varad, Urvashi, Janaki and I will wait for you below,' I pointed to the trapdoor that led to the foundations. 'From there, we will move to Tunnel 3. The horses will be further down. If things go according to the plan, it would take you very little time to reach the forests and disappear there. Then we wait till Vidur gives us the signal.'

'And if things don't work out?' Kunti asked.

'Then depending on the nature of the crisis, we'll go to Tunnel 1 and swim through the Ganga. Or, if things are very bad, we take Tunnel 2 and seek refuge at the ashram. From there, we will work out how to get out from there as soon as possible.'

The silence was broken by the chirping of birds, now awake. In the distance, a horse neighed. Physically, we were silent but our minds were buzzing with possibilities and probabilities. Our bodies were tense.

I allowed everyone to explore the tunnels of their own making. They had to go through them.

Nobody else can walk through your darkness, your fears.

Nobody else can experience the excitement either.

'While Bhim and Varad burn the palace, the rest of you will wait in the foundations below. Once the job is done, they will join you. Then, we hit Tunnel 3.'

One by one, I looked at them. 'Have I left anything?'

'Purochan,' Bhim was looking outside through the window of the eastern room.

We turned to him. 'What about him, Bhim?' Yudhishthir asked, his arm behind his neck.

'I can't leave without killing him. I have to.'

'This is no time for foolhardiness, Bhim,' Kunti hissed. The retort was sharp enough for Bhim to move back physically as she empowered her words with a glare that could have killed. 'I want no more of such risky and stupid ideas. Our first dharm is to save ourselves. You can kill Purochan on a later day.'

Bhim looked away, his jaws clenched. He looked at me, that mad look back in his eyes. I knew he wasn't finished. He was consumed by the idea of killing Purochan. It was like he was calling destiny itself. Irrespective of Kunti or Yudhishthir, he would make it happen, he would will it. I had to get this thought out of his mind. A shiver that had suddenly entwined around me like a python was now asking a suffocating question.

*What if Purochan killed Bhim instead?*

# Farewells

### *One day before the fire: third muhurt*

I held her tightly, my head bent against her spine, feeling the smooth texture of her body, one that I had held for as long as I cared to remember. Tomorrow, we draw blood. Again. A surge of energy passed through the iron, filling me up with an intimate strength. *We will protect.* I put her down gently. Then picked up the second spear and repeated the mantra. *We will kill.* The third. *We will hack.* Fourth. *There will be no hesitation.* Fifth. *He, whose time has come, will move on.* Sixth. *He, who still needs to grow, will stay.* One by one, I empowered each of my spears with the death mantr. Then prayed for strength, unshakable resolve. And finally, peace. When I put them down, I sensed them vibrate, ready to slash, aching to kill.

### *One day before the fire: ninth muhurt*

In the foundations of the palace, when he finally emerged, I met the giant with relief, and assurance that exceeded the strength of my arms or the victory of my mind. 'Bhim,' I said to the Pandav, as we tested and re-tested the walls, the floors, the ceilings of Tunnel 3. 'This is our final tunnel. This is our escape route.' He looked around aimlessly, his eyes still adjusting to the darkness. 'Escape, we will,' he looked long in the distance. 'But it is Purochan I want. I will not leave without killing him.' The determination was a command of destiny.

### *One day before the fire: thirteenth muhurt*

Near the tributary that flowed through the ashram into the Ganga, I stood before the future king of Hastinapur, perhaps even Aryavart. 'Yudhishthir,' I spoke to a gentle soul, who had now put his family's future in my hands. 'The festival is two nights away. But we escape tomorrow night. Please tell everyone to be alert.' Yudhishthir nodded. 'You have done enough, everyone knows what to do. I am aware of your thoughts about Damyanti and her sons. I feel the same way. But sometimes we need to bow before a larger dharm. Maybe, one day we, you and I,' his voice turned graver, 'will remember this and change the laws.'

### One day before the fire: first muhurt

The owl hooted again. The cold had spread and reptiles were beginning to hide. Hunger would haunt the forest for a few months till spring. 'Janaki, I...Hastinapur will be beholden to you,' I said. She kept silent but her eyes burned me. 'Once this is over, I will take you to Hastinapur and you will be welcomed like a hero.' She shook her head. 'I need nothing for myself. Just that my people must get our lands back and those who violated us must be punished. That's it, Badri.' Hesitatingly, she took two steps towards me, the angvastr slipped, revealing arms that wound around my neck, holding me in a python-like grip. 'I may not come out alive. There may not be any Hastinapur for me, any future for us.' She kissed me passionately, then paused for breath. 'But let us not waste the present.'

### One day before the fire: fifth and sixth muhurts

Within the open and transparent confines of Kedar's room, I sat, empty of all thoughts, all urges, all desires...even the desire to win. 'Gurudev.' I sat before one of the greatest warrior-Brahmins of Aryavart. 'I need your blessings and spiritual strength. After that, it's my destiny.' His eyes were closed but as I felt the force of his tapasya, new vitality began to flow through me. 'Only in death there is life. In death lies destiny. The final goal is to express spirit in the body, in matter. When you fight with dharm, your body becomes the instrument through which the spirit will reveal itself,' he paused to smile, compassion flowing through his eyes. 'And remember, death is not your dharm. Not in this life.'

### *One day before the fire: seventh muhurt*

As we walked around the ashram, on the last watch of the night, I was full of unease. 'Urvashi,' my voice cracked, uncertain whether my conviction, my truth would reach the only woman I loved. 'This could be my last battle. You need to know, I love you and always will.' She looked up, 'Every battle looks like the last.' A thick wall of memories appeared, then melted away. 'Your love stays with me, but I'm no longer yours alone. The ashram has embraced me. I belong to it. If I die, tell the children, I loved them.' We sat in silence. 'But Badri,' she looked at a diya in the distance, 'you need to live, the aspiration of martyrdom is behind you.' I opened my mouth to speak. Her eyes twinkled, reminding me of our youth. Slowly, she brought her hand up and stroked my cheek, 'you should shave.' We laughed.

### *One day before the fire: eighteenth muhurt*

The darkness in the forest was as thick as Tunnel 3. Veer sat before me, alert. A large group of wolf-dogs surrounded us, each deadlier than the next, all looking at Veer for a signal. Veer turned to his left and a grey-skinned wolf-dog walked towards me, smelt me, then walked away. In a surrealistic ritual of beasts, others followed in a circle. Veer and I continued to look at one another. Not a sound anywhere. Finally, he came to me, licked my foot. *A few more days.* I petted his head, then held him close, almost like a last embrace. *I know, I'll be there.* In the darkness I let my tears fall on Veer's head. He gently licked my cheek.

# Escape

*Night of fire: twentieth muhurt*

Crackle of the fire thundered across Varanavat. Muted within the gasps of its breathing were the frantic cries and wails of the town's citizens lamenting the 'deaths' of the Pandavs. I was in my tunnels but reports that flowed in, days after The Blessed Home had turned to ashes, said the orange-yellow-red flames were as tall as the neighbouring mountains, consuming everything and everybody that came in their way—the soldiers in the palace, the tribals, Purochan.

And the Pandavs.

Such a fire had never been seen. Purochan's planning, Varad's workers and a long trail of dark and secret bloodshed ensured that Varanavat danced to the tune of Pashupati's tandav. Its beats reached all the way to Hastinapur and gave Duryodhan the tempo to run and embrace the throne he so desperately sought.

Tonight's task was to ensure that these sounds and lights of Varanavat reverberated throughout Aryavart.

Love and sacrifice eased the task.

Murder and betrayal brought frictions.

And in dharm's books of account, empty entries disturbed a balance only deaths could fix.

We provided the bodies.

*Night of fire: fourteenth muhurt*

'Are all preparations in order, Purochan?' Yudhishthir asked, his voice resonating to the gaiety of the moment outside the palace. It was difficult to believe what we proposed to do later.

'Yes, prince,' Purochan's voice boomed with an extra edge of confidence, a certainty that all was as planned. 'Everything is in order. The priests, the people, the musicians...not a prasad vessel is unaccounted for. I have never seen so much preparation for the Pashupati festival.'

'Good,' Yudhishthir smiled and turned towards Vishnu and Varad. 'All of you need to relax now. You've worked very hard on this. What was that som you brought that day, Purochan?'

Purochan laughed heartily. 'Oh, that was Nasiva's poison, the best brewer in Aryavart if you ask me.'

'I agree, Purochan. I agree. Now, ask Nasiv to bring all his stock to the palace by evening. I want everyone here completely drunk tonight. Tomorrow is going to be a very hectic day, right from the morning. So, we'll retire early tonight. But not before Nasiva's som renders us senseless,' Yudhishthir smiled to himself.

Vishnu looked at Purochan, confused.

'Don't let him stop you. Purochan,' he turned to the giant, 'I am disappointed that you don't allow your soldiers the delights of som.'

Purochan began to open his mouth to speak.

'Nothing doing,' Yudhishthir looked up at Purochan. 'If you want, here's the royal announcement.' His tone became serious. 'I announce that every soldier, every worker, every person in this palace must be given a free supply of Nasiv's som, the best in this area.' Behind him, Arjun looked as if he needed to throw up.

'If I may...' began Vishnu but Yudhishthir silenced him with a look. Vishnu looked furtively at Purochan, who smiled at him. 'He is the future king, Vishnu,' he said smiling. 'It is in our best interests to follow his instructions.'

Yudhishthir nodded, and with a slight smile on his lips, let out his last command. 'And I want all of you to stay the night here at the palace. All soldiers, workers, attendants,' I sensed tension rising from my left where Vishnu stood. 'My brothers and I will walk through the palace to personally thank as many of them as possible for the excellent work and immense effort they have put in over the past months to make our stay so comfortable at The Blessed Home. We are indebted to you.'

For a moment, I thought Yudhishthir was going too far. But his sincerity could not be questioned. Even I, who had planned the entire defence, felt that perhaps he meant it. For a fleeting moment, I wondered if he realized the gravity of our situation.

He looked at Purochan. 'You too, Purochan. Luckily, you are still single, so I don't have to seek your wife's permission.' Instantly, the stress that had been building up in the past few moments, lifted. All of us laughed. Not merely to flatter the prince but in relief.

'Whatever you say, prince,' he caught his breath. 'But I still would need to go and ensure that the children of the state are well fed and sleep in peace.'

With the mention of children, the warrior Purochan suddenly gave way to a human being. Here we were, planning an escape, maybe even killing him. And now, there were children. To his credit, we never heard of them nor did he ever bring them over. A mark of a dignified man, devoted to the cause of running the territory. Killing him was going to be difficult. I saw Yudhishthir melting. My mouth dried.

'And you, Badri.' Yudhishthir turned to me. 'I know som is not part of Kedar's ashram life, but do join us if you can in the evening.'

I cleared my throat. 'I thank your concern, prince, but rules of the ashram are strict,' I glanced at Vishnu through my veil. The ugly glare was back—it is one thing to laugh at a prince's joke, quite another to indulge someone who you plan to kill. 'Even at my age, I dare not disobey them. Please forgive me.'

'Off you go then, Badri. This is no place for those not indulging Nasiv. From this moment on, only sinners will stay here,' over another round of laughter, Yudhishthir nodded at me signalling towards the gate. I folded my hands and turned to leave. 'Give my pranam to gurudev,' he said. 'Tell him, I will personally be standing at the gate to receive him at dawn tomorrow.'

From the corner of my eyes, I noticed Vishnu and Purochan glance at each other.

'I will, prince.'

'Wait,' a voice filled the air. It was Bhim. A scowl was beginning to form around his lips as he walked up towards us and got closer to Purochan, who moved aside to widen the circle and accommodate him. I had told the Pandavs to keep Bhim away from Purochan. He turned to me, 'Mother wants to speak to you.'

'The queen?' I wondered what new torturous plans she had thought up of. 'Let's go, prince.'

'Badri,' Kunti's voice shook and for the first time I realized that behind her strong poise stood a woman, vulnerable, afraid, uncertain. 'Is everything going according to the plan?'

'Yes, queen,' I pulled my voice, a note or two deeper, to comfort her. The truth is I wasn't sure at all. 'I think Purochan will ensure wine flows like the Ganga here. All of you,' I turned to Sahadev, who was holding her hand and Nakul at her feet, 'will have to stay alert.'

Three pairs of eyes, innocent as puppies, looked at me as though I was their saviour. The burden was heavy. I had to brush it aside. A rustling outside. We turned. It was Urvashi, guarding the entrance. We exhaled.

'Bhim,' I turned to the giant, 'you will decide the time to light the fire. Better to light it from the first floor. Just make sure everyone is drunk.'

I turned back to Kunti. 'All will be well, queen. I have taken it upon myself to keep you safe. Only my death will change any of that. And even then, I would have left you in safe hands. Urvashi, Varad, Durjan, Janaki...all of them know what to do. Besides, in the worst case, you can take the short route to the ashram and stay there until we decide what to do. In my view, our defences are strong,' I paused for the hard facts to sink in. 'And the gods are with us.'

'In case we don't meet again, Badri,' Kunti spoke gently, her eyes trembling, 'I want you to know that if we survive this, we will remain eternally in your debt.' Nakul put his arm around her, looking at me with fierce conviction that echoed his mother's words.

'I'm only doing my dharm, queen,' I said. 'As far as I am concerned, there is no debt.'

Overcome with emotion, Bhim stood up. Clearly a physical man, there was only one way for him to display all emotions—anger, hatred, frustration and now love, devotion, gratitude. He almost crushed me in his tree-like arms, transferring some of his emanative strength into me. I tried hard but could not control the involuntary grunt.

With tears in their eyes, Kunti, Bhim and Nakul laughed. Sahadev looked on, a light smile on his lips. 'Stop it, Bhim,' Kunti said between sobs and laughter, 'or else we'll lose our protector.'

When Bhim released me, I felt as if I was part of a family. Their warmth flowed into my being.

What was I saying? This was the royal family—the Pandavs. My task to save the future of Hastinapur was becoming more complex. I felt myself getting trapped in a new tunnel, warm no doubt but a tunnel still, of difficult relationships.

### Night of fire: twenty-first muhurt

'Something's wrong,' I whispered to nobody in particular. Janaki and Urvashi sat next to me.

We had been waiting in the foundations for a very long time, right under the room opening. Why was it closed? When you are inside a tunnel, it gets impossible to see how the sun and the moon, the light and the darkness, move. So, we had only estimates of time. Besides, waiting stretches time.

'Relax, Badri,' Urvashi's light touch on my shoulder was comforting. From Tunnel 3 came a familiar snort—Kadak was getting restless. Vayu had refused to enter the tunnel. For the first time, he just wouldn't listen. It's not just men who have fears. Finally, the substance that gives men life and mind is the same for horses, dogs, elephants. 'Give them time.'

'How much time do they need?' I hissed impatiently. 'Something's happened. Varad is never late.' And then I realized what was bothering me. I had taken Durjan's word as truth. What if he betrayed us? I squeezed my eyes and winced, clutching tightly at my spear.

'What's bothering you?'

I looked at Urvashi. 'Durjan,' I paused to let the weight of that word sink in. 'I think I made a mistake. I must save Varad.' I stood up. 'I have to go.'

'No,' a cool voice came from the other corner. We turned to see. In the faint glow of embers of our small torch, we saw the whites of two eyes rise as Janaki stood up. Flames of raw energy hit us as she moved closer—she was ready for battle. Perspiring, her body reflected the embers, her skin smooth and golden. The dull gleam of her sword peered behind her two shapely legs tapering below a short lower garment. She was barefeet. 'You stay. I'll go.'

I started to object. 'She's right,' Urvashi said calmly. 'You need to be here with the Pandavs.'

'Wait,' I stood up, my eyes now seeing clearly the grim features of her face. Her hair was tightly-knotted behind, held together by a wooden clip, just as all warrior-women did when they hit the battlefield or protected queens. 'We need no heroes tonight, Janaki. Our task is to get the Pandavs across the forest. We have a long night. So, the slightest sign of danger and you return. We don't need unnecessary distractions.'

She smiled indulgently and threw a soft knowing smile at Urvashi that said, 'Men will be men'. Then, without the slightest sound, she merged into the darkness of Tunnel 1.

The horses were not happy with the darkness and were fidgeting. Every few moments, I would go and calm them. It kept the blood flowing. Besides, they were vehicles that would carry the Pandavs and needed utmost pampering. There was no food or water in the tunnels. But surely, they deserved attention. Urvashi and I gave them that.

'What's bothering you?' she asked. 'Think backwards.'

Intimacy of our past years had become her first instinct. So many times, as we negotiated life's so many problems, thinking aloud was our refuge.

'Before we converged here,' I said slowly, thinking hard, 'I had walked through all four tunnels. All was fine. A few rough edges grazed past, some by geology, some by errors, and a few by design.'

She remained silent, allowing me to speak to myself.

'To be sure that exits were clear, I had told all of you to walk inwards from the exits.'

'Yes, and that's what we did.'

'Right. Janaki came through Tunnel 3 from the forest side. She brought these two stocky mountain horses,' I said, stroking the neck of one. He was missing Janaki and was not happy with me. It took me some time to calm him down. The other one followed him blindly.

I turned to Urvashi. 'You rode in with Kadak and...what's her name? He's become too fond of her.'

'Rani,' she said, an invisible smile underlining her words, as she calmed the new couple.

'Yes, Rani. You rode in with them from Tunnel 2.'

'That leaves Tunnel 1.'

'Varad and Durjan were to come from the Ganga side through Tunnel 1. This is the shortest tunnel. It is also the most dangerous one. No horses here, there is no space. I have tried to keep it as safe as possible, opening it a little distance from the river, in a cluster of bushes.'

'The shrubbery?'

'No, the tulsi trees are around it. This one opens out into some wild bushes. Tunnel 4 is an escape tunnel, so no need to bother. Let's return to Tunnel 1.'

'But river banks, even if they are exclusively for the royal families, are cluttered with soldiers, guards. That makes it doubly dangerous.'

'That's a gamble I had taken. I thought Purochan would be overconfident on this side.'

'Why?'

'The five brothers routinely go there for swimming and their weapons practice. The spot is always too noisy and has too many soldiers. So it would be an unlikely escape point. Not a place that needs much guarding.'

'Makes sense.'

We were silent again but had decades of togetherness behind us to feel the discomfort. How can a man and a woman love one another and yet...the thought trailed off.

Was our relationship based on love? Had time decayed it? Did we move so far apart that the only intimacy between us came from memories? Or was it climbing the next summit of growth, a point where we transcend the physical, live in the past, and move towards equilibrium of peace and unity that only the inner countries of our vast beings could fathom?

Urvashi limped back to the foundations. Her body was straight, supple, and strong. She had been trained so many times before. First in the Aryavart war academies where she had gathered her skills and now they were being sculpted by the ardours and rigour of ashram life and her duty to protect it. Brahmatej was in consonance with Kshatriyatej to create a woman who could kill with compassion. She too was dressed like Janaki. Except that she had an additional belt of knives around her.

And that limp cut my heart. It was accentuating with age.

'Promise me one thing, Urvashi,' I said.

She pulled out her leather strap and began to sharpen her sword. 'I'll see.'

'No, this one time, give me your word before I ask for it.'

She continued to run the sword down the strap. The sound comforted me but her answer was clear. The battle was beyond redemption. Behind us one of the horses began to get fidgety again. I calmed him down with a cluck.

'What is it?' she asked.

As I began to speak, Tunnel 1 rustled and killed the moment. By the time I stood up, Urvashi was already next to the entrance, her sword ready. 'It's not Urvashi, you fool,' I told myself. 'It's you who's getting old.'

I pulled out a knife in my left hand, the spear ready in my right.

Varad stumbled in first, almost tripping over a stone. He turned to look at me, his eyes ashen. Gently he walked to a corner, leaning on the wall of the foundations.

Janaki followed next, carrying Durjan on her shoulder. Her hair was dishevelled. She saw my look, as I rushed to take Durjan from her. 'I'm All right, help him.'

Durjan was in pain. There was an ugly wound on his back running through his body. I brought the torch closer, blowing into it to revive the flames. He was bleeding. This was serious. 'What happened?'

'We have been discovered,' Varad said quietly.

'How?'

'All was fine,' Durjan gasped, as Urvashi began applying herbs from her small emergency pack, 'until we entered the tunnel. They were hiding. We fought. I killed them all. Except one, Varad…'

'Before I could do anything, he had cut through Durjan from behind,' Varad said slowly. 'When he turned to kill me, an arrow flew past. Janaki reached us just in time.'

'I went out of the tunnel and checked. The place was empty, there were no more soldiers,' Janaki said. 'But I don't like the feeling. If they could send six soldiers to this tunnel, it means they know about us. Maybe there are more.'

'Most of them would be within the palace gates, drinking. Besides, they don't expect us to escape tonight. Tomorrow is their big day,' I was thinking as I spoke. 'But for now, Tunnel 1 is behind us, which means the most dangerous path is clear. If all goes well, we can take this short tunnel. Tunnel 2 in the ashram is secure. That leaves Tunnel 3.'

'But how did this happen?' Varad asked. 'Where did the information slip from? As far as I know, apart from the Pandavs only we know about the tunnels. And,' he said slowly, 'Kedar.'

The pause was laced with an allegation. Urvashi spoke calmly. 'Are you suggesting gurudev...'

'No, no, no...no not at all,' a hint of panic filled Varad's voice. 'But maybe someone in the ashram?'

'Apart from gurudev and me, nobody knows. The opening is in gurudev's personal room that has been guarded by him or me.'

'Then...how?' Varad's voice softened as we heard the marble slab move above us. The Pandavs were coming.

Something was not adding up. And it was too late to fix it. I wanted to hide it in some dark tunnel of my mind, but couldn't. This was something I had to face. Now. No tunnel, however deep, could capture and endanger the future of Aryavart.

The slab shifted and sounds of confusion began to flow down. Through that chaos, I came face to face with an enemy I had no control over.

We had, among us, a traitor.

## Night of fire: twenty-second muhurt

A flood of light attacked me as the slab moved aside. It carried the sounds of men and women burning within the constant crackling and a loud, dull hissing. Yudhishthir's face, tense with anticipation but laced with faith, looked down. 'Surangraj,' he spoke urgently, 'are you ready?'

An icy knife of cold sweat slashed my back.

'Where are Bhim and Arjun?' I asked.

'They've gone to set the house on fire,' Yudhishthir said, his face reflecting light and shadows from the flames outside. He looked worried. 'They should have returned by now.'

'Then...?'

'I think, Bhim wants to kill Purochan. I'm worried, Surangraj.'

As we spoke, Kunti and the twins jumped into the foundations. Urvashi helped Kunti find a corner. The twins, instinctive healers, were next to Durjan, applying some paste they had. The eyes of both Nakul and Sahadev were closed in deep concentration, as if nothing mattered but the health of Durjan. They were healing him with an ethereal technique.

The sounds of soldiers, staff and attendants were loud. Above them all was the neighing. 'The horses!' I said in horror.

'Don't worry, Badri.' Kunti's voice was calm, strange for a woman who had endured so much. Or maybe it was because of that endurance. 'Sahadev and Nakul opened all the stables and cowsheds. They will not burn. The entire focus of the fire is within.'

'Yes, queen.' I looked at her with relief. Like Janaki and Urvashi, Kunti too had given up the angvastr and wore a firm bodice. All of us were dressed to run—our dhotis tightly tied around our loins, above the knees. We were ready.

I turned to Yudhishthir. 'Come down, prince. I'll go and check.' Behind him, the flames became more intense. I tied two layers of my veil around my head.

'I think it would be better if you stayed with mother,' he said.

'No, prince.' I was firm. Before entering the tunnels, gurudev had strengthened my concentration. I was in the warrior zone, my being firmly stable in my solar plexus. Yudhishthir was still dithering and a little uncomfortable climbing down from his swinging perch from heart to head. He has a long way to go. 'Come down. We can't risk your life.'

He gave me a strange look, as though he was seeing me for the first time. Then, without a word, he jumped down.

I turned to Durjan. He was sitting now. The twins were working their magic. He tried to get up, but winced. 'You stay there, Durjan, I'll take Varad with me,' I said, nodding at the Lakhera leader to join me.

Did I sense some hesitation in him? Or was it just the flames?

I signalled to Yudhishthir. He clasped his hands, allowing me to place my foot there. I braced myself on one foot and with the momentum of my leg as well as the push from Yudhishthir, I was suddenly waist high in the chamber. I grabbed the floor edge and stood. The room was hot.

I looked at the doors and windows. The lak was beginning to melt like thick reddish dew. Anytime now, the flames would embrace it in a love lock.

There was very little time.

Below me, I saw the whites of Varad's eyes. He looked frightened. 'Come.'

He looked around like a trapped animal. Something was wrong. Was he the...before I could complete the thought, a loud sound filled the air. I turned and rushed to the outer gallery beyond Arjun's room.

Pashupati was burning, the Ganga flowing from the lak statue was melting and had turned into three tributaries of flame, lighting up the ground floor. A small wall of fire was building around the main palace. It was getting hotter. I looked up, the ceiling above seemed to be softening. Where was Bhim?

The horses were creating the chaos we needed to keep the attention outside. Beyond the thundering of the horses, I could see dazed men, trying to stand up and help douse the fire. But the huge overdose of Nasiv's wine had dulled them. I wasn't worried about the soldiers at all. My concern was elsewhere.

Bhim and Arjun were nowhere to be seen.

As I looked down impatiently for Varad to join us, I found him engaged with Yudhishthir in a conversation. Suddenly, Urvashi pushed the prince aside and leaped up, trying to grab the edge of the floor.

She missed. I didn't.

My grip on her scarred arm was firm. We looked into each other's eyes. The hunger of our youth filled us. She pulled herself up in one graceful swing. A stray strand of hair brushed her nose. She blew it aside, smiling at me. 'Let's go.'

I looked down. Janaki put her right hand on her heart and spoke with her eyes. 'Don't worry, I'm here.' Further down, I could see Durjan sitting up, folding his hands before the twins. He was reviving. Varad was standing next to Yudhishthir, his head hanging.

A log covered in flames thundered down with a thud at the front gate beyond the window of Yudhishthir's room. As it fell, it broke into fragments, spreading its rage in every direction like a fountain of burning embers. 'Come on, Badri, we have very little time,' Urvashi was at the door.

I joined her. 'The stairs,' I pointed to Urvashi as we reached the outer chamber, watching the flames lick the walls outside. The outer rooms were already in flames. We rushed towards the stairs, passing through the burning ante-room.

The corner of my eyes caught movement. Damyanti. There were three burning bodies there. One was still moving, but so drowned in wine that he was unable to get up, or even call for help. He just looked at us, his eyes pleading, as he pointed towards his mother. Urvashi paused to help. I held her hand. Her eyes were filled with pain. We turned to the stairs. Neither of us looked back.

It's one thing to be a party to cold-blooded murder. It's quite another to see it with your own eyes.

We were running. The flames were now larger than ever, blinding me. Two more turns of the veil. As I saw Urvashi leap on the stairs, I tripped. There were two completely charred bodies next to each other. I looked up. Two more bodies had barely dragged themselves to the door but could not open it. I looked closely. The door was locked from inside.

Forgive us, Damyanti...forgive me. Little did I know that this murder, this organized slaughter of a woman and her five sons would haunt me till the end of my years. It brought me face-to-face with a part of myself I didn't know existed. I sensed a tunnel lying dormant within my being.

Looking up the stairs, I saw Urvashi, her body glistening with sweat, taking three steps at a time. In a moment she was gone. The fire was coming closer. It was getting difficult to breathe.

When I reached the first floor, I saw Urvashi dragging Arjun down with her. He was a great warrior, strong. But right now, he lacked the concentration needed. Urvashi was clearly the more poised. He was crying.

'Stop those tears, Arjun,' Urvashi shouted above the crackling. 'Kunti is waiting. Your brothers are waiting. Badri will take care of Bhim,' she pushed him down the stairs with superhuman force. 'Now go!' She glanced at me and nodded me forward, following Arjun below. 'Bhim...,' his voice was muffled in the creaking of the palace and the hissing of fire.

Above me, the staircase began to crumble in thick streams. This palace was melting faster than any candle I had known. We had underestimated the materials.

I rushed ahead, stood at the entrance of a door and looked inside. Purochan stood there to his full height. He was a born warrior.

He bent down and picked up a body, Bhim's, and threw it across the room. Bhim fell against a burning wall. He singed but got to his feet, his dhoti carrying a trail of fire. His face was fierce, his eyes bloodshot, his mouth open in a roar that filled the room.

Purochan shook his head. The wine was strong and he had drunk much. He probably didn't expect us to attack a night in advance. He looked for his sword. There it was, hanging on the wall. He tottered towards it. Before he could get his hand on it, I kicked it away. He glared at me like a lion whose prey had been taken away by a jackal.

He swung his arm and hit me squarely on my chest. I staggered across the room, stopping only when I banged against a burning window. His shadow loomed over me. He caught me by my neck and pulled me on my feet, choking me. My kicks were like twigs on a tree. The power of his iron arms felt as if two huge maces had grabbed me. It was getting difficult to breathe.

Suddenly, I saw Bhim's face above Purochan's. He had jumped on him from behind.

Purochan's neck pulled back. His grip on mine loosened. Slowly, Bhim dragged him behind. He probably had a knee on Purochan's back. Bhim could have done that. They fell, shaking the entire floor. Some loose flakes of lak rose up. The flames covered them and the floor was on fire now, burning with passion.

'Bhim!' I shouted, 'leave him, let's go! The floor will fall!'

Purochan heard me and bent forward with a grunt that muted the burning sounds, throwing Bhim over his head through the air. As he fell near the burning door, Bhim rolled over on his feet. He began to move towards Purochan but tripped. He looked down. His foot was trapped in the melting lak. He pulled his hands out of the lak, grabbed a metal stool and dragged himself up.

Purochan waited, squeezing his eyes shut and opening them again. He had drunk too much. Before I could look at Bhim, he launched himself on Purochan, kicking him with both feet. Purochan fell, tried to roll but banged against his burning bed. The lak on the bed broke loose and stuck to Purochan's back. When he stood up, shaking, his back was a wall of fire. In his eyes, I saw the recognition of death.

Puzzled, he looked around the room, as if gauging where he had gone wrong. Through the window, he looked out at the mountains, his eyes now softer. He was in a trance.

Bhim was roaring. He looked around like a madman, his arms bent, his face contorted. His eyes settled on a burning log from the fallen staircase. The giant picked it up and turned. Purochan shifted his eyes from the mountain outside to the one in front of him, bracing himself. Bhim swung the log with all his might.

Purochan caught the burning log and fell back on the floor now on fire, pulling the log and Bhim with him. The floor gave away and they crashed through it on the ground floor, next to the inner chamber below. A fountain of burning lak rose as high as the floor above.

I looked down through the broken floor and saw two giants, Purochan in flames and Bhim staggering. Next to them stood Urvashi and Arjun, their bows drawn, but afraid to let their arrows loose.

I rushed to the stairs. As I turned, the entire staircase collapsed before me, taking a chunk of the balcony with it. The sound overpowered that of the flames.

Returning to the room, I looked down through the large breach in the floor. Purochan had ensured that Bhim's back was to Urvashi and Arjun. Still burning, Purochan roared and pounded Bhim, one powerful blow after another. Bhim wouldn't be able to take that punishment for too long.

No time to think. I jumped down, landing on Purochan's shoulder, kicking him with all my might.

My legs felt as though they had hit an iron pillar. Purochan shifted a step or two but nothing more.

But Bhim got a few moments of respite. Purochan gave me a contemptuous look of insignificance and turned back to Bhim, who was reeling now.

Before anyone could blink, he grabbed Bhim in a bearhug, tightening it. Bhim began to pound his face in panic. Purochan just buried his face in Bhim's chest. The blows bounced off his massive head. Bhim was losing strength. I saw his eyes roll upwards, his body loosen a bit. Anytime now, he would be gone.

'Get him, Arjun!' I shouted above the crackling flames.

Purochan heard me and looked up.

As Arjun jumped into the fire surrounding them, Purochan simply took two steps forward and kicked him on his chest. Arjun lost his balance, tottered over forcefully and tumbled through the trapdoor into the foundations below, falling on Yudhishthir who caught him and softened the drop.

I glanced down and saw Kunti's terror-struck eyes.

Behind them, was a wall of calm, where the twins were fighting for Durjan's life on another plane, almost in another space, another time.

Bhim was losing consciousness. His flailing arms were weakening. This couldn't be happening. Everything was going wrong. Bhim's head fell on the side.

Suddenly, Purochan flung Bhim away, who fell like a sack of wheat. Purochan rushed ahead, his eyes like a wounded tiger's, his mouth open in a roar that was louder than the fire and shook the palace.

It was a frightening sound that was suddenly cut abrupt as Purochan's attention shifted.

A boy, Damyanti's youngest, had dragged himself into the room, pleading for help, crying. Instantly, Purochan's face softened.

His attention diverted for the briefest of moments and the inner beast in him began to disappear. I almost saw him rise towards the compassionate part of his being.

Purochan looked at Urvashi and me. 'Let me save this child,' he said tenderly, his back still on fire weakening him as it burnt deeper. 'I promise to return.'

'That's not possible, Purochan,' I said, my knives out. Urvashi drew her bow, ready to unleash death.

His eyes filled with surprise. 'You won't let me save a child? What sort of Kshatriyas are you?'

From the corner of my eyes, I saw Urvashi's hands pause, they were shaking. The fire below us was beginning to hurt my feet. I was flitting from foot to foot, holding my heavy knife but unable to throw it.

It was a bizarre sight, a man holding a half-dead boy in his arms, his back burning, his hair dishevelled, his focus on the boy, completely unaware of the fire or the way to escape.

'Not very different from you, Purochan,' Bhim charged into his thighs, throwing him against the wall. The boy fell from his arms and tumbled down on the burning floor.

'Wait, Bhim!' Purochan shouted, barely noticing the fall, 'this boy has done you no harm. He is not part of our fight. Let me save him. I promise to return in a moment,' he was pleading. 'You can kill me then.'

'No, Purochan!' Bhim was roaring. 'You die now.'

Bhim kicked a burning beam that held the palace. It cracked, falling down with a muffled thud. The ceiling above shook dangerously. His hands burning, Bhim picked it up, lashed it across the room to hit Purochan's face. Bits of lak scattered, like fireflies dancing on the giant's body.

His one eye destroyed, Purochan looked at the boy, writhing in pain, trapped in the melted lak, unable to move. Bhim raised the beam. Purochan rushed to cover the boy with his body. The beam fell and broke on Purochan's head.

For long moments, Purochan lay where he was. Then he raised his head and looked at the boy. He was still. Purochan shook him. No movement. He was dead.

Then Purochan turned over. Blood flowed out from his mouth. He coughed.

His face was calm.

Grief. Out of nowhere, deep grief gripped me. I saw it choke Bhim and Urvashi too.

The end of any warrior, even your greatest adversary, is a moment of anguish. You kill because you have to, you need to. You kill because it's your dharm. You kill because you're born to do it.

But after you kill, something holds you from within. Perhaps it is Yam, the god of death. It squeezes you somewhere deep. You celebrate your victory but more than the celebration, you mourn the loss.

One of Kuru's greatest warriors now lay burning, bleeding...dying. A few more years and Purochan could have been one of Aryavart's foremost warriors. He had the potential to become a shoulder of Hastinapur. Such men are not born easily. They take their time to come.

Now he stood a few moments away from his last steps. Bhim was catching his breath. It was difficult to do that now. The smoke was thick. We were coughing.

Purochan's head was like Pashupati's linga symbol. Instead of milk, we had given an offering of blood. He lay on his back, one eye crushed, the other barely blinking. Small flames, smothered on his back, now danced around his chest. He didn't seem to notice. With great effort, he raised his arm and called us.

The floor was still dry, though flames from Purochan's body were beginning to get erratic. Bhim and I went towards him. As I knelt and held his hand, my eyes were filled with tears. Between the terrible sounds of the burning palace, behind us, we could hear Urvashi sobbing loudly.

'You fought well, Bhim,' his voice was clear, strangely effortless. He paused to cough. 'Please ask Prince Yudhishthir to forgive me. I was only doing what I felt was my duty, my dharm. Tell him, at another time, in another age, Purochan would have died for him. But now, I had to think about my Varanavat,' his good eye looked in the distance with longing. 'Varanavat...'

'Bhim!' Yudhidhthir's voice came from the foundations. 'Bhim, what's going on?'

Urvashi looked down and silenced him with a signal.

Bhim's anger was subsiding, his breath getting even. The demon of hate was leaving him, the Kshatriya was taking over. He suppressed a cough.

'You are the greatest warrior I've fought, Purochan,' Bhim's voice shook with an emotion that I didn't expect him to have. 'And you know as well as I do that if it was a fair fight, if you hadn't drunk the wine, if you hadn't been so confident, if we hadn't hit you suddenly, you would have crushed me.'

'No, Bhim,' Purochan smiled. Blood hung from his mouth, joining the lak now emerging from the floor below in a dribble of red. He winced in pain. 'It wasn't the wine...or the surprise.'

We looked at him with an intense curiosity.

Purochan coughed, scattering the blood on his chest. 'Victory, warrior Bhim, goes where truth stands,' he said with great effort. 'It is good that I lost...it is right that I die. I...I didn't know Yudhishthir. I wish I did. Only he is fit to be the king of Kuru.'

Purochan took a few deep breaths, accumulating a last burst of energy. 'Even if I had killed all of you,' his voice was strained, 'my life would have been miserable. I wouldn't have been able to sleep even one night. In my success lay my defeat. And now, in my defeat, I see success—grander, higher, vaster success. Death is my redemption, Bhim,' he paused to turn his face down and feebly spit out the blood that had accumulated there. It merged into the red, lak floor. He turned back to Bhim. 'I am grateful to you.'

A tear spilled from Bhim's eye and evaporated even before hitting the melting floor. He held Purochan's hand firmly.

'Be safe, Bhim' Purochan said. 'Be safe all...all of you.' For a long time we only heard the crackle of flames.

I could sense air entering the palace from the foundations below, as the fire above gulped it down, drawing it completely to burn. It was a steady flow.

'Come Bhim,' it was Arjun.

'Wait,' Urvashi said firmly, wiping her eyes.

Death was hovering but Purochan had asked Yam to wait. And the god of death stretched his last few moments. His eye now moved slowly towards the charred body of the boy next to him. With great effort, he tenderly put his large hand on the boy's head, covering it completely with love, as if protecting him from the fires. He turned to Bhim, 'Why didn't you allow me to save this innocent boy...he had nothing...nothing...to do with...our fight...'

Bhim and I looked at each other, our eyes heavy with tears, partly from the smoke and partly from the deed. When we turned, Purochan was gone. He had a peaceful smile on his face.

### Night of fire: twenty-fourth muhurt

'Ideally, we will face nothing,' I addressed everyone in the foundations— the Pandavs, Janaki, Urvashi, Durjan and Varad. 'Most soldiers did not expect us to escape. They didn't even expect the fire. So, right now their attention would be on the palace. Our aim is to run across Tunnel 3, all the way to the forests beyond. From there, Araak will take over.'

I turned to the Pandavs, the flames above moving across their faces. 'Follow Araak and Janaki to the northern bend of the Ganga. There, a boat will carry you across into the darker forests.'

Yudhishthir nodded.

Suddenly, there was a sound. Naked swords clanged against the stray rocks. A group of soldiers was coming in from Tunnel 1. The fire above was pulling all the air from every possible source. Right now, wind from all the three tunnels was gathering strength. From Tunnel 1 it carried the sounds of swords.

I turned to Durjan and Janaki. 'I thought you had cleared them all?' Durjan began to speak but I turned away, there was no time.

'Arjun!' I shouted, 'pull out your bow, kill them all. Not a single soldier must remain alive.' Arjun flashed a smile of relief, pulling out three arrows out of his quiver and moving towards the mouth of Tunnel 1.

'Be careful, Arjun.' It was Bhim. 'I want you fighting next to me.' The love between the two warrior brothers was palpable every moment. Arjun smiled.

'Urvashi,' I looked at her, standing next to Kunti like a disciplined solider. 'You guard Arjun, do what he says.' The two archers looked at each other across the darkness with the satisfaction of finally being able to do what they did best—kill. They also had a look of anticipation, the pride among their kind...who was better?

As I saw them enter the darkness that was Tunnel 1, for the thousandth time I longed to be trained in archery.

I turned to Bhim. 'Take Kunti and the twins with you to Tunnel 3. Let them ride those tall horses, but you lead on foot.' Bhim, wet from the sweat and blood after his fight with Purochan and still getting his breath back, nodded. His face was swollen from the beating.

'Yudhishthir, ride Kadak.' The mule snorted with anticipation on hearing his name and looked at the approaching prince with a puzzled look. He looked at me for clarification. But I had no time.

'Janaki, guard their backs,' I said walking over to Kadak and allowing him to nuzzle against me as I stroked him. 'And once you reach the exit, go forward and hand them over to Araak.'

Satisfied, I looked at the two parties, Arjun and Urvashi towards Tunnel 1, the others in the opening of Tunnel 3.

'Durjan, can you fight?' I asked the mercenary.

'Yes,' he said, convincingly, his slowly-swinging sword gleaming with hope. What magic did the twins do? I wondered. Durjan walked towards me, his swagger back, ready.

'Take Prince Yudhishthir and follow Bhim into Tunnel 3.'

Everything was ready. Everyone knew what was to be done.

Except one.

'Durjan,' I stopped him on his way to Tunnel 3. 'There is one thing you need to do before you enter that tunnel.'

He turned back, expressionless, and raised his head.

I turned to look at the traitor sitting in the corner. Then I nodded towards Varad. 'Kill him.'

'What?' Durjan said, visibly surprised. The two of them had become close friends during the past few days.

'Surangraj...why?' Yudhishthir asked. 'Why...?'

'What is wrong with you, Badri?' Varad was on his feet, his sword out, for the first time since I met him. He was every inch the warrior I had suspected him to be.

But he had given up these skills to become one who fed on others' talents. His sword carried no conviction. He could have been carrying a toy.

'There was no way anyone could have known about our tunnels,' I said to Yudhishthir. 'Every one of you carries that knowledge in a contract sealed by death.'

'And how is it different for me?'

How was it different? I didn't know. I had taken a gamble, based on little but an inner instinct. 'You tell us, Varad,' I tried to buy time. 'Tell us where you went in the nights. Who you met in the forests?'

Varad's voice began to shake. 'I don't know what you are talking about.'

'Is that so?' I looked at him through my veil. 'For a long time I didn't believe it.'

'So, what's the reason for the change?' a hint of sarcasm laced by fear entered his voice.

'You talk too much when you drink, Varad.' That was another gamble. It worked. His eyes widened. I pushed further. 'And when you're asleep, with a woman around you.'

'Rasilee,' Varad hissed.

Now, I knew I had him. I sent a prayer of gratitude to the gods above. Now, there was no stopping from revealing his truth.

'Most of what you did can be understood,' I said. 'Except the part when you're cheating on your own tribe, killing them systematically, offering them as helpless fodder to Purochan's cannibals.'

Bhim's face was changing. The animal he had left above with Purochan was coming back. He took two steps towards Varad.

'Bhim, you wait. This is not for you...'

I was too late. Bhim hulked his way towards Varad. Varad pushed his sword towards Bhim. 'He is lying, Bhim,' his shrieked. 'Let me explain...'

'You chose wrong, Varad,' I said firmly. 'You thought Purochan would let you go. You thought offering one or two people every now and then would satisfy the cannibals. You thought nobody would notice that Lakheras were leaving, but with your permission—there was no other way for them to leave. You allowed your brothers to be eaten alive so you could prosper.'

'That's not true. These small sacrifices were needed so that a larger number of people in my tribe could escape alive.'

'You thought by sacrificing a few of your brothers, you would win the confidence of Purochan.'

'No, I had only wanted to help my people escape. He had promised.'

'You thought by helping to kill the Pandavs, you would win yourself the favours that only adharm offers.'

'No,' his voice rose. 'By offering some, I traded for the lives of a larger number. I did what statecraft had taught me—the death of a few for the benefit of the many is right,' he looked down. 'But...but they just kept asking.'

That godforsaken statecraft, again. 'And you kept offering! You fool, it would have been better if you had died fighting. You thought you would return to your tribe as a hero. You assumed the Pandavs would be killed.'

In the silence of that dramatic pause, we heard the raging fires above. The lak from the palace was now dripping into the foundations, small fires were lighting up the darkness here.

Varad was muttering something that made no sense to anyone. He was trembling.

'You didn't realize that couldn't happen as long as dharm rules Aryavart and protects the righteous.'

'This is not how it happened!' Varad shouted, raising the sword higher, as he saw Bhim close in. His sword arm shaking, Varad took a step back. 'Stop...wait, let me explain.'

'There is nothing to explain,' Bhim bellowed and in the brief moment when Varad's eyes closed with fear, he kicked the Lakhera on his chest. We heard a bone break with a crunch.

As Varad hit the wall behind, with a thud louder than the fire above, his sword bounced against the wall and fell with a ring. Varad bounced right back at Bhim's feet. Bhim picked him up, and gave him a slap that resounded in the tunnels. A blow followed on his midriff that silenced Varad.

Without waiting, Bhim lifted him bodily, bundled him into a large ball, his knees meeting his head, held him over his head and with a loud grunt threw him into the reddish-yellow burning flames above.

Varad's scream tore at our hearts. He tried to claw back. We saw his fingers trying to pull back into the foundations from the edge of the opening. But the melting lak had gripped him. His screams continued in the foundations for a long time. Then gradually, they could be heard in spasms. His head was on fire as he looked down, trying to escape from the palace that he had helped build.

The last we heard from Varad was a moan. A Lakhera who had built the house of lak felt its force and possibly carried it with him to the realms beyond.

Wind from the three tunnels was racing in, as the fire above burnt violently, pulling out every breath of air towards it.

I turned to Bhim. 'Let's go.'

### Night of fire: twenty-fifth muhurt

I watched the group go through Tunnel 3. Between Bhim, Janaki and Durjan they were safe. Besides, the twins and Yudhishthir were warriors too. Not as good as their two brothers, but warriors still. They had been taught by Dronacharya. In any case, we were not too far.

Turning to Tunnel 1, I followed Arjun and Urvashi. This was the shortest tunnel and for one where I had expected a major fight, it was strangely silent. The snakes and the rats and the entire ecosystem two dhanush below the ground were quiet, as though awaiting the great war in their realms, a war that could crush them if they stepped out.

'Urvashi, retreat,' Arjun's voice broke the sacred silence.

'I can't leave you, prince,' she sounded weak.

I ran forward, all my five spears raring to go. In the darkness, Urvashi couldn't see me but to me this was clear as their daylight.

'Step aside!' I shouted, checking the belt around my waist. My knives were all there, ready to fly.

A group of soldiers was walking towards Arjun. Urvashi was behind him, leaning against the wall of the tunnel. She was hurt.

The twang of Arjun's bow carried death every time it rang. But before him the soldiers were protected by their shields.

My first spear flew between Arjun and Urvashi, bored through the lead soldier's shield. I heard two loud grunts. Possibly, the spear had passed through the first soldier into the one behind. Their steps faltered.

A small volley of arrows, rained past us harmlessly. The tunnel was short but twisted. The arrows hit the walls. Suddenly, Urvashi rushed to embrace me. Then I felt her stiffen. I looked down. Three arrows had buried themselves in her back.

I put her on the side. 'Wait for me, Urvashi,' my voice shook to the death-fear lurking within. 'Just a few moments...'

'Arjun, are you fine?' I reached next to him.

'Yes, but my arrows are not going through.'

'It's their shields. Wait for me to break through, then let your arrows fly.'

Two more spears flew through, boring through shields and soldiers. The shields fell with loud clangs on the stray stones that I had uncovered.

There was an opening, as five wasted bodies lay still. The soldiers behind, as I had expected, were not carrying shields, only swords and maces. I laughed at the crude tactic. To send your men with maces in a tunnel was as stupid as you could get. But that meant they had exhausted the swordsmen.

'Now, Arjun, now!' I had made the opening.

Six twangs sang their music next to me, ending in songs of agony. This was truly the greatest archer I had seen. He could shoot in the dark with a precision that many in light couldn't.

We were half-way into the tunnel. Urvashi lay on the side, her arm trying to reach one of the arrows buried in her back.

I rushed to her. 'What happened?' My arm around her waist felt the blood.

'Nothing, it's just a few scratches.'

The wounds were not scratches. But before I could say anything, she had limped ahead, her jaw clenched in pain which she wanted nobody to see.

'Urvashi, wait!' I shouted, running to her. 'Go back.'

She looked at me strangely and turned away as soon as a dribble of blood began to fall from her mouth. This was serious. An internal injury.

Before us, a shadow got up with a raised sword. Something swished. It was Arjun's arrow. The arm fell, the man shrieked in pain. I rushed ahead and kicked him in the chest. Without my knowing, my spear bored him into silence.

I looked ahead. Exit into the Ganga was just a few steps ahead. I walked through the debris of bodies, slipping on blood and mud, but not falling. I counted eighteen bodies. I stood at the exit. The roar of the Ganga was muffled by the flames behind. I stepped out and turned to see the palace. It was a mountain of fire. But this was not the time to ponder over death. It was time to escape.

Returning to the tunnel, I walked to where Arjun and Urvashi were waiting, a third of a distance from our base at the foundations.

'Arjun, go and join your brothers and Kunti in Tunnel 3.'

'I can't leave her. She saved my life.'

'Sure she did. But we want to keep it that way. You need to stay alive. Go join your brothers in Tunnel 3. I will see you beyond the Ganga.'

I pulled the scaffolding and Tunnel 1 began to collapse before me. A rumbling that silenced the fire behind, a flurry of earth and rock and in a few long moments, the tunnel had caved in before us, burying the soldiers. The tunnel destroyed, we were safe.

Suddenly, the fire in the palace began to tug at the air. I felt the strong pull. Now that the tunnel was closed, the fire was pulling air from where we stood.

I turned to Urvashi. 'Can you walk through Tunnel 2 to the ashram? You are in no position to fight.'

She smiled. 'Badri,' she paused to let the tone sink in. 'It is time.'
Time? 'For what?'

'It is my time, Badri,' she paused to gather strength.

The shock hit me like a mace but this was a private grief. I turned to Arjun. 'Prince, you'll have to go alone.'

He didn't move. 'And you?'

'Go now,' I shouted above my grief.

'No, I can't leave you. Let's go to Tunnel 2 and leave her at the ashram.'

'No,' Urvashi's voice cut through the shrill wind blowing. 'You need to go now, Arjun. Otherwise, all our work would be a waste.'

Arjun looked at me deeply. 'Let's go.'

Panicking, Urvashi turned to me. 'Gurudev told me, Badri. And I am ready.'

Between the tears that flowed, I shouted above the wind and the Ganga and the fire. But there was no sound. A dam of helplessness broke and I didn't know what to do, where to dump my stranded pain. I pulled out two arrows, one on her left near her lung, the other below that. The third was lodged in a bone.

'Take a deep breath Urvashi, this could hurt.'

She closed her eyes. I slashed the arrow, letting the head remain inside.

'I'm going to put you on my shoulder,' I told her 'brace yourself.'

'Why don't you listen, Badri?' she pulled me towards her.

I felt Urvashi's hands around my head as she pulled me towards her bosom. I hugged her tightly, not wanting to let her go, helpless against destiny. I heard myself roar with pain. Years of pain, control, poise broke down and I didn't know what to do, how to express it.

'No!' I screamed. 'No, no, no!' I was sobbing loudly. 'You can't go, Urvashi. I will change it.'

We had to return to the foundations, enter Tunnel 2. Then carry her to the ashram. All this while, danger gnawed at us from various points in the tunnels. Arjun was refusing to leave. There was only one thing to do.

'Arjun, run to the ashram, and bring gurudev halfway. Tell him to get his medicines and mantr. I'll get Urvashi.'

Arjun disappeared in a moment.

'What's all this drama, Badri?' she smiled at me, a mocking look in her eyes. There was reddish froth around her mouth. The lungs were punctured. She kept the pain under control.

'As long as you are alive, you will remain alive. I'm going to lift you. It will hurt,' I looked into her eyes. 'Ready?'

She nodded.

In one, clean movement, I lifted her. She seemed heavier. Maybe I was older.

I began to run softly, ensuring that I landed on my toes, not heels to keep the jerks in check. Urvashi needed no further jolts. The run was slow. The pull of the wind was in my favour and I made the best of it, riding the momentum of the suction. This was a short tunnel, so it should get over quickly.

My breath was getting heavy with the burden of Urvashi and the lack of air.

She was still.

A few steps more.

I reached the foundations and gently put her on the ground, at a part where the horses had stood and made the earth softer. I was panting, trying to squeeze out air from the recesses of the tunnels, fighting the fire in the palace.

The flame above was raging. The lak was dripping down in a trickle, some of it carrying sparks that died by the time they touched the ground. Almost like a trail of stars. It was a dangerous sight.

And yet, so beautiful.

Any time now, they would catch fire. And if the ground above fell, that fire would fill the tunnel for many dhanush. I had designed it that way. If we entered Tunnel 2 towards the ashram, we might not be able to return. We would have to go around the ashram from the outside and meet the Pandavs at the opening of Tunnel 3 in the forest. Would we be too late?

No time to think. I gathered my energies.

'Living in palaces, you've forgotten the lessons gurudev gave us,' Urvashi spoke gently. 'We are all transition beings. In the cycle of evolution, the next step for this body,' she put her hand on her chest, 'has arrived. Let me go in peace.'

Her head suddenly fell behind.

'Wait, Urvashi, wait just a few moments.'

I picked her up again with a grunt. Entering Tunnel 2, my head was reeling, my feet shaky.

'Let me go, Badri,' she said. 'Save the Pandavs.'

I held on tightly, the blood from her back was flowing down her thighs, making it hard to hold on. Below me, the flattened soil was an advantage. But now, the wind was against me—the fire was pulling it. My breath was quick, my feet slow.

I could see light in the distance. It expanded like dawn and filled the tunnel. Two torches, one each with Arjun and Kedar.

'Badri, what have you two been upto?' Kedar's voice boomed, filling the tunnel and bringing light into the rapidly-increasing darkness within me. I put Urvashi on the ground, waiting for them.

I held her, my hand slipping from the sweat and blood. I sat down, Urvashi's head in my laps. I was sobbing, my shoulders shaking with new, unexpected pain. 'Why didn't you tell me, Urvashi? I would have kept you out of this.'

'Leaving me to die a mediocre death by old age?' She smiled.

Urvashi raised her arm and caressed my face. 'You should shave, Badri.'

We burst out laughing. That one line captured our entire past and in a handful of moments we relived the decades behind us. The academy, the wedding that was broken when Panchal attacked Hastinapur, the battles we fought, the lovemaking we enjoyed, the children we raised...

She began to laugh, pausing only to cough blood. I held her close, but joined the laughter. Then she was silent. I brought her close and kissed her lips.

Then, Kedar and Arjun reached us. 'Save her, gurudev!' I begged him. Kedar looked at me.

'But it is her time, Badri,' he said gently.

'No, hold her...hold her for some time.' She was losing consciousness.

'We will breach the cycle,' he said compassionately.

'To hell with the cycle!' I heard myself shout. 'Save her! We have to break the previous cycle. She has died too many times this way. Lifetime after painful lifetime, she has reached here, only to return to the cycle. She was Asmi the last time!'

'I know, Badri,' Kedar's voice didn't change. 'But she has chosen this,' he paused to look up in the darkness as the fire behind us tugged at his angvastr. 'She chose it up there, in the moment when her soul decided to be reborn. At a time when she could have chosen differently. It is her destiny. She has decided not to move forward.'

The cracking filled the vacuum of our thoughts.

'She is waiting, Badri.'

'For what, for whom, for...'

'You.'

He said that simply.

Behind us, a thick stream of lak poured into the foundations, burning all the way and filling it with smoke.

'Me?' I was confused.

'Yes, you.' he said, 'Unless you decide to walk with her, she won't go further.'

I was confused and looked at him, pleading.

'Unless Jambu walks with her, Asmi can't go further. She just won't. You are bound together in a bond that was sealed up there,' he pointed to the skies. 'You have to travel together. She needs to evolve but is holding back her own evolution for you. You need to rise up before both of you can walk further. Until then, she'll wait. She will continue to die.'

'What am I supposed to do?'

'Live. You have to shed the skin that you love so much, you need to reject the constant repeat of the karmic cycle. You were Jambu the last time. Before that you were Dridheyu, Sampati, Yat, Ahas...you were all of them. Urvashi travelled with you through journeys across births.'

'But what do I need to do?'

'For her to live, you have to stay alive, you have to want to stay alive. You need to give up on the love for martyrdom you're so addicted to.'

'My martyrdom, sacrifice to the nation, to the king is...is an... addiction?'

'Yes, you're so deeply wedded to the idea,' Kedar smiled with love, 'that you've ignored your soulmate, your wife or should we say wives across time. It is time for you to look within, Badri. But it's not me, not Urvashi, not the king...nobody but you have to decide that. Evolution is waiting for you and you are fighting a losing battle. You have to want to cross this threshold, this hurdle that you have consistently avoided.'

I knew what he was saying. 'What hurdle is this?' I still asked to hear it from him.

'The hurdle that stops you from moving beyond serving the sword, living by killing, dying by it. That which prevents you from moving to the higher realms of knowledge, realms that are now ready to absorb you. Realms of the rishis. They are waiting for you, Badri.'

The fire-laced lak continued to drip into the tunnel, stretching long before falling in the foundations to congregate, hungrily devouring air. Arjun shifted as it fell, throwing smoke around us.

Arjun! In all this, I had forgotten about him.

Pandavs...Kuru...Hastinapur...

Their safety...I had to go.

'Gurudev, hold on to her,' I felt my voice change. 'I'm ready to cross the threshold. But I need to finish this last assignment. After that, I'm yours,' I looked at Urvashi. 'And hers. We will rise together.'

Kedar smiled as he opened his bundle of medicines, I took one long look at her.

She smiled weakly, rising to speak. 'Don't...' she winced at the effort, 'don't do it for...me. Do it because...you,' she stressed the word, '...you feel it.'

I held her hand tightly and looked deep into her eyes. 'I do,' I said, feeling the vacuum pull me up.

In the battle within, my consciousness was being pulled up towards the heart from my solar plexus. 'But this one thing I have to finish. I'll be back.' I let go of her hand, slowly placing it on the ground to her side so that the embedded arrow didn't hurt, and with a glance handed her over to Kedar.

'I will seal the tunnel from there,' I said pointing towards the foundations. 'But the ventilation is clean in this tunnel. You can stay here.' Kedar nodded.

As we walked back, smoke was beginning to gather in the area. Arjun coughed loudly. I turned to look back. Kedar was bent over Urvashi, applying his magical herbs.

Then, like the notes of the veena, Urvashi turned to look at me, on her face a glow of peace, an ethereal compassion flying through the darkness and enveloping me. I enjoyed the feeling for a fleeting moment. Then, I pulled down Tunnel 2 into a crashing heap of rubble.

## Night of fire: twenty-sixth muhurt

Freedom was a few steps away.

With Tunnels 1 and 2 closed, the fire behind was pulling the wind violently from Tunnel 3, the only one left—Janaki had pulled down the escape Tunnel 4. Arjun had reached the opening and lay on the ground, gasping for breath, enjoying the open space. The boy was not used to living in darkness. The twins were upon him, refreshing him with their celestial force, before he could even sit.

The clearing was as I had visualized it. There was just enough space for all of us to sit and rest within a circle of horses and mules.

I picked up some long dry grass, walked up to Kadak and rubbed him down. As he nuzzled me towards Rani, Vayu walked up. I rubbed them down too.

From under the tree behind the horses, Durjan glanced at me silently. He was slightly bent to the right because of the wound there. I began to walk towards him. He raised his hand, told me to not come closer and pointed towards the Pandavs. I understood.

The Pandavs were waiting, their grim faces reflecting the fire in the distance. I turned to look at The Blessed Home, where its creators, Purochan and Varad, lay. The flames were as high as the distant mountains.

Pashupati had melted, burning the Ganga of lak with him. The area around the palace was a rising ball of yellow. Screams of victims filled the air, sometimes rising above the thunderous sound of the fire. The scene was straight out of a painting, unbelievable, fantastic.

Varanavat was awake, weeping for the Pandavs, grieving for Purochan.

The Pandavs...my task was not yet over. I threw the hallucinating reverie away.

Bhim was pacing around the entrance. Behind them, Araak held Janaki closely, sitting patiently for orders.

'What took you so long, Arjun?' Yudhishthir asked as Bhim bent down and embraced his brother, stretching out next to him. Kunti followed Bhim, caressing Arjun's hair, his face, holding him. The love was a delight to see.

'Urvashi...' Arjun looked at me.

Over Araak's shoulder, Janaki threw a glance of concern at me.

Yudhishthir turned to me, 'Is she fine, Badri?'

'She is with gurudev,' I said but didn't want to ponder on that thought. I knew she would be safe now.

'Araak,' I turned to the young warrior with whom I suddenly had a strange relationship. We loved the same woman, which in his case was as normal as breathing. For me it created an irrational resentment that the Aryavart morality brought with it. Why can't a woman love more than one man, if a man can explore many?

The balance of dharm was still tilted, in favour of men.

But there was no time for that now. 'Are you ready?'

Araak nodded.

All of us were in a circular huddle, the horses surrounding us for stray arrows.

'Araak and Janaki will lead us to the forest,' I said generally, pointing to the thick, dense trees ahead. 'They will take us to the Ganga,' I turned to Araak for confirmation. He nodded. 'There, a boat will be waiting.'

Araak held Janaki's hand and nodded at me with quiet, strong confidence. For the first time I noticed his eyes. On his young, almost boyish body, they were old. He had seen much in his short life.

'We need someone to take the horses to the ashram from the outer perimeter,' I told Araak.

He whistled. Out of nowhere, three archers emerged from the thicket. He spoke to them in their language. The men began to gather the horses. Araak turned to me.

'You too, Durjan.'

He rose weakly, a question in his eyes.

'Yes, you go with the horses. Gurudev will bring Urvashi to the ashram from Tunnel 2. Be with them and let them know exactly what happened.'

'But I can fight.'

'Go!' my voice was sharp. 'You are weak and there is no more fighting to be done. I'll meet you at the ashram.'

Durjan followed the horses, his head hanging near his chest.

For once, it appeared everything was going according to plan. The Pandavs were out of danger, ahead lay further safety. The fire was behind us. It would burn for days together.

I looked at Yudhishthir. 'Ready?'

He nodded, a smile around his face. 'Yes, but you need to return to Urvashi.'

'I will, prince, I will once my task is over.'

I looked at Janaki and Araak. They nodded.

'Let's go,' I said firmly, but found no conviction in my voice.

The ascent of the consciousness had begun.

I was steady physically, but felt strangly light. It was in that moment that I decided to live and rise. After Kedar's explanation, the being within me had shifted his stance and had taken the next step, towards the heart.

Almost like a rebirth, I could feel the warrior in me lose strength. New love was beginning to fill me up from within. This love looked beyond the delightful curves of a woman, the warm binds of family ties, the innocent laughter of daughters and sons, the unquestioning embrace of a friend, the blind faith of a fellow warrior.

My heart was opening out, towards new light. I was still in the shadows, in the dark, deep tunnels of my own making. But with each tunnel I destroyed, I came closer to this light—gentle yet strong, blinding yet comforting.

As we began to walk, I found worry lurking at the back of my mind. Something was not right. I could almost sense it physically, but couldn't put a finger. But all our dangers were behind us.

The palace fires were burning high and loud. Varanavat was busy there. What could it be?

And yet, it was there, running up and down my spine—the sense of menace. It was almost as if the forest we were entering was filled with it. Something inside was talking to me.

It must be the movement of the being.

I was wrong.

Araak led us into the forest. He took no known trail and I was happy for that. The boy knew what he was doing. We followed him silently.

Behind Araak was Bhim. Kunti followed next with Janaki in tow. Then, the twins, Arjun and Yudhishthir. I guarded the end.

The only sound we heard was that of the burning palace, the victims the fire was claiming as its own.

Less than six dhanush into the forest and it was darker than any tunnel I had ever built.

'Light up,' Araak said, stopping. 'But no flames.'

Janaki lit three torches. She handed one to Araak, then came towards me with the other. The dull light of the embers accentuated the shadows of her sensuality. But it stirred nothing in me. She handed the torch to me and returned. We continued.

Yudhishthir's angvastra got caught in a branch and I bumped into him. We looked at each other silently. He pulled it out and walked on.

'Hold on to each other,' Araak's voice broke through the crickets chirping. I held Yudhishthir's hand and felt the power of the chain.

Cold leaves brushed us, sometimes an extended branch tugged at my dhoti. In the silence, I heard loudly the clashes of the struggle within.

*It's over, Badri.*

*What?*

*Your time here. We need to rise. You need to.*

*But rise where?*

*From the clutches of the earth to the freedom of heavens.*

*Heavens?*

*Yes, heavens.*

*How?*

*By allowing the natural course to flow through you. Realize that you're merely an instrument.*

*Instrument for what?*

*For the ascent of consciousness.*

*Consciousness?*

Silence bound us.

The sound of the fire was behind us, mellow now. Ahead, I could hear the Ganga. Instantly, it brought peace.

*That's right. You're getting it.*

*Getting what?*

*The peace you've been seeking since lifetimes. You're finally allowing it to flow.*

*I can't understand.*

*You don't need to. No...don't let the mind interrupt. Let it go. Let it go. Let it go...*

We reached the river. Reflection of the moon above was in shreds of blue, moving in waves and ripples. The Ganga, powerful and young, stood waiting for us.

Araak move aside, allowing all of us to come. Someone whistled.

From under the overgrowth partly hanging over a tree and partly from a bush at the sandy banks, I could see the silhouette of a small but sturdy boat. A short man, holding a single oar stood straight.

He reached near us, got off and began to pull the boat to the bank. Araak helped him pull it further, then turned to us. He stood still, his intense eyes boring through us—a young body holding an old soul.

'We're ready.'

The Pandavs turned to me. It was too dark to make out the details, but not dark enough to miss their eyes. They were misty. Yudhishthir stepped forward.

'We are deeply grateful, Surangraj,' he said, bowing his head mildly. 'Without you, we would have been there,' he nodded towards the glow of the burning palace behind us over the trees.

'I just did my duty, prince,' I said, my hands folded, 'my dharm. But let's not waste time. You need to leave.'

'Not so fast, Badri,' Bhim grabbed me from behind in a hug that almost broke my ribs. I felt a wet tear fall on my left shoulder. He held on to me like he would never leave. I could feel his affection within me.

'Bhim, you'll crush him,' Arjun warned. He stood in front of me with the twins, waiting. They laughed. Bhim let go.

Then the warm love of Arjun and the twins flowed through me. These two, Nakul and Sahadev, definitely had something magical in their beings. I felt my weariness fading as they ran their fingers on my head, my shoulders. Was it a skill or a gift? I didn't know, and even today I don't care. All I remember is that when they stepped back, I was fresh as just having woken up.

Kunti looked at me and smiled. 'We are in your debt, Badri,' she said, wiping her perspiring forehead. 'We will never forget it.'

'You don't need to, queen,' I was standing straight now. 'It was my dharm and I did it to the best of my ability. I would do it again. And again.'

'I know, Badri. That's why we are born—to do our dharm. That's how kingdoms run. That's how the balance of the earth is maintained. We could have been burnt to death. You could have been somewhere else. But that wasn't to be. This was the tunnel,' she paused, her eyes sparkling, smiling delicately, 'the tunnel,' she stressed the word, 'that all of us had to pass through together.'

We smiled our tiredness away.

'And now that we are out of it, let us pray we never enter it again.'

'We have to go, queen,' Araak's voice carried the urgency of discipline.

I could sense danger around us. But there was nothing. What was going on?

The Pandavs stepped into the boat, now swaying to their weight. Bhim went in first. He turned to me and I felt the force. I folded my hands. The boatman pushed with his oar. The Pandavs stood, their heads slightly bowed. They settled down after some shuffling.

Bhim, always ready for the next challenge, stared beyond the silver streaks of the Ganga. Yudhishthir sat at the end, looking at us, holding the boat's tail for support, next to the boatman.

Beyond, a dolphin screeched its delight.

Slowly the boat floated away. Then it gathered speed. A blanket of solemn silence covered this departure.

We looked on. Then the boat turned around the bend.

My assignment was over. The Pandavs were safe.

A sense of strange peace had descended around us.

But that feeling of danger still lingered.

*Night of fire: twenty-seventh muhurt*

The last prahar of the night was on us. All was quiet. Even the crickets had stopped singing their songs. Barring the occasional flight of an owl, nothing moved. The moon had shifted. The only sound was from beyond the forest, where The Blessed Home stood burning, still gnawing at lives and the wailings of Varanavat citizens.

But above the darkness, beyond the stillness, that feeling of danger lingered.

We sat there, gathering our breath, releasing the accumulated tension from our bodies, loosening the muscles, easing the mind. The sandy banks of the Ganga were soft, inviting. I lay there, enjoying the coolness.

I looked at Araak, now gently braiding Janaki's hair. Their love was strange. Or perhaps mine was.

She smiled at me and a dart of longing embedded itself into me. But nothing moved within me. The moment was gone.

My love lay elsewhere. Waiting for me. It had waited for lifetimes now, calling me gently, softly. No demands, just a silent, deep yearning which I had smothered. Now, I had no option.

Like the Ganga before me, my life as a warrior was flowing away. I had spent many lives fighting, killing. I had died for kingdoms. This strange dharm had brought me to these crossroads. Time after time. That thumb-sized being within had its own mechanisms. It chose new bodies. But the savagery of a Kshatriya was too exciting to give up. To live with kings, to protect the weak and the strong alike was a strange, heady mix. Trust me, nothing can give you that high.

And now, I had to give it all up.

Give up the warrior's path. The thought was so alien that I fought it. Someone deep was holding out a hand.

I turned away. Janaki and Araak were locked in a deep kiss, the gentle breeze caressing their bodies softly. They were true warriors. Janaki sensed me and opened her eyes over his shoulder. Her lips continued to kiss Araak, her eyes mine. I didn't turn away.

Through the distance, we embraced with passion. Her eyes turned misty. A strange dance of beings was in play. Physically, she held Araak. Subtly, she made love to me. Within, she knew I was gone.

I sent her a wave of compassion. She closed her eyes to receive it from within. When she opened them, her smile carried the sadness of a lover's separation as well as the joy of knowing he was going where he belonged, where he ought to be, a signal that all was how it should be.

Then, she shut them tightly, and in a physical frenzy returned to Araak.

I turned back to the river with a deep breath. There, on the banks across, standing firmly, wearing a robe of bright light stood someone, waiting for me. I leaned forward, opened my veil. Even though I could feel it, knew it, the image was unclear. I stood up and walked to the Ganga.

Still fuzzy.

Taking a few steps into the river, I was almost thrown down by a strong force. Its vitality shocked me. It hadn't felt so violent when I entered Varanavat. What had happened?

The light continued to call me. But I was losing my strength. I felt too weak to swim, I was about to return, when something smooth brushed past me.

The dolphin.

I waited for him to return. He did and offered himself. I grabbed him. A few powerful strokes and we were in the middle of the river. My eyes didn't move away from the light across the shore. I nudged the dolphin towards the light. It followed. The light was now closer, glowing more strongly but as unclear as ever.

But it didn't hurt my eyes.

The man's face was hidden in the bright light of his shining robe. He looked familiar. I had seen him many times, and I knew him. Who was he?

A thousand celestial stars followed the movements of his arms as he raised them to call me. Something within me was being pulled towards him by an unconscious force. A force I didn't fight. I couldn't fight. I didn't want to fight. I was tired of fighting.

The cold water was slicing my body. Gliding over the water with the dolphin, my eyes ached from the effort to see the man across the river. We had now crossed the middle of the river. The face was still blurred.

Holding tightly, I put my head underwater to clean my eyes. We were now closer. The dolphin paused, bobbing in the water. I looked up at the glowing man, now less than a dozen dhanush away. As he smiled, I felt something open within me and recognition speared me.

But instead of drawing blood, it pulled something that was lying in a closed tunnel of my being. I felt something travel through me, clearing all the dark crevices lying within, brushing the cobwebs that had gathered over time.

I shut my eyes and opened them again. His face was now clearer. When I finally recognized him, I almost lost my grip.

It was me.

## Night of fire: twenty-eighth muhurt

Janaki's eyes held a question, a demand.

'I know my promises, Janaki. Go on, now. I'll meet you at Rasilee's shack in two days. We may not have to go to Hastinapur. Hastinapur will come to Varanavat and give you justice,' I said.

'What are you talking about, Badri?' Araak looked confused. 'I don't understand these things. You said, you needed our help. We told you we want justice, we want our lands, our rivers, our sacred mountains. You promised to take us to Hastinapur,' he paused, trying to overcome his annoyance. 'Now, what is this?'

'I will do everything I promised,' I began slowly. 'The Pandavs are dead, burnt in Purochan's palace of lak. Barring Dhritarashtr, Duryodhan and few generals, everyone will be here. Most of all, Vidur will be here.'

Araak turned to Janaki. She closed her eyes and smiled at him.

'They will not come alone. Soldiers will accompany them. I will get Vidur to the ashram. You will meet him there. So will Rasilee and her people. Tell her that the Lakheras need not worry anymore. They will get safe passage.'

The sky was developing a purple hue. Ratridevi was leaving, taking the darkness with her. Ushas would be up anytime. I had to leave.

'I will meet you in two days at the ashram. By then, I would know precisely when Vidur would be here. You have nothing to worry about. You don't need to go to Hastinapur,' I repeated gently. 'The kingdom will come to you.'

Janaki squeezed Araak's hand and nodded at him to wait. She walked up to me, the dry smell of blood and sweat lingering. She put her head on my chest and held me closely, her warmth flowing into me. She looked up, her mouth open, inviting.

As I began to look at Araak, she pulled me gently down. She kissed like no woman ever has, almost like leaving a final memory before warriors went to battle, and held it for a long time. I held her back tightly, my hand stroking the scars on it.

She stepped back, her eyes still closed. I opened my arms.

When we parted, she ran her hand round my head. Then, she turned away, wiped a tear, reached out to Araak, gripped his arm with both her hands, and silently walked into the forest.

# Vishnu

The crack of the twig told me that the time to think was long gone. I had to act. Kill or be killed. There was only one recourse—ride my instincts, honed over lifetimes. I fought the new movement within with the perfected old instincts. I felt my body harden, my back straighten.

Still weak, I tried to gather my scattered self. I had to kill Vishnu. It was too risky to leave him and his soldiers alive. But the love in me was flowing too fast, too deep, transforming all my past into a fluid future, where neither weapons nor their wielders existed.

If I didn't kill Vishnu now, I would be wasting another lifetime. Kedar had pushed the realization in me and I could feel the consciousness within. I could not betray my destiny any longer.

For the future ahead, my past had to be erased. I may be weak. Possibly on another plane. Perhaps only death would finally grant me the release I had been seeking. But I didn't want to die now.

I had to face my fears.

'So, what are you doing here?' the confident sarcasm sounded stronger than ever. 'You should have been there,' Vishnu nudged towards the burning flames in the distance.

I kept quiet. Five soldiers materialized behind him. All armed. The first thought that hit me was if he knew about the escape.

'What happened? You lost your voice?' He laughed. 'Now, what will you do, where will you go? The Pandavs are dead.'

He didn't know.

'Allow me to grieve, Vishnu,' I played along. 'We've lost everything. Purochan has won.'

He laughed loudly. 'Purochan?' he sneered. 'That vain warrior, who wanted to change the face of Varanavat? You're talking about him?'

The men behind him laughed.

'He's dead too, Badri.'

'I thought...I thought you worked for him.'

'That's what I thought. That's what all of us thought.'

'You mean...'

'Of course,' he laughed, his sword dangling like death. Like many warriors, Vishnu was a talker. With Purochan around, he could do nothing. Now, he was possibly the next in line. 'Purochan was too focused on the future of Varanavat to watch his back. He died with the Pandavs.'

'You mean, you...'

The soldiers behind him had circled me. I did not have my weapons. There was no escaping.

'No, I wouldn't do that. Nobody needed to do it. He was getting softer. He was losing his core and yielding to that of Yudhishthir's,' Vishnu turned his head and spat, 'that prince's goodness. No, I didn't have to do anything. Purochan killed himself.'

'Allow us to grieve, Vishnu. It is a big loss to Aryavart.'

'Yes, of course,' he said and laughed. 'But why waste the tears here?' His chin came up slowly. 'Why not join them?'

I looked around. The soldiers were enjoying themselves.

'I have no weapon, Vishnu...'

'Oh, that's all right. I have no problem.' He laughed. 'Do you?'

As he laughed, he looked away. I found a gap between two soldiers, one of who was grinding tobacco on his palm. I rushed.

The other soldier tried to block me. I leaped, but couldn't jump over him. My knee slammed into his face. I heard the crunch of his bone breaking. I fell, and rolled over in one motion. I had to escape.

But my body was not moving fast enough.

'Catch him!' I heard voices behind. Then sounds of running feet filled the forest. Birds began to shriek. The sun was coming out. I had very little time.

My weapons...I ran as I had never run. But I was panting faster than ever. My body was no longer supporting my past life. I was already in the kundalini of the heart. I tripped over a fallen branch and fell flat.

Someone kicked my side and I rolled in the grass. It was a young soldier. I tried to get up but before I could, a foot crashed into my chest that emptied the wind out of me.

A group of three young soldiers, all toughened by mountain life, attacked me. My back, my thighs, my face...nothing was left. Two soldiers held me as one of them smashed his fists into my face. Within moments I was broken and battered.

My body hurt. Outside the forest, I could see the sun. If I ran there, I would be running blind. I was closer to my weapons now but not close enough to touch them. I got up wearily and faced six spears around me.

'You're not going anywhere,' a voice said.

They were waiting for the kill.

*Forgive me, Urvashi. I tried.*

*I know. But why give up so easily? You still have your life.*

*You've got to see me. Life is just a moment away from death. Maybe, we'll try next lifetime. But don't wait for me any longer. I might not return.*

*Wait I will. But you don't give up on me. Not yet. Get up. Get up, Badri.*

The soldiers around me parted a little. In the distance, I could see Vishnu coming. With Purochan gone, he now behaved like a king, his natural swagger accentuated by the knowledge of being the next in line at Varanavat. He took his time.

A family of langoors swung on the trees above, looking for fruits. I looked above them. Vultures had sensed death. And I was meat.

Vishnu swaggered in. 'Enough?'

I continued to pant, glaring at him. This is not how I was to die. Mine was supposed to be a hero's death. Not this. Not by this bunch of...hyenas.

Vishnu gave me a look that soldiers give before the final death blow. 'Kill him.'

I looked at the six men around me. They came closer, their spears ready to invoke Yam. I closed my eyes to wish a final goodbye.

Nothing hit me for some time. I opened my eyes. Then I heard the growls.

The men before me began to tremble. 'They're here.'

'Who?'

'The wolves.'

'Wolves...'

They began to look around in fear. In their heart, I sensed panic.

'What madness is this?' Vishnu shouted, his voice a few notes higher. 'Kill him!'

The growls became louder. Then there was the hiss of of bodies against bushes. In less than a moment, there were four large dogs between the soldiers and me. The soldiers tried to run back but six more dogs stood waiting there. They were silent, waiting for a signal. The soldiers froze.

*Do you want this fight?*

*Veer...*

*We don't have time. Do you still want to fight?*

*Yes. It's going to be my last.*

*What do you want me to do with them?*

*They can't be allowed to live.*

*All right. I'll handle them. You look after this creature.*

Before me, Veer walked in majestically into the clearing and glared at Vishnu. Vishnu didn't move a muscle. Veer's head was as high as Vishnu's waist.

'He's asking you to take your sword off,' I fumbled, rising to my knees.

Vishnu looked at me stupidly. Then at Veer. Then, very slowly, he loosened the leather belt around his waist that held his sword and gently kept it before Veer.

I stood up, holding my chest. It felt as if my rib was cracked. Maybe, two.

Veer growled a signal. The dogs around us attacked the men. In a few moments, they were a mesh of blood, flesh, hair. Their screams died in their throats, as the dogs jumped at them, tearing them down.

The fight in them had died long back. In the final attack, only their bodies were butchered.

One of them found a gap and began to run. In one long leap, Veer was on him. Before he hit the ground, his neck was torn off, the head rolling over to Vishnu's feet, fearful eyes staring at him. Vishnu stepped back in disgust.

Another soldier was dragging himself away, a bloody dagger in his hand. One dog lay still next to him. He reached a tree trunk and braced himself there. Two dogs turned to him. He began to shout for help. The dogs calmly walked up to him, growling softly.

He began to slash his knife, the blade glinting in the semi-darkness. The dogs waited. Then pounced towards him and backed off. They were playing with him, filling him up with fear he had never experienced. He tried to wind around the tree but a third dog awaited him.

The solider was a mess, seeking the protection of god on one side, threatening the dogs on the other and shrieking for help at the same time. He was staring at the jaws of death before him.

The three dogs looked at Veer, seeking permission. Veer turned towards them.

An unspoken signal passed. The dogs attacked. The sounds from the man died with him. Silence returned to fill the chaos of a few moments ago.

Vishnu stood near a tree, frozen before Veer.

Four dhanush away I was still reeling from the beating.

Between us lay the six soldiers in various states of dismemberment.

The only sounds were the gushing of the Ganga and the cracking of the palace.

'Come Vishnu,' I grunted, 'we need to finish this.'

'And him?' he pointed at Veer.

'As long as I am alive, he won't touch you.'

Vishnu's eyes widened. So, it was either death in my hands or between Veer's jaws.

He chose bravery. In four quick steps he walked towards me, raising his dhoti and tying it above his waist, ready for hand combat.

I limped ahead slowly.

He was fresh. I was tired.

I was beaten down. And I was weakening within. I just had one advantage. In the darkness of the forest, I had sight.

Suddenly, he rushed at me, a thick shoulder slamming into my chest, throwing me bodily away. He stopped to relish the moment. I got up slowly. Kshatriya blood had begun to flow again. I felt my strength return.

Holding a branch for support, I got up. Before I could turn, his fists slammed into my ribs. I bent over. But he didn't allow me to fall, driving an elbow into my face. I felt the salty blood fill my mouth. I spat it out.

He grabbed my neck with his left hand and was drawing back to thump his right into my face. I let my feet apart, falling. Vishnu missed and followed his fist over me. I fell on my back, held his left arm and kicked him in the stomach before throwing him over me.

I got up to my knees.But Vishnu was the quicker warrior. As I took a moment to cough, I felt an ox-like arm around me, his other arm on my head, trying to break my neck.

I tried to bend forward but he was too powerful. I felt my breath shorten and my neck stretch. A little more and I was gone.

Bringing all the strength I had into my legs, I pushed back with my body. Lashing out, my right leg found a tree and pushed hard. We fell. His grip loosened. I twisted away.

Instead of running away as he expected, I met his face with my left and flattened his lips against his teeth. A small shower of blood flew on me. I still didn't relent, throwing in a right into his ribs, then a left into his solar plexus, drawing air from him.

He bent down. I threw my right knee into his face and in that one moment jumped and kicked him with my left foot. He fell back. I leaned on a tree to catch my breath and regain my strength.

Rising slowly, Vishnu blinked. This was not what he expected. He was a head taller than me and much heavier. Younger too. In the darkness, he tried to locate me and found me leaning on the tree.

Like an angry bull, he charged at me, swinging his iron fists. I caught the blow from the right fist on my head and fell. As I fell, his left dug into my right shoulder. But I turned, reducing the power of his blow. We fell.

He got up almost instantly, but I was waiting on my knees. Joining my hands together, I threw them into his lunging frame. The air went out of his lungs, as he began to fall. I turned a full circle and slammed him there again. He was on his knees, holding his stomach.

As I walked in to attack his open face, he threw a right into my face. Specks of blood flew as I felt my teeth rattle.

Without even so much as a pause, he was on his feet, swinging his left. I got under it and elbowed him into his solar plexus again. That was clearly his weak spot. He grunted in pain.

I was losing strength. He was still fresh.

He got up, smashed his knee into my stomach, completing the attack with an elbow on my back.

I fell on my fours.

Vishnu began to circle around me, taking time to catch his breath. I could hear him panting behind. Youth may give you strength. But for stamina, you need to work hard.

Suddenly I stood up, turned around and faced him. He didn't expect me to.

I grabbed his hair, raised his head and threw a full-blooded fist into his open neck. His eyes widened with shock. I kneed him in the stomach again. And again.

He stood up, holding his neck. Pain stabbed at me from all the beating I had taken. This was my only chance.

Slowly, I walked behind him, kicked the back of his left leg. He fell on his knees. I stepped aside. Taking a deep breath, I grabbed his neck, pulling it up. He began to rain blows on me.

But this was it. If I let him go this time, there would be no future. I was at the end of my tether.

The faster man, Vishnu grabbed my head and pulled me over him. In trying to catch my balance, I lost his neck and went over him, landing near a soldier's severed arm.

I grabbed the arm and swung it like a gada. The shoulder slapped blood all over Vishnu.

More than the pain, it was disgust that he backed away from, tripping over another body.

I jumped on him, pounding his face. He tried to protect himself, shaking me away with his chest.

I fell.

Out of nowhere, I saw the glint of metal. In a moment, my mind travelled back all the way to our first meeting. The asidhenu—he had been holding that killer three-edged weapon.

Even with my spears I had no chance against this weapon of close combat...or maybe I did.

I waited, crouching on the ground.

He held the asidhenu in his right hand, not hiding it anymore. Slowly, Vishnu began to get up. Behind us, Veer growled. Vishnu got distracted. He was still on one knee when I leaped onto him, roaring, driving the knuckles of my left fist into his throat, breaking it with a crunch.

The asidhenu fell. He stood up shakily. His hand went to his throat, a puzzled look in his eyes. He stared at me as he stood there. Then, like an old tree, he fell slowly.

He didn't get up.

Another warrior was gone. His eyes continued to stare at me. But this time, I had no regret.

As I fell on my back, something within was celebrating.

I wasn't dead.

*Veer.*

*I know. I'll get help.*

*Yes. But I need to be near my weapons.*

*No, you don't. They're all dead.*

*Take me to that tree.*

*I felt Veer's fur as he lowered his head. Every bone in my body felt like it was broken, every muscle felt torn. I was a mass of pain. I grabbed his thick neck tightly. He dragged me gently towards a tree.*

*Now, go and get help.*

Veer looked at me for a moment. Then he was gone.

I had passed through this last tunnel. Even as I was ready to die, I chose life. I chose Urvashi.

I chose me.

# Epilogue

Vidur looked at the ashram gate, where ashramites were going about their work. 'So, are you ready to leave? We start in the early second prahar.'

'Do I really need to? You have kept your promise in spirit. My parents will understand.'

'I'm sure they will. But you didn't promise,' he smiled. 'I did. Come and light the second diya and then return.'

A group of eight young boys, clad in white dhotis, their heads shaved, passed us by. One of them looked at me and smiled.

'And don't you want to see Hastinapur for one last time?' Vidur asked. 'See your sons and grandchildren—Sumati?'

Something burnt in my heart. Vidur was pressing at the right spots.

'Vidur,' I looked at him indulgently, 'I think it's time you dropped your diplomacy. I'll go.'

He slapped my back. I winced. And then we laughed.

We reached the enclosure of the Lakheras.

'How are your wounds treating you, Badri?' Rasilee swayed towards us, smiling. 'Are you ready for tomorrow?'

'I think so. With Vidur here, you don't need me...'

'...says who?' she cried, turning to Vidur. 'Please don't mind, prime minister, but if Badri won't come with us, we won't go.' A few other Lakheras began to gather around her.

'He will, he will,' Vidur said.

'But only till Hastinapur,' I interrupted. 'After that, you don't need me. Actually, you don't need me at all—the Himavat Patth has been cleared of the cannibals. So, there's no danger.'

'It's not danger, Badri,' Rasilee said. 'It's you. All of us here want you to come with us till all the way home.'

I shook my head. 'It's Hastinapur, and no further. I had promised to lead you to safety and that promise will be kept.'

'One last thing.'

I looked up.

'Our king sends his regards to you and the ashram. He has also asked me to tell you that you will be a royal guest if you ever pass our way.'

'Please give him my gratitude.'

'We will meet at breakfast tomorrow and leave by the second prahar. Are all of you ready?'

A celebratory 'yes' filled the ashram.

In deep concentration, I felt the presence. Slowly, I opened my eyes.

'The governor is here, Badri.' It was Kedar.

'Yes, gurudev,' I folded my hands and looked beside me. Urvashi was waiting. I smiled at her. A heavy presence hung in this meditation room.

Three months into the tapasya, and my beard was now close to my chest. 'Do I need to shave?' I asked her, mischief in my eyes.

'Only if you want to impress the governor. Not for me.'

Kedar led the laughter.

The governor sat in the dining room, straight. He stood for nobility, so naturally, that I wondered how I missed it.

'Badri,' he got up, leaving all decorum behind and clasped me in his arms, now covered with the paraphernalia of officialdom. I held him close.

He gazed at me for long moments. 'There is something about you, Badri. Something has changed.'

'My bandages?'

'Stop fooling around, it doesn't suit your new life. You have a…a presence…of sorts. I can't describe it.'

I nodded. It was the intensity of the tapasya gurudev had directed me to. An inner transformation was on and it could no longer stay hidden.

'Where are your bodyguards?'

'I don't need them, Badri,' he said, sounding offended.

'You don't. But the governor of Varanavat does.'

'Not here, not in this ashram.'

'Come then.'

We took our places on the floor. I looked at him. Only yesterday, he had been a mercenary for hire, for whom loyalty was for sale.

Yesterday, he had sought justice. Now, Durjan would deliver it in Varanavat.

Janaki...

I looked at Vidur to ask a question.

'Don't worry, Badri,' Vidur's tone was gentle. 'Janaki and her tribe are being taken back to their lands. I have deputed Mangal as the new governor, with clear instructions. The old governor is being pulled back into Hastinapur, he will now oversee some harmless department,' he looked at me in the eye. 'Janaki will be the new general of the Khasianis.'

'And all cases of murder and manslaughter against them...'

'...have been withdrawn. We were strongly misled. Now, we have to make amends. Apart from setting them up where they rightly belong, I have given the district a three-year moratorium on all tax revenues. That should give them enough time to rebuild the tribe.'

I relaxed. Under the banyan tree we sat, relishing the gentle breeze.

'Yes, Janaki can rebuild the entire tribe the way she wants, how she wants.'

Vidur was smiling.

'What?'

'Nothing,' he looked away, the flutter of his silk angvastr flapping as the breeze yawned for a brief moment.

'Tell me, Vidur.'

'She sent you a gift.'

'So, what's the mystery?'

'It's a dagger.'

I looked at him, puzzled.

'A dagger of love, one that a Khasiani woman gives to a man she loves.'

I closed my eyes. 'That chapter is over, Vidur.'

'For you, yes,' he said, handing me the dagger. 'But she continues to love you.'

I looked at it. A sharp dagger, about nine dhanurgarh in length, built with iron that had been tempered to perfection. It was heavy, with a handle chiselled by hand. If I knew my tribal studies right, Janaki must have cut it herself. A seal of sovereignty looked at me from the end of the dagger. It was no different from the amulet I had kept in the small box of my worldly possessions, in the ashram store. The dagger would follow.

It was a simple, almost austere weapon. Pure in its intent. Unassuming in its being. Dangerous in its action. Sensual in its feel.

Just like Janaki.

I opened the dressing on Urvashi's back. As I pulled it gently, I knew it was hurting her. But she did not make a sound.

The cuts had begun to heal, but still needed a week or so to close. It were the wounds inside that would take longer.

Urvashi turned her head to look at me. Gently, I turned her over, put my hand under her head and helped her up. She winced towards the end. I gave her a vessel of herbs. She drank it silently.

My body was tightly bound by cotton strips. Kedar said I had three broken ribs that would take their own time to heal. My cuts and bruises weren't so serious, largely on the surface. I felt stronger. But the recovery was not going to help me retrieve my warrior body. Something inside me had shifted and all my energy was focused on my heart.

'It never felt so difficult to leave the ashram as it feels today.'

'You need to finish the last few tasks. Take time out and fix the lands, the horses, the cows, the gold,' she said, her eyes clear. 'We don't want to burden the children with problems of inheritance.'

'Do you want anything?'

She looked at me and put her hand on my bandaged chest. 'I have everything.'

Urvashi looked into my eyes and sent her calm right down into my soul. The time for violence was behind us. Now we were to fight the more difficult wars within.

'So, that's it. No more wars, no more blood, no more killing,' I said.

'Yes,' she eased out a delicate smile. 'We will die inglorious deaths, probably by tripping over a stone and banging our heads.'

We laughed. Then, slowly, something enveloped us. That invisible presence was back. It was doing something to us within.

In silence we sat.

In complete surrender we waited.

Eternity would carry our souls up. And this time, our journey would be together. Bound by time, sealed by space, this journey was preordained.

Destiny had waited for us. We couldn't betray it now.

Outside, the Lakheras were waiting, each of them getting a personal blessing from Kedar. Ahead in the distance, Durjan waited to lead us to the outskirts. The best soldiers of Varanavat would accompany us, along with the Hastinapur contingent that followed Vidur.

Strangely, neither Dhritarashtr nor Bhishm had come to Varanavat. They paid their respects to the 'dead' Pandavs from Hastinapur. Bhishm closed himself in his inner chamber, in silence. He did not come out for forty days.

Dhritarashtr cried with sorrow. He sent Vidur and a contingent to Varanavat for the funeral rites of 'those heroes'. He offered oblations at the Ganga in Hastinapur.

The citizens shed genuine tears.

Our mission was over. I thought about the Pandavs and my heart was instantly transported to Bhim. With him around, no harm can come to them.

Ushas was threatening to paint the purple skies with bright colours. I pulled one layer of veil around me and turned to Vidur. 'Ready?'

He nodded.

*Shall we go, Veer?*

*Another adventure?*

*No. This time, it's going to be peaceful.*

*Peace? For us?*

*Yes, Veer. Our days of war are behind us. The nights of planning are over. Dances with death are long gone. Peace is the way forward. Peace.*

*We'll see.*

# Glossary

**Dhanurgarh:** a unit of length, about 3/4ths of an inch

**Dhanush:** a unit of length, 6 feet; the height of a bow

**Gurukul:** a centre of learning, led by a guru

**Krosh:** a unit of distance, 4,000 yards or 3.7 km

**Muhurt:** a unit of time, 48 minutes; each day is divided into 30 muhurts

**Nadik:** a unit of time, 24 minutes

**Prahar:** a unit of time, 3 hours; each prahar divides the day into eight parts

# Acknowledgements

In my attempt to reimagine the Mahabharat for the modern mind, I stand at the feet of three gurus.

First, Ved Vyas, who captured India's ancient glory in his mega-treatise, the Mahabharat and provided the canvas to paint my stories on. Through him, I experienced the breadth of India's history, the expanse of its varied geography, the depth of its complex culture and most important, the eternal idea that encapsulated ancient India: dharm. I reached him through several translators but finally used Kisari Mohan Ganguli's work as my base text.

Interpreting dharm is not easy for people in an age that worships the mind and discards anything that extends beyond the narrow confines of reason and matter. For this, I bow to my spiritual gurus, Sri Aurobindo and his collaborator Mirra Alfassa (better known as The Mother), who explored the higher realms of spirituality through their Integral Yoga. They've taught me the evolutionary place of the spirit in the troika of matter-life-mind and how man as we see him today is a 'transitional being'.

My Mahabharat takes the story of Ved Vyas, fills it up with subaltern characters and holds them together in the powerful expositions of Sri Aurobindo's and The Mother's works. The basic story remains Ved Vyas's; the new characters are mine. The principles of spirituality are Sri Aurobindo's and The Mother's; their applications are mine.

As a journalist for several years, I have tracked the worlds of money, power and faith and have used that training and draw from several fields—economics, politics and history; culture, psychology and science—to explore contemporary yet timeless themes like marginalization, inequality and justice. I am grateful to several teachers, practitioners and thinkers in each of these fields.

Spread across the world, the good wishes of my family and friends have accompanied me on every journey, including this. Words are inadequate to express my gratitude to all of you.

Finally, Monika—without you, there's no me.

And Meera—a privilege to be your father.

www.ingramcontent.com/pod-product-compliance
Lightning Source LLC
Chambersburg PA
CBHW060429030726
47495CB00003B/799